The Prophet Walker

Book I:
The Trans-Burgeoning Pathways

By Dan MacElReavy
Tales From Trails / Awen Books
Temple, NH

The Prophet Walker

Book I: The Trans-Burgeoning Pathways

By Dan MacElReavy

Cover Art and Illustrations by Angus Ryan

1st Illustrated Edition
Copyright 2013
All Rights Reserved

Published By
Tales From Trails / Awen Books
94 Brown Rd
Temple, NH 03084

ISBN 978-0-9841248-1-7

Acknowledgments

Special acknowledgment to my friends and former students; *Stella, Patrick, Clarsah, David, Andy, Tom, all their classmates...*and *all* **the characters** who have walked with me upon the pathways. You are more wondrous than any characters the wildest fantasy could ever hope to portray.   You are mythic!

To *Tom Brown, Jr.*. who first showed me Coyote's path, and much, much more...so long, long ago...

To *J.R.R. Tolkein*, and *G. Edward Griffin*, whose works enlightened the way for me to grasp the real Rings of Power.

To *James Fitch* and *Gloria Flynn* who volunteered their time, their thoughts, and valued perspectives.

To my bardic ancestors....

To Awen....

Above all—to my ever amazing, loving family who have sacrificed more than can be acknowledged.

*For those who will
look to the sky
and ask questions...*

Table of Contents

Foreword..7
The Great Prophesy..10
Prologue 11

Part I: From the Innocence of Childhood

Chapter I: The Mysterious Creature 19
Chapter II: The Shadow Beast 47
Chapter III: Field Guide..63
Chapter IV: Homework..87
Chapter V: Nightmares...111

Part II: Through Chaos

Chapter VI: To Believe Not Or To Not Believe..........................125
Chapter VII: Forest Terror 147
Chapter VIII: Faas...169
Chapter IX: The World Wide Web.................................201
Chapter X: Memories, Madness, and Dreams.... 247

Part III: Toward The Awakening

Chapter XI: The Flight..283
Chapter XII: Between 293
Chapter XIII: The Prophesy...301
Chapter XIV: The Beast's Monster Conspiracy 327
Chapter XV: The Journey Begins..... 351

After Word 383

Beware, Oh Traveler, who treads this trail—
For nought on this way is what it seems....
Not rock nor root nor footprint stained
with soot, snow, blood, nor heavy metal
fallen from poisoned rains.
Beware, Oh traveler, who dares these paths.
for when ye turn and look ye back—
nought will be same....

Foreword
By Uncle Ken

Nothing you are about to read is *just* what it appears to be. No tree is just a tree—no footprint just a footprint—no thought just a thought. Each and every thing *is* what it appears to be—but simultaneously, in many layers, on many levels, it is much more.

Of course, this could be said of any piece of writing— most poignantly here, any piece written in that most ancient form of literature still printed each day upon the trans-burgeoning pathways—*track and sign*—whether from animal footprints or geological, and/or meteorological imprints. On the pathways, reevaluation and discernment always remind us; nothing in observed reality is *just* what it appears to be.

The difference here, from the very beginning of this journey, is an initiative to openly engage a new generation of awakening minds: those who will cross the boundaries, those who will question, and when necessary, break the rules.

These *Pathways*, like The Great Prophesy intertwining within them, work in a truly organic fashion to educate and inspire this new generation toward their own awakening, that they may become the game changers, the reality changers. This is a tale of true education. Not that which happens at school, but that which happens naturally—outside the system (which is rather designed to prevent true education).

Embedded in every chapter (both apparent and invisible) are keys that unlock doors to new layers and levels of consciousness— new dimensions of mind. Unlike the typical genre smoke and mirrors, with hooks and lines crafted simply to captivate readers in fruitless fantasies, or instill subliminal messages—here, as awakening minds read deeper, in collusion with the obvious Fantasy, hard truths emerge to plain view.

This may be disturbing to the faint of heart or fixed of mind. Certainly, to the genre establishment. Yet most disturbed will be those who will to keep our minds trapped in their constructed illusions. It is unthinkable to them that common people, especially young people, may come to realize the hidden truths revealed in the Prophet Walker's footprints and on the myriad pathways upon which they tread.

Yet unstoppable are those who will know the truth. So while some will be horrified, others glorified. The props are falling down—getting taken out as the fantasy progresses and expands into reality, a reality becoming ever more amazing as its own illusions and make-believe (made by belief) dissolve. Setting this curtain-less stage, for example, is the initiative for a character from the story to write the Foreword.

On its surface *The Trans-Burgeoning Pathways* reflects the journey of a supposedly "less than" ordinary person awakening to her true potential; she is after all, "extra" ordinary. Her will and imagination heed no bounds. She may be delusional. Or she may be the greatest prophet in the history of the world, whose revelations could change the future course of humanity. If the latter is true, she and all who follow her tracks will be targeted by *It*.

There have been many mythic beasts the world has experienced in various manifestations throughout history. If the one known commonly, and simply, as "The Beast" cannot control this young woman (and all her ilk) by the means vested in labeling them "less than." *It* may instead label them "the world's most wanted terrorists," and stop at no end to have them destroyed.

This is no mere children's story—though Part 1, by Natural Law,* must at first appear so. Nor does it hold to any of the establishment's "acceptable subtleties" in expressing views. Finally, this story could not be told within the confines of any existing genre. Thus, from it, a ***new genre*** emerges. Consider yourself briefed.

To young and old alike who seek deeper meanings and insights, who push for expanded truth beyond that found in mere text books...or genre Fantasies....

To those who would graduate from Hogwart's, and who might leave college for higher learning....

Don't bother trying to hold onto your hats. Throw your cap off now!

What you are about to read is no mere Young Adult Fantasy, but rather, a ***Mythic Reality....***

Ken Owing, 2020

*Natural Law: one must be grown up enough to discern and remain comfortable, yet child-like enough to get into the kingdom.

The Great Prophesy...

*of the myriad futures of humanity
was written not by the hand of a god.
Nor even by the hand of a man—
but by two feet in molten stone.*

It foretold of the ages....

*And, of due course, of the End Times;
of the arising of The Beast—
of The Illumination—
of The Shadow—*

of the World Freedom Revolution—

*and of The Return...
of The Prophet Walker...
at the beginning of The Terrible War;*

the war for the minds of all...

ᚦᚻᚦ · ᚦᚻᛏᚻᛖ-ᚻᚻᚢᚢᚦ ᚦ ᚠᚢᚦᚢ · ᚻᛏᚦᚻᚻᛏᛉᛖ
ᛏᚢᚦ · ᚦᚻᚦ · ᚻᛏᚦᚻᚻᛏᛉᛖ · ᚦ ᚦ · ᚻᚢᚦᛏᚦᚢᚦ ᚠᚦ

A near future— in wild-lands very, very close to home...

Prologue

It was dark—in the thickness of the forest, the utmost dark; pitch black. Yet darker still were Stella's thoughts, her emotions, her suspicions, her fears. A confusion of memories raced through her mind.

"The worst sort of nightmare is the sort you wake up in the middle of, and realize, to your horror—it is real!" The icy voice of *The Shadow Beast* echoed in her memory.

Stella was running for her life. Her bare feet were bruised and bludgeoned, but she barely felt them. Her pursuers were many. Their tracking devices were of a technology whose invention most people had not yet even imagined.

Death—in a free world, she thought, *would be far better than what will happen if they catch me.*

If only she could wake from this terrifying nightmare. But there was no waking, because Stella wasn't sleeping. This *was* real.

She would have cried if she had a moment. *How did it change so fast?* Her life had been good. Sure, there was school and homework and all that—but she'd take it all back in a

11

heartbeat if only she could leave this horrible nightmare her reality had become.

Stella remembered: *Blinding beams of light—strange doctors examining her, prodding her with alien-like instruments—the Nazi scientist, and those terrible eyes....*

This pitch black forest had been comforting compared with the memories racing through her mind as she ran through the darkness —at first. But any sense of comfort, and even the memories were driven from her by the rising sounds of engines and the terrifying vision of flashing lights. *They* were closing in—and not only from behind her now, but from ahead and all around.

Stella stopped short—almost in a panic. She had to get off the trail! Trembling, she left the path and felt her way into the brush.

But if she had been afraid while she was running, it was nothing to the fear that came over her now. The sudden pounding, clattering vibration of a helicopter came raging out of nowhere, and hovered—barely over her head! From it, a sonic weapon discharged.

Stella's mouth opened—and all breath left her lungs. But she did not know if she actually screamed. For what may have been the loudest outpouring of emotion ever to come out of her was like silence under the all consuming and terrifying sound of the helicopter's deafening clatter.

Yet it was the highly focused sonic beam that ravaged her nervous system. Frozen on her feet, her face turned up in pure shock and awe, her head tilting back. Her treasured knife dropped from her hand. All terrain vehicles and foot soldiers closed in from every direction. It was over. They had caught her. Overloaded completely, her terrified body went limp. And Stella fell.

She did not feel the ground. She felt nothing. She neither saw nor heard anything. She lay on her back, her eyes and mouth open, as though dead. No thoughts. No dreams.

When the soldiers closed in, it was apparent their quarry was unconscious. Their leader, Commander Grey, shone his flashlight beam onto her face. The second in command, Lieutenant Green, was standing right over her. He removed his goggles, shaking his head at the sight of the young girl, then looked questioningly at Commander Grey.

"I know. It's hard to believe," Commander Grey answered his look. "But terrorists come in all shapes and sizes. And *this one,* as I have been *most clearly* informed, is extremely dangerous—and...*of the utmost importance.*"

Lieutenant Green shrugged. Whatever she supposedly was, it was all over for her now. But she, *most clearly*, was not looking so impressive. He gently pushed her eyelids shut, then signaled to his troops. They turned on their flash lights and approached.

Yet even in unconsciousness, even through closed eyes, even through the cover of clouds—photons from distant stars pierced the veil about her and entered Stella's vision. Through her subconscious came an awareness of blue and white swirling sparks; they were all about her and upon her, touching her skin, absorbing into her—dancing, swirling sparks of *life.*

From this energy there came a voice, powerful and compelling. Stella knew this energy, and the voice, *sub*consciously. But she was *un*conscious—until the moment, when suddenly, this life force exploded throughout her body, jolting her wide awake. And then she had no memory of swirling sparks—but with a bolt of energy, leapt to her feet and ran like she had never run before.

There was a gap in the circle of flashlights closing in on her. Maybe she could make it through.

For her pursuers, she knew, there would be a moment of confusion. She had fallen and lain unconscious. They must have been confident she was captured. Perhaps they were wrong. They had underestimated her. Perhaps they weren't as efficient and all powerful as they believed. And in their overconfidence they had revealed *their* positions by turning on their lights. Now she could see where *they* all were—and now *she* was not so foolish as to turn on her own flashlight.

Stella charged between the widest gap in the circle of flashlights—and was no longer surrounded. She ran with new strength.

But the helicopter tore after her—and the lights of her pursuers, again, went dark. She could no longer see where they were. *Oh no,* she remembered. *Infrared. They can see me in the dark!* Of course they'd be tracking her by her thermal emissions. If only she was a snake, *or even a turtle,* Stella thought, maybe she could escape. But all warm blooded animals emit heat—and no matter how dark it was, *they* could see her heat signature.

Still, there might be a way. She would rather die trying than be taken. She would *not* fall victim to fear again. She would follow all her senses. She slowed down a little, that she might hear or smell or some other way *sense* them.

All sound, however, was overwhelmed by the helicopter hovering above her. *Taller trees,* she thought. *Maybe I can lose it if I get under some taller trees.* But even as she paused to search through the darkness around her, she became aware of an unnatural mist descending upon her. She was being sprayed! By exactly what, she could only imagine. But it was obviously coming from the helicopter—and it wasn't vitamin water. She had to run. Fast!

Stella stumbled from the thicket into an opening. She recognized this place at once. She was on the old railroad path! Here she could more clearly see. Heartened to have navigated so well through the dark woods, she ran with all her might.

But the helicopter stayed on her, now spraying her with greater intensity, almost knocking her down. It was disgusting. Whatever poison it was, she thought....

She hardly got to complete the thought when the poison took effect. Suddenly, she was confused. Her head was in a fog. She was stunned—as though she had been sledge-hammered on the side of the head.

She staggered, stopped running, and walked—almost in a full circle. Fear came over her once more—not intense as before, but with a confusion now that grew worse each moment. Where was she trying to get to?

Her head ached. Then it throbbed. In moments the pain in her skull grew almost crippling. *Why was I even running?* She wondered, but barely. For the pain and disorientation were worsening each moment.

God...God! She panicked. *Where am I?* She cried, wondering; *What is this horrible banging over my head...or is it in my head?* She put her hands on her face—and noticed sweat and saliva all over her hands. She wiped her hands on her pants and felt for her face again. Liquid was dripping, oozing, secreting from her mouth—her nose—her eyes—her ears—the pores of her skin....

The spraying had stopped. But now the foot soldiers were closing right in upon her. Stella saw one of them. In the darkness, with his protective clothing, helmet, gas mask, and infrared goggles, he looked like an alien. For all she knew, perhaps he was. Staggering, she ran in the opposite direction.

She was still on the old railroad path, though at the moment did not know it. Her memory was almost completely gone. She knew only that she was chased—that her pursuers were more terrible than any nightmares she had ever conjured from her own unconscious—and that she was confused. Somehow, she knew she was confused. And that in spite of her pain, she had to keep running—running with all her might.

Somehow, she did keep running. And though staggering, she did not relent—until the moment. A huge, dark shape lunged onto the path—directly in front of her! Stella froze in her tracks. This was no mere human. *But what?*

She'd been afraid to turn on her flashlight. But now she had no choice. For whether or not her light revealed her position, *she* had to see….

Throughout her entire life, Stella Childs had been leaving tracks. This fact, in and of itself, is nothing out of the ordinary. We all leave tracks—from every step we ever take. And just like most of us, Stella was completely unaware of the vast majority of tracks she left behind.

But Stella's tracks were noticed. In fact, every track she ever left was touched, sniffed, and observed. Of course, this fact, though perhaps more intriguing than the first, is no more unique. Every track ever left by any one of us is touched, sniffed, and observed—by at least some one or some thing.

But Stella's tracks were not only touched, sniffed, and observed—they were studied, pondered over with the deepest of thoughts, even talked about and debated upon in various obscure and mysterious languages.

Clearly, Stella's tracks were followed. So too, were those of her friends. But not all those who followed were of like mind. Some were benevolent—which of course means good. Some were ambivalent—that is, of mixed or undetermined configuration. Others…well, *they* were rather made up of the dark persuasion. Sinister, you could say. Diabolical. In fact, down right evil. Evil to the core—to the very heart of darkness. The most wicked of the wicked.

You think you get the picture? But I doubt any one truly does. For what I have failed to relay thus far is the deceit. Above all, *they* are great deceivers. So whatever image or perception we have of them is probably incorrect. *They* are not what they appear to be.

Now comes my warning: As you read or listen to these words —you, yourself, are following Stella Childs' tracks—and those of her friends. For *words* and *sentences* are types of *tracks* and *trails*. As you've been informed, *others* are following this maze of trails already. *They* may be in front of you. *They* may be behind you— perhaps both—or even beside or above you. Keep wide your eyes. Keep an ear to the ground. And keep all your senses on full alert. For as difficult as it may be to even imagine how this could be possible—some of these other trackers may notice *your* footprints following Stella's.

I hope, first, you notice theirs. For depending on who you are and what you might become—*they* may be interested in *you*. I will not comfort you falsely. At this juncture you have already placed a foot on *the pathways*. If you continue—your tracks, inevitably, will lead through some very dark places….

Part I:
From the Innocence of Childhood

ᛃᚼᛂᛅᛅ·ᛐᛂᛅ·ᛐᛐᚠY
ᛁᛐᛂᛁᚼᛐYᛂ·ᛃᛐ·ᛁᛅᛃᛐᛅᚠᛅ

When all life was innocent...
but an illusion lived.
When sweet Childhood graced
the stains of a world...gone totally mad
in the cold, steel grip of greed and fear;
"Oh look! Oh look!" she cried.
But they don't look.
Now The Shadow Beast is here.

Chapter I:

The Mysterious Creature

Stella sensed nothing unusual about the day as she and her friend, Patrick, stepped onto the path leading from her sunny back yard into the dark wood. It was the first of May. All around, burgeoning buds of trees and shrubs swelled with potential and promise. Green leafy plants, unfolding ferns, and new blades of grasses were sprouting everywhere—especially in the vast mud and swampy areas alongside the path.

Of course these two seventh graders never noticed the amazing animal tracks of all types that got printed throughout the abounding woods and wetlands each night. For like most two legged shoe-wearers, they generally stayed on path and talked a lot, barely ever seeing anything that wasn't right in front of them.

That's partly why they didn't hear the footsteps of The Mysterious Creature sneaking up behind them. But also, it was because The Mysterious Creature knew how to stalk, dead silent, through the woods.

"So," Patrick asked, "by the time we get there, how far do you think Andy will have gotten? On his new game?" he pressed, as he noticed Stella was not paying attention.

"Oh—I don't know," Stella sighed, her eyes drifting about from tree tops into clouds and various places in the atmosphere. Her body swayed as she spoke, animated as were her facial expressions, by spontaneous thoughts and emotions moving through her. As was her way, she resembled a wafting wildflower in a field, moved by the subtlest winds, rains, and bursts of sunshine. "I'm not sure if *David* is so nice a person," she sighed. Then her starry gaze descended from the clouds suddenly and fixed onto Patrick. "Do *you* think I'm a space cadet?"

"Uhh..." Patrick hesitated. "Well...I doubt *you* are in training to become an astronaut," he smiled. "But...I'm betting Andy is already passed the third level of *Star Seeker Three*! So that qualifies him—"

"He said I'm an air head!" Stella snapped. "Half the class heard him. Can you believe that? I mean, maybe I *am* an air head —from *his...sophisticated perspective*," she mocked. "But he didn't have to say it." She stumbled over a forked branch lying in the middle of the path as she glanced sideways at Patrick. The other side of the branch popped up and hooked Patrick's ankle.

"Uhh...*well*—" Patrick stumbled. "*David,*" he replied, regaining his balance, "is probably just trying to get you to go along with *his* ideas for that script you guys have been writing. So —how far do you think Andy is?"

Stella rolled her eyes and shook her head. "*You* are so clueless."

"It's not just a dumb video game, Stella. The creators of *Star Seeker Three* consulted with *Stephen Hawking*," Patrick paused, eyeing his friend. "Do you even know who Stephen Hawking is?"

Stella glared at him. He was so clueless he didn't even get what it was he was clueless about. *She* had written the script for that play. It was *her* idea. *David* was just helping her edit. As for who the creators of a meaningless video game had consulted with —she could not care less.

"Do you know who the Maharishi Bodhisattva is?" Stella retorted. "Do you know who Ram Daas is?"

Patrick crinkled his brow. "*Rom Dos*? I know *what* Rom is. And I know what dos is."

Stella shook her head. "Obviously—you only know what *you* know, Patrick—which is infinitely less than you think...."

Now, Patrick was so focused on the game he was hoping to play when they got to their friend, Andy's house; and Stella was so consumed by her feelings about David and their whole class, that neither of them were even attentive to each other, much less to anything else in the forest. So, on top of being oblivious to the forked branch they had stumbled upon, *or* the Mysterious Creature —now stalking right behind them—they didn't even notice the tracks.

Embedded clear as a flashing neon caution sign in the smooth patch of mud crossing the path right before their eyes were the perfect tracks of this forest's most ferocious hunter; *Martes pennanti.*

As was typical of Martes pennanti when he bounded across a trail, his tracks were printed in three sets of threes—as though they were some type of magical symbol or conveyed a numerological significance.

Stella and Patrick trampled right over Martes pennanti's exquisite tracks, smearing them into illegible muck. In each print, every one of the five long sharp claw marks embedded in front of each of the perfectly printed toes, were now obliterated by sneaker tracks. They never knew what they had missed. They just kept walking and talking.

But The Mysterious Creature who was following in their footsteps saw everything. Not only had he spotted the tracks of Martes pennanti—and sniffed them, touched them, tasted them, and read from them the stories of where Martes pennanti had come from and where he was going—but also, he saw how *oblivious* the humans were.

At such oblivion, The Mysterious Creature was appalled—incredulous! But further, he was *summoned*. His eyes flashed and his nostrils flared, his lips parting. The Mysterious Creature was enthralled by animal tracks of all kinds; the fresh, clear type like these *exquisite* prints Martes pennanti had so recently scrolled out were deserving of reverence, of awe—and worthy of following. But to be smeared without a thought....

Narrowing his gaze and clamping his jaw, The Mysterious Creature bent low, squinting at the two legged *unawares* as though ready to pounce. He grasped the silver branch Stella and Patrick had unconsciously stumbled over. He sniffed it, stroked it reverently. It was silver birch—quite hard and dense. For a moment, a wild smile streaked across his face beneath the flashing of his enormous eyes. Then his gaze snapped forward, to the quirky, unconscious hominids walking the path.

Primal instincts crawled and clawed within this Mysterious Creature, alerting his brains to one certainty; the humans needed to be taught a lesson. The time had come.

Although this Mysterious Being was most often out of sight, dead quiet—even invisible—and normally his own tracks were not seen on human trails—at this moment he raised the silver branch over his head, and ran straight for the two seventh graders. Stamping his own tracks clearly and purposely into the mud, on top of their sneaker tracks that were stamped on top of the tracks of Martes pennanti—and wailing out a high pitched scream, he slammed the branch down! It jolted the ground like lightning—just behind their feet.

The two seventh graders froze in their tracks. Stella almost screamed herself, but just managed to hold it inside. Neither she nor Patrick moved. Their very thoughts froze. They stood, still as statues, mesmerized by shrill echoes of the wild scream now reverberating inside their minds.... Or was it a thunderclap?

It was like no sound they had ever heard or imagined. Yet reverberating from it as it faded came every buzz, chirp, scratch, screech, thump, bump, bark, howl, and growl of the forest. For a long time neither of them moved. Their eyes were wide—their ears and all their senses on full alert.

The forest was alive with an amazement of sounds and colors—as though it had been awakened—or Patrick and Stella had suddenly been awakened from a dull dream they'd been walking in half their lives. Now the forest was dazzlingly bright. Ravens croaked overhead. There were the shrill cries of an eagle, high in the sky. Bees buzzed. Insects of all varieties swarmed and flitted about. Bull frogs croaked. Tree frogs peeped. The breeze whispering through the pine trees seemed almost certainly to be forming words.

Throughout her childhood, Stella had sensed—or rather, imagined—she was being followed. This had caused years of strange dreams and some rather annoying diagnoses from her old school psychiatrist. She remembered the reptilian humanoids who used to follow her in her nightmares. But she had grown out of *that. This* was no dream!

A strange scent filled the air. Beyond the insects, Stella heard something else buzzing...ringing...humming. The air itself was fuzzy and alive, electrified with tiny blue and white swirling sparks. What was it? She sensed she had seen the air looking like this somewhere before and, more than once, but she could not remember exactly when. Yet not only could she see and hear it, she could actually feel it.

As though breathed upon by the cold breath of The Mysterious Creature, Stella felt the hair standing up on the back of her neck, her whole scalp tingling with trepidation—as ever so slow and cautiously, she and Patrick turned around, unsure if they truly wished to see....

The Mysterious Creature was not in sight, but their wide eyes were immediately drawn to the Creature's steaming tracks, freshly stamped into the mud—right on top of their own. Sunlight glistened brightly in the dark, wet mud, making the tracks appear to glow—as if magically, from their own sparkling light.

"What could have made that horrible scream?" Stella asked in a hushed voice as she eyed the peculiar tracks.

"I thought it was more like a growl," Patrick half- whispered. He was already on his knees, examining the strange prints more closely. "Right on top of *our tracks*," he whispered hoarsely, "which were right on top of something else's tracks!" he gasped, now noticing also, the tracks of *Martes pennanti*. His eyes were clearly seeing things he had never noticed before. "Oh my word!" he stared in bewilderment, "look at all these tracks!"

"Oh your *Word*?" Stella shot Patrick a look. "*God*—"she shook her head, a part of her thinking; *he is such a geek.* But her eyes were scanning about, also—rather apprehensively—as she, too, detected the previously unnoticed network of various animal tracks all around them.

"An absolute..." Patrick faltered, searching for just the right word: "*plethora* of animal tracks," he finished, looking quite pleased with himself, Stella thought, in spite of the pervading sense of dread he was obviously striving to cover.

"Wow..." Stella half-whispered. "*Plethora*.... Impressive word, Patrick. Do you even know what it means?" But in spite of her habitual and irresistible temptation to critique Patrick's every quirky word and way, she was actually more focused *on* the plethora of tracks—her whole body still shaking in the wake of the horrible scream and whatever it was that had made it.

"Of course I know what a plethora means," Patrick whispered defensively, his eyes carefully and cautiously scanning about.

"Well, Einstein?" She whispered, raising her brows. "What *does* it mean?" she asked, as though the meaning of a word was the focus of her attention.

Yet not only was her heart still racing and her mind still perplexed about whatever it was that had made the horrible scream; at the same time she was growing more and more mesmerized by something her eyes could not quite focus on. The air was still abuzz with tiny swirling sparks—like the whole atmosphere was electrically charged.

But maybe it's just a trick of my own eyes, Stella reasoned to herself. And even if this explanation fell infinitely short of the truth, it *was* somewhat reasonable—as she *had* been rather affected by the shock from that horrifying scream—or electrical discharge, or whatever it was.

"A plethora means: *a whole lot*," Patrick answered.

Stella had forgotten she had even asked, which made her aware; she had many layers to her being—each like a personality unto itself. Only the personality on the surface was speaking and relating to her friend, Patrick, while other layers of herself concentrated on deeper matters.

"Oh. Then why not just say: *a whole lot?*" her surface personality asked—while trembling, Stella got to her knees, like Patrick, to look more closely at the weird set of prints he was most mesmerized by—those of the mysterious creature.

"Because..." Patrick paused, obviously trying to think up what more he could add to *because*. "A *plethora* has more pizzazz than *a lot,*" he whispered. "It's an *over* abundance—an overflowing," he explained.

Stella was no longer listening. Her surface personality was overcome by deeper awareness. Her mind focused, and she was struck by the reality before them. Her eyes widened, her mouth hanging open. "They look like bare foot human tracks!" she exclaimed. "Only—" her voice went quiet, "the toes are really *long* compared to the foot."

Stella's eyes widened in further amazement as her vision followed the myriad of tracks of all sorts of creatures, interwoven like strands of scrolls, each telling a tale printed by its own author

—all part of a great ongoing saga that she and Patrick, all the animals, and some Mysterious Creature, were in.

At last, Patrick's surface personality seemed to have submerged, also, overcome by deepening awareness. For a quiet time they both studied the tracks and listened intently to the sounds of the forest.

From the silence of the shadows behind them, without warning, came a sudden raspy whisper.

"If wants ta have ye two, *really* a close look at those tracks, ought ye to lie down on yer bellies and look sideways—so does na' the glare o' the sun obscure yer view."

Startled, their hearts racing, Patrick and Stella looked up behind them. And there stood the Mysterious Creature—or at least, *a* mysterious creature; a tiny old brown-skinned *man* wearing a cap of green leaves.

A fog they had been unaware of swirled suddenly about the atmosphere and evaporated. Sunlight burst through the trees, illuminating the Earth as though dawn, for the first time ever, put death to an unfathomable night—and awakening to the whole wide world.

The mysterious little man held up the silver branch, but in his grasp it now shone gold under the brilliant sun. Smiling, he tossed it over their heads. They did not hear it land behind them. Nor did they turn to look. Their eyes were fixed on this mysterious creature.

Furry and curly eyebrows and sideburns protruded from his pointed little face. His head, narrowing at the long chin and nose, was strangely wide toward the tall pointed ears and furrowed brow extending over enormous dark eyes. He wore a mottled gray and brown—rather tree bark colored cloak over scraggly tattered knickers. His feet were bare, and his long, dexterous toes tapped the ground like fingers.

"Better still," he continued, "ought ye ta sniff them prints. Yes!" he nodded, smiling at their dumbfounded expressions, "and ofter takes ye a good look, should ye feel 'em wi- yer fingers."

Patrick and Stella neither spoke nor moved, but stared in shock and disbelief.

"Is what the matter?" the little man asked, "got cat yer tongue?"

Stella felt her jaw drop open, her eyes blinking. There was an aura about this little man—a blue and white light.

"Oh—" the little man nodded in sudden realization, "yes—o' course—is't yer strange custom o' putting subjective nouns before their verbs. Confused are ye by my usage. Try will I—or rather—*I will try*—ta form my sentences so can ye—hum," he shrugged, "rather—*so ye can* understand me. How's that?" he smiled, apparently thinking they were only confused by his odd use of language when in fact they were shocked by his very appearance.

"Who are you?" Patrick asked from his frozen position on the ground.

Stella eyed the long muddy toes on the little man's feet. "You made these tracks!" she spoke in sudden realization. "Was that you that made that horrible scream?"

"Horrible?" The little man looked positively incredulous. "The alarm that saved ye from a lifetime o' trance—horrible?" There was a quiet moment while they stared at one another.

"If wants ta hear ye—or see ye, *really* something horrible," his eyes lit up, "show ye can I the tracks o' the most horrible beast ever ta tramp on the face o' this Earth."

He nodded, and then whispered, "has been it following right in yer very footsteps." His eyes darted about. "Lucky are ye that saved ye, I, wi- that li'l scream o' mine—else ne'er would ha'e ye escaped from...*The Shadow Beast.*"

"The Shadow Beast?" Patrick stood up, his eyes darting about. Stella froze. The way this little man said that name, *The Shadow Beast,* struck a haunting cord at some deep, dark place inside her. It had an eerie ring about it that was strangely familiar, disturbing, and chilling.

"Frightened it off, did I—for the moment," the little man explained. "But will be it back. Once on yer trail, ne'er will it leave ye alone—unless," his eyes flashed, "follow ye *its* tracks—and learn ye *its* ways. Only then can know ye how ta avoid it."

"Is it really dangerous?" Patrick asked, his eyes surveying up and down the little man's form—as though still hardly even believing *he* was real.

"Deadly!" the little man answered.

"Then I don't think we should follow its tracks," Stella half whispered with raised brows.

"Is't following *yers*!" the little man snapped. But, noticing the intensity of fear in their expressions, "Oh—worry not—*too much*," he assured with a downward wave of his hand. "Won't get it *too* close ta ye whilst wi- ye am I." He smiled.

They looked questioningly at him. "Magic," he stated, as though it explained everything. They raised their brows in uncertainty at the little brown man. He shrugged—then his large, gleaming eyes narrowed, slowly closing. As he did the whole forest grew dim as night, for a moment. Then, his eyes flashed open—wide. And the forest lit up even brighter than before.

Patrick and Stella's jaws dropped in amazement. Patrick stepped backwards, shocked. But Stella was simply enthralled. This Mysterious Creature was magic! Or he knew magic. She stepped forward, eagerly.

Somehow, as Stella stood before him, she felt—more than anyone in the world, she could trust this mysterious being—creature—whatever he was. She sensed his magic was good. In fact, she could see it in his aura. And the more she focused on his aura, she realized, it was made of the same blue and white swirling sparks she was seeing in the air all around. Only it was concentrated around this Mysterious Creature.

Now she remembered; she used to see auras when she was young. But everyone else had said she was just imagining—so she'd stopped looking. Like everyone else, she learned to focus on other things. She still saw intangible stuff from time to time, but shrugged it off as tricks of light on her retinas, fuzziness in her eyes—or whatever. But *this* was not just *whatever*!

Whether Patrick regained his better senses or simply could not stand Stella being one up on him, she wasn't sure. Either way, in moments, he had stepped up beside her, now facing the Little Brown Man as though he was as eager as Stella.

"Ahum," the little man grunted with satisfaction. "Now—keep wide yer eyes," he instructed, "an' awake yer senses."

"But...*magic*," Patrick stumbled over his words, "is scientifically impossible."

"Shows how much know *ye* about *True Magic*," the little man rolled his eyes, "or *true* science." He stuck his face right in front of Patrick's. "Is *True Magic*," he whispered, "at the root of *all* science." That silenced Patrick—or at least, his surface personality —much to the satisfaction of Stella's, which now reemerged, thinking, *Patrick thinks he is **such** a scientist.* Even her surface personality was a bit changed, however, wet by the waters of her deeper consciousness.

"Are you a leprechaun?" Stella asked.

"Ha!" he laughed. "Called that have I been before—and lots of other things. Like *Mysterious Creature*," he said mysteriously. "*Supernatural Being,*" he added, his eyes blazing up as though a great fire lived hidden inside his head. "*Goblin,*" he grunted. "And—more properly, Sir Mac Awen. But may ye just call me, MacAwen," the little man smiled.

"Mac…Awen?" Patrick repeated with raised brows. "I'm Patrick."

"And I'm Stella."

"As if didna' already half the forest know that, and yer life's stories, from all yer bletherin'," MacAwen retorted. "But well pleased am I ta meet ye." He removed his green cap and gave a bow.

Patrick turned to Stella. "We *have* been accused of being overly imaginative," he said, turning again to MacAwen with a puzzled look on his face. "And of acting rather young for our age," he sighed, frowning. "But..." he glanced back to Stella, "we are...none the less...a bit old to believe in leprechauns."

"Told ye I already that a leprechaun am I *not,*" the little man snapped.

"Patrick," Stella added, "how old you are shouldn't have anything to do with being able to see what's right in front of you." She shook her head, thinking: *He...is the one who acts young for his age. People just think I'm weird.*

"I see what I see," Patrick confessed. "But I don't believe in *any* kind of mysterious creatures."

"Well! Glad am *I* ta hear *that!*" MacAwen shook his head and rolled his eyes. "And yet—" his gaze penetrated through Patrick's eyes, as though he could see right inside him, "as smart as do ye think yerself, still do believe *ye* in the strangest, most fantastic—and utterly *ridiculous* theories," he pointed an accusing finger—a humored if disgusted look on his face. "And *no* understanding yet do posses ye 'bout the true nature o' that which *perceive* ye ta be this *Mysterious Creature.*"

There was a moment of silence. Patrick and Stella were obviously confused by MacAwen's words. The little man shrugged.

"Not that would expect I, any typical pair o' modern, shoe-wearin' humans ta have even a chance at graspin' me meanin'—but —in case one day might catch one o' ye, a ray or two o' the Central

Sun...ought ye ta be prepared...ta realize; is the solid Earth ye walk upon more hollow beneath than the belly of a whale—and is the world that believe ye ta be livin' in...pure illusion upon layers of illusion."

Patrick frowned, turning his puzzled eyes to Stella, then back to MacAwen. "Well—" he shrugged, his expression lightening, "no offense, Sir MacAwen, but your verbs are still coming out before your nouns." Patrick smiled.

MacAwen's eyes widened and his mouth opened, but no word came out.

"I like the way you talk," Stella cut in quickly. "It's not confusing at all," she said, sticking an elbow into Patrick's side and shooting him a sharp glance.

"Ah. Hum..." MacAwen grunted in contemplation, tapping a long, pointy finger to his chin.

"Uh—are those the tracks of the Shadow Beast?" Patrick changed the subject quickly, pointing to the five toed prints with the sharp claw marks left by the ferocious hunter, Martes pennanti.

"Martes pennanti? Oh no," MacAwen answered. "My *friend* is *he*—very pleasant."

"Martes…what?" Stella asked.

"Martes *pennanti*—scientific name," MacAwen shrugged. "A bit of Latin gibberish, really. Just thought I ta round yer education a smidge. Is a fisher what is it commonly called."

"A fisher! That's what ate my uncle's chickens!" Patrick exclaimed.

"And I've heard they eat cats," Stella added with a disgusted and accusing look.

"Well—a ferocious hunter, yes," MacAwen acknowledged. "Even are porcupines on his menu from time to time. But a playful and funny rascal is he, too. Come. Follow his tracks will we for a bit. Heading is he for The De Da Mua," MacAwen smiled, his eyes aglow. "Is't the perfect place for tracking—and for tricking—the Shadow Beast."

"The *De Da Mua*?" Patrick inquired with raised brows.

"Is *the De Da Mua* short for the Deep, Dark, Muddy Area—or so is it said," MacAwen gleamed. "Come," he beckoned with excitement, as he started after the tracks of the fisher.

"What do you think?" Patrick whispered to Stella, as he eyed the back of MacAwen, heading into the deep, dark forest.

Stella sighed, clutching the silver amulet she kept in her pocket. She took it out, glanced at it, then held it tightly to her heart. Caution told her they should not follow *any* mysterious creature into the deep, dark woods. Yet, something else told her otherwise.

After a short debate, Stella and Patrick followed, apprehensively. The Shadow Beast *was* frightening, but they decided that for the moment it was better to be *tracking it,* than to be *tracked by it.* If the Shadow Beast never left you alone once it got on your tracks, as MacAwen had told them, then they'd better do as MacAwen had instructed; learn the ways of The Shadow Beast, by tracking it, so they could know how to avoid it. Besides, they might get to learn some true magic!

Once off the path, MacAwen paused, raising a finger to the air. "First must learn ye ta *stealth walk.*"

"Stealth walk?" they repeated in unison.

"Ahum," he nodded. "As walks the fox. Is't a bit different than elephant walking, tramping, tromping, lumbering...or *bumbling*—as have I been noticing is yer usual mode of travel," he imitated their walks in a rather humorous, if insulting manner. "But now—" he gestured to the forest about them, "will appear a whole new world before yer eyes—and ears—when *stealth walking.* Partly because much more keen will be yer eyes and ears. And partly because not running and hiding from ye will be so much of the rest of the forest's population! Observe—" and he demonstrated the stealth walk while explaining it.

It seemed to Stella that MacAwen floated or flitted about like a hummingbird, if she only watched the little man's upper body. But MacAwen's legs were in constant flowing motion—his feet, especially the toes, moving *most* fluidly. Yet he never needed to look at his feet, for they felt their way over the terrain—and were actually better than another pair of eyes, telling him every detail of all that passed beneath him. "Yer turn now," he stood still to observe his new students.

Stella and Patrick gave it a try.

"Ah...hum—not bad," MacAwen smiled. "*Very good!*" he chuckled. "Failed ye both perfectly, to know even what was the first lesson."

Stella and Patrick stopped, eyeing him questioningly. "Well?" Patrick raised his eye brows, "what *was* the first lesson?"

MacAwen said nothing. His eyes seemed to go so wide they went out of focus. His ears pricked up. His nose twitched and his nostrils flared as he sniffed. His hands slowly went out, wide to either side of his body, his fingers moving as though he was feeling something in the air.

In silence, Stella and Patrick studied him closely. They too, listened intently to hear what he might be hearing. They too, sniffed the air and felt it with their fingers.

"Now are ye getting it," MacAwen nodded.

"We *are*?" Patrick questioned.

"Ye *were*," MacAwen shrugged, "when ye were observing me."

"Hey," Patrick smiled, "you got your nouns in front of the verbs that time."

"*Now* are ye getting it again," MacAwen smiled.

"I am?" Patrick, clearly, was confused about what he was getting.

"I know," Stella lit up; "observation."

"Ahum," MacAwen nodded, his eyes gleaming. "Is the first lesson, observation."

Stella beamed. She didn't know how she knew. She just knew. Patrick rolled his eyes, nodding and forcing a smile. "Before begins any real education," MacAwen continued, "must come first, *the failing to observe*."

Patrick crinkled his brow. MacAwen eyed him questioningly, raising *his* brows.

"I get it *now*," Patrick said. "I think. But you said the *failing* to observe. What you must mean is; first comes the *succeeding* to observe," Patrick corrected MacAwen's words. "I think your *usage* is still getting a bit mixed up."

"Ah.... Inquisitive is he," MacAwen smiled, "observant of *words*—and *articulate,* even *scientific*."

Patrick was looking very pleased with himself now. "It is imperative to ask questions," he smiled importantly, glancing at Stella as if he was MacAwen's assistant teacher.

Stella gave him a look that said, wow—you're so impressive, Patrick.

"But not *yet* do ye get it," MacAwen laughed, shaking his head.

Patrick stared at MacAwen, clearly disappointed—and confused. Stella observed them both, curiously.

"How could be it true learning if succeeded one the first time?" MacAwen asked. "What would be the point ta learning what already know ye? Hum?" he stuck his neck out, his eyes bulging. "How would even know ye what success was if did na' fail ye first? Is it not better ta fail first, and get it right later, than the other way around?"

"Now," MacAwen smiled, his hands again stretching out wide to either side of his body, his fingers gently feeling through the air. "*Observe*," he said, his outstretched hands drifting backwards, behind the line of his shoulders. "Do as do I, and observe both hands at once."

Stella and Patrick tried it. Stella noticed right away that she could see both outstretched hands at the same time, no problem—if she let her eyes go out of focus from any one thing. "Wide vision are ye using now," MacAwen nodded. "And so must be observing ye ta properly stealth walk. Especially if wants ta see ya some creatures before are seen ye, yer selves. For already are most of the creatures in this forest educated in wide eyed observing—as well as in techniques of sniffing, listening, and feeling that not yet ready are *ye* ta learn." He observed them practicing their wide peripheral vision. "Good," he nodded. "Now do it while stealth walking." Again, they tried the stealth walk.

"Patrick—no slouching or hunching forward," he snipped. "Not long enough are yer arms ta make a proper chimpanzee! Notice how straight is my body as walk I?" he demonstrated. Patrick and Stella emulated his movement. "Good," he nodded. "*Better.* But relaxed be—not stiff, Stella," he laughed. "Not just a robot are ye. Move with the *flow*," his eyes widened, "like the *wind*. And while walking," his voice hushed to a mystical tone, "wide must be yer eyes ta all around ye at all times—never just focused on the stretch of ground in front of ye. For a wide world, yes," he nodded, "wide eyes." MacAwen's eyes went wide as a frog's.

"Now—taking short steps—come down on outsides of feet, rolling in as apply ye pressure ta the Earth. See?" He showed how his feet gently conformed to a oneness with the earth in every step he placed—and gestured for them to do the same.

"Not heal toe, heal toe," he barked, "but outside of foot, rolling in. And walk in balance—" he demonstrated further, "no lunging. Each moment must be able ye ta freeze without falling, on one foot or the other. Patrick—slow down!" he put his hands on his hips. "Should not be swinging yer arms like some kind of locomotive steam engine are ye! Alert will ye every creature of the forest that traipsing toward them is a bumbling human. Let hang low yer arms, close ta yer body—so like a moving tree stump do ye look."

"I'll *try*," Patrick consented defensively, "but *tree stumps* don't usually *move*."

"Not that would any *modern human* notice!" MacAwen shrugged. Yet at last, as he observed Patrick and Stella practicing their stealth walks, he nodded his approval. "Ahum. Very good," he conceded. Now may begin ta learn ye a tracking lesson or two —without bumbling in pure oblivion—straight in ta the Shadow Beast, itself!"

Still, he frowned at their shoes. "Shoes..." He sighed, shaking his head. "Best is it ta be barefoot," he stated flatly, his toes tapping and wriggling into the mud. "When on rough terrain, *okay* are soft soled shoes—*without* heals." He stared at their sneakers again, as if pondering deeply. "Hum. Not bad... *for factory made*," he admitted, reluctantly, though clearly impressed. "Now —are ready ye?" he smiled wide eyed.

"Okay," Stella smiled brightly in return. "Tread the word, Little Brown Man."

"Stella!" Patrick snapped at her.

"Ah..." MacAwen shot her a wild gaze. "Hum!" he nodded, his eyes gleaming. "See shall we who treads what words!" He turned and lead them further into the forest.

"*Where* did you come up with *that* one?" Patrick asked quietly in Stella's ear, as they followed MacAwen.

"Oh...it just came to me," Stella smiled. But as Patrick shook his head, rolled his eyes, and headed down the path after MacAwen, Stella recalled how it *had* come to her:

Two eighth grade boys were talking about a certain shirt one of them had bought on their class trip. On the front of it was a picture of a hand with the middle finger sticking up. Apparently, their teacher had noticed it. "We weren't even at school," Andrew had complained to his friend, Graeme, "and Mr. Rimen wouldn't let me wear the shirt."

Stella had misunderstood when Andrew said, 'wear the shirt'. She had thought she heard him say, 'tread the word'. "Wow! That's such an awesome saying," she cut into their conversation.

They looked at her like she had three heads—and not one screwed on quite straight. "What are you talking about?" Andrew asked, as Graeme stared at her, smiling.

"Tread the word!" she answered. "It's such an awesome saying. Where'd you get it from? Did you make it up?"

They eyed her oddly. "I didn't say *tread the word*," Andrew laughed at her. "I said *wear the shirt*."

"Oh. Well—*wear the shirt*. Yeah—that's a pretty cool saying, too," Stella smiled. "But isn't *tread the word* just the coolest saying ever?"

Graeme and Andrew continued to stare at Stella rather oddly for a few awkward moments. Then they turned to one another. "It *is* a pretty cool saying," Graeme offered with a smile.

"*Tread the word*?" Vaguely amused at first, Andrew pondered the phrase. Then suddenly, it seemed to strike a cord within him. "Actually, that is cool," he now agreed. "We could use that for the name of one of our songs."

"Yeah, we should," Graeme chuckled. "We will," he added, as he and Andrew carried on, discussing how many songs they had already written for their first CD....

"Mind ye the *pathways* that *treading* are ye *now*, Stella!" MacAwen's voice snapped her back to the present, as the Little Man approached from ahead on the trail where he and Patrick had been staring back at her. "Are there pathways enough in *there*," he pointed to her head, "ta keep ye busy enough for a lifetime, without ever *treading a foot*. But is education the act of coming *out* of oneself—not just wandering within."

"Oh...." Stella swirled from her daydream, striving as quick as she could to return her senses to the present. There was an awkward moment. Then, "Yeah!" she lit up brightly. "I totally do get it!"

MacAwen's large eyes widened, his brows raised, and a stifled sound halfway between a laugh and his typical "Ah...um" issued from his opened mouth as he turned back to the trail and led them onward.

Patrick glanced at MacAwen, then half-whispered to Stella, "*I* have formulated a theory on how *Tread the Word* came to you. We are both *walking* in *Converse* sneakers. To *converse* means to speak. Therefore, we are *Treading the Word*."

36

Stella shook her head in disgust and continued after MacAwen, striving to ignore her geeky, chatter box friend who never ceased impressing himself with facts and theories which made no sense to anyone but him.

They followed the tracks of the fisher—winding, turning, hopping, meandering. Over logs, he went, upon every available stump, under branches, through the mud, into the water, up and down trees. Clearly, this was an inquisitive and fun loving creature. It wasn't always easy tracking this *four-legged hoodlum*, as Patrick called him, but it was intriguing—and fun.

"Look closely here," MacAwen pointed to an especially clear print. "Can tell ye that is he a *he* by the fact that registering consistently are his hind feet a deeper impression on the outsides of the heels than on the insides. Gently feel these tracks wi- yer fingers. Then look forward into the next ones, the next ones, and the next ones." Stella and Patrick took turns looking closely, and feeling the tracks with their fingers.

"The back prints are deeper on the outsides of the heel than on the insides! I can see it!" Patrick exclaimed.

"And I can feel it!" Stella whispered in awe.

MacAwen then pointed to another set of tracks crossing those of the fisher. "Now who do suppose ye printed these?" he asked with an impish gleam. Neither Patrick nor Stella had a clue. These prints were smaller than the fisher's, and they had only four toes. Also, the walking pattern was quite different.

"Walks this gray fox in a diagonal pattern," MacAwen informed. "Is't even easier to tell that is he a he. For is he very *he-ish. And*, in diagonal walkers—which, when relaxed, are all dogs, cats, and hoofed animals—register the male's hind feet usually a narrower straddle than do the front." He turned to Patrick and Stella. "See ye how closer together are his hind feet than his forefeet?" He pointed to the hind prints which landed almost directly on top of the fore prints, only a bit to the inside.

"*Those* are the hind feet tracks!" Patrick exclaimed in realization, circling a couple of prints with his finger. "And that's what's left of the front tracks," he added, pointing to a couple of the slightly longer prints that were almost directly stamped on by the rear ones, and thus erased, except for the claws

and outer edges. Stella and Patrick were both nodding, amazed they could read such a thing in a set of tracks. They had previously thought only the rare expert hunter with a lifetime of experience could read sign like that. Now they could.

MacAwen then pointed to a set of tiny tracks. "White Footed Mouse," he informed, "not quite grown up. Can tell ye whether male or female is it?" Patrick and Stella studied the tiny tracks. After a bit they shook their heads. These prints were just too tiny.

"Look closer," MacAwen urged. And, for example, he lowered his head sideways, right onto the ground in front of one of the tiny sets of tracks. Then he shifted his head to the other side. Stella and Patrick tried it. They stared, for a long time, at the track pattern and into the individual prints. They were on their bellies, their heads tilted this way, then that way, to study the prints from different angles. After a while the light seemed to change somehow-- and then the tracks appeared to be glowing.

"I can tell!" Stella suddenly whispered. "It's a female."

"I see it, too," Patrick whispered. But they both continued staring, amazed by their own ability, not only to read the tracks, but to *see* so vividly. For they knew it was the way they used their own eyes that made the tracks appear to glow, not just MacAwen's magic.

"This is just like...*amazing,*" Stella breathed reverently, her eyes widening, "I mean...*tracks* are like...a *living* manuscript," Stella's arms and whole body swayed about—in her typical fashion—animated by emotion, as though she was *feeling* to the depths of the meanings of every word she spoke. Patrick rolled his eyes and shot her an odd glance.

"Ahum," MacAwen raised his brows, smiling at Stella and Patrick, then turned back to the mouse's trail. "A happy mouse is she," he nodded. "Full is her belly with sprouted red oak acorn, nibbles of mushroom, grass seed—and the moth that ate she while back on the trail, tromping unconsciously on the tracks of Martes pennanti, were ye two," MacAwen whispered hoarsely, as he continued along the trail of the fisher.

"How can you tell all that?" Patrick asked, unconvinced.

"Easy as read ye, yer books," MacAwen answered. "Study tracks as do ye yer letters and sentences, and learn will ye also ta read tracks as I."

Stella opened her mouth and lipped the phrase, "*wow...awe...*" but no breath came out to make the sound, until the final syllable of her phrase; "*some!*"

"*Some* what?" Patrick eyed her inquisitively. But Stella barely heard him. To her it was obvious *what*. It was *awe*-some. Mesmerized by MacAwen and his ability to read tracks, now she just wanted to see more.

Along the way they saw a place where the fisher took a running slide. "Cool," Patrick whispered. Stella smiled.

Her smile vanished, however, as she noticed the black, wet scat Mr. Fisher had neatly placed on top of a log just before he entered The De Da Mua. "Ooh," she scrunched up her nose. "That's disgusting."

"Has he left a sign post for us," MacAwen explained. Patrick smiled. Stella rolled her eyes.

As she walked along behind MacAwen and Patrick, Stella's attention was drawn from the fisher's tracks, to an amazing purple mushroom she spotted alongside the trail. Mesmerized, she knelt to observe it. But her attention was now captured by a strange and beautiful moth that crawled from under the mushroom's cap and took flight. She stood up, following the moth's meandering course, high into the trees. Through an opening in the canopy above she saw a jet, streaking across the sky. It left a contrail behind it....

Stella remembered her Uncle Ken describing the formation of contrails to her. It was during a party in Stella's back yard. The sky was clear and Stella had commented on the *fumes* she thought she was seeing, trailing behind a jet.

"What you're seeing are not the fumes," Uncle Ken corrected her. *That* is a contrail. And there is another," he pointed to another jet, also leaving a short trail behind it.

"What are contrails?" Stella asked.

"Temporary cloud trails formed by otherwise invisible atmospheric water vapor, usually in the form of ice crystals, that condense on the exhaust particles streaming from the engines of jets," Uncle Ken smiled, grabbing a hazel and a nutcracker from a bowl on the picnic table. "Depending on altitude, temperature, and atmospheric conditions contrails can last anywhere from the usual few seconds, up to—in rare conditions—several minutes." Uncle Ken had cracked open the hazel nut while he spoke, and now plopped the contents into Stella's hand.

"Wow... You know so much—" Stella said, staring in awe at her Uncle Ken— "about everything."

Uncle Ken shrugged with a mixture of a grunt and a laugh. "It only seems that way, Stella," he shook his head, "because real knowledge is forbidden. And your Uncle Ken chooses to be an outlaw," he smiled, then turned to the grill where he was cooking a rather massive fillet of salmon.

"Forbidden?" Stella was struck with wonder and confusion. *Knowledge?* "By who?"

"The Shadow Government," Ken turned to her with a chunk of salmon, held out on a fork. "Take a taste of this...."

Stella never got to ask Uncle Ken what *The Shadow Government* was because her Mom had walked over to them, and the subject had changed. It was understood; asking Uncle Ken questions about certain categories of strange things he mentioned was not appropriate.

For Stella, watching *this* contrail *now* was mesmerizing. It was magic. Studying it ever more intensely, she was completely captivated. She forgot all about Uncle Ken—or the pretty moth that had drawn her attention to the sky. Her consciousness followed the vapor trail as it formed and, almost as quickly, dissipated, vanishing into the clear blue.   It was beautiful....

"*Stell...la*—" Patrick called to her once more from ahead on the trail, "you're *eyes* are in the *clouds*. *Tracks* are on the *ground!*"

"Oh!" Stella's consciousness came crashing back to Earth in a panic as her vision jolted from the sky to Patrick and MacAwen, once again, staring back at her from ahead on the trail. She expected MacAwen to scold her for allowing her focus to stray. But it was upon Patrick that the Little Man turned his ire.

"Are tracks *everywhere!*" MacAwen snipped. "Not only on the ground, young whip snapper. Just as important is it ta look up —and all around. *Especially* when is the Shadow Beast afoot." He gave Patrick a scrutinizing gaze. "Though limited be yer head ta two eyes, at least endowed is it with a neck. Ought ye ta use that neck more often perhaps—ta help yer eyes connect more of this universe ta yer mind. Hum?" He extended his own neck so his face went right into Patrick's.

Patrick rolled his eyes, but his neck *was* getting more usage now, Stella noticed, as he was looking everywhere other than into MacAwen's face. "Much better," MacAwen smiled. His eyes darted from Patrick, to Stella, to the last wisps of visible vapor that had been the contrail moments before. Then he spied the very moth that had brought Stella's attention to the sky. As if the moth had left a trail in the air behind *it,* MacAwen tracked its exact flight with his eyes, back to the purple mushroom that had drawn Stella's attention from the trail. "Ahum," he nodded, smiling, then turned and continued on the fisher's trail.

Stella stared at the back of him, amazed, realizing that MacAwen had back tracked the very trail of her thoughts—from the clouds, to the moth, to the mushroom, and back to the footprints of the fisher. And he did it so quick, with such ease. She could only imagine what else further he could read. But more than anything else, she felt a great and unusual sense of satisfaction —and a gratitude toward the little brown man. People were always reprimanding her for having her head in the clouds; now she was being commended for it.

Stella looked back up at the sky. Now she saw a different sort of cloud. It was long and narrow—like a gigantic contrail. Yet this cloud was not dissipating. Through three different openings in the forest's canopy she could see that this strange cloud extended the entire length of the sky.

"Whoa! What's that?" Stella asked, still staring— mesmerized.

"Jet stream." Patrick answered, as a matter of fact.

"You mean like—from a jet?" Stella asked, glancing at him just long enough to realize, MacAwen had gone ahead of them. "Or like—*the* jet stream?" she continued staring at the sky in lingering bewilderment.

"Well—I think it's from a jet," Patrick answered.

"But...*contrails* dissipate in a few seconds," Stella stated, puzzled. Uncle Ken had explained this to her. This cloud did look like a gigantic contrail, only it wasn't disappearing.

"I've seen jet streams like this," Patrick answered. "And I'm pretty sure I've seen them being made. They come from the exhaust of jets." He nodded.

"That's weird." Stella frowned. "I thought contrails only lasted a few seconds."

"Actually—" Patrick lit up. "Now that you mention it—I did hear something about the existence of *persistent contrails*—at science camp, last summer. There are certain conditions that cause this phenomenon."

Stella raised her brows. "Seems more like pollution than condensation trails, if you ask me. But now that *you* mention it—I think I've heard Uncle Ken talk about something like this."

Patrick rolled his eyes and shook his head. He was about to comment further when they both noticed MacAwen, standing with his arms folded, staring back at them them.

"Seems it now that growing ever more urgent is it, for *ye* two-leggeds, ta be focusin' on the path before ye—and ta get in ta the De Da Mua." He glanced to the sky, shaking his head. "Clearly, is the Shadow Beast afoot. Now come!"

All Stella's thoughts and feelings were abruptly changed. As she and Patrick followed MacAwen, the forest opened suddenly —to a vast and strange area of tall grasses, variable bushes, and dwarf trees. Here there were only islands of dry earth. From the woodland border, the ground dropped down about a foot—into a black, wet mud. Stella's heart seemed to drop with it—her consciousness drawn in. She felt a great energy—a presence, rising up into her. All throughout there swirled streams and billows of mist. Yet within and beyond the mist, Stella's eyes perceived the swirling, fuzziness she had noticed before—yet now more vivid, more lively. It pulsated and emanated from everywhere.

"Now shall we enter the De Da Mua," MacAwen announced with a deep, resonant breath and a gleam of great joy in his eyes. Patrick and Stella stared—wide-eyed—into the mysterious, weird, wet swamp-wood. It *was* enchanting...and enticing. Yet Stella felt certain—once she stepped in, she would never be the same. And for she and Patrick both, rising from abstraction in the depth of their minds was the dark realization; lurking...somewhere in there...was the Shadow Beast.

Behind the veil of all that's seen
a monster lurks...through eyes between
the here and there, and the you and it.
But Bright the light and change a bit!

Chapter II:
"The Shadow Beast"

"Well—it's not as big as I had imagined," Patrick stated, in spite or denial of the eerie sense of awe he had obviously felt at his first glimpse of the De Da Mua.

"Bigger is it than think ye—" MacAwen laughed. "Think ye is the far side that island over there?" he gestured to the tall trees on the other side of what Patrick thought was the expanse of The De Da Mua. "But one of many, many of the larger islands in The De Da Mua is that," he whispered with a strange, awe filled pride. "Not in a lifetime could explore ye the depths and breadths of myriad labyrinths that make up The De Da Mua."

"Its just a swamp," Patrick blurted out. "I mean—it's awesome. Don't get me wrong," he added, so as not to offend the Little Brown Man. "But if it was really that big we would have heard about it. I mean, it would cover half the map of Lilton—our town," he explained.

"Yer maps—ha! Not even do show they but a scratch on a stone—if shows they even the stone!" MacAwen snapped at Patrick, though Stella perceived a twinkle in his eye. "Think ye contained is The De Da Mua within yer town? Think again, young-on'! And whilst thinking—keep opened *wide* yer eyes...to The De Da Mua." MacAwen's eyes widened like headlights and stared off into the mist.

"But...I *love* maps," Patrick stated, eyeing MacAwen pleadingly. "And though it has often been said: *the map is not the territory*, the latest computer technology does provide me—and my Dad—with the most outstanding maps."

Stella shook her head, hardly able to believe her friend could continue babbling about maps and computer technology when they were surrounded by such enchantment. But MacAwen somehow seemed suddenly reverent to some aspect of Patrick's nerdy personality.

"Ah...." MacAwen returned his wide, gleaming eyes to Patrick. "Hum...." He stared at him thoughtfully. "A well rounded stone on the cutting edge is this young jewel," he nodded. "Is more ta wonder. And yet is it no wonder that joined have our pathways at this moment," he smiled. Patrick smiled also, quite pleased with himself.

"Yet see shall we soon what happens to young Mr. *Leading Cutting Edge,* and all the jewels who follow," MacAwen added with a gleam, "when meet they face ta face with the molten iron of the Central Sun!" MacAwen's face appeared suddenly fiery, like a great unknown power was blazing within.

A sudden confused and concerned look overcame Patrick's expression. MacAwen smiled with satisfaction.

"Is't nae fairy tale that are ye walkin' in ta now, young-on', but rather—*a Mythic Adventure*."

"Uhh..." Patrick shook his confused head. "What's that supposed to mean?"

"Use yer imagination," MacAwen retorted.

"Wow!" Stella's eyes lit up. "Mythic Adventure! Yeah!"

Patrick shook his head, in annoyance at Stella and in bewilderment to MacAwen.

"Is a *Mythic Adventure*," MacAwen explained with a shrug, "in terms that might even by *ye* be understood; a real world experience enhanced beyond ordinary reality...by expanded consciousness."

Patrick had to pause to ponder MacAwen's words.

MacAwen nodded and smiled. "Soon shall see ye how much of what believe ye ta be fantasy is more real than what believe ye ta be reality. And how is most of what modern people believe ta be reality, in truth, pure fantasy. Now come." He leapt, precisely where Martes pennanti had, upon a small log embedded in the mud.

Stella and Patrick realized right away, their sneakers, socks, and pant legs would be completely wet and muddied within their first few steps. It was inevitable. Patrick simply shrugged, smiled and stepped right in. Stella removed her sneakers, tucked her socks into them, and tied them to her belt loops. She also rolled up her pant legs, though it was clear she would get them soaked anyway.

Once in The De Da Mua, the fisher's feet had sunk deeper, making his trail easier to follow. Yet in this deeper, mucky substrate it was almost impossible to clearly see any of his individual prints.

After a while MacAwen veered off the fisher's tracks, whispering, "now must be ye fully alert—soon shall come we ta the freshest tracks...of the Shadow Beast."

Now they noticed that MacAwen left no tracks at all, when he didn't wish to, even though the mud was so deep. The Little Brown Man could swing on the reeds, leap from log to log, and even seemed to step on the mud occasionally without making any apparent mark.

If there had been strands of scrolls in the muddy areas of the upper woodlands, here there was a collage—a vast and complex artwork, created and recreated by hands and feet beyond counting.

"I never imagined in all the world there were this many tracks!" Patrick exclaimed. "What do you suppose made these, MacAwen?" he pointed to a set that resembled the mouse's, only much larger.

"Clearly is it a rodent," MacAwen whispered. "Can tell ye by the U-shaped pattern— small front feet with four toes, larger hind feet with five toes," he pointed.

"But if those are the front feet," Patrick asked, "why are the hind feet in front of them?"

"Are most rodents bounders—most of the time," MacAwen answered. "After leaping from their big hind feet, land they first on their front paws which are close together here, see?" he pointed. "Then swinging past the front paws ta the outsides come his big hind feet, landing side by side, in front of the front feet—and leaps he off again."

"Like a rabbit!" Stella blurted.

"Like a rabbit," MacAwen folded his arms, "sometimes. But notice how change this fat creature's walk into a diagonal pattern? Belong these tracks here ta a pack rat named Pat. Humph!" he snorted. "Stolen more than a few jewels of mine has this rodent!" MacAwen narrowed his eyes. "A real thief is Pat," he nodded with a sigh. "And a great collector."

"He steals? Stuff?" Patrick asked.

"What would expect ye of a pack rat?" MacAwen snapped. "Every now and again must inspect I his nest," MacAwen nodded. "At least knows I where ta look when gone missing has something or another. Pat's Nest!" he accused. "But a likable fellow is Pat," MacAwen added. Another time will I introduce ye ta him."

Stella's eyes lit up. She so wanted to meet this great collector.

"But now," MacAwen turned, pointing to a much larger set of tracks, "what do suppose ye left these?"

No individual prints were discernible in this set of tracks, yet it was clearly a large creature with a very strange walking pattern—impossible for Stella or Patrick to comprehend.

"Is it the Shadow Beast?" Patrick asked, staring at the strange tracks.

"Those look really weird," Stella noted, "kind o' scary."

"Not from any Shadow Beast are these

50

tracks!" MacAwen asserted with a laugh. "Left were these yesterday, by a mother coyote on the way back ta her den— dragging the remains of a deer carcass that had she cached after a winter's hunt. Is't what are all those strange marks, see?" he pointed out all the drag marks from the carcass.

Eyeing Stella's disturbed expression, MacAwen explained: "Four growing pups has she. Hungry all the time. Ought ye ta see 'em. Do look they just like their father. A real wolf is he—biggest coyote in these parts since his great, great, grandfather twenty seven times removed. But come—off track are we getting."

In a short distance they came to another set of suspicious tracks. These were enormous. The stride was very long, and the tracks sunk very deep into the mud. Their senses heightened to full alert, Stella and Patrick looked to MacAwen with wide questioning eyes.

"Yes—a most intriguing creature is this moose," he answered, "but time do we not have ta follow it now." And he continued leading them along.

After about twenty more minutes with no further sign of anything larger than a weasel, Patrick voiced his impatience. "We've been meandering for quite some time—"

"Hush!" MacAwen exclaimed. "Another set of fresh tracks are ye about ta discover. This time," he whispered, "will be they the tracks of the Shadow Beast!"

"How can you...*know*?" Patrick's voice faded to a fearful whisper. Then he went silent. Stella also felt suddenly vulnerable —so far removed from anything formerly familiar, other than her geeky friend.

Sure enough, in another ten paces they came upon a set of tracks—much larger than those of the moose—very fresh, and unlike anything they had come across before. Stella noticed a strange scent in the air—like that of something rotting.

"It's a heavy creature," Patrick whispered, pointing to the depth of the tracks.

"And it moves with an irregular gait," Stella added with a disturbed expression as she pointed out the bizarre and changing pattern. Sometimes it appeared to go on all fours. Other times it seemed to be walking upright, on two legs.

Now their senses grew super alert. Each little sound— whether bird or insect, grew to monstrous proportions. Every dark stump or stone or shadow might be a part of The Shadow Beast's hidden form. And every breeze hinted at the cold breath of the thing that could not be seen.

"It just stomps right over everything in its path," Patrick noted. "Even that lumbering moose showed a little care in the way it placed its hooves."

Stella found a squished frog in one of The Shadow Beast's tracks—and then another. "Oh my god!" she exclaimed, though very quietly. "It's terrible!"

At that moment, the world seemed suddenly to grow a little bit darker. The fog filled air went still as death. "What just happened?" Patrick whispered, as he and Stella shot startled looks about them. But they both seemed to realize at once, while tracking other things, they had lost track of time. Could it already be growing dark? Or was it only the density of the fog?

"Stalk silently!" MacAwen warned with a whisper. "Very close are we ta the Shadow Beast. Shall see ye it soon."

Stella and Patrick hesitated, almost frozen.

"Cautious—" MacAwen nodded, "and intensely be alert, yes," his eyes lit up, "but be not frightened out of yer wits! Expanded are the illusionary powers of The Shadow Beast by *too much* fear. Feeds it on terror and panic."

"*Illusionary powers?*" Stella trembled, feeling for her amulet and giving it a squeeze in her pocket. Patrick and Stella both froze in their tracks, eyeing each other the same concerned look. Then Patrick turned to MacAwen.

"I was sort of thinking this thing to be like—like some kind of, maybe a *slightly* supernatural sort of *animal*," he whispered intensely, "not some *being* with magical powers!"

"Magical powers—*well!*" MacAwen's eyes widened. "Anyone that the power to imagine has—and anything that the power to inspire imagination possesses, endowed is with magical powers."

Patrick and Stella's eyes were as wide as MacAwen's. Neither made a motion to continue tracking.

"Come now," MacAwen reassured. "Underestimate ye, yer own powers. Endowed with the powers of imagination are ye, also. Is it *ye* who empowers this Shadow Beast—with yer fears— with yer lack of awareness."

"Ta tell the truth," he whispered, "much safer are ye from The Shadow Beast now than when stalked I first up behind ye. As a matter of fact," he added, "whilst wi- me on the trail of this Beast, safer from it are ye than ever have been ye in all yer lives. Furthermore, after seeing it, as disturbing as may be it, know will ye at least what takes it ta avoid it. Now come," he commanded. And he led them forward, toward the shadowed source of the tracks.

A pungent odor of something rotten now, without a doubt, permeated the dense, moist air. As they walked, the odor grew stronger. Patrick and Stella were unsure whether it was the smell of the beast or of the muck getting stirred up under their feet, but it made them feel uneasy—and their tension was growing.

MacAwen quietly urged them along the way until they came suddenly upon another set of tracks—very similar looking, and continuing alongside those of the Shadow Beast. Here the foul odor grew twice as strong. "Another set," Stella whispered. "There's two of them!"

"So appears it," MacAwen nodded. "But maybe is it just in two places at once," he raised his brows, a bit of an impish smile on his face.

Stella and Patrick's' breathing quickened—as though they had been running. Their hearts raced. Stella felt the drumming in her chest so strong it hurt. Her head felt it was spinning as she wondered, what *was* this terrible beast they were about to meet? What would it look like? And when at last they discovered it, how would MacAwen ensure their safety? Their eyes scanned the landscape very carefully, striving to spot the beast—or beasts— before it, or they, spotted them.

"Wait a minute—" Patrick whispered. "I recognize this place. This is where we first spotted the Shadow Beast's tracks." He looked left and right, studying the second set of tracks, the surrounding landscape, and the direction the tracks came from. "It's leading us in a circle," he stated in realization. "That set of tracks is mine and Stella's," he pointed, "and there we go, following The Shadow Beast."

"If we're going in a circle," Stella whispered intensely, "that means the Shadow Beast is also tracking us. It could be behind us —or in front of us."

"Maybe both," MacAwen added.

Behind us, and in front of us. That thought sank quickly into Stella's mind—penetrating as if MacAwen had dropped a heavy rock—through the De Da Mua's water, through its soft mud, to a solid depth where it was no longer a moving thought, but a settled realization.

Now they followed their own tracks, following those of the Shadow Beast. Yet as their feet plunged cautiously through the water and mud of the De Da Mua, another thought formed in Stella's mind. She turned and studied the tracks *they* were now making. "*Our* tracks—" she whispered aloud, "are really similar to the tracks of the shadow Beast. The way we walk...."

"Of course!" MacAwen exclaimed, as Patrick and Stella turned questioning looks to the tracks behind them, to the tracks before them, to each other, and finally to MacAwen. "Who do think ye is it following? Who, or what, do expect ye it ta resemble?" he asked them, his gleaming eyes now wide as tea cups. "Be aware!" he whispered, nodding intensely. "Are about ta behold ye The Shadow Beast!"

They halted in their tracks, searching with eyes and ears. All was quiet and still. Patrick's gaze shot upward. He froze. Stella's gaze followed Patrick's. High in the tree tops, she saw something moving—a large, dark shape. Suddenly, it was descending toward them—gigantic and snake-like!

Stella almost screamed, her heart pounding. But as adrenaline intoxicated her body and the throbbing beats in her chest slowed, she realized—it was just the shadows of branches, moving down a tree trunk—an illusion, caused by sunlight and wind...and her own imagination.

She turned to Patrick. Now he was eyeing something in the bush behind them—rather concernedly. She looked. Nothing. They waited—looking, listening, sniffing.... All she heard was her own heartbeat and breath—unnervingly loud. The fog filled air, the water, the trees, the grasses, the shrubs—all were quiet and unmoving. Too quiet. Their own awkward movements and sounds struck into the silence and stillness like a pronouncement; here we are—nearly deaf and blind, but obvious for whatever is out there to see and hear. Her only sense that did not betray her was her scent. Yet she rather wished it was not so keen. The odor had grown to a pungency that was almost overwhelming.

Stella's eyes fell to the deep, dark, motionless water covering the muck just below their knees. She could see her reflection—befuddled and clueless. But as she looked deeper, beneath her reflection, she could see something moving in the dark muck below. This was not caused by wind. Something, beneath the water, was definitely moving. She glanced at Patrick; sure enough, his eyes also were now fixed, on something moving in the depths of the De Da Mua's water and mud.

Stella's gaze shot back to where she had perceived movement —and there, beneath the water, was a face! Petrified, she gasped —and her vision blacked out. Time seemed to stretch between one heartbeat and the next; yet it was not until after the third pound in her chest that she realized her eyes had been shut. She opened them—expecting to see the Shadow Beast, risen from the water. But whatever it was had disappeared in the depths of the mud. Fog swirled and moved about in clouds and billows that hinted at shapes of various size and form. But she held her focus to the spot where the face had appeared. She bent down, searching closely.

For a moment, the fog directly above Stella thinned—and sunlight burst down. The face reappeared—right beneath her! Terror, in that moment, gripped her motionless. She could feel the cold, slimy hands of the Shadow Beast with its sharp claws clasping her ankles! It would pull her below!

But as she caught her breath, and got a grip on herself, she realized—it was only sticks and mud on her ankles. And again, she could see...the face was her own reflection.

"See ye the Shadow Beast?" MacAwen asked.

"Are we tracking ourselves?" Patrick asked, both terrified and thoroughly confused.

"Of course!" MacAwen answered. "Always are we tracking ourselves."

"What?" Stella's head swirled. "You mean— You little trickster!" she exclaimed, staring incredulously at The Little Brown Man. "I was wondering if that—"

"Wonder some more!" MacAwen snapped, "but quietly!" he whispered intensely. "A greater trickster might be I than are ye guessing, yes!" his eyes gleamed. "But greater still may be the trickster that is The Shadow Beast itself—for guessing are ye only at the part of this riddle that reflects on the surface of The De Da Mua's water."

MacAwen held his hands just above the water, so Patrick and Stella could see them and their reflection just below. Then he slowly lowered his hands into the water where the reflection disappeared, and his true hands only could be seen below the surface. There they pressed into the mud, disappearing without ever having made a ripple. "Is't the wonder of wonders. Be aware, be aware," he chanted. "Tracking ye for a long time has been this Shadow Beast. Now at last have tracked ye it."

"Uhh…I don't get it," Stella surrendered, staring into the muck below the water where his hands had disappeared—then back at the tracks. "Aren't these our own tracks?"

"Yes—" MacAwen turned to her, eyeing her as though she had just floated down to Earth from Planet Bubble Head. "But very real is The Shadow Beast. Walks it in yer very tracks—yes! Supernatural is the Shadow Beast—paranormal. And deadly can it be beyond yer imagining."

"Wait—" Stella reached down for MacAwen's shoulder and froze. "Is there actually a beast out there? Or are we just imagining?"

"Certainly, yes! And yes!" MacAwen thrust his wide-eyed face in her direction, his hands still submerged in the muck. "But," he toned down, "never is it just what imagine ye. In fact," he scanned the surrounding landscape and the tree-scape above, "exactly what never imagine ye—yes," he nodded, "exactly that is what is The Shadow Beast—what *unaware* of are ye." He worked the muck with both hands, continuing his speech, "But notice how awake are ye now." He pulled up two dark wet globs of mud and lobbed them at once, splatting Patrick and Stella square on the foreheads. Stella and Patrick's jaws dropped. A whispered shriek issued from Stella's opened mouth while a cold breath filled her lungs.

"Notice how feel ye alive, and see ye that alive and awake is the forest, too?" he continued on regardless of their astounded gestures. "Remember how asleep were ye before, and unaware of the abounding life?"

That moment, a layer of illusion dissolved. Patrick and Stella looked at each other. Their foreheads were tingling. They looked around, then down at the tracks beneath them—their tracks. Then they looked at MacAwen. "But...I guess I'm still a *little* perplexed," Stella admitted, mud dripping from her face.

"Is tracking the Shadow Beast a way ta clear yer mind, and come ta understand," MacAwen explained. "Is't the Beast of yer own unconsciousness. Yer own self is it, yes, but not yer awakened self. Is't yer self that half asleep is in a trance, and unaware of yer own walk—of yer own tracks, much less those of other creatures."

"Oh—so The Shadow Beast is not a physical creature," Stella sighed, relieved at last to have sorted the mystery out.

"Wrong," MacAwen answered. "*Is* a physical creature The Shadow Beast. For a part of ye, is it—that which know, *ye* do not —that which unaware of are ye."

"But—if it's a part of us that we're unaware of," Stella asked, "then how can we avoid it?"

"Strive always ta be ye aware," MacAwen nodded, "and always ta stretch yer awareness—and ta spread this awareness. For belongs this awareness ta ye alone no more than does the Shadow Beast. Belongs it ta everyone in the universe. And just as more powerful is the Shadow Beast than know ye—so also is this awareness as powerful as will ye ta imagine."

"Lurks the Shadow Beast everywhere," he whispered, his arms raised to the air, "always when and where expect ye it least. Now that are ye aware of it, have ye a chance at least ta avoid it—by keeping wide yer eyes—and yer ears—and on full alert, all yer senses." MacAwen nodded with a sigh. Then he sniffed the air inquisitively, his eyes going wide to all around, his ears extending, his arms outstretched, his palms upward, his fingers moving as if working an invisible force in the air.

As the full reality began to sink in at last, Patrick and Stella felt dumbfounded—and yet profoundly awakened. Their senses truly were enlivened as never before—and their eyes were wide. They understood, basically, and were grateful to MacAwen for the gift of wisdom he had bestowed upon them—even if it was a rather mucky brand of wisdom.

"But that's not quite a full explanation," Patrick ventured to state, "nor exactly a straight answer—"

"Ha! About time is it, fostered somebody a sense of wonder in ye," MacAwen retorted. "Not a good teacher would be I if cheated I yer inquisitiveness. Comes true wisdom from solving yer own mystery—not from any textbook. But tell ye will I this—if know do ye not already," he paused, eyeing Patrick intensely.

"Much bigger and greater is The Shadow Beast than the small aspect of it that following has been in *yer* two sets of tracks on *this* day. For as long as have walked humans in the flesh—so too has followed the Shadow Beast in their trails. Cast all souls of all creatures their individual shadows. Is The Shadow Beast made up of them all—yet independent of the individuals who cast their wee facets of its great darkness."

MacAwen's expression softened. "Now learned have ye, from experience, not ta fear it—rather ta pursue it, study it. For shrinks the Shadow Beast ever ta the light of growing awareness."

At last the lesson hit home. Not that they grasped the full meaning of MacAwen's words. That would take a lifetime of study. But they had a new sense. They were onto something. For a long spell, they stood in silence.

Now, like never before, Stella and Patrick heard the resonant tones of the peepers, the deep croak of the bullfrogs, the chirps and songs of birds and insects—and further, on some level they could sense the deeper meanings of all they heard and saw.

They listened ever more intently. And simultaneously, their vision was enlivened as well. The light of the sun, the shadows of the trees, the abounding colors, and all that reflected on the water took on dazzling new significance.

They began to see—or perhaps to notice what they could always see but were never conscious of; they were seeing the *living energy* that was usually invisible in the atmosphere all about them. And with the vision of this energy they were most mesmerized.

MacAwen noticed how they gazed in wonder at the thin air, and he smiled. "Not so thin nor empty is the air that breathe and walk we through, is it?" They shook their heads in silence. "Seeing Awen are ye now," he nodded approvingly. "Is't that which have I sprung from. Is't that which have begun I ta train ye ta see wi- yer wide eyes—and ta work with. Another time will I show ye, perhaps, techniques for enhancing yer vision, so that seeing will be ye, much more."

"Another time?" Patrick shook his head with disbelief, returning from his trance.

"More?" Stella asked in amazement and wonder as she noticed how auras and energy fields around every visible object were connected to, and part of, the living Awen.

"Always is there another time," MacAwen answered. "And always is there more." His eyes went wide as dinner plates, staring off into some place Stella and Patrick could only imagine. "Barely yet have glimpsed ye the air around us." His eyes narrowed onto Patrick and Stella. "For but a few moments only have eluded ye The Shadow Beast. Barely yet have grasped ye even a speck of the infinite magic."

"Infinite…magic?" Stella asked, still mesmerized by the pulsating energy in the air. "Oh...yeah..." she sighed, her eyes aglow, observing MacAwen's brilliant aura pulsating in perfect synchronicity with the energies all around. "Where do we go from here?" she asked excitedly.

"Home," MacAwen answered. "Much homework do have ye before any point can there be ta our next lesson." With his toes, MacAwen drew a perfect paw print in the mud. "Will be the animal who leaves this track yer teacher and guide, until find ye me again."

"It will?" Patrick raised his brows, his face blank.

"What animal leaves that track?" Stella stared wide-eyed and intrigued at the print MacAwen had drawn.

"That must find ye out on yer own," MacAwen eyed the air above the track as though looking at the animal itself. "On his path will find ye also, the tracks of four other creatures," he nodded. "Must remember ye the numbers of toes in each of their prints, and whether or not have they claws. Observe their track patterns," he squinted intensely at Stella and Patrick. "Find out about them all that can ye."

They scrunched their eyes in confusion, as though just returning from another realm. "Detectives must be ye," MacAwen explained. "Draw the prints that find ye, and the track patterns. And then, remembering that endowed are ye, with magic," he gleamed, "allow yer imagination ta bring ye the answers. All on yer own must find ye out who belong the tracks ta," he folded his arms. "Only then shall have we our next lesson."

"But—" Stella looked around at the vastness of the De Da Mua. "How will we find you again?"

"Find *me*?" MacAwen smiled. "Ah…um," he closed his eyes, placing a hand on his chest. "Prepare yer selves simply," he nodded, "and when return ye ta the De Da Mua, find *ye* will MacAwen," he smiled.

"Is there a bit of a trick though," MacAwen informed, "ta regaining access in ta the De Da Mua. Out here are there…*things* that guard the perimeter," he peered about, looking this way and that.

"Things?" Stella looked about with alarm. Patrick also, was peering about wide eyed.

"Not the kinds of things that need ye ta worry about," MacAwen assured. "Only are there forces out here that keep the De Da Mua hidden—*the guardians* of the doorways," he whispered, with his hands extended as he looked about in the branches above.

"I didn't notice any *doorways*," Patrick shot MacAwen a sideways glance.

"But are there many doorways out here," MacAwen nodded, folding his arms. "Several have walked we through this day." He raised his bushy brows. "Protected must be the De Da Mua," he nodded. "But created are special keys for those who have earned them."

He reached into the branches of a dwarf white birch growing beside them and pulled down a wide, dead branch. He dug his thick fingernails into one end and split the branch in half. From his trousers he produced a stone carving knife, and within a minute had fashioned two perfect little boards, faced with birch bark parchment. Onto each, he carved a unique inscription.

"Ta gain access back in ta the De Da Mua," he handed the parchment faced boards to Patrick and Stella, "these special Ogham codes will ye need."

Patrick and Stella grasped the boards and stared at their codes in confusion. "Tree letters," MacAwen informed. "Are yer personal keys on these boards. Just touch em wi- yer fingers while searching for the De Da Mua, and access will have ye ta the next level—if have earned ye it. For are there many layers ta the De Da Mua," MacAwen's eyes widened, "many levels above and below where stand ye now." Patrick and Stella quietly pondered the meaning of MacAwen's words. Stella imagined tunnels leading down under the earth, beneath the swamp level on which they now stood. But she could hardly imagine how levels *above* this place could exist—at least not physical levels.

"Ofter touch ye the code on yer key board, know who are ye will the De Da Mua's guardians. And open will they for ye, the doorways ta the realms that ready for are ye, and earned access ta have ye."

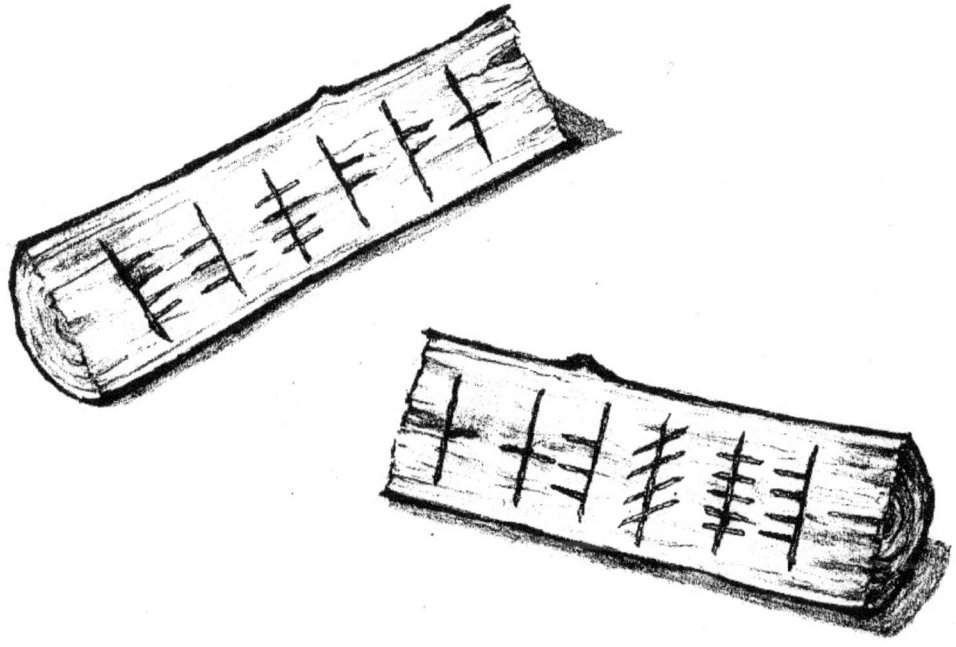

"How do we *earn* access to other levels," Stella asked, intrigued by the possibility.

"By spreading awareness," MacAwen breathed in a resonant half whisper— "awareness of the Mysterious Creature…awareness of the Shadow Beast…awareness of The Web of Tracks that connects them ta each other and ta everyone else in this world— even beyond this world," his wide eyes went to the heavens.... "And—" he gazed directly into Stella's eyes— "by spreading awareness of *The Terrible War* that brewing is even now—between those forces opposed ta what believe they is this Mysterious Creature—and those opposed ta the domination that planned has been by the Shadow Beast's *manipulators*."

Stella went silent, her eyes wide also, under raised brows. This was a bit more awareness than she could fathom all at once. *The Terrible War?* She thought to herself.

A war for your minds, she heard MacAwen's voice answer her thoughts—only his voice was *in* her thoughts. Or perhaps it was her thoughts in *his* voice. Either way, she sensed this was much bigger than just Patrick and her—or the small aspect of the Shadow Beast that they had observed. This was a war for the minds of everyone in the world. Now she rather wished she could get the thought *out* of her head.

Patrick on the other hand seemed to have let that last bit go right *over* his head. He was still staring at the strange symbols on his birch bark *key board*. "These are our personal codes?"

"Yes," MacAwen answered. "Hold them sacred. For as well as being keys ta the De Da Mua's doorways, hidden within each symbol are long forgotten powers. When ripe is the time will understand ye."

"A keyboard," Patrick stated. "Hm. Makes it seem…modern."

"Keyboard? Modern?" MacAwen shook his head, his eyes rolling. "Have keyboards been in use more than ninety thousand years!"

Patrick shot him a look—of amazement. Stella smiled. She and Patrick studied the tree letter codes on their keyboards so closely now that MacAwen was no longer in their view, as he concluded, "enough is that for now—until our next lesson." And with his last words, in a blink, a fleeting shadow and a flash of light flitted from the corners of their eyes. They thought afterward, they had heard something like a splash. And MacAwen was gone.

ᚦᛄᚡ ᛡ ᛏᚦᛞᛂᚼᛏᚤᛂ ᛂᛄᛏᚼᚦ ᛏᛂᚦ ᚦᛄᛏ ᛂᚷᚷ ᚦᛄᛏᚦ
ᛁᚦᛂᚷᚦᛂ ᚦᛄᚦ ᛁᚼᛏᚠᛢᚷᚷ ᛏᛂᚼᚦᚷᚷᛂ ᚦᛏ ᛏᚦᚦᛏᚦ

What's not absurd
does stand no chance.
What's unbelievable
must be seen.
Search for signs
near and wide
in brook, in bog, in green....

Chapter III:

Field Guide

Stella had never felt more alive or awake in her life. She felt inspired, ecstatic, like she could take on the world! And re-create it! At least in her imagination. She looked up, breathing in deep. The evening air was crisp. The stars were brilliant—pulsating! Stella stealth walked with wide eyes, barefoot. She felt strong and healthy—vibrant. The whole atmosphere was pulsating....

Time slipped. Stella walked alone on the path. It had grown very dark. A strange, alien or stealth sort of aircraft was flying high, high overhead—leaving a long, thin cloud trailing behind. In moments, another craft just like it appeared—then another. In the darkness, Stella could not actually see any alien crafts—nor any ordinary ones. But she could hear them. And she could see the vapor trails they left behind, for it seemed they snuffed out the very stars: huge, expanding, contrails that seemed somehow more unnatural than normal ones. They obscured the previously brilliant heavens now, like a foreboding sign. Stella lowered her eyes to the ground....

The Shadow Beast came to her mind. Not as it had come to Patrick and her. It was much bigger now. The more she thought of it, the more it seemed to be everywhere—lurking in every corner of the world, even pervading her very thoughts.

Stella forgot what it was she'd been thinking about, what it was that had inspired her, and why. Her head went foggy. Her thoughts were confused. A depression came over her, and a feeling like she just wanted to sleep. She glanced back to the sky. There were no alien crafts now, nor smog trails—only a massive, dull haze spread out over the dark sky. Not a single star could now be seen.

It was only somewhere in her foggy subconscious that Stella had an inkling this smog was unnatural. And now she only vaguely remembered hearing sounds of air craft in the sky, and perhaps she had only imagined them. But *something*, she felt, *was* clouding her brain. What if something in the atmosphere above her *was* unnatural?

Stella grew frightened. She remembered *The Terrible War* MacAwen had told her about—*a war for the minds of everyone on the planet*. Even now, it was brewing. *Who was it?* Stella tried to remember, *that was waging this war?* She thought she remembered MacAwen saying something about *those forces opposed to what believe they to be this Mysterious Creature—and those opposed to the Domination that planned has been by the Shadow Beast's manipulators.*

The Shadow Beast's *Manipulators*? Who or what could *they* be? Stella wondered. Then, as had happened before, she heard MacAwen's voice—*in* her thoughts:

"At the height of The Terrible War will come *The Singular Confrontation...*between the Shadow Beast's *manipulators*—and *the one whose tracks have foretold all."*

Again, this clue; *The Shadow Beast's Manipulators?* She still had no idea as to who or what they were. But they clearly had plans; *The Domination.* It didn't sound good.

But at the height of The Terrible War, MacAwen had now informed her, they would be met—in the *Singular Confrontation*—by *the one whose tracks have foretold all.* Something about that intrigued her. Logic told her this *one* must be MacAwen. For *the Manipulators* were opposed to *what believe they ta be this Mysterious Creature.*

She strove to remember all MacAwen had told her. But she could not concentrate. For her thoughts kept getting drawn to the clouds above her. Real or imagined, they seemed to have descended upon her and taken hold of her mind. She walked in the fog now, with growing uncertainty—until it seemed her life, in its entirety, might be nothing more than a dull and meaningless dream....

This was so opposite to how she had felt before. How could her mind have fallen to this? Within a few breaths, even that thought left her. Now she no longer had the thought or inclination to wonder why. She just walked, almost mindlessly....

The sudden snapping of a twig behind her jolted Stella from her trance. She turned toward the sound, but in the darkness could see nothing. Yet she *did* hear something. Her heart pounded. Someone was stalking her! Or some *thing....* Perhaps both. Perhaps many! Her thoughts raced. Her pace increased—almost to a run. But she stopped herself. Her thoughts weren't helping. *Too much fear,* she remembered MacAwen's voice, *serves only ta increase the illusionary powers of the Shadow Beast.*

Yet the sudden fright *had* reawakened her. She reached for the silver amulet in her pocket and gave it a squeeze. As always, it was comforting.

Stella stealth walked very carefully now, with all her senses on full alert. She *was* being tracked. *Not only by the Shadow Beast,* she sensed—but by *others.* And *they* had great tracking abilities— almost like MacAwen. Only, Stella sensed those stalking her now were *not* so benevolent. They were rather, diabolical. And for some reason, they wanted *her....*

A tall, dark figure suddenly appeared on the path in front of her. She halted and stepped backwards. But *others* were coming from behind. She could feel it. The dark figure in front of her was as terrifying as those behind her. But it was not one of them. It was something else. Stella froze. She sensed them closing in on her from behind, but she did not know what to do. She could not move!

As she awaited the inevitable, frozen in terror, a rather detached part of herself simply thought; *well—this is going to be interesting....*

With a shock of adrenaline, Stella opened her eyes...and sighed. It had all been dreams. Or rather, nightmares.

Well, not *all* nightmares, she pondered, noticing the first glow of dawn coming through her window. And a growing excitement overcame her as she remembered; *MacAwen is real!* They had been with him all yesterday afternoon! She and Patrick had never even made it to Andy's house!

They would have to go see Andy this morning, instead. Certainly, not to play his new video game—but so they could all go out to the wetlands together, to discover the tracks— their guide — MacAwen.... Stella was so excited she sat bolt upright in her bed. But then she realized; it was only like four o'clock in the morning. No one else would even be up yet.

Stella sighed and plopped back down onto her bed. Her vision was drawn to the shadows behind her half opened closet door, retreating from the morning light with a slowness she could hardly bear to watch. She closed her eyes and strove to remember her dreams. Most had vanished into the fog of subconsciousness. *Dreams, of course, have meaning.* Stella knew that well enough. *But when we remember them,* she pondered, *those memories—* as she sometimes did, Stella made up facts for herself as she went along— *those memories are windows into other worlds....*

Stella remembered being tracked in her dream. And as she lay in her bed she had a strange feeling, an old feeling, she *really was* being tracked—not only by some *one*, but some *thing*. And not just the Shadow Beast. There was something else. There were *others*. *The Manipulators*. Maybe it was *they* whom she sensed had been tracking her all her life.

Ah...hum—maybe even longer, she heard—or imagined MacAwen's voice answering her thoughts.... But at this point she caught herself—feeling suddenly very self conscious... and weird. What crazy thoughts she was having! She needed to get a grip on her imagination—as so many *other* voices had so often reminded her. There was a word for people who thought *others* were out to get them; paranoid.

The psychiatrist had reminded her of that, just as his prescribed drugs had helped her to forget—about anything that might be stalking her (when she didn't spit them out).

Now she focused her thoughts, instead, on the little brown man. Of course no one would believe her or Patrick about MacAwen. Thankfully, they had both met him together. *And...*they could meet him again! He would teach them more about tracking and other sorts of magic! But first, they would have to do their homework; identify the tracks.....

The tracks of *the Mysterious Creature*, as well as those of *Martes pennanti*, were still clearly embedded in the mud, on the pathway to Andy's house.

But when they got to his house, no matter how they tried, Stella and Patrick could not convince their friend about the existence of a little brown man named MacAwen.

Of course they couldn't blame him for not believing. The entire adventure that the little brown man had led them on sounded like, seemed like, smelled like, and smacked of pure fantasy. Andy laughed when Stella and Patrick showed him their little birch boards with tree letters carved into them.

"Nice job though, Stella," Andy added, earnestly, as he glanced at the key boards. "You did a nice job carving these runes."

Stella sighed, shaking her head. All their friends had seen her drawings of runes, which she had copied from books. As for the giant bog which was somehow magical, or at least, inter-dimensional—Andy could only take it as a joke.

"It's called *The De Dumb Wah?*" Andy asked, laughing.

Studiously, Stella scrutinized her seemingly skeptical friend—a short, dark-skinned boy with curly hair and a radiant smile. Andy was nice enough. He *was* really cute. *And* he was quite the little athlete. Outside of sports, however, he was rather clue-less. Harmless, but clueless.... She could persuade him—at least to come have a look, even if he didn't want to. She had methods.

Grasping Andy by the arm and putting her face right in front of his, "You *have to* come see for yourself," Stella half pleaded and half commanded. "MacAwen's tracks are still there, on the path," her eyes widened. "We just saw them on our way over."

"How about after you guys try out my new game," Andy smiled, wriggling free from Stella's grip and turning to Patrick. "It's really awesome, but you have to get past the first three levels before it gets good, and it'll take you hours to catch up to where I am—"

"Andy! Pleeease…." Stella stretched the word with her brows raised in just such a combination that Andy should surely sense his resistance was a lost cause.

Still, not lacking in the powers of persuasion himself, he made one last effort. "Okay," he smiled brightly, his brown eyes sparkling under his curly, dark haired brow, "after you just get through level one."

"*David!* Wake...*up*—" Stella squinted at him, shaking her head. There was a moment of silence. Patrick raised his brows. Andy stared at her, confused. They did have a friend named David, but he obviously wasn't here. They couldn't tell if this was an insult, a mis-speak, or Stella's weird way of making an effect.

"Whatever your name is," Stella shrugged. She shook her head and sighed, looking down. "It's already raining," she glanced out the window, then back at Andy, "soon the tracks will be all washed away. And all you care about is a stupid computer game you can play any time." She turned and stared out the window, revealing nothing more of her expression, but that which is obviously stated by a girl's back, turned in the face of a stubborn boy refusing to see eye to eye with her.

Andy looked to Patrick. Patrick raised his brows and shoulders, glancing toward Stella. Andy rolled his eyes reluctantly in Stella's direction. He shook his head in quiet rebellion—but only at an unflinching back, draped with long, blond hair. Stella imagined all their little gestures just as easily as if she had eyes on the back of her head. It was pointless for him to argue any further.

"Okay," Andy surrendered, though clearly unconvinced. If there really were any creature tracks in the mud, he'd be inclined to suspect they were fraudulently made by Stella and Patrick themselves—though at this point he dared not say so aloud.

As they left Andy's yard there was a clap of thunder. The clouds seemed to burst—and what was a gentle rain now became a downpour. "Oh no!" Stella eyed the ground with grave concern. "We have to hurry!"

The three of them hit the trail at a fast trot—Stella leading the way, barefoot, Patrick and Andy just behind her. It was raining hard. A brilliant flash of lightening was followed immediately by a shocking crack of thunder. They all froze—for a moment.

"Come on!" Stella called, glancing back at the boys as she took off running again. Patrick shrugged at Andy's wide eyed expression—and the two of them followed together.

This part of the path was on an ancient railroad, though there were few remaining signs; an odd piece of iron here and there and the occasional remnant of a railroad tie, usually quite rotted and barely protruding from the Earth. It was about a ten minute walk between Andy's house and Patrick and Stella's houses, which were next door to each other. Patrick and Stella had met MacAwen on the previous day, about halfway between. It seemed they'd been running quite long enough to Andy, as was evidenced by his slackening pace. He was the most athletic of the three, but his motivation was just about depleted. Following a goose chase, in pouring rain, for what reason he couldn't grasp... But then, miraculously, just as sometimes happens with thunderstorms, the rain stopped as quickly as it had started.

"Come on," Patrick motioned Andy forward from a bend in the path. "It looks like Stella's found something." He waited as Andy trotted up to him, then the two of them trotted toward Stella who was bent over low, staring at something on the ground. The boys slowed to a walk as they approached.

"I can't find MacAwen's tracks anywhere—or any of ours from yesterday, but look at these," she stated, still staring at the ground beneath her. There was a perfect set of fresh tracks crossing the path, embedded in just the right spot of mud—as if intentionally, for them to find. This animal showed a heal pad and four toes in its prints—a perfect claw mark extending from each of the toes.

"That looks like the print MacAwen drew with his toes,"
Patrick stared excitedly.

"It looks like a dog track to me," Andy stated, clearly
disinterested.

"It's not a dog, Andy," Stella scolded. "The creature who left
these tracks...is our guide," she stated with reverence and awe.

"It looks like dog tracks to me," Andy retorted. "I should
know, since I own a dog and you don't."

"It looks like coyote tracks, if you ask me," said Patrick.

"It *is* coyote tracks," Stella added as a matter of fact. "Of
course! That's who our guide is!"

"A *coyote*—is your guide?" Andy gave an incredulous look.
"That's stupid."

Stella shook her head, rolling her eyes, "Andy..." she sighed,
as though he was a small child. She turned and began following
the tracks—away from the human trail.

"Where are your shoes?" Andy asked, eying Stella's footprints
and shaking his head.

"MacAwen says it is best to be barefoot," Stella spoke over
her shoulder. "Shoes dull your senses—and disconnect you from

the Earth." She glanced at Patrick's shoes, then went back to her tracking.

"MacAwen said these aren't bad for factory made," Patrick defended himself as he watched Stella move further into the woods. She did not reply, but continued her tracking. Patrick turned to Andy. "In fact, MacAwen was rather impressed by our Converse All Stars—the only factory made shoe you can actually stealth walk in...and tread the word!" he raised his voice, hoping Stella would hear.

Andy just shook his head and shrugged, staring at Patrick in disbelief.

"Come on, Andy," Patrick pleaded, "you have to admit, these are fresh made tracks. Otherwise they'd have been erased by all that rain. Even if it was just a dog, don't you wonder what he was doing out here—and where he might be heading?"

"I guess," Andy shrugged. "At least they're real tracks—not just some weird thing you guys drew in the mud."

"Wow—" Stella breathed reverently, inspired. "Just think about all the tracks in the forest, Andy," she called back to him. "It's like...all the animals are like—characters in a great play. Only they each get to write their own part."

Andy rolled his eyes, shaking his head and smiling as he approached. "I don't think *animals* have any ideas about what they're doing."

"Clearly, *some* don't," Stella shot back.

Andy smiled innocently, apparently unaware of the fact that he had just contributed to his own classification amongst the lowest order of nonthinking creatures. Yet in spite of his overtly clueless nature, he did know how to press at least one of Stella's buttons: "It's not like when David puts his ideas to paper— like on that play you guys have been quarreling over—"

"It was *my* idea!" Stella snapped. "I wrote it!"

Well, originally... she thought to herself, as she halted her steps to scan the forest paths. *David just thinks he knows everything about script writing*, she smoldered within, *and that I'm just some extreme case of ADD who like...they don't even bother prescribing medication to any more.* She shook her head.

"David just wants to...*perfect the writing*," she made a face, "*so much,* it's like—it won't even be the same story." She forced a sigh, shaking her head—then scanning the forest once more for any further signs. "He just doesn't get it," she whispered.

"The story—or you?" Patrick ventured to cut in, raising a brow.

She shot him a look—then her eyes drifted into the trees as they talked. "He doesn't understand the story—or the main character—in any *deep way,*" she over accentuated her *deep way.* "So, of course, he couldn't *possibly* understand the writer." She continued following the tracks of coyote.

"Well—" Patrick shrugged, with a hint of a smile, "you are a bit of an enigma."

She halted again and raised her brows, her arms folded.

"What I mean by an enigma, in case you don't understand the word," Patrick added smugly, "is...well—few people *can* figure you out, Stella. *I can,* of course," he added quickly. "But David, for example, doesn't know you so well." Patrick continued walking.

"What do you mean—*few people* can figure me out?" Stella demanded.

"Uhh...well—" Patrick smiled nervously, but impishly. "Take this purple *hippy shirt* you're wearing—"

"It's not purple," Stella cut him short. "It's indigo."

"Uhh...whatever," Patrick rolled his eyes. "It's not that unusual by itself, but—" he pondered. "Most *Indigo People* don't go to school carrying Army-Issue backpacks with six inch blades in the side pocket." He smiled his typical smug smile.

"Hum," Stella sighed, shaking her head and rolling her eyes, but inwardly smiling, feeling rather happily expressed in the shirt her older sister had given her—and the *fully equipped* backpack that was a gift from her Uncle Ken. "I find it all fits together perfectly," she said. "Uncle Ken told me he's going to teach me to be a survivalist," she boasted. "To be prepared...for *the day the doo doo drops on the fan,*" she added.

"Whatever *that* means," Patrick rolled his head as he walked. "You know—your Uncle Ken has a rather... *interesting* reputation."

"Yeah? So? What's wrong with interesting?" she frowned. "Like—I wouldn't be *interested* in anyone who wasn't interesting." She eyed the two boys, giving each other smart looks as they stumbled along. "*You* wouldn't understand," Stella sighed. "It's like Uncle Ken says; at the cozy little private school we attend— we're sheltered from the harsh reality that is coming down."

"I have *no* idea...*what* you're talking about," Patrick came back.

"Me neither," Andy agreed.

"Unless..." Patrick added, his tone brightening daringly, with a quick glance to Andy, "she is referring to the lunatic ravings of a mad man....or a religious zealot," he added, sighing smugly.

"Oh...*wow*—you're *so* smart, Patrick," Stella came back, "such...*sophisticated* vocabulary! I wish I could be *just* like you." She felt like ripping into him. How dare any *twerp* insult her *amazing* uncle? But she stopped herself. Patrick was a good friend, really. They were just letting surface personalities take over. Before them awaited the most amazing mystery. The silly stuff wasn't worth arguing about. Besides, she was not exactly sure what *zealot* meant. She got the sense it meant someone who was overly passionate about their beliefs.

She *had* heard Uncle Ken say he was Christian—but also, that he did not *subscribe to organized religions—nor to their controlling ways. Only to the teachings that make sense.* Her Uncle Ken *did* tend to think he was always right. Of course—he probably was; he knew so much. He certainly *was* rather unique.

Probably other kids think of me the way adults think of Uncle Ken, Stella thought as she followed the trail of the coyote. But if others were confused by *her* at least she had *something* in common with *them*—ordinary people, that is. For she felt completely perplexed by the *bulk of the human species* and much of what she perceived to be their mean, thoughtless activities upon the Earth.

Not that she was a bit surprised by *Patrick's* little perceptions. She eyed him, scrutinizing. Wearing one of his typical *safari adventurer* outfits, he was about as transparent as a fish bowl—and as predictable as a puppy. She *did* questioned him a lot, because she liked hearing him trying to describe things. As for Andy— well, if he wasn't so small and cute he'd not be so tolerated by her nor anyone else.

As she turned from the boys, Stella noticed the swirling sparks in the air again—Awen. This energy, she realized, was in the air all along, but her attention was so taken up by their...*conversations*, she had forgotten to notice. Now she noticed something else.

"Hey, look!" Stella called. "There's another set of fresh tracks here. Our guide has already led us to another set of tracks—just like MacAwen said he would!"

Patrick and Andy hurried to where she was. After staring for about a minute, Patrick blurted: "That's not just another set of tracks—that's two sets of tracks! Look at this print—then look at this one." He pointed back and forth. "These are twice as big, and have four toes. These little ones have five toes."

Andy stared at the tracks Stella and Patrick had found and was mesmerized...for a few moments. Then, with a sudden inspiration, he ran ahead of the other two.

As if drawn straight to the spot by an invisible magnetic force, in moments he too had found something. "Look!" he shouted back, "I've never seen anything like *this!*" Stella and Patrick exchanged looks of surprise at *Andy* suddenly being hooked on tracking. They ran up to him. He was pointing at a full set of four paw prints. "And I think this bigger animal is following it," he added, pointing now to a diagonal walking pattern of the larger set of tracks.

"But the coyote tracks have turned off this way," Patrick added from behind.

Stella was looking at the tracks Andy had pointed out. "That's awesome, Andy!" But which way do we go now?" She turned back toward Patrick. "I wish we could see where they *all* go."

"How about I stay on the coyote tracks, while you two follow those two sets?" Patrick answered.

"I guess so," Stella replied.

"We should stay together!" Andy piped in, clearly *quite* concerned at the thought of splitting up.

"Well, as long as you two are still within ear shot—I'll just stay on these coyote tracks," Patrick stated, clearly *un*-concerned. "It seems they're all going in the same general direction."

Without a further word they continued tracking—Stella and Andy, side by side, on the two trails with two sets of animal tracks each—and Patrick on the coyote.

Stella and Andy's two sets of tracks ran basically parallel to one another. The undergrowth was thick, and here and there Stella and Andy lost sight of each other. But after a while their two sets of tracks joined, forming a wider trail. Now it was a mottled jumble of prints that, for the most part, were indiscernible—at least as individual tracks. But the trail as a whole was very well trodden.

The forest was dominated above by a varying mix of red oak, beach, ash, hemlock, pine and maples with a few odd birches, black cherries, and hornbeams. Beneath the larger trees in this area was an undergrowth of twisted and jaggedly formed mountain laurel with rust colored stalks and a dense, dark green canopy ranging from six to twelve feet high. Stella and Andy weaved their way through the tangles of laurel until their four sets of tracks re-joined with the trail of the coyote, which Patrick was still tracking, now just ahead of them. Here, the undergrowth thinned.

"Patrick, you're stepping on all the tracks," Stella protested, noticing his sneaker prints trespassing directly on top of their trail of interest.

Patrick turned, looking at his tracks and then back to Stella and Andy and their tracks. "You're walking right on the trail too," he noted.

"Oh *no*," Stella sighed. "How could we be so stupid?"

"I guess from now on we better keep our feet on the *sides* of the trail," Patrick added. And with nods of agreement the three of them continued tracking.

The undergrowth of laurel had thinned to small patches here and there, interspersed with golden birches, witch hazel, and swamp maple. After about five minutes more Andy stopped abruptly and said, "Let's head back."

"What?" Stella exclaimed, turning toward him. "We just started, Andy. And this trail could lead to the most amazing moment in your life—and you want to turn back? Just to play some stupid game that will be there any time you want it—even when you've grown totally bored of it?" She shook her head. "These tracks are here only for one moment in all of time. Another rain storm—and they're gone forever. I can't leave this trail now, Andy. We have to find out who left these tracks or we might never see MacAwen again."

"He did say there would be no point to our next lesson," Patrick added, "until we identified the four prints that our four toed guide, who I'm pretty sure is this coyote, would lead us to.

Andy shrugged. "I'll go *a little* further." And so they continued....

It wasn't long before the tracks of the animals they were following entered a bog. "Is this the Dum-Dummer-Area?" Andy asked, as innocently as possible.

"It's called the De Da Mua, you idiot!" Stella reacted.

"And this is definitely not the De Da Mua," Patrick added. "But," he stared into the deepening water running through this grassy place, "it looks like all the tracks disappear into there." For a moment they all stared into the bog in silence. "All except for one set," Patrick smiled as he noticed where one of the animals had circumvented the bog.

"Good find, Patrick," Stella smiled. Andy rolled his eyes.

"I guess we'll just follow the coyote then," Patrick piped out. "Anyway, he's our guide."

"You don't know it's a coyote," Andy shrugged. "It still looks like a dog to me."

"It can't be just a regular *dog*," Stella insisted. "This is our *guide*."

"Well—no use arguing about it," Patrick interjected, "there's only one way to find out." And he started around the bog, on the trail of whatever it was.

"Come on, Andy," Stella beckoned as she continued after Patrick. Andy followed, but his feet were dragging.

"Bang!" A gunshot rang out, freezing all three of them in their tracks.

"That was close!" Patrick exclaimed, his wide eyes searching about.

"Let's go home," Andy pleaded, clearly shaken.

"We can't—yet," Stella asserted. "We have to seek our guide —even through danger." She looked about, defiantly. "They better not be shooting at our guide."

"It's not hunting season," Patrick stated. "They must be just target shooting."

Andy was not convinced, but reluctantly continued following. The coyote tracks led them to a field where suddenly, they just disappeared.

"Okay then, let's head back now," Andy urged. "There's no more tracks."

"We just can't see them in the grass," Stella stated. "Maybe if we lie down and put our heads near the ground—" She got to her hands and knees, then lowered her eyes right down level to the grass. Patrick knelt and did the same.

"Come on you guys, I'm going back," Andy stated.

"Wait! I see the tracks perfectly," Stella exclaimed.

"I see them too," Patrick added excitedly. "Andy, look!"

Grudgingly, Andy knelt and lowered his eyes, just to the height of the grass. As if by magic, the trail of the coyote, if it was a coyote, could be seen winding through the wet grass. Not that any individual footprints were clear, but where the animal passed through the meadow its body smeared the dew glazed grass. Andy sighed, looking back in the direction from which they had come.

"Andy, we have to go on," Stella pleaded.

"I thought you were supposed to *draw* the four sets of tracks," Andy argued. "Shouldn't you go back for paper and pencil before it rains again and washes away all the prints."

"Now that's a good point, Stella," Patrick agreed. "It looks like it might rain again."

"Oh...but we've come so far. How about you two go back for paper, and I'll follow our guide."

"I think we should stick together," Patrick answered.

Stella squinted, almost imperceptibly—her jaw clamping. She turned from the boys, releasing a quiet sigh and following the tracks with her eyes.

"Anyway, we'll need *you* to draw the tracks," Patrick persisted. "You're the best at drawing." Stella didn't respond, but walked further into the field, slowly—not exactly on the tracks, but more in a wandering sort of way.

"We could use mud," Andy shouted with a pleading tone, "to draw the tracks." Stella continued meandering away. Andy searched his pockets. "I think I have a little piece of paper—" Patrick raised an arm to silence him.

"Shh," Patrick whispered to Andy, "just wait a minute." They stared at Stella's back as she wandered yet further.

As was often the case for Stella, it was as if she had eyes in the back of her head—for these two boys were entirely predictable. But also, very great was her ability to imagine others' perspectives —subconsciously, at least. So not only was it like she had eyes in the back of her own head—but also, it was like she could see out of the eyes that were in *their* heads—sort of. Not that she was concentrating on *their* perspectives—rather, it was just something in the back of her mind. She was searching for a sign from nature —or the universe...or something. She wasn't sure. But she sensed it was coming. She had just to wait for that right moment—when inspiration would find her—and move her.

Stella looked to the sky—to the expanding forest about them —then around and throughout the small field they were in. She paused, standing motionless. Her hand came up to her chin. Her head turned. Then her body swayed, her head and her arms swimming slowly about, this way and that—as though she was in a trance. The boys stared, silent and unmoving. After an uncomfortable passage of time, suddenly, she turned. "That's it!" she shouted.

Patrick and Andy stared at her, expectantly, impatiently. "Well —" Patrick called. "*What's* it?"

"It's a *field!*" Stella shouted back. They continued staring at her, fully expecting her to add a little more explanation to her revelation. She didn't.

"So what?" Andy shouted.

"Don't you see?" she started back toward them.

"See what?" Patrick asked, searching around.

"It's so obvious," she stated as she rejoined them. "MacAwen said this animal is our *guide,*" she widened her eyes, gesturing toward the field with an outstretched hand—as though it made perfect sense and should now be obvious to the boys.

They stared at her like she had three heads, and not one of them screwed on quite right. "Well—our *guide* took us straight to a *field*," she nodding, raising her hands and her brows. Patrick and Andy stared dumbly. "This is our sign," she explained, open mouthed, as though they were stupid. "Our sign that we need a *field guide*—" she nodded again, as though they might get it. They didn't. "A field guide...*to tracks,*" she rolled her eyes. "It's so obvious, it's brilliant!"

Patrick and Andy exchanged odd glances. "Okay," Patrick shrugged with a smile. "Let's go get a field guide."

"You mean a book?" Andy asked, hopefully—obviously relieved, if confused.

"First I have to draw all five sets of tracks," Stella informed, "the individual prints and the track patterns." Andy took out his piece of paper. "That's too small," Stella stated. "Especially with mud. I could barely draw one print on that paper."

"Not to worry," Patrick stated proudly. "*I* know where there's some fine parchments of birch bark," he said, with a finger in the air, "which happen to be right near the best prints we've seen—in the muddy area just near the spot where we first left the old railroad path."

"Alright. Let's head back before it rains," Andy blurted in relief.

Stella shot Patrick a look—tempted for a moment to tear into him for being so impressed with himself. But then—it *was* impressive—a *bit.*

"Bang!" There was another gunshot, this time much closer and followed by a loud yell: "Woo...hoo!" they heard a shout, followed by raucous laughter and raised voices.

"It's those crazies," Patrick whispered—"the Cambulls!"

"The Bad-Ones?" Andy froze for but a split second, then was quick on his way, at quite a speed. Stella and Patrick followed close and quietly behind him. Of course they had all heard about "*the Bad-Ones.*" And whether or not half the murderous tales were true, none of them cared to find out. They spoke not a word until they had run all the way back to their own safe trail—which took them but a fraction of the time it had taken to track the animals out to that field.

"They better not be shooting at our guide," Stella stated, catching her breath. Patrick said nothing, but went straight for the birch bark parchment he had promised. Andy didn't speak again, but waited patiently while Stella drew the tracks. The mud in this area was ideal, both because it preserved perfect prints and because it worked well as paint. Stella drew the five unique prints—and under each one, drew the track patterns with a stick she dipped into the mud. Then they all headed back towards Andy's house.

It was a silent walk on the old railroad path at first, for they were unsettled from their near meeting with the Cambulls. But before they got to Andy's house they saw three figures approaching from ahead. "Look," Andy tapped Patrick's arm. The three of them froze. They were about to make a run for it when Stella spoke.

"Wait a minute," she said. "That's not the Bad-Ones." And there was a smile on her face. "Look guys, it's Tom and Robert... and Craig." Greatly relieved, they ran to meet their other three friends.

"Hey!" Tom yelled with his typical loudness. "What are *you* guys up to?" He was a tall, auburn haired kid, fairly freckled, wearing a yellow tee shirt and long, blue jean cutoffs. Stella studied him for a moment. Here was a loud, obnoxious kid— overflowing with wit and humor that he was all too proud of. He was a rude, insensitive boy who clearly made no habit of thinking any deep thoughts. Nor did he take the least moments here or there to consider the thoughts and feelings of others. To sum it up; Tom, quite simply, was *not very nice*—in a word; *clue-less*.

"You won't believe it," Andy exclaimed, "we almost just got killed by the Cambulls!"

"The *wacko's?*" Tom raised his brows.

Craig smiled wide—an even taller kid than Tom, thin, with blond hair. A one syllable laugh escaped through his large, bright white, and perfectly straight teeth.

"They're not just wacko's," the third kid, Robert, cut in with his usual quiet monotone. "They're murderers," he stated as a matter of fact, his lips puckering into his typical contortion as his eyes searched left and right for response or rebuttal. He was a mousy, thin kid of average height, long brown hair and large brown eyes. His face and clothes were decorated with his usual dust and grime. "Even the cops don't go near them," he raised his brows.

"I've always wanted to meet them!" Tom blurted, as loud and sarcastic as ever—or so Patrick was hoping by the look of concern on *his* face. You never could be quite sure with Tom.

"Let's go find them," Robert piped in. "All we have to do is follow Patrick, Stella, and Andy's tracks, and they'll lead to the Cambulls' tracks—unless you guys were lying to us."

"What do *you* know about tracks?" Stella eyed Robert distrustfully.

Robert's lips puckered up in his strange way, the rest of his expression unflinching. "My dad is a hunter," Robert retorted dryly. "So is my uncle. They taught me how to track." He bent down and put his hand into a footprint, then scooped up a bit of dirt and sniffed, eyeing the path where Stella, Patrick, and Andy had come from. Craig laughed quietly at his friend. Robert's tracking skills were brand new news, but Robert's reputation for making things up was well known.

"I wouldn't advise following those tracks," Patrick warned, eyeing Robert concernedly as the skinny and dirty faced boy studied the prints Patrick, Stella, and Andy had just left. "One thing for sure, they'll lead to no good."

"I'd like to find *no good*," Craig responded in a monotone a bit deeper, but even more perfect than Robert's. "It'll be fun," he continued, sounding robotic, yet still bearing his gleaming smile. "But I'm not highly optimistic about Robert's ability to find the path to the Cambulls'. How about you just show us where your tracks left the main trail."

"Yeah!" Tom cut in with a laugh. "My Dad's a hunter too, but I'm not going to waste my time trying to follow *your* foot prints on *this* busy trail. Just show us the path you came from."

"No." Stella answered abruptly. "Don't." she ordered, giving Patrick and Andy each a stern gaze. "First we need to identify these animals," she held up the birch bark. "Then we have to continue tracking our guide—so we don't want his prints all trampled on."

"They're already trampled on," Andy answered with wide eyes on Stella, "by *you know who*. But I'm not going back there," he glanced at Tom. "And you shouldn't either," he frowned at Stella.

"But following our guide is the only hope of meeting MacAwen again," Stella responded.

Craig's bright white smile widened. "We heard about your little brown man."

Stella shot Patrick a look. He shrugged.

"Did they tell you that one, Andy?" Craig asked.

"Yeah," Andy shrugged.

"Craig—you don't even deserve to *know* about MacAwen," Stella shook her head.

"Ma-*caawww*-en," Tom mocked loud and abrasively.

"Can you show him to us?" Craig persisted.

"Are you kidding?" Stella replied. "You wouldn't believe it if he was right in front of your face."

"Yes I would," Craig retorted. "Come on—introduce us to the little dude—to MacAwen."

"Just forget it," Stella shook her head. "We probably made it all up anyway," she mocked in return. "Besides, *we* can't even see him again 'til we solve the mystery of these prints."

"Ooh—wow," Tom mocked, eyeing the birch bark paper.

Craig smiled. "It looks like you drew some tracks with some mud, Stella. That's impressive."

"She did draw the tracks with mud," Patrick retorted to his tall, blond friend. "How else could we get them identified before they got rained on?"

"So, tell us about Ma-*caawww*-en," Tom prodded—again, mockingly with his ever loud and abrasive tone.

"It's just some little leprechaun they made up," Andy answered.

"We didn't make him up," Stella protested. "He's real. And he knows *everything* about the forest," she looked up and her eyes went wide with wonder. "He told us *this animal* would be our guide," she explained, holding up the *mud-on-birch-bark track* that matched the print MacAwen had drawn for them, with his toes. "And he told us our guide would lead us to four more sets of tracks —and that's exactly what our guide did. And now, only after we identify all the tracks and learn all we can about them will MacAwen come back to teach us more."

They all stared at her in disbelief with varying levels of humor —from Craig who could barely contain himself, and Tom who was making the most fun of it that he could, to Robert who was not smiling at all, and finally Andy who was downright frightened. Clearly, *the Cambull's* were foremost on Robert and Andy's minds —not any little brown leprechauns. Yet even Patrick had a look of near disbelief on his face. Though he was right by her side, and it was only yesterday—it was just such an incredible, unbelievable story.

"Everything has happened just as MacAwen said it would," Stella concluded. "Now we have to get our field guide. Then we can continue tracking our guide."

"Okay. So when will you track *your guide*?" Craig asked, still unable to contain a bit of a smile.

"Probably not until tomorrow—after school," Stella sighed. "We have to get a ride to the Toadstool," she paused, her thoughts searching—"and enough money for the book."

"You're going to get a ride to a toadstool?" Tom stared in disbelief, his head shaking. "You really *are* insane, Stella."

"*The Toadstool Bookshop*, you idiot!" Stella shook her head. "Don't you ever read...books?" She raised her brows.

Tom busted out laughing. "I was just kidding! You are so gullible, Stella! Don't *you* ever read...into a joke?"

Stella shook her head and rolled her eyes, sighing and studying the rest of the group—other than Tom. Tom's jokes were a waste of time—and only funny to those who found humor in ridiculing others. Of course, Stella did like to pick on Patrick. But that was different. Patrick needed a compassionate person to show him how stupid he acted sometimes. Besides, Patrick loved the attention.

"Can we come with you, when you go back to your tracks?" Craig asked.

Stella studied him with a scrutinizing gaze. There was a bit of a suspicious looking smile on his face, but his eyes seemed sincere. "Sure," she answered, "if you promise not to act like idiots."

"I promise," Craig answered earnestly.

"We promise, too," Tom spoke on behalf of Robert. They didn't look as convincing.

Stella eyed them scrutinizingly. "Promise not to make fun of MacAwen— or our guide," she commanded. They all promised. "And to be careful not to trample on any tracks," she added. Again, they all agreed. "Okay," she eyed them quizzically, "can any of you contribute some money for our field guide?"

"Field guide?" Craig asked.

"To tracks," Stella answered.

"Oh. Cool," Craig responded. "Yeah, sure." He reached into his pocket. "I've got five bucks."

"I've got three bucks at home," Tom added.

"My mother can give us a ride," Andy added, eager to get out of the woods. "She takes my sister to karate anyway, at four O'clock."

"Great," Stella concluded, "let's all meet at Andy's house, as soon as possible, with all the money we can get."

"But I'm not going back out there," Andy added.

"It really was the Bad-Ones?" Craig asked.

"It definitely was," Patrick nodded with wide eyes. "But I don't mind seeing their tracks—as long as I don't have to meet up with *them*. On the other hand," he glanced at Stella, "whatever I have to do to meet MacAwen again—" his eyes drifted out of focus, a hint of a smile of amazement returning to his face, "I think I'll risk it," he nodded.

Stella returned a nod to Patrick. Then she threw up a peace sign at the others and said, "tread the word," scrunching her peace sign fingers twice—once when she said *tread*, and once when she said *word*—as if she was making the hand gesture for *"quotes."* They shot her a few odd looks, and some sideways glances to each other. Then they all headed off, to gather what money they could. They would rendezvous at Andy's house, for the quest for the field guide to tracks. And then, if they could solve the riddles on Stella's birch bark, the real quest would take shape. Though at the moment, not one of them had a real clue as to what they were truly beginning to get into.

Stella, however, did have an inkling—inwardly. For she now remembered MacAwen's cryptic words: "the terrible war that's brewing—between those forces opposed to what believe they is this Mysterious Creature—and those opposed to the domination that planned has been by the Shadow Beast's manipulators." And she recalled what his voice said when it was in her thoughts: "A war for your minds."

Further, she remembered what MacAwen's voice had said when it came into her dark dream:

"At the height of The Terrible War will come The Singular Confrontation...between the Beast who manipulates the Shadow Beast...and the one whose tracks have foretold all."

Somehow, Stella sensed, she and her friends had been living in a child's illusion. And somehow, it couldn't last.

Nothing ever—just what seems
Awaken now while still in dreams
and watch reality grow.
A battle of will—who would imagine
beyond the beast's machine.
Imagine brilliance beyond the bounds.
Crash and rip and run, run...free!

Chapter IV:
Homework

Tom, Craig, and Robert had been generous enough to contribute what they could—but didn't want to waste *their* time driving all the way to Milford just to browse a book store. So it was just Stella, Patrick, and Andy. They entered the Toadstool Bookshop and started to look around. It was not as vast as the giant book stores in the city, but this place was packed tight with all the best books.

"May I help you find anything?" a squat woman with short, dark hair asked from behind the counter. Her glasses hung low on her nose, pinching her otherwise huge nostrils into an almost shut position—a spectacle which the three kids could not help but stare at.

"Well—" Patrick raised his brows, "we're looking for a field guide to tracks."

"We have quite a few of *those* to choose from," the woman informed with a rather nasal voice, "on the back wall," she pointed, "just to the left of that couch."

"Alright," Patrick replied, quickly turning and heading in that direction.

Stella glanced at Patrick, back to the woman, and then her eyes seemed to swim as through an ocean or a far off cloud circling above the store. "Yeah—" Stella smiled at the woman, "that's great. Thanks." She turned toward the back of the store.

"Thank you," Andy smiled brightly at the store clerk, with his typical over-the-top politeness—though he only looked her in the nose, never in the eyes. Then he and Stella followed after Patrick. The woman smiled, but gave them a rather odd look.

Sure enough, there were quite a few field guides to tracks for them to choose from. In fact, there was a whole section of the wall devoted to field guides of all kinds. They found it quite mesmerizing and fun browsing through them.

"I wish we could get one of these," Stella was holding A *Field Guide to Mammals of North America.*

"And I'd like to get one of these," Patrick had a *Field Guide to Reptiles and Amphibians.*

"We don't have that much time," Andy reminded them.

"You're right," Patrick agreed, "or that much money," he added putting the *Field Guide To Reptiles and Amphibians* back on the shelf and focusing on the tracking field guides. The three of them sifted through all the choices and quickly had it narrowed down to four of the most colorful books, with beautiful photos as well as illustrations.

"We can only buy one," Andy stated.

"So, what do you think?" Patrick looked to Stella.

"Oh—I don't know," she hesitated. "This one has amazing photographs," she held up a copy of *Tracking and the Art of Seeing,* by Paul Rezendes. "But this one seems to have the most information," she now held a copy of *Mammal Tracks & Sign; A Guide To North American Species,* by Mark Elbroch.

"I think this one's better," Andy had *Mammal Tracks and Sign of the Northeast,* by Diane Gibbons. "It's more for our area."

"On the other hand, this one is more compact—for carrying in the field," Patrick held a small book titled, *Animal Tracks of New England,* by Sheldon, Hartson, & Elbroch.

"Oh, it's so hard," Stella stammered.

"I have copies of all those books," a man's voice cut in. They all jerked around, and there stood a rather wild looking middle aged fellow with long curly hair contained by a brown, cloth headband. He had an auburn mustache, a generally scruffy face, and bushy brown eyebrows. He wore a tee shirt with a Celtic design on it, cut-off camouflage army pants, and moccasins without socks. There was a tooth missing from his mouth, but he none the less had a pleasant smile. "They're all great books, and I'd recommend *all* of them," he nodded, "if you could afford it," he smiled, turning to another rather wild looking gentleman who was just approaching the field guide section.

This second man was taller, a bit older, and had even bushier eyebrows. He had great bones in his face, graying hair, and a beard like a mountain man. He wore a leather vest, shorts, and hiking boots. He spoke with a deep, booming voice. "That one has been especially handy lately," he pointed to the small book Patrick was holding, "as it's all local and it fits right into my pocket." This man squinted at their books. "You've left out the Peterson's Field Guide," he noted. "Whether it be trees, tracks, frogs, or whatever," he lectured, "you should always supplement your references with the Peterson's Field Guides."

"We can only afford to get one," Stella replied. Then studying these rather scholarly seeming woodsmen thoughtfully, she asked, "If you could have just one book on tracking—which one would it be?"

"They're all good, mind you," the shorter, curly haired man answered, "and the more you have, the better. But if I *had* to choose only one..." he paused. "Well—that would be me, not you." He frowned. "Are you trying to identify *specific* tracks?"

"Yes. Five distinct sets of tracks," Patrick answered.

"Five sets?" he raised his brows, turning to his friend.

"Serious stuff," the other nodded.

"Okay," the man returned, "will you be comfortable carrying a big book?"

"Well, actually—it's no problem," Patrick shrugged. "I usually carry a pack. Anyway, we can identify these ones from home, because we have them drawn."

The curly haired man turned to his friend with a smile, his hands extended and an expression on his face that seemed to say, *there you have it.* And as though the meaning of this gesture was perfectly clear to *the mountain man guy*—and he was in full agreement, he gave a nod and a squint. "Take Elbroch's book then," the curly haired man nodded, turning back to Stella. "It's the most extensive—if you can afford it."

"Alright—thanks for the advice," Patrick concluded. Stella and Andy also thanked him, and his friend.

The curly haired man nodded, pulling one of the *least* exciting looking tracking books off the shelf—the one with the non-glossy, beige cover, no photos, and barely any illustrations—which the kids had passed over quickly without a second thought. "Happy trails," he said, and headed for the checkout counter.

"It's a good path you kids are on," the bearded *mountain man looking guy* jolted them with his booming voice. "Keep it up," he nodded. "Follow the tracks and you'll be studying the most ancient—and the very best—literature on the planet," he nodded with a gleam in his eyes, *"Inscribed woods lore!"*

The three of them stood transfixed, mesmerized. Though Andy, being Andy, seemed to be staring rather into the Man's *beard* than his eyes—not really comprehending any of his words. He got a deep impression of their essence, however, simply from the vibration of this voice that seemed to echo the resonance of great mountains and wild, far off places.

The man's final phrase left the clearest impression emblazoned in Stella's mind; *"Inscribed woods lore."* It resonated in a way that was unforgettable--as if a sudden bolt of lightning had flashed in a dark night, revealing a carved sign on a post. In her mind's eye, a grizzly bear's claw marks appeared on a tree stump—and she translated the meaning of the bear's carved inscriptions to the man's exact phrase: *"Inscribed woods lore."*

He gave a final nod and squint—and was on his way....

After coming out of their trance, Patrick, Stella, and Andy agreed to take the advice; *Mammal Tracks & Sign,* by Mark Elbroch.

Once at the checkout counter, Patrick and Stella strove to fix their gazes anywhere other than the woman's nose. Andy on the other hand seemed to be probing the inner regions of her nostrils. Looking behind her, Stella noticed this and gave him a little kick to the side of the foot.

"What?" Andy stared at her, genuinely clueless.

"Never mind, Andy," she replied, turning her focus back to various places on the ceiling. After Stella paid for the book, the woman behind the counter plopped it—and another book—into a paper bag and handed it to Stella.

Once the three of them were in the back seat of Andy's Mom, Mrs. Amera's Car, Andy asked, "What was that other book she put in the bag?"

"What other book?" Stella asked as she opened the bag and, to her amazement, pulled out two books. *Mammal Tracks & Sign,* by

Mark Elbroch—and *Tom Brown's Field Guide to Nature Observation and Tracking,* by Tom Brown, Jr..

"Where'd that come from?" Patrick asked.

"The lady gave it to us," Andy answered.

"What? Why?" Patrick asked.

"I don' know," Andy replied. "I guess—"

"Wait—"Stella interrupted—"the lady didn't give it to us. That man gave it to us. There's a note in it. Listen." And she read:

"Dear Fellow Trackers, the book you bought may have more information about *tracks* than any book in the store. But this book has the most information about track-*ing*. I thought you should have both. May your trails be filled with tales."

"Wow—that's awesome," Andy exclaimed. "Can I see?"

"That was a really nice guy," Patrick added. "And his friend was richly endowed with woods lore."

"*Richly endowed*? Wow, Patrick, impressive words," Stella rolled her eyes.

"What guy?" Andy's older sister asked, turning her head from the front seat of the car.

"Just some guy from the book store that likes field guides," Andy answered flatly. Then smiling impishly, "He's too old for you." She didn't bother responding, but turned back to whatever she was reading in the front seat.

The three of them flipped through the two field guides until the car approached their neighborhood. "I don't know about you two," Mrs. Amera said, "but Andy has homework due tomorrow—which he has thus far neglected this weekend," she shot him a look through the rear view mirror. "He'll have no more time for visiting."

"But Mom—" Andy protested.

"But nothing," she silenced him. "Do you two have the leisure to take the trail-or shall I bring you right to your houses. Perhaps you've *also* left some of *your* work for the last hours?"

"I didn't neglect my homework," Andy butted in. "I just didn't finish it."

"Well, I guess I haven't exactly finished mine either," Patrick admitted.

Stella was feeling distraught—and it must have shown, because Patrick and Andy seemed to have gone stiff on either side of her and were giving her sideways looks. A sudden great heaviness pushed down upon her. "How can we ever learn anything important when we're forced to do so much useless...*meaningless*...homework?" she exclaimed. The thought crashed out of her brain like a two ton granite domino, starting a whole chain reaction of heavy thoughts—each pounding the next into motion as Stella expressed them out loud. "It's bad enough we have to be...*imprisoned*—inside the same four walls for five days every week. But then—even when we're finally freed...we're not really—because they...*shackle* us down...with all these stupid assignments. It's *torture.*"

Mrs. Amera was listening to Stella's speech, and watching her expressions through the rear view mirror. Her own brows were raised and her mouth hung open in an almost smile. She was obviously amused—but also, filled with empathy. After Stella's last word, *torture*, Mrs. Amera swallowed hard and sighed. "I know just how you feel, Stella. I sure do remember how that was for me when I was your age—but it hurts a lot less when you just get it done."

Andy's older sister pulled her nose from the book she was reading from her slouched position in the front seat. "When you were a kid, ma, you didn't get half the homework we do."

"That's true," Mrs. Amera admitted. "But *we* were expected to do it *all on our own.* Nowadays it's expected that your parents will work with you on your assignments. In a way, it's like *I'm* still getting homework—if I think of the amount of time *I* have to spend on it each week...."

"Doesn't that make you angry?" Stella asked.

"I do get *frustrated* at times," Mrs. Amera admitted, dodging the *angry* part of the question, "just like you. But that's part of our training. Sometimes we have to overcome our feelings, and rise up, and do our work," she sighed heavily, "even when it's the last thing we'd ever choose to do on our own." The car went silent.

Stella thought to herself now: *It's not her fault. She's just been beaten...taken over....* Stella surprised herself with her own thoughts as they formed in her head. *Taken over by what?* She wondered, for she could not quite grasp what *it* was. *School? Society? The Government?* She barely understood what *society* or *the government* really were. She *had* learned *some* things at school. But she heard very different things from her eccentric uncle, Ken—*and* her radical, teen-age sister, Ari, who were ranting and debating about it all the time. But then another thought entered her mind: ***The Shadow Beast.***

After dinner Stella retreated to her bedroom to do her homework. She had one of the two field guides and three of the five track drawings on birch bark. Patrick had the other book and the other track drawings. She forced herself to look at her math workbook, to open it. *Nothing* to stimulate her imagination resided within—no exploration, no adventure, no discovery. Nothing. Nothing but drudgery. A heavy feeling came over her. Her mind went blank. Suffocating. Trapped. *Math is so boring...and meaningless*, she thought, shaking her head. She slammed the workbook shut.

Now she eyed the field guide—enticing—exciting—inspiring —full of wonders and discoveries—but forbidden. She was supposed to be doing her homework. In fact, if she didn't get it done she'd get a yellow slip. Stella already had two yellow slips— one more and she'd have to stay after school every Thursday for a month. A whole *month*. That was the reason she had to do it—the only reason. But she was drawn to the field guide now, as though pulled by some magnetic force. On its cover was the photo of a fox, overlaid with smaller photos of tracks, trees with shredded bark, *and*...at the base of the trunk of a great moss covered tree... there was a large dark opening—easily big enough to be the entrance to the den of a bear. Reluctantly, apprehensively, she opened the book—and all the heaviness left her.

Inside were tracks and tracks and tracks. Tracks of every kind of mammal that walked on North America—and photos and drawings and stories to go with them all. It was so good—she didn't care about tomorrow. Also, it was so organized and meaningful, she was sure she'd be able to identify her tracks. Besides, identifying the tracks *is* homework, she laughed—from MacAwen.

Why did this homework feel so different? Obviously, there was a great mystery here, and she felt with all her soul that she just had to solve it. And that was the key to her motivation. It didn't feel like work at all.

Yet really, there was a thousand times more work involved in MacAwen's homework than there was in the whole math workbook. There was so much more to be learned from *this* book —and this book really just barely scratched the surface...of the greatest book—the book that *was* the world, written in the most ancient and ever evolving form of literature: tracks.

MacAwen's homework was so complex and involved, yet it was stress free. It wasn't just that MacAwen's homework was more interesting and meaningful. But there was no deadline—no punitive consequence if she didn't do it. He didn't say *when* they had to do it. He didn't even say they *had* to do it. Only that there'd be no point to their next lesson until they identified the tracks. They were free to go at their own pace. But—he inspired them so much, Stella just had to do this homework—now. She couldn't stop herself. She was just burning to find out who and what made all these tracks—and what it might mean.

The first track to identify was that of her guide. Sure enough, it was coyote. Not that her mud drawing could be distinguished between coyote, dog, or wolf. But there were no wolves in their area. And all the characteristics described in the book hinted toward coyote and not dog. The way it moved, the places it went....

"Are you doing your homework?" Her mother called to her.

"Uhh. Yes."

"How's it going? Do you need any help?"

"I'm fine. It's going great!" she answered. Which was of course, absolutely true—in regard to MacAwen's homework. She had positively identified her guide. He had four paws, each with four toes and four claws—sixteen toes and claws in all, she thought. How wonderful. It was about two feet between each set of the coyote's paw prints. So every two feet he left sixteen claw marks. *Wow*, Stella thought, *I wonder how many claw marks he leaves every mile*. Her mind raced: eight claw marks per foot— five thousand, two hundred and eighty feet in a mile.... She jotted down the multiplication on the back of one of her math book worksheets. *Over forty thousand claw marks every mile!* Of course, many of those claw marks would not show as they landed in leaves or on rocks. But knowing the measurement of his stride and straddle, and his track pattern, she imagined she could figure out where his hidden prints would be—and in her mind, reunite them with the ongoing pattern. And what patterns!

From the field guide she learned of the various shapes and patterns that coyote prints make when walking, running, trotting, galloping, etcetera, over all kinds of terrain. She also learned to notice the subtle differences in the geometric shapes between various canine footprints. Canine prints were generally oval shaped—clearly more so than the roundish feline prints. But within the canine family there were subtle differences as well. The coyote's two inner toes were situated slightly more forward in comparison to the two outer toes than that which was generally observed in domestic dogs. Also, with the coyote, those two inner toes tended to show more pronounced claw marks more often—depending on the dirt, mud, sand, leaf litter, rock, root, or moss as the coyote traveled up hill, down, or along level terrain. The coyote tended to be more *on his toes* than the typical lazier dog who allowed more weight to rest on his heal pads.

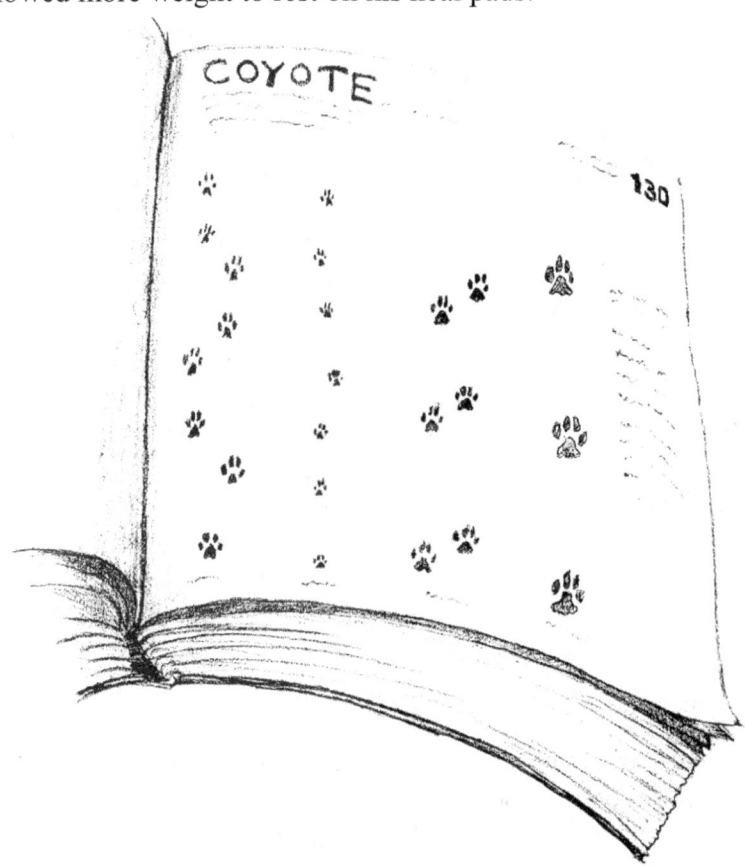

Stella studied the 1-2-3-4, 1-2-3-4, 1-2-3-4...pattern made by a galloping coyote. In the field guide it was just a few simple illustrations. But in her mind she could see the actual tracks being made. She could hear the rhythmic pitter-patter of paws. She thought of *her guide*, and wondered upon what patterns he had left since she saw his tracks, how fast he had been going—*and where*

was he right now? Her mind was filled with the most intriguing possibilities—encompassing, but not limited to statistics, multiplication, division, algebra, and geometry—to the truest living sense of the words. She followed the shapes: ovals, triangles, sharp lines, X's, H's, Z's—all in living patterns, laid out by pulsing paws, on perhaps real, but in this moment imaginary landscapes that Stella could only wish to be a part of.

But already she was flipping through the pages, hot on the tracks of the second animal—which she quickly concluded, had to belong to the common pack rat. That inspired a new mystery, because according to the Field Guide, the pack rat was not supposed to dwell in this range. But these tracks were found quite close to the De Da Mua, which, according to the map of the town, didn't even exist. MacAwen had already pointed out a set of pack rat tracks that belonged to that infamous collector named Pat, and Stella was pretty sure these were the same type—maybe from Pat himself. MacAwen had said he would introduce them to the plump little thief. Stella could hardly wait to meet him. Somehow, she imagined him to be almost like a strange little person.

The third of the three sets of tracks Stella had to identify showed four toes with a single pad behind them. But these were smaller than the coyote's and there were no claw marks. With the field guide it was quick and easy work. They were clearly from a member of the feline family. Too big for a house cat —too small for a mountain lion, these tracks fit exactly the size and description of the bobcat.

Now she had identified all three tracks. It seemed to take no time at all.

"How's the homework coming?" her mom asked from outside her door.

"I've got it all done," Stella answered gleefully.

"Oh good," her mother sighed, entering her room. "I didn't realize how late it was. You need to get to bed." She smiled and kissed Stella on the forehead.

"Goodnight, Mom." Stella looked up lovingly at the tall, slender, and very beautiful being drifting out of her room. Then she glanced at her clock, and realized with a shock how much time had passed.

Identifying the three tracks seemed so quick and easy, but there were so many other tracks and sign in the book that drew her attention—took her from her focus. In that rapture time had flown —and suddenly she felt very tired. She had done none of her math, for which she would be in trouble tomorrow. But she had learned so much—it was like she had taken a great drink from the well of knowledge. A deep satisfaction flowed through her being. Tonight she would sleep well. Deep peace came over her, and she drifted into a sea of dreams...

That night Stella had seen MacAwen in her dreams. And it was more than just a dream; because in the middle of the dream she became aware that she was dreaming, and MacAwen told her that being aware of her dream while dreaming meant she was "*lucid dreaming.*"

"An' further—when become ye aware that are ye dreamin', an' lucid dreaming are ye—then may begin ye ta control yer dream. An' ofter master ye the control of yer dreams—then may begin ye ta master reality...."

That was so amazing and inspiring to Stella, she could hardly think of anything else. MacAwen had come to her, in her dream, and was teaching her true magic! But MacAwen had been trying to tell her something else—something about being aware of her surroundings....

Though the night's dreams ended, for Stella, daydreaming continued....

Staring into the sky, once more she was seeing the energy MacAwen had pointed out to Patrick and her—the Awen. As it swirled about in the atmosphere it formed into ghostly figures. *Angels*, Stella thought. But they dissipated into raw energy as quickly as they formed. Then new ones formed. A concentration of this energy approached her, forming into a familiar shape—it was MacAwen!

But MacAwen's image disintegrated into pure energy, spiraling and pulsating throughout the atmosphere. Stella stared, mesmerized—now seeing brilliant patterns forming from the raw energy; there were waves of various size, pulsing and vibrating in the sky—there were swirling sparks of blue, white, and red, spiraling in and out of vortexes—there were geometric forms... Through her subconscious mind came mathematical equations that perfectly summed all the dynamic geometry moving through her vision. It was beautiful!

In the image of God, Stella thought. She didn't know where that phrase came from. It just came to her. She imagined the Creation of the universe; The Big Bang.... An explosion of Awen, swirling from the Will and Imagination of The Great Consciousness—the Infinite Consciousness that Stella suddenly realized, her consciousness was a part of. It was the same consciousness that hers was, only unlimited. And the more she imagined of it, the more she became of it—and it, of her. The most powerful feeling of love permeated her being—from her head to her toes, throughout her consciousness, expanding the infinite, and returning infinitely greater....

"*Stell...la...*" Mrs. Caledon's voice cut at last into her trance. "We're waiting..."

Stella's focus snapped out of the clouds beyond the window and back into the classroom. Not only was Mrs. Caledon staring at her, but so was half the class. "Oh—yeah," Stella answered, trying to look attentive.

"Yeah—what?" Mrs. Caledon called Stella on her bluff.

"Uhh—I didn't get the question," Stella fumbled.

"Did you *hear* the question?" Mrs. Caledon asked.

"Um—not really," Stella confessed, feeling like a cornered mouse.

"Number thirteen," Mrs. Caledon repeated. "What did you come up with for an answer?"

"Oh—" Stella scanned frantically over the opened page of her math workbook. But nowhere could she see a number thirteen.

"*The next page, Stella,*" a tall friend named Iona, whispered over her shoulder, stretching from the seat behind her. Stella flipped the page quickly, but her gaze glazed over. She blinked and strove to focus.

Mrs. Caledon had risen from the big desk at the front of the class and was now approaching. Stella's heart pounded. A terrible, hot sensation came over her whole body. She could feel every eye in the classroom upon her. She wished she could just disappear. Nervously, almost unconsciously, she reached into her pocket and clutched her silver amulet. Mrs. Caledon was standing over her now, staring down. Stella could feel the piercing eyes, penetrating her cover. It was over. She was found out. She had done none of her homework. A blank page. She was doomed.

This moment would never end. She had experienced this moment many times before. And in the eternity of this horrible moment, she was always just *about* to be utterly humiliated. The whole class would laugh at her when the teacher's glaring accusation exploded into the room like a bomb. Stella had done nothing. Stella was not even on the same page as everyone else. Stella was the odd ball. Somehow, Stella just wasn't good enough. Stella was different. Stella didn't even belong at this school. She was frozen, cringing, waiting for the biting words. Mrs. Caledon was still standing above her, staring down. All attention in the classroom was fixed on Stella's position. *Here it comes.* The wrath that so many teachers are just made to give—and the humiliation.

But it never came. Instead, Stella felt a warm, gentle hand rest on her shoulder. "Alright," Mrs. Caledon said nonchalantly. "This is a tough one. Let's take this problem to the board ladies and gentlemen." And as she spoke, Mrs. Caledon moved toward the blackboard, taking with her all the focus of the class. Stella sunk in her seat, breathing out at last. She hadn't realized she'd been holding her breath. Mrs. Caledon was writing the problem out long hand, and explaining it as she went. The terrible moment had passed.

Stella's *old* teacher, *Mrs. Yandel,* would have pounced on such a moment as that—like a lion on a rodent. She would have devoured all joy from Stella's life. A tear came from her eye as she caught her breath, staring in awe at Mrs. Caledon, staring in admiration, with gratitude—even with love—at least, for the moment.

Still, it was like she had been struck a *dolorous blow* to the side of the head and was dazed in such a way that she might not recover for days.

When at last the class was over and it was time for recess, Mrs. Caledon told Stella to stay. It was time for a chat.

"I *am* going to have to give you a yellow slip, Stella," Mrs. Caledon informed. "That's three this month already. So you *will* have to stay after on Thursdays." Stella nodded. "It's not a punishment, Stella. We're trying to help you. You know—it gets a whole lot tougher in eighth grade. You need to be prepared. I know it's hard for you, but you've got to try harder to focus, and stay on the same page as everyone else." Stella was still staring at the floor. "Chin up, kiddo," Mrs. Caledon smiled. "Now go get some fresh air." That, Stella did in a hurry.

"Stella! Stella!" A small flock of girls rushed to greet her as Stella emerged from the classroom. At the front were three very wide-eyed friends—Clarsah, Brighid, and Jessie—followed by Iona, a tall loner who Stella always perceived to have a wise and benevolent look about her—and then several more smiling girls, but with less benevolent, rather smirking, and questioning looks about them.

"Is it true?" Clarsah McKinnon asked—a slender girl with light brown hair. "Is he real?" Jessie and Brighid, the two girls by Clarsah's side said nothing, but waited hopefully for the answer.

"Yeah," Stella smiled, remembering MacAwen. Though it seemed like a dream now, and she'd completely forgotten about the little brown man and all his magic while getting hit with the hard reality in the classroom. Now, just as suddenly as when it seemed she'd been struck the *dolorous blow* to the head, she recovered. Her head cleared. The air was fresh. The sky was blue—and once again she saw the dancing, swirling energy in the atmosphere. "He's totally real!" her eyes lit up like a blaze. "I can bring you to him. You can all meet him!" Stella smiled wide.

"When? When?" Clarsah was jumping up and down, unable to contain herself.

"*Oh* my *God*!" Tom's loud voice cut in from somewhere behind Stella. "Please—oh please, Stella," he begged sarcastically, "can I meet your little brown figment of imagination, too?"

Stella did not bother turning around to see Tom approaching. In fact, none of her friends responded to his obnoxious and uninvited presence with more than a quick roll of the eyes, as they carried on their conversation with unchecked enthusiasm. Clarsah *had* stopped her jumping, however.

"Are you sure—he's *really* real?" Brighid asked with wide eyes and raised brows, clearly hoping beyond hope that the Mysterious Creature was real, though it was awfully hard to believe.

"He really is real," Stella answered. "You'll see," she smiled.

Patrick approached now, followed by Craig, and Robert. "Sorry about your homework trouble," he raised his brows. "I guess you did MacAwen's homework instead?"

"I got it all done," Stella stated proudly. "It was costly," she sighed, shuddering as she remembered the trauma she had suffered in the classroom. "But it was worth it," she breathed deeply, imagining an incredible next adventure with MacAwen.

Clarsah looked upon her friend in awe and admiration—but without envy. "You *are* brave," she smiled.

"Crazy, more like it," Gretchen cut in, rolling her eyes and shaking her head. Gretchen was a tall girl with long, brown hair. "Are you really that stupid, that you believe her?" she eyed Clarsah, Brighid, and Jessie with a smile of amazement.

She thinks she's so perfect, Stella thought. *So pretty. So smart. Such a lovely student.* "Gretchen," Stella smiled at her, "why don't you go fly a hot air balloon?"

"What?" Gretchen laughed. "It's a *kite*, you air head! You're supposed to say, *go fly a kite*," she smiled. "But in your case, Stella, hot air balloon is perfect."

"Either way, it's over *your* head," Stella sighed.

"Wow, Stella! You're getting so smart—for an air head," Gretchen turned and started away. "I guess they've been teaching you some common phrases in your special classes," she added over her shoulder with an air of *I'm leaving you gullible children behind,* as she walked off.

"I know you won't let that bother you," Jessie encouraged with a bit of a smile. "You've survived through *much worse* today, already." Jessie's eyes widened. "*I* know what *that's* like—to be humiliated in front of the whole class." Jessie was a rather naive, but lovable friend. Not the quickest of wit—but she knew that, and seemed not at all bothered by it. *Because* d*eep thoughts are more important than quick ones,* Jessie had said to Stella during a recent Academic Support class.

"I don't know *how* you can recover so fast from such an *awful* moment," Jessie continued. "You must be like, *psychically, really* strong, Stella. I'd have just *broken*," she shook her head dramatically, with sympathetic eyes. "I'd still be crying."

"Yeah, me too," Clarsah hugged Stella tightly.

"Me too," Brighid gave Stella a sympathetic smile, and put a warm hand on her cheek.

"Ah—that's so sweet!" Tom blasted in with his usual sarcasm. "I just wanna cry, guys," he turned to Craig and Robert with a smile. "I'd be a broken man...for the rest of my life...if I spaced out and forgot to do my homework!" he laughed.

Stella almost reacted, but had more urgent business on her mind. "So Patrick, how far did you get?"

"Well..." Patrick slowly admitted. "I tried to do some—but my mom and dad found me out and made me do my school homework. Then I didn't have any time."

"Oh." Stella did not hide her disappointment. "You have to do it tonight."

"No worry about that," Patrick answered. "There's nothing more I want to do in the whole world than discover who made those tracks. So—" his eyes widened, "who made the tracks you had?"

Stella's eyes lit up, remembering the coyote...the pack rat...and...the bobcat! But before she had time to open her mouth, a boy's voice came from behind. "Hey Stella. How's the little brown man?" And there stood David.

David was a short guy—and had a very pleasant face. Not that looks meant anything to Stella. The ugliest person in the world could be the nicest. But David *was* really smart. Not that being smart made anybody into a nice person. Of course, David was a super talented actor—*and* he was a brilliant writer. Not that any of that made him be a nice person. You had to be *nice* in order to be a nice person. And David usually was nice, but—

"You're not still upset with me, are you?" David asked, in response to Stella's blank expression and dead silence—in spite of the fact that he'd said hello and asked her a question.

"Oh...no..." Stella's focus returned suddenly, from some distant place. "Why should I be upset with *you*? I hardly know you," she added with a casual shrug. "So—who are you?"

"Um—David Montague," he smiled, "last time I checked, anyway."

"Oh, him—yeah," Stella nodded with a bit of a smile. "He seemed like a nice guy," she looked off, somewhere into the blue above. "But aren't you the one who said I was an air head?" Her gaze fixed suddenly upon a point, dead center, between David's eyes.

"Oh—*that,*" David sighed with a frown, his head turning away as if to deflect some invisible laser beam that had just struck him on the forehead. "Well, actually, being an air head—once in a while—is not really a bad thing," he stated cleverly, attempting to schmooze the whole thing over with his typical charming and sophisticated style.

"Oh—really? Hey, thanks," Stella nodded convincingly. "You shouldn't feel too bad then— 'cause maybe being a conceited jellyfish once in a while isn't such a bad thing either."

"Oh..." David's eyes darted about. *"That* hurts." His eyes widened. "I guess I deserve it though," he nodded with raised brows. "Jellyfish—wow. Ouch," he cringed. "But I hope you don't *stay* mad at me," he said with pleading eyes.

"Stay mad at you?" Stella rolled her eyes, pretending she couldn't care less about him, like he wasn't worth being angry with. Yet somehow she was irritated with him for having the ability to make her be angry in the first place—and to manipulate her into *not* being angry now. "I wouldn't waste my energy," she said nonchalantly. Though in truth she was feeling a bit exhausted and confused from trying to figure out what it was exactly that she was feeling and trying to pretend that she didn't care.

The Bell rang, and the conversation ended—for now. Though for the rest of the day, at any opportunity, the little brown man and Stella and Patrick's adventure in the De Da Mua had become the talk of the seventh grade.

The next day it was the same. And once again, Patrick had not done his homework for the tracks because he had too much homework from school—and no spare time. Mrs. Caledon was laying it on—and so were their other teachers. "To teach you responsibility," the English teacher had said.

"To prepare you for eighth grade," the science teacher had added.

"It builds character," their class teacher, Mrs. Caledon had topped them all with that one. "Someday you'll thank me," she insisted.

Stella was just fuming as she walked onto the playground. Respons...ibility, she thought. Response-ability.... Homework doesn't teach us to have any ability to respond to anything. It just teaches us to shut up and do what we're told without questioning. And it robs us of all our free time—when we could otherwise be learning so many things that we'd remember for our whole lives— not just stupid, meaningless facts that matter for nothing in the world but scoring high on some stupid test. It's just like remembering who scored how many points in some stupid sports game. Who cares? What's wrong with these people? Stella's thoughts, once again, were crashing from one to the next, in domino fashion.

As Clarsah and Jessie approached on the field, Stella's thoughts formed into words, "They think they're preparing us for *eighth grade*? That was their excuse *last year*—to prepare us for *seventh grade*. Next year it will be to prepare us for *high school*— then for *high school* to prepare us for *college*."

"College homework must be to prepare us for what then?" Clarsah asked.

"To prepare us for life?" Jessie pondered.

"No way!" Stella asserted. "Don't you guys get it? It will have caused us to *miss* life—to not have a life! To never see an animal track—to step right on the most amazing tracks and never know it! That's how we're being trained—to never think for ourselves what to do with our time. I guess, to be servants to some corporation...." Stella thought deeply, and soon enough she came to a realization; "Now I understand how homework builds character," she looked intensely into the faces of her friends. "It turns you into an obedient slave—an IRZ!" Stella added with a possessed look, her eyes going out of focus to the hazy sky.

"What's an IRZ?" Jessie asked

"An Idiot Robot Zombie," Stella answered. "Someone—" The bell rang, cutting Stella's sentence, blasting her train of thought and her nervous system. Automatically, her friends turned and headed toward the building. "Someone!" Stella continued, before even taking a single step— "whose whole life is dictated by ringing bells, schedules, and assignments!"

Her friends stared at her, open mouthed, their expressions frozen, dumbstruck. Though within moments, a *sadness* could be read in Jessie and Clarsah's stricken looks—a realization of the undeniable truth.

Stella was almost as shocked by her own words. For she knew not where the term, IRZ, came from—nor how it came *through* her. She knew only that it was true—and like so many inklings that seemed to just flow *through her*, it was barely a ripple in the gulf stream that carried it. Though her *conscious* mind, almost immediately, completely forgot the term and its meaning— *sub*consciously, she sensed the spirit of her older sister, Ari, near the source of her momentary inkling.

"But it doesn't *have* to be that way!" she asserted. "We can change it. We just have to...*think free*—and be willing to fight...*the war for our own minds,"* she raised her brows, her eyes wide. "Tread the word!" Stella said defiantly, throwing up her

104

peace sign, and scrunching her fingers twice. The other girls smiled at Stella's gesture, and they all headed slowly back to the building.

Wednesday came—and it was the same thing all over again. Too much school homework, and Patrick made zero progress on the tracks. Stella could take it no longer. As soon as recess came, she exploded. "That's it, Patrick! You've had your chances! I want those track drawings back—this afternoon! I'll identify them myself—tonight!"

"Calm down—it's not my fault," he protested. "You know what it's been like." He sighed heavily. "I promise I'll bring them in tomorrow morning—no matter what—even if I have to get up in the middle of the night and sneak with my flashlight to study that field guide. And even if it takes me all night until tomorrow morning—" he held up his right hand, "on MacAwen's honor," he promised, "I'll find the identities of the tracks."

Stella sighed, shaking her head. "I'll give you one more chance—but I'm coming over after school to make copies of the drawings, just to be sure."

"My mom still isn't letting me have anyone over—or letting me out, until all my homework is done."

"This *is* your homework!" Stella snapped. "You have to be strong!" her voice broke. She turned away, tears filling her eyes.

And just at that moment—there was Tom, Craig, and Robert. Tom had a bit of a smile on his face that looked, to Stella, like a smirk. "Whoa," he stared at her, "this doesn't have anything to do with the little brown dude, does it?"

"Shut up, you idiot!" she lunged at him and almost struck him, but just stopped herself—her arm raised and a wild look in her eyes. Tom, Craig, and Robert all froze—for once there was not a smile on any of their faces.

Stella stormed from the playground and sat on the edge of the woods with her field guide. No one else understood the importance of MacAwen's homework—not even Patrick.

Three girls who had been standing nearby now approached. Two were very tall—a blond haired girl named Cindy, who always seemed pleasant enough—and Gretchen, who never seemed pleasant at all—at least, not to Stella. Though she did *usually* seem to be nice enough to everybody else—especially the teachers who all thought she was so perfect. The shorter girl had wavy, coppery hair. Her name was Jasmine.

"You *can* read!" Gretchen exclaimed with a mocking enthusiasm as she smiled down at Stella, holding her field guide. "Tracking?" Gretchen made a disgusted face as she looked at the cover of Stella's book. "Oh my *God*—that is *so* stupid. Why are you reading *that*, Stella?"

Stella breathed in deep, her jaw clamped. She closed the book with a sigh, and looked up at Gretchen. "You wouldn't understand —*obviously*," Stella responded. "It's beyond your realm."

"*Realm?*" Gretchen mocked. "You're such a tard."

Stella put the book down, then stood up and stepped toward Gretchen, eyeing her up and down. "You're a snake," she said, as a matter of fact. "I can see your scaly skin. And I sense the cold blood in your veins."

"You are *such* a freak," Gretchen shook her head, her nose turned up.

"Whoa! Let's not get violent now," Tom shouted, approaching from the middle of the field.

"You have *got* to be kidding," Stella responded, glancing at him over her shoulder. Robert and Craig were coming warily behind him. Just behind them, David, Clarsah, Jessie, and Patrick were meandering over, as well.

Stella sighed, turning back to Gretchen. "If a snake has venom, it may decide to strike. If it's not sure, it may be wiser for it to just slither away."

"What a *weirdo!*" Gretchen made a disgusted face. "Can you believe her?" she turned to Cindy.

"*Can you believe her?*" Tom mocked Gretchen's voice.

"Why are *you* sticking up for *her?*" Gretchen snapped at him, accusingly—and clearly surprised as well as disappointed.

"I'm *not,*" Tom answered defensively. "I'm just trying to keep peace on the playground," he smiled. "It looked like it was about to spill over, into violence."

"It would have been a crazy fight," Craig added with his perfect monotone and gleaming smile. "Who do you think would have won?" he asked, turning to Robert.

"I don't know," Robert answered dryly, " but I wouldn't want to be around to find out."

"So what's this all about anyway—huh?" Tom asked.

"*She* just can't keep her scaly nose in her own business," Stella said. "And she thinks tracking is stupid."

"Gretchen," Tom nodded, "You *are* right about a lot of things —*almost half* of everything you say," he added with a mischievous smile, still nodding. "But you're just *dead wrong* about tracking." He shook his head.

"*Really?*" Gretchen questioned him. "I thought following some *filthy*, tick infested animal's trail...through the *mud* was for like—weirdo, fat, cigar-smoking *losers* who just like to shoot things because they're just like...*too stupid* to think of anything better to do with their time—and they're like, *social misfits*. I can't believe *any* body would make *a book* about tracking."

"That is such crap!" Tom laughed. "You *are* joking—"

"You're gonna get a *strike*—for *swearing!*" Jasmine cut in.

"*What?*" Tom smiled at her incredulously. "*Crap* is *not* a swear."

"Yes it is!" Jasmine answered, doubly vehement now since Tom had said it again.

"*No...*" Tom explained very slow and mockingly, as though she was mentally inept, "*Crap*...is a slang word for *poop. Shit,*" he emphasized, "is a swear. "

Jasmine stared at him, flabbergasted. Robert and Craig broke out laughing.

"You could go tell on him," Gretchen suggested. "He deserves it," she added, looking at Tom with an air of satisfaction, as Jasmine stormed off to tell Mrs. Caledon.

"Now *why* did you have to go and egg her on?" Tom frowned at Gretchen.

"I don't know," Gretchen shrugged nonchalantly. "Why'd you have to stick up for Stella?"

"I wasn't sticking up for *her!*" Tom snapped. "You're just wrong about tracking."

In a moment, Mrs. Caledon approached. "What's going on Tom?" she prodded.

"Nothing!" Tom answered defensively. "We're just having a normal conversation—and she gets offended 'cause she thinks *crap* is a swear word."

"Tom—we *don't* use that language here."

"Oh my *God*—" Tom shrugged, as though in pain. "This school is so *weird*. Just because she's too immature to hear every day words used in the real world—"

"Tom!" Mrs. Caledon asserted her authority. "Stop." She stared at him until he stood still. "*Listen,*" she raised her brows.

"Do me—and yourself—a favor—please. Do *not* use that kind of language around Jasmine—or anyone else on this playground whom it might offend. You got it?"

"*Okay.*" Tom conceded. "I *won't,*" he added, shrugging, as Mrs. Caledon gave him a final *look.*

"I'm glad to hear it," she nodded, then sighed and walked away.

"God! I wish I could just be back at public school—where people are normal!" Tom glared across the field at Jasmine. "She is such a—" he hesitated, "B-I-T-C-H," he spelled out the word.

"*Ooh*—such a big word, Tom," Gretchen mocked, "It's amazing how you could spell it."

"Ah, get over it! You're an even bigger bi—" Tom halted, then his eyes lit up and a big smile spread across his freckled face. "*Gritch!*" he said with great satisfaction. "Gritchy Gretchy!" he added, his smile spreading. "Don't be so gritchy, Gretchy!" Tom shouted. "Now that's a good one; *Gritchy Gretchy.*"

"Let's get out of here, Cindy," Gretchen shook her head. "These *children* are *lost* causes!" And she stormed away.

Cindy shrugged, smiling uncomfortably at everyone, then following Gretchen across the field.

Stella had all she could do to let it go another day. But Friday morning, at last, Patrick had come through.

"I have positively identified the tracks," he assured her. "I double checked—I triple checked—and I checked and checked again. I'm sure—the track drawings I have were of *White-Tailed Deer...and Snow Shoe Hare.*"

Now at last they had identified all five of the animal tracks—their guide and the four other animal tracks their guide had led them to. Now at last there would be a point to their next lesson—and hopefully, they would meet MacAwen again. And he would teach them true magic! Patrick and Stella were more than ready to get back out to the woods.

Now they could earn access to other levels, as Stella recalled MacAwen's words, "By spreading awareness of the Mysterious Creature...of the Shadow Beast...of The Web of Tracks that connects them to each other and to everyone else in this world—even beyond this world.... And then she remembered The Terrible War. A war for your minds.... Stella remembered, this was a war for the minds of everyone on the planet.

Yet for now, she let that thought slip away. Knowing, or sensing things that others didn't, made her feel different—kind of unique and powerful, but also, alienated and alone—maybe even crazy. Logic told her she was probably fantasizing. Thank goodness she was not alone when she met MacAwen—thank goodness for Patrick!

There were a lot more than Patrick and Stella who were ready and eager for the weekend's adventure. There was quite a troop hoping to rendezvous on Saturday morning—over a dozen. For some of them, this was figuring to be the biggest adventure they had ever embarked upon on their own.

Certainly, there was the mystical element. The whole class was emotionally charged—even those who weren't coming. But also, there had been talk of *the Bad-Ones*. And though that brought in the element of danger— for most kids, it seemed to excite rather than frighten. For Patrick and Stella, all the danger in the world could not stop them. For though they did not know what it was, their eyes had glimpsed the Great Mystery of *Awen*—the energy that seemed to be moving in all things. And beyond all else now, their spirits longed to see and experience more.

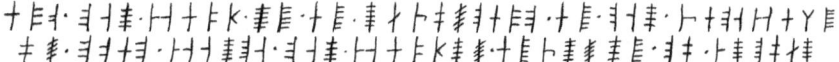

In darkness watchers watch.
In brightness shadows scream:
The most terrible nightmares ever dreamed
are never what at first they seem....

Chapter V:

Nightmares

A strange, wispy, metallic sort of smog floated across the sky. Stella had seen clouds like this before—but only in dreams. Or rather, nightmares. And she barely remembered them when she woke up—until now.

There was something hidden in this smog—something sinister. She sensed, as the cloud came over her, something invisible was falling out.

Suddenly, she realized, this had happened before. In fact, this had been happening all her life! But usually, it only happened in dreams she did not recall in her waking life—repetitive nightmares where she had a dreaded sense something was trying to destroy her mind.

Yet now it occurred to her, maybe it had not just been in her dreams, but also, in her real life—while all her life she had walked oblivious—as *though* in a dream.

Now, as always, the affect of the fallout from this cloud took hold—completely. Stella forgot what it was she'd been thinking. Her head went foggy—her thoughts, confused. She walked in a daze—barely conscious of where she was going as the twilight turned to darkness.

A full moon was on the rise. It's bright glow penetrated the hazy atmosphere. In the distance, from somewhere deep in the forest, a haunting and mysterious sound pierced the fog. In the darkening night a shrill howl was detected—though only by Stella's *sub*conscious. Her conscious mind was lost in the fog. Thus she did not know why, and was barely aware that in spite of the suffocating smog, something deep within her was awakening—something wild....

Stella was completely alone in a strange, dark forest. It was a chill, damp night. An eerie glow from the full moon, filtering through swirling fogs, cast large, dark shadows all about her—looming shadows from tall, silent trees—shadows that moved unexpectedly through the forest, as though alive and aware of her presence. A shiver ran down her spine. She glanced up to the moonlit treetops, high above her dark path. Pine, hemlock, and newly unfolding yet still leafless deciduous branches swayed about —*the source of the moving shadows*, she reasoned. Yet it was not altogether reasonable. For she could feel no breeze at ground level and, on second glance, the tree tops were not swaying about at all. In fact, they were dead still.

Stella walked slowly, cautiously. The forest was silent—so silent it was loud. It was a fuzzy, electrical sort of sound—like she had heard immediately following that terrible scream MacAwen had used to startle her and Patrick to a heightened state of wakefulness. But there was no scream now. There was no MacAwen. And there was no Patrick. Stella was all alone.

Ahead, to the side of the path, she saw a dark shape moving. Then it was still. Stella froze. *It must be an illusion*, she thought, *the shadow of a tree, moved by the wind, over a big rock...or a stump...or something.* She looked back up to the treetops. One tall tree *only* was moving, slightly. As she studied it, it went as still as the others.

There must have been a small gust of wind, she thought. Why the wind only moved that one tree, she could not fathom. *But winds are strange and invisible, yet explainable*, she assured herself.

She continued, her pace slower now. Stella walked very cautiously, straining all her conscious focus on the dark shadow ahead that had appeared to move—striving to discern the log, the stump, or the something *explainable* that she hoped it would be.

But subconsciously, she could not help focusing on the something *unexplainable* that she hoped it would *not* be. She did not know what that something *could be*. She did not know what that something *might be*. She could only imagine. Of course, to the infinite imagination—especially as it whirls through a wide open mind, like that which belongs to Stella Childs—*everything* is possible. And every possibility in the universe flits through the subconscious in less than a millisecond. If the conscious mind gives over to belief...*it could be anything;* it *might* be anything.

Stella knew only that whatever it was scared her—which she also knew was ridiculous, of course—as she assured herself. It was illogical. It was unrealistic. It was childish. It was just a stump—or a big rock. It was not even moving now. It had probably only appeared to move that one time. It *hadn't* moved again, even as she drew closer—as she strove to make out the details of what the object *was* in reality.

Still, to the subconscious, there is no difference between reality and imagination. And when fear takes over the subconscious, it is more powerful than conscious belief. Stella remembered the Shadow Beast. Whether it came from inside her own mind or not made no difference. She felt inside her pockets, for her amulet. It wasn't there! With a heightened sense of fear and helplessness she realized she'd left it at home.

Stella's eyes were fixed on the base of a huge tree, ahead on the trail's edge, where whatever it was *that it might be* lay still in the shadows. As Stella got closer, it now appeared to be a stump protruding from the bottom of the tree.

She let out a sigh of relief, but her heart was still racing. She hadn't even noticed her heart racing before, as she had been so focused on the shadowed object. Now she felt it beating painfully inside her chest. It was as though her heart had stopped along with her breath as she had approached the shadow—and now it was pounding desperately to make up for lost time.

She stood a moment, breathing deep to catch her breath now and ease her heart rate. Yet even as she did—again, the object moved.

In the darkness and tricky fog, it appeared as though a hooded face protruded from the side of the tree and turned toward her. Then it was still again—dead still, staring directly at her. In Stella's imagination the shadowed *stump* had now taken on the appearance of a hooded figure, standing still as a ghost—staring toward her from the base of the tree. *But it couldn't be,* she reasoned, *it's just a trick of the shadows.*

Stella stood frozen, staring. The stump had such an appearance of a hooded figure, she almost laughed. Because of course it couldn't be real. She was maybe twenty feet from it now. Surely its real features would come into view as she got closer. She took another step, then another. Focusing on the *wood* of the *stump* that looked so like a hooded figure, but would any moment be revealed of its true identity as she drew closer, Stella walked. But her steps grew shorter—and slower—as her vision grew clearer. It looked even more like a hooded, cloaked figure now. Stella stopped. She held her breath again, staring. Her body trembled. She was so very close now. *It should not still look like a person,* she thought to herself.

"*Who said it's a person?*" a voice answered...from inside her head. At least, *she thought* it came from inside her head. She assumed it was her own thought. But she wasn't sure. And as each second passed from the time she heard this voice, it seemed more and more unlike her own. "*You don't get it, do you?*" the voice spoke again—this time it definitely *was* inside her head. She sighed.

"I get it now," she spoke out loud to no one but herself. "It's my subconscious. I'm just imagining."

"*You get it halfway,*" the voice answered. But this time, the voice came from the hooded figure in the shadow of the tree. "*Come closer,*" it said, "*and I'll show you the other half.*"

Adrenaline shot through Stella's blood stream. Her body trembled uncontrollably. She was afraid beyond belief. Yet she could not resist. As if in a trance, and pulled by a magnetic force, she moved toward the figure, shaking like a leaf.

With every step, she searched within herself for some place where she might realize how the voice could be her own. And as she strove to be reasonable, more and more she thought, *maybe the voice did come from inside me.* And yet, with every step, it became more clear to her eyes—the hooded figure was real!

What she hadn't realized before was that the figure had been *kneeling* at the base of the tree. Now, as the last breath she would ever breathe in this forest left her lungs, and her body froze in terror, the figure stood up before her. Tall and powerful, its face still invisible within the shadowed hood, it looked down at her and spoke in a more potent version of the voice that she, in her confusion, had thought *maybe was her own*:

"Some people wake up from their nightmares and think; *oh, thank goodness—it was only a nightmare,*" the tall figure hissed. Its voice was neither male nor female, child nor adult. Nor was this figure a mere ghost, monster, or any natural sort of beast. It was something else. That, Stella knew without thinking. But she could not think. She could only listen, as its voice continued;

"When you're having the nightmare, you don't know it's a nightmare. Thus, when you're *in* the nightmare, the nightmare is completely real."

Frozen, staring up at the invisible face—open-mouthed, without breathing, Stella took in these words—and was overcome. She was conscious of nothing but the figure before her and the words it spoke, as each moment, its words grew more terrifying: **"The very worst sort of nightmare, though, is the sort you actually wake up in the middle of, and realize, to your horror —it is real! In fact, it is the happy reality you believed in all your life that was but a dream."** And with that, the figure reached up and threw back its hood.

Stella beheld a face that was at once amazing and terrifying. Its head was bald. Throbbing veins bulged from its pale skin. In a moment it appeared as an ancient, shriveled person, a reptilian creature, a newborn baby, an alien being, and uncountable other things to Stella's imagination. It was both dead and alive.

The tall figure bent down and stuck its face in front of hers. She would have screamed if there was a bit of air in her lungs, but they were empty. She stared wildly into its eyes. Those eyes— terrifying, mesmerizing, alien, and yet familiar. She had seen those eyes before—somewhere. They had watched her. And when she was not consciously aware, they had penetrated to the depths of her soul. She sensed this. For this beast, she suddenly realized, had stalked her all her life. Her subconscious had glimpsed it here and there—but in fear she had blocked it out, turned from it, and forgotten.

For what seemed an eternity, she was frozen in that one moment—terrified by the supernatural beast that felt so alien and unthinkable. Yet, in another moment of time, or perhaps in another layer of her consciousness, in this Shadow Beast's expression—she saw a disturbing likeness of herself. And then, in her own voice, it shouted, **"Wake up!"**

A great rush of air filled her lungs as she opened her eyes. It was as though she had fallen flat on her back from a great height. "Wake up!"she screamed, as she sat bolt upright in her bed. All was pitch black. Her heart pounded once—then went silent. Then, boom, it thumped again, and she could feel the blood pump through her body and brain as though by a powerful electric shock. One more time, her heart pounded. Then her room suddenly was filled with a blinding light.

"Stella!" her mother's voice called out to her. "Stella—darling," her mother's arms wrapped around her, as Stella's eyes adjusted to the light. "Are you alright, honey?" Her mother searched into Stella's stunned features. "It was just a dream," her mother's voice soothed. "It's okay now."

Stella looked at her mom, at the room around her, then back at her mom. She searched under her pillow, frantic for a moment, until she found her silver amulet and clutched it tight in her palm. She let go a heavy sigh. "What time is it?" she asked, pleadingly.

Her mother sighed. "It's the middle of the night, honey. I *don't know* what time it is."

Stella sighed again, searching about her room. She let out an exhausted bit of a laugh, a dreamy smile forming on her face, though she almost rather felt like crying. "I had the most *crazy* nightmare."

Now her mother sighed again. "It's been a while since you had one of your nightmares—thank goodness," she smiled. "I've hardly thought of it—though we *have* all been sleeping much better lately."

Stella nodded, wide-eyed. "But I think it was actually, really good to meet the Shadow Beast." Her Mom raised her brows, questioningly. Stella shrugged with a bit of a smile. "Mom—" Stella asked, "Tell me again, what was my father like? What did he *look* like?"

Stella's mom looked startled, for a moment. Then she sighed, shaking her head. "I've told you all there is to tell—and so many times. Yet it *has* been a while since you asked." She gave Stella an odd look. "What makes you think of him now, honey?"

"Oh...I don't know," Stella answered, glancing quick at her amulet, then clutching it tight again— "It just came to me."

Her mom shook her head, then smiled. "You're a funny one. More and more, I think, as you grow..." her voice trailed off. "You are just like your father...an angel." Her mom stared off into some other place and time, a faraway look filled with both joy and sadness. "He was the most beautiful man I've ever seen." She sighed, and then returned her focus to Stella. "You have his eyes," she said, "and his smile."

"I still feel..." Stella faltered. "Are you sure? I mean— no one ever found his body."

Her mom sighed, closing her eyes and shaking her head. "I know he's not alive...*in the flesh*," she answered. "At least, not on this planet," she smiled. "For if he was, he most certainly *would* be here with us."

"I wish he was."

"I do too, honey. But he's always with us...in spirit."

Stella's older sister appeared in the doorway, squinting in the bright light. "Hey," she smiled—then came in and sat on Stella's bed, opposite the side of their mother.

Stella smiled at her, then turned back to her mom and asked, "He wasn't exactly an *angel* then, was he? I mean—if he could die?" Her mom sighed, but didn't answer. "Mom?"

"Oh—I'm sorry, honey. It's very late," she sighed. "Your father *was* an angel...in a *man's body...*" she sighed again, very heavily. "But how many times have I told you that?" she shook her head. "I need to get back to bed. Are you going to be okay now?"

"I got this, Mom," Stella's older sister cut in.

"Thanks, Ari," Her mom answered. "Sweet—uh...*sweeter* dreams," she smiled as she got up. She blew them a sleepy kiss and left the room.

Stella turned to her elder sister, Ari, whom she idolized—who was about the coolest big sister she could possibly imagine. Ari who was a rebel, an activist, a radical—kind, gentle, and thoughtful to Stella, yet tough as a tiger out in the world—afraid of no one and always demanding "*social justice.*" Though she did get into a bit of trouble now and again.

"Your father *was* an angel," Ari said. "A *true* angel," she nodded.

Stella smiled. "I wish I could have met him." She stared off, into some space beyond the ceiling. "It's so cool—he actually built *boats*...for a job."

"He could build *anything*," Ari replied, "the coolest tree forts, go-carts, toy boats, doll houses, *real* houses. "I remember him *so* vividly," she shook her head. "I was only like, five. And he was only in our lives for like, maybe a few months. But it seemed like so much more. It was such a happy time. And I have so many memories from that time. It was like...a big part of my life—like a few years packed into a few months."

"What's it like to know your father?" Stella asked.

"Are you serious?" Ari raised her brows. "I don't even *want* to know *my* father," she shook her head. Stella shot her a surprised look. "I would rather we both just had *your* father for our Dad," Ari said, "even if he did have to die."

"I wish I could have known him," Stella sighed. "Why did he *have* to die?"

"I don't know," Ari answered, softly, shaking her head. "It just seems like—like all the best people—like Abe Lincoln, Gandhi...and Martin Luther King...and John Lennon..." she sighed, "they all get killed. Probably, by the MIF," she added with a low, suspicious voice. "At least, that's what Uncle Ken says," she added with a raise of her brow and a bit of a smile.

Stella sighed. "I think it was one of Uncle Ken's stories that caused part of my nightmare. But what exactly *is* the MIF?" Stella asked.

"It's just a secret part of our government," Ari answered. "An organization of spies. *The Middle Information Front.* But it's so big...and so powerful...with so many agents all over the world— and no one knowing who they all are...or where they all are...or what they're *really* up to—even the president is scared of them."

"The *president*? But I thought he was the boss of everyone in the whole government?" Stella questioned.

Ari laughed, shaking her head. "Oh yeah—*right*. Well—the president, the congress, and the supreme court...they make up the three branches of our government—the executive, the legislative, and the judicial. They're *supposed* to watch over each other—and be the bosses over every lower level of our government," Ari answered. Stella stared at her in awe and admiration. Ari knew so much. "But how can you be the boss over an organization that is so big and secretive, you don't even know who's in it, or what they're up to? If the MIF doesn't like a member of congress—or a president—they can just kill them."

"What?" Stella responded with disbelief. "Really?"

"Well, *I* don't know for sure," Ari answered. "But *Uncle Ken* thinks *he* knows for sure," she smiled, "though I wouldn't advise asking him, unless you're in the mood for a long, twisted story."

Stella nodded and smiled, knowingly. "But how *could* it be true?" she asked. "If our government was controlled by like— some evil force—wouldn't everyone know? I mean, we wouldn't allow it, would we? And like, why would we have ever invented an agency like that in the first place?"

"*We...the people*—never created the MIF," Ari answered. "And they don't work for *US*—everyone should know that.

Actually, the MIF is not a legitimate part of our true government. That's why our government can't control it. According to Uncle Ken, and I don't doubt him on this one, the MIF was created by the multi-national *Triple Leverage Corporation*—as part of their secret plan to take over our government—which is part of their secret plan to take over the whole world. The MIF spies on *we the people*, it terrorizes *we the people*, and basically does whatever the Triple Leverage Corporation wants it to do...to *control* us...to take away all our freedom—" Ari stopped herself. "Oh— I'm sorry," she sighed. "You don't need to be worrying about all this stuff. And Mom would *not* be happy if she knew I was telling you all this." Ari sighed again, smiling and putting a hand on Stella's shoulder.

"Why don't people do something about it?" Stella asked.

"*Some* of us *are* trying," Ari answered. "That's what political activism is all about. That's what was intended by the founding fathers when they created a government *by* the people, *of* the people, and *for* the people. They made it clear that it's our *duty* to participate in *governing ourselves*—by watching over those we elect to serve us, by questioning everything they say and do, and by demanding that they serve us exactly as we wish to be served. Otherwise, the founding fathers warned us, when *the people* don't *control their government*, it will turn corrupt—and inevitably, *the government* will *control the people; a Tyranny*. We have to be vigilant. But—" she rolled her eyes, shrugging and shaking her head. "The world is populated by a vast majority of...*non-thinking scaredies.*"

"Uh...what?" Stella's consciousness snapped back suddenly from some other world she had drifted into, and now puzzled over the meaning of that which she *thought* she heard her sister say: IRZs. "IRZs? Oh, I get it," she laughed. "Idiot Robot Zombies. *IRZs* stands for Idiot Robot Zombies."

Ari gave her an odd look, then smiled. "IRZs? Where'd you come up with that one, Stella?"

"Uh...you just said it—didn't you? That the world is populated by a vast majority of IRZs?"

Ari laughed, shaking her head. "That's my little sis," she smiled. "What I said was *non-thinking scaredies*—not *IRZs*. I don't know *how* you got IRZs out of *non-thinking scaredies*, but...

Idiot Robot Zombies," Ari laughed, "that is a good one, Stella. That pretty much sums it up."

After Ari left her alone in her room, Stella remembered her dream—how she had felt so awake, so alive, so knowing—and then the fog came over her. In real life, she often *did* have fleeting moments when she felt so alive and so awake that she just seemed to know things. She would feel such inspiration—such creativity.... It was like, there was a great...*fog* that stifled ninety percent of her brain—and at times it would just be lifted away from her. But other times, for no apparent reason, the fog would come over her again.

Suddenly, Stella remembered a whole series of her dreams that had something about strange clouds in them—and how, when she was *in the dreams,* she always remembered the other dreams in the series, as though they were real life. But, when she was *awake,* she never remembered any of those dreams. It was like she was living more than one life. Perhaps many!

But then there was her Uncle Ken—she had heard him say something about unusual clouds, also. Maybe *that* had caused her cloud dreams. But now that it came to her consciousness, it seemed she'd been having those dreams so long. And maybe it was only *in one of her dreams* that Uncle Ken had said something about strange clouds. She was not sure. She would have to ask him next time she saw him.

Stella recalled the short time she was on ridacull, for her ADD. How pleased her teachers were. "She is so much more present," was the most common phrase Stella remembered from that time. And she *was* more present. It *did* help her to focus—*on the things she was supposed to be focused on.*

But there was a sacrifice for *"being present"* when and where others wanted her to be. It was like she was *cut off* from other aspects of herself. It was like, there were whole other worlds—worlds of imagination—worlds of her own creation—other dimensions of her mind. And when she was drugged, and made to focus—like, on a chalkboard at school—she was totally cut off from those other dimensions. And then, she no longer was fully herself. It was like she was turned into an IRZ. Like so many.... These memories haunted her as she drifted back to sleep....

Stella popped the pills into her mouth, but secured them under her tongue before tilting back her head and swallowing a gulp of water. "Ah..." she breathed. The nurse smiled. "Bye," Stella said, returning the smile as she left the nurse's office.

120

And Stella was free—not only in body, but more importantly, in mind. She darted into the girl's room and spat the pills into the toilet. A quick rinse of her mouth, and she was on her way....

"Stella! Did you take your medication?" Mrs. Yandel demanded, with her robot-like voice—in front of the whole class. Stella stared wild eyed and mortified, but said nothing. "It certainly doesn't seem like it!" she scolded. "Because the chalkboard is up *here,*" she pointed, "in *front* of the classroom," she mocked. "But you seem to think we have a chalkboard outside the window somewhere. If you *are* taking your meds—then it seems you need a higher dose."

Time and time again, Stella played this memory back in her head. There were so many things she imagined herself saying back at Mrs. Yandel: *you seem to live, your whole petty existence, inside a chalkboard.... I know perfectly well where your little chalkboard is Mrs. Yandel—it's just that staring out the window is far more interesting, and stimulating, than listening to you.... I* **would** *have to be drugged to sit here and listen to* **you** *for a whole hour...*

Imagining herself coming back at Mrs. Yandel with phrases like that took the edge off the memory. But it didn't actually change it. And the worst part wasn't just that the woman said those things, but that she said it in front of the whole class.

Stella slipped back into dream, and once again, was reliving that memory: "You seem to think we have a chalkboard outside the window somewhere.... If you *are* taking your meds—then it seems you need a higher dose...." Stella heard kids laughing. Maybe it was only two or three, but it felt like the whole world. She sat, in her chair, at her desk, frozen. In that moment she felt totally stupid—like a hopeless case.

"But you are as you feel you are," a frightening, yet now familiar voice hissed into her ear. "And that's what being in this class **now** is all about—reminding you...teaching you how stupid and worthless you really are." Stella turned to the source of the voice. And there—standing behind her—was the tall, hooded figure she had seen in her nightmare—the Shadow Beast!

But it didn't make sense. This tall figure was from a recent dream. And this classroom was from a time in her past—years before she ever saw this figure—or heard of the Shadow Beast.

"I must be dreaming," she thought.

"*Then wake up!*" the voice cracked. And her old classroom disappeared—along with Mrs. Yandel...and the hooded figure.

"Thank goodness," Stella sighed, as she opened her eyes once more in her dark bedroom.

Yet, even as she lay awake in her bed, the voice of the Shadow Beast echoed in her head: "*The worst sort of nightmare is the sort you wake up in the middle of, and realize, to your horror, it is real.*" And again, Stella was haunted by the image of the Shadow Beast's face—un-hooded. Consciously, she could not clearly see the face, nor understand its significance. Yet subconsciously, it unnerved her. She wished the image would just go away. She wished she had never seen it. But she sensed she had been seeing it all her life, only subconsciously. And now, at last, some part of her that had only slept, or awakened in dreams, was waking up in the real world.

Stella lay in the dark for an uncomfortable time as the slow seconds ticked. The air in her bedroom was charged—disturbed. There was a fuzziness—a buzzing, ringing static electricity. But as she focused her vision and hearing upon it, the energy changed. The swirling sparks of Awen danced into her consciousness. And then she remembered MacAwen....

At the thought of the little brown man, the image of the Shadow Beast disappeared. And at last she slept in peace. In the morning she had a sense that MacAwen had come into her dreams and had taught her some more magic. She wished she could remember. Perhaps if she could be more awake in her dreams.... Perhaps if she could be more awake when she *was* awake.... These thoughts rekindled a vague memory of MacAwen telling her something about "*mastering dreams...ta be mastering reality....*" She was so excited to learn more. But there was the Shadow Beast to contend with, also. She would have to be aware with all her senses.

Part II:

Through Chaos

ᚸᛁᛁ ᛁᚾ ᚻᛁ ᛁᚾᛁᛁᛈ ᛁᚾᛁᚿᛁᛁᛈ ᛈᚻᛁᛁ ᚸᛁᛁᛁ ᚻᛁᛁᚲ
ᛁᛈᚻᛁᚻᛁᛁᛁ ᛈᛁᚹᛁᛁᛁᚾ ᚸᛁᛁᛁ ᚻᛁᛁᚲᚹᛁᚸ ᛖᛁᛁᛁ

A fine line there is
and yet a gap of eternity
between not believing and believing not.
And so she thought;
this gap's nae filled with one's perceptions—
one's perceptions are filled with it.
Read between the lines.

Chapter VI:
To Believe Not Or To Not Believe

"Free...dom!" Stella yelled at the top of her lungs, her arms flailing high in the air, "at long last!" She spun like a whirling dervish, then leaped and planted her feet firmly on the trail— gazing intensely at her friends for a moment, then smiling wide. "I can't *believe*—I am back out on the trail—*finally*, after such an *excruciating* week."

Short, dark-haired Jessie was giggling as usual. So was the coppery haired Jasmine. Excitement was writhing through the whole gang. Stella felt a gigantic sense of relief that the week had ended—also, a bit of pride that she and Patrick had identified all the tracks. But most of all, she felt exuberance. At the moment it was like time didn't exist. So free and lusty she felt for the intrigue of further discovery and adventure that this day might last forever. With their homework for MacAwen all finished, now they could have their next lesson—and prove MacAwen's existence to their friends.

It was a perfect Saturday morning—not too hot, not too cold, mostly sunny. Clarsah, Jessie, Jasmine, David, Brighid, and Iona had gotten dropped off at Stella's and Patrick's houses. Now the eight of them were footing it for the halfway point on the old railroad path to rendezvous with Andy, Tom, Robert, Craig, and whoever else would be able to join them.

Stella felt like a changed person from whom she had been only six days earlier when she and Patrick had first encountered MacAwen. By the air about him she could sense the same about Patrick. The others also noticed a transformation in their two friends, but clearly had varying opinions about it.

"You seem so different," Jessie stared at Stella with a look of awe as they walked. "Since your lesson with MacAwen," she glanced at the path, her short legs struggling to keep up—"it's like you know things no one else does—kind of like Iona," she glanced at their very tall and aloof, brown haired friend. Iona smiled.

"Yeah," Clarsah agreed. "You *are* different." Her brown eyes lit up from behind her glasses, "I hope MacAwen shows me how to see things, too."

"I hope," Jessie added, "more than *anything*, that MacAwen will offer us all a lesson."

Jasmine shrugged. "I *do* hope it's real," she spoke with her typical fast and fiery tongue. "And I'm not saying you made it up. But—" she sighed. "To be perfectly honest, it's just really hard to believe."

"Oh, that's okay, Jasmine," Stella assured. "I'd have a hard time believing too—if I hadn't seen." She smiled. "You'll see."

Iona just smiled. She was obviously happy for her friends, and she had said that she did believe, but was without expectation. Now she seemed pretty much carefree about the whole event— pretty much how she always seemed.

"I believe," Brighid's eyes were wide with hope under her great mane of wild, dark hair. "I guess." Doubt fell over her face and into her voice. "Are you really sure?" she turned her head sideways, glancing back and forth between Stella and Patrick.

"I know *I'm* sure," Patrick answered with his typical air of confidence.

Stella smiled, getting distracted for a moment in the glistening sunlight dancing through the amazing waves and curls of Brighid's hair. "You have such...*amazing* hair, Brighid," Stella sighed. "It's like, just wild and beautiful," she smiled, her hands outstretched, almost *in* Brighid's hair.

"Thanks," Brighid smiled, "but are you really sure, he's *really* real?"

"Oh—yeah," Stella smiled. "well, you'll just have to wait and see Sir MacAwen for yourself."

"I know you wouldn't lie," Brighid added. "I really do hope MacAwen is real." The other girls seemed all to be nodding agreement on that point.

Then there was David. He was nodding most vigorously. Stella looked at him. "Oh yeah," he stopped his eyes in mid-roll. "Of course I believe you, Stella…and Patrick—whole-heartedly," he nodded, almost convincingly. "I mean, little brown men, three feet tall," he nodded some more, raising his brows, "although seemingly rare, actually—" his mouth hung open for just a second, "well, quite common…in Grimm's fairy tales, Irish legends, even in modern literature and popular film," he nodded, in a pretentiously supportive manner.

"As for the New Hampshire woods—" David now frowned very seriously, barely a hint of a smile leaking through his mask, "I think this is a first," he raised his pitch in feigned enthusiasm. "If I snap a photo of you two, arm in arm with this leprechaun," he nodded, "I'm almost positive you'll make the front page of the Milford Cabinet. Of course, since your—"

"Shut up, David!" Stella glared at him. "You're nothing but an arrogant little, pea-brained—" she stammered— "ninny wit!"

"A ninny wit?" David raised his brows, almost smiled, but quickly faked a shocked, hurt look. "Me?" he put a hand over his heart.

Stella shook her head. "MacAwen probably doesn't like to be filmed—so try and show some manners. Anyway," she turned to her other friends, "he's got magic abilities and probably wouldn't show up on film if he doesn't want to—especially if some arrogant person tried to film him. In fact," she turned back to David, "I'm sure he won't even show up for your dim witless eyes."

"Ouch," David replied, holding his shoulder as though he'd been hit by a stone. "Must we ever be so combative?" He put on a perfect pair of puppy dog eyes. "I try for a little friendly dialog—and then you react the way you sometimes do—and then..." he trotted theatrically in front of the group.

"Put a cork on it, David!" Jasmine demanded.

"A cork?" he raised his brows.

"It means, *shut up,*" she informed. "The show's over."

"Oh..." David sighed. "Thank you very much," he added with a bow. "Such combative, young...*ladies*..."

"Just in the nick of time!" Patrick stated, looking ahead on the trail. "Here comes the other half of our class."

They all looked up the path. This was the long, straight section of the old railroad path. And sure enough, there was a group of kids approaching that was as big in numbers as they were.

"Hey y'all!" Tom shouted from the distance. "See any little brown men?"

Stella shook her head, eying the bunch. "I'm not sure this is such a good idea," she said. "I mean—I don't know. MacAwen doesn't seem like the type to like—like crowds." Tom was accompanied by Robert, Craig, and Andy, of course. Then there was Cindy, Gretchen, Anna, Evan, and Roxie. The two groups joined into one.

"Wow, this looks a lot like—whew," Stella sighed, her head swimming this way and that, looking at the crowd around her. "Well," she glanced at Gretchen, "at least the ticks will find plenty of extra hosts to choose from." She smiled. Gretchen smiled sarcastically in return.

"How about that," Patrick stated, "we met almost at the very spot we first encountered MacAwen's tracks. Well met, indeed," he stated with a princely air.

The kids all mingled. Half a dozen conversations started at once. Half the Spruce Hill seventh grade was here and fully absorbed in the group—and fully absorbed in the moment. For a little bit of time it was like there were no separate individuals, just a big boisterous group. And time didn't exist. There was a feeling in the air—like this day would last forever.

Everyone was talking and joking, and it was pretty loud. Nobody was paying any attention to anything that might be going on around them. "I'm not too sure about this," Stella stated, looking apprehensively into the woods. "Maybe just Patrick and I should see if we can find MacAwen first. He might not like crowds."

"Oh yeah—right, Stella," Gretchen cut in. "Like, you two go off and come back with another story, right?"

"Whatever," Stella shrugged, eying the tall, olive skinned girl with feigned disinterest. "Like I care whether you believe us or not. The point is I just doubt MacAwen is the type that likes big crowds."

"Oh...*kay*—fair enough," Tom shouted, spreading his arms like a referee. "Here's the deal: Since I'm not here to find Ma-*Cow*-en, anyway," he said with his signature insulting slur, "I don't really care. It's the Bad-Ones I'm after—the *Cambulls,*" his eyes lit up. "Cause they, at least, *might* be real." He squinted around at the crowd. "But here's the deal—to be fair to everyone else here, you two," he pointed at Stella and Patrick, "have to bring one of *us* with you as a witness when you go off to find the little brown squirt."

"As long as it's not a *rude* person, I'm sure he wouldn't mind," Stella agreed with a nod, "if we just brought one other person with us."

"Oh please, can it be me?" Clarsah's eyes widened. Then she turned suddenly, thinking of Jessie.

"It's okay, Clarsah," Jessie conceded, "you go first. I know I'll get to meet him after."

"I don't think so," Craig cut in. "No offense, Clarsah, but—like, we all know you're honest and everything—but you're almost as dreamy—and even more gullible than Stella." He smiled genuinely, not in any way meant to be insulting. "You might get fooled—by these two," he pointed at Patrick and Stella, "into thinking you saw something you didn't. I vote we have someone else—like Andy go."

"Andy and Clarsah should both go," Iona broke her silence. "Everyone trusts Clarsah to never lie. And we trust Andy not be fooled by any tricks—or see anything that isn't real. I'm sure MacAwen wouldn't mind if you just brought two friends. He didn't sound like he was that shy."

"That sounds like a *great* idea!" Tom shouted. "You four go after the little brown dude," he pointed, "whoever's up for hunting down the Cambulls—come with me and Robert."

"And me," Craig added, not to be over-shadowed by his boisterous, auburn-haired friend.

"I want to *track* the Cambull's," Robert added, "I don't want to *meet* them."

"Show us where the Cambull's tracks were last week," Craig said. "While you guys are looking for the little dude, we can be tracking some big dudes."

"Big trouble, more like it," Andy added.

"Oh come on!" Tom demanded. "Just point us in the right direction. Or else—or else we'll get a net and hunt down your little leprechaun."

"Ha." Stella laughed. "*You*—are so stupid, Tom. You wouldn't stand a chance against MacAwen. Anyway, the only way anyone can see him is if he allows them to. And you can't even find the De Da Mua unless you have a code."

"Oh yeah, your *secret symbols,*" Gretchen mocked. "That was a good one, Stella and Patrick," she shook her head. "Talk about stupid."

"So I guess we wouldn't be able to find you," Robert nodded with dry sarcasm, "even if we followed your tracks, right? Because we don't have *keys,*" he raised his brows, making quotes with his fingers, "into the...*De Da Mua*?" Gretchen burst out laughing. Cindy smiled, but strove to remain polite.

"Gretchen," Stella glared, "you...are such a total...complete. ..." She stammered.

"Go ahead, Stella," Gretchen mocked, "complete...?" She raised her brows.

"*Completely,*" Stella continued, "not worth talking about—" she said, unable to think of anything else to say.

"Just promise to give us fifteen minutes," Patrick cut in, "after that, if you think you can track us—good luck," he smiled confidently.

So it was agreed upon. Stella, Patrick, Andy, and Clarsah would try to make contact with MacAwen and see if he was willing to meet the rest of the group. Tom, Craig, Robert, and whoever else intended to go tracking down the Cambulls with them would refrain from their adventure for fifteen minutes—by which time the word on MacAwen was supposed to have come back to the larger group.

So the four of them set off; Stella, Patrick, Andy, and Clarsah.

"Don't get lost, Stella," Craig called from behind. "I mean, don't get distracted following like, a leaf blowing in the wind or anything."

Iona responded to Craig, in Stella's defense. "Her Uncle Ken *is* teaching her to be a survivalist."

Tom laughed loud. "Then I guess she'll have to give up vegetarianism! And learn to hunt! Now that would be a sight, eh boys? *Stella...hunting?*"

Stella wasn't going to bother responding, but now felt compelled to defend vegetarianism. "There are many edibles to be gathered from the forest," she informed, "that you idiots don't know about."

"You mean like, pretty flowers and mushrooms and things," Craig asked.

Tom burst out laughing. "*You'd* last really long in the woods, Stella!"

Stella shook her head and continued on. They left the old railroad path exactly where they had followed the coyote tracks six days before—and exactly where, one week ago, they, along with MacAwen, had followed the tracks of Martes pennanti—the fisher.

"I can't believe everybody in our whole class is here to see your little brown man," Andy stated from the rear of the group as they ventured into the wood.

"Andy, he's as real as you are," Stella responded over her shoulder.

"But not everyone is here to see *MacAwen,*" said Patrick, who was leading the way. "Tom and company would rather track the Cambulls."

"Did you tell your parents...about—*MacAwen*?" Andy asked.

"Not me!" Patrick exclaimed from ahead on the trail, not even pausing or turning his head.

"Don't be ridiculous, Andy!" Stella turned on him. "Only a small child would try to convince their parents of such an amazing thing. You don't want to be thought of as crazy, do you? I mean, come on, Andy. You must be wise enough by now to know when to keep your mouth shut."

"Look who's talking," Andy retorted.

"Stella," Patrick laughed, "you have to admit—*you* say some pretty crazy things."

"Yeah, but I don't make a big deal about it," she explained as they walked. "And no one takes me seriously anyway. Except for Clarsah." She smiled and put her arm around Clarsah. Clarsah returned the gesture and they continued walking arm and arm, as they often did. "It's only when you make a big deal over crazy stuff," Stella continued, "that you get into trouble. They'd never let you out into the woods again if you told all about the Crazy Bad Cambulls, or The Mysterious Creature, or The Shadow Beast. You tell the wrong people—and they'd put you in an insane asylum, probably—or keep you under constant surveillance—maybe even insert some RFID chips under your skin to follow your every move —even keep tabs on your emotions and control your mind."

"What?" Andy frowned. "What's an RFID chip?"

"You don't want to know," Stella answered. "I learned about it from my Uncle Ken—and I've researched it on-line, probably while you were blowing up innocent people in one of your dumb video games. But I'll tell you this—if they ever try to put one in you, run for your life and never come back."

Andy rolled his eyes. "But you *have* said some pretty crazy things to Mrs. Caledon," he said.

"Oh yeah—" Stella answered. "Well—*she* just thinks I'm airy fairy, *a dreamy child—young in the mind* and all that. I've got it all figured out. I know who it's safe to say what to."

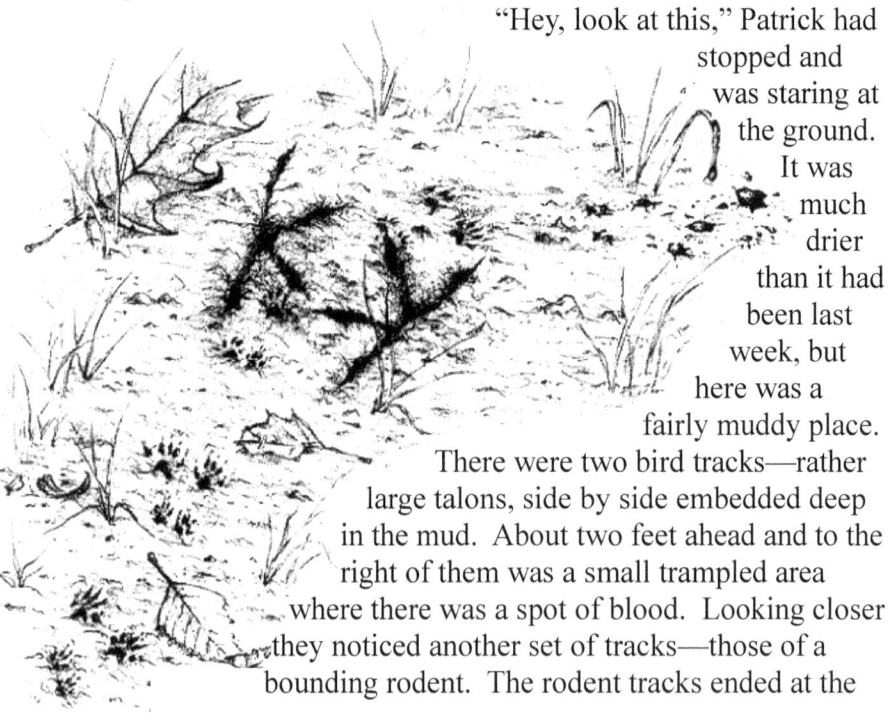

"Hey, look at this," Patrick had stopped and was staring at the ground. It was much drier than it had been last week, but here was a fairly muddy place. There were two bird tracks—rather large talons, side by side embedded deep in the mud. About two feet ahead and to the right of them was a small trampled area where there was a spot of blood. Looking closer they noticed another set of tracks—those of a bounding rodent. The rodent tracks ended at the

132

trampled place in the mud with the blood—and for Patrick the conclusion was obvious. At least, part of it.

"Some sort of a bird of prey," Patrick stated as though he was a scientist, "swooped down here," he pointed at the talon prints, "and having missed at the first attempt, it leapt to this spot," he pointed to the blood stain in the mud where the rodent tracks ended, "where it clutched a hold on some type of rodent and carried it off for a meal."

Clarsah was staring, mesmerized by the tracks and Patrick's story. "I wonder what kind of rodent it was," she questioned.

"Too large to have been a mouse," Patrick answered.

"Oh, I hope it wasn't Pat," Clarsah said with great concern—as though he was an old friend. For she had gotten Stella to tell the full story of the Mysterious Creature and the Shadow Beast over and over—and she had it memorized, almost as though she had been there herself. She'd even had a dream with MacAwen in it.

"Much too small to be Pat," Stella answered. "Probably a chipmunk.

"I wonder who exactly it was that made the kill," Patrick stated. "My guess, by the size of those talons, is the red tailed hawk."

Stella looked into the treetops. The sky seemed suddenly darker. There were wisps of mist wafting amongst the branches. Her eyes were drawn to one great limb extending horizontal from a gnarled old ash tree. "It was an owl," she stated as a matter of fact.

"What makes you think that?" Patrick asked, his eyes following Stella's to the great limb of the gnarled ash.

"I just know," she answered. "*She* perches on that great limb at night," Stella pointed. "And she sees *all* below. Sometimes she brings her catches back up there to feed in peace."

Andy was frowning and shaking his head. He was also looking around—and was beginning to look a little nervous. A mist was rising off the forest floor and it seemed to be having an eerie affect on Andy. "I've been thinking," Andy said, "I'm not saying I believe you guys—but if your story was true, how would you know if MacAwen wasn't the Shadow Beast himself?"

"Andy!" Stella turned forcefully toward him, "that is the stupidest thing you ever said in your life!" She advanced upon him. "MacAwen is as opposite from the Shadow Beast as you can get."

Andy seemed to shrink before her. Clarsah stepped up next to Stella and stood shoulder to shoulder with her. Andy *was* a short kid, but now he seemed suddenly the size of a first grader. "I was just wondering," he said, as though pleading forgiveness.

"Oh yeah, well—you'll find out soon enough," Stella relaxed her countenance. "You'll be seeing MacAwen for yourself—any minute now," her eyes went wide, scanning the woods all about them. Andy and Clarsah's eyes followed Stella's—though Andy's had a dread in them unlike the intrigue that sparkled in Clarsah's and Stella's.

They saw only the twists and tangles of branches and twigs on shrubs and trees bursting with new spring buds, dangling fuzzy catkins, and a few early unfolding leaves. And, of course, they saw mist, which had varying affects on their emotions and imaginations.

"It's okay if you guys made up the whole story," Andy said in a small voice. "I wouldn't be mad. I'd be glad if you told me."

"I see," Stella answered him. "you don't want The Shadow Beast to be real."

"Ah, don't worry Andy," Patrick consoled. "The Shadow Beast wasn't *exactly* real," he raised his brows, "it was just us."

Andy's face lit up. "I knew it wasn't real—"

"It is real!" Stella cut Andy short. She turned in astonishment to Patrick. "Don't you understand, Patrick?" She stared at her friend, dumbfounded. "It does *come from* our own *unconscious* minds, but not just from yours and mine. And it's not what we think it is. It's what we don't think. It's what we're unaware of. That's why we have to keep all our senses awake and alert."

"Well, I know that," Patrick quickly took out his keyboard and started tapping it with his fingers. He turned and slowly walked further into the forest, his eyes in the branches above.

"I don't think we're quite there yet," Stella said.

"I don't think it matters," Patrick responded, continuing to tap his board. "The boundaries of the De Da Mua are not precisely synchronized with any constant existing in our space-time reality."

"Wow," Stella rolled her eyes, "you're so…*impressive* with your technical wisdom, Patrick. I mean, I just want to *worship* you. If only you knew how incredibly smart it sounds like you're trying to sound—and how totally stup—" she paused—

"stupendous you *really* do sound," she added, smiling— "you'd be just as amazed at yourself as I am." She stared at the back of him. "But probably you're even more impressed with yourself than we could possibly imagine." Stella rolled her eyes, glancing at Clarsah and shaking her head. But she took her birch *key* board out as well, and also began tapping *her* fingers onto the *tree letters* MacAwen had carved.

Though his back was turned to her, Stella sensed Patrick's eyes and ears had been wide, taking in all she had said. In the side of his face she now saw a mixed expression. There was a bit of a smile in his confusion—exactly as she imagined there would be. He was totally predictable. He clutched his keyboard hard, pondering. Then he glanced at her and his eyes lit up. She shook her head. He obviously couldn't figure what measure of her words were actually insults or compliments. So, knowing Patrick, he'd take Stella's rhetoric as a whole to be a testimony to his vast knowledge of practical things. She could see it clearly in his smile, as he quietly and contentedly continued his tapping and searching.

Stella and Patrick were both tapping now, their eyes going back and forth from the symbols on their boards to the visions of the forest about them as they walked. Clarsah walked tight beside Stella, intently eyeing the magical code on the birch keyboard while striving also, to keep all her senses alert to everything in the forest about them. The mist was thickening further, seriously limiting the distance of their vision into the forest.

A sudden coldness came about them in the damp air. It was just then, Andy, who had lagged behind, noticed a very strange and disturbing set of tracks. At first he didn't say anything. He just stood and stared. Oblivious, Stella and Patrick wandered further into the wood, busily looking like they knew what they were doing. Clarsah, mesmerized, followed close behind Stella. "Hey!" Andy finally called. "Do you guys know what made these?"

Reluctantly, the others came back to Andy. The four of them studied the tracks. The imprints were quite deep, but none were clear. In the softer earth and mud there was so much dirt torn up and flung about that whatever it was must have either been of gigantic size or moving very quickly. There were enough trampled plants along this confused looking trail that the creature that made it could have been dragging something. On the other hand, there was an unnatural look to these tracks. There appeared to be what might be treads at one spot. None of these four kids could make heads or tails of this set of tracks. This was most frustrating to Patrick and Stella who thought they had learned so much tracking since last week. There was a long silence.

"Well," Patrick said at last, "whether man or beast or machine--or," he raised a finger to the air, "some combination of any two...or perhaps all three—I say we follow this trail and get to the bottom of this mystery."

"No," Clarsah protested. "I want to see MacAwen," she eyed Stella, pleadingly.

Stella nodded agreement. "These tracks are interesting, Patrick. But we can always follow them later. Our task right now is to find MacAwen."

"I think we should head back," said Andy. "It's been way more than fifteen minutes and we haven't found anything—"

"Don't even waste your breath, Andy," Stella cut him short. "You can go back alone if you must—that is, if you're not too scared. There's no way *we're* going back—until we find MacAwen."

"What could have made these tracks?" Andy asked.

"The Shadow Beast," Stella answered. "It usually circles around until it finds some lone idiot who's turned back—from his quest—from his friends—and like a scaredy-cat is skulking home all alone."

"Don't say that," Clarsah pleaded. "What if these are the Shadow Beast's tracks?" She looked up and down the strange trail. "How do we keep it away?"

"That's easy," Patrick stated with an air of authority. "All we have to do is stay aware—like MacAwen said. *And*," he added with a sudden light, "*tracking it* is the best way."

"You think you know everything," Stella accused. "The Shadow Beast is not what you think it is, Patrick. It's what you're unaware of—what you never imagine."

"It could be tracking *us*," Andy said, his eyes wide.

"It's always tracking us," Stella assured, her eyes as wide as Andy's. "That's what it does."

"But it isn't real," Andy added, trying to remind himself as much as to convince anyone else. Patrick raised his brows, but said nothing.

As if in answer, a frightful sound came suddenly from the forest behind them. They all froze. It sounded like a low moan or a growl, no more than fifty yards away. Now all went silent in the forest. Their eyes and ears searched in the direction of the sound— the very direction they themselves had just come from. It seemed they really were being followed. Perhaps the thing that had made these strange tracks had doubled back on them. Certainly, this time, it was not their own footprints—but something completely alien.

As they stared through the mist and trees and shrubs, into a patch of tall ferns, they saw a movement. Something was crawling toward them. They stayed frozen, staring. Whatever it was, it was very long. They could see that by the movement in the ferns.

After a bit, the movement stopped. "Maybe it's Tom and those guys," Andy whispered hopefully.

In answer, a hoarse whisper leaped from a swirl of mist right behind them, "Yer friends is it, yes—bumbling ta ye along the very path o' the Shadow Beast."

Stella spun around to see the figure of MacAwen, standing behind them with his arms folded. But before she could say anything or notice what was happening, there came a sudden great raucous of yelling, screaming, and crashing footsteps. She spun around again—and charging from the ferns came Tom, Robert, and Craig.

"Oh my God, you idiots! Would you shut up," Stella scolded.

"Ah, shut up yourself," Tom answered, catching his breath as they approached. "What took you so long?" he asked. "Couldn't fool Andy into going along with your story?"

Just then, Stella noticed David also, casually walking toward them from the ferns. She shrugged and turned away from them all, to where MacAwen had appeared only moments before. As she expected, he was out of sight now. Though she suspected he was still close by. "Did you see him?" she asked Clarsah, Patrick, and Andy. No one else had. "You did hear him though, didn't you?" No one answered. "You didn't just hear MacAwen's voice?" she asked, staring exasperated at Patrick.

"Ah…yeah," Patrick smiled, nodding. "I heard him."

"Oh, that's *so believable* guys," Tom mocked, "especially the way you make it up on the spot," he smiled shaking his head.

Craig just shook his head, sincerely disappointed. "I really did *wish* that MacAwen was real," he gave over. "It actually wasn't a bad story. Anyway, you should write it down."

"Clarsah," Stella asked, "didn't *you* hear MacAwen's voice?"

Clarsah was looking most distraught. "I didn't hear it—but these guys were so loud—I don't know."

Stella looked at Andy. "I did hear something," Andy admitted, smiling. "There *was* a hoarse whisper. But it was either Patrick or you," he accused, eyeing them both.

"We know your tricks, guys," Robert stated flatly. "We're not stupid, you know," he stared levelly at Stella and then Patrick.

"You *are* stupid," Stella responded. "Because MacAwen was standing right here in front of you, and you were all too dense to notice."

"Actually, *I did* see the little man," David said as he walked up. Stella shook her head and sighed. "No, really," David stated casually. "You guys all had your backs to him—and these guys were running like mad—I was the only one looking."

"Oh, shut up, David," Stella sighed.

"Okay," he agreed with a shrug.

"Say, what do you suppose made these tracks?" Patrick asked of their newly joined companions, as he pointed out the strange trail they had been studying before the ambush arrived.

"Good question," Tom answered. "what do you think, boys?" he turned to Robert and Craig.

"I have no idea," Craig answered right away. "Stella and Patrick maybe?"

Robert studied the trail from where they all stood. Then he followed it a little way. He looked up and down the length of it as far as he could see. He continued to follow it. "It might not be the Cambulls," he called back to Craig and Tom, "but it is rather interesting—and it definitely *wasn't* made by Patrick and Stella."

"Let me see that," Tom joined him. Craig followed. "Okay boys," Tom let loose, looking further up the trail. "I think we're on our quarry!"

138

"It *may b*e the Cambulls," Craig added hopefully. Stella, at that moment, had a vision of MacAwen, springing up from behind a rock. He was waving his arms in alarm, trying to warn the boys against following the trail of the Shadow Beast. But no one could see or hear him. Anyway, it didn't make sense to her, because tracking the Shadow Beast was the way to knowing how to avoid it. She blinked her eyes and the vision was gone—there was just a dense patch of mist rising from the moist rock.

"So long, suckers," Tom gave his kindest farewell with a quick wave, and he was off, down the trail.

"Aren't we going to meet somewhere?" David asked, as his other three companions moved away.

"Back at the rendezvous point," Craig answered. "The others are still there. We'll meet you…in one hour," he eyed his watch, "at eleven thirty." And he turned and followed Tom and Robert.

"See you later," David replied with a quick raise of his brows and a subtle shrug.

Stella sighed some relief that the noisy ones were gone now. But as she watched them disappear on the path of *whatever it was* she got a sudden dreaded sense about *the Beast who controls the Shadow Beast*. And David, an obvious nonbeliever, could pose an obstruction, she feared, to MacAwen's reappearance. Her fears were unfounded. No sooner had their three loud companions disappeared than MacAwen reappeared. She spotted him, standing in the mist not ten feet away. "Clarsah," she took her friend by the arm. "Look!" and with a glowing smile she pointed directly at the little brown man.

"I don't see anything," Clarsah said, though she was certainly straining with all her heart to behold.

"What?" Stella looked at Clarsah, amazed—and disturbed. Clarsah wasn't seeing MacAwen. Stella could not comprehend why. A sudden sense of sadness came over her—and panic. What if no one else could see? She shot a glance at Patrick. He was looking in the direction of MacAwen.

"Good to see you again, Sir MacAwen," Patrick gave a bow.

Stella felt a sense of relief that Patrick at least was seeing MacAwen now. Andy was shaking his head and looking away, then back to where MacAwen was. He didn't seem to be seeing anything, but that was no great surprise. Stella didn't care *so much*

139

if Andy didn't see anything, because Andy didn't care if he saw anything. In fact, he seemed rather to not want to see anything. Clarsah, on the other hand….

"Clarsah—" Stella looked into the face of her friend. Clarsah was practically trembling with confusion and disappointment. "Poor Clarsah," Stella put an arm around her, staring back and forth between MacAwen and Clarsah. "Oh no! Why can't she see you, MacAwen?" Stella looked pleadingly at the little brown man. "She definitely *does* believe. I know Clarsah. She believes as strongly as I do."

"Believes she *more* strongly than ye," MacAwen's eyes lit up. "Is *this* the very problem."

"But I don't understand," Stella pleaded. "Seeing is believing. And believing makes seeing possible."

"Wrong," MacAwen snapped. "Misinformation have ye been given. Told I ye once. Now tell ye will I again. Is belief neither necessary nor helpful in true seeing. In fact, only aids it in the reinforcement of the illusions that have agents of the Shadow Beast built. See?" He pointed to Clarsah. "Believed Clarsah in something that am I not. Thus could not her eyes fathom that which truly *am* I."

"But—" Stella almost cried

"Luckily," MacAwen interrupted, "a smart girl is she—and quick ta grasp a lesson."

Stella turned to Clarsah. "Don't *believe* in MacAwen, Clarsah," she urged. "And don't *make believe*. Just let...*inspiration* come to you. Let imagination happen *without trying* to form it in any way you might have ever thought before."

"Ah...hum," MacAwen nodded approval, his eyes wide and his brows raised. "Wise words, Stella."

"Yeah," Clarsah smiled, tears streaming down her cheeks, "wise words, Stella."

"You can hear him?" Stella looked hopefully at Clarsah.

Clarsah nodded, staring at MacAwen. She took off her glasses, put them back on. "And I *see* him," she stated in awe, "with or without my glasses."

"Thank heavens!" Stella sighed.

"Ahum," MacAwen nodded, "and the Great Spirit moving in all."

"Glory be to God and everything!" Stella shouted, laughing with joy. She hugged Clarsah.

"You guys are nuts!" Andy laughed, shaking his head.

"Andy! What's wrong with you?" Stella walked up to MacAwen and threw her arms around him, hugging him tight. MacAwen smiled, seeming to grow giant-sized for a moment. "Wow—MacAwen," Stella smiled at the Mysterious Creature. "You're so magic!" She laughed. Andy smiled, looking straight at MacAwen. "So, you do see him now," Stella exclaimed, studying Andy's eyes.

"Yeah—I see him," Andy answered, "sort of. But we're just imagining him, right?"

"Are you kidding, Andy?" Stella and Patrick both stared at Andy, questioningly. Clarsah was too mesmerized with MacAwen to turn from him.

"Believes me not to be real, this one," MacAwen interjected, "therefore, truly can see he not."

"Is it true, Andy?" Stella was amazed. "Is it really true you can't see him? You can't even hear his voice?"

Andy looked puzzled, but the fear was gone from him, and he was smiling. "I just imagined that he talked and he said, *believes me not to be real, therefore can see he not,*" Andy imitated MacAwen's voice.

"You *can* hear him!" Stella exclaimed. "Thank goodness."

"I can *hear* him," Andy answered with a frown, "but he isn't real. He *can't* be," he shook his head. "I'm not like *you*, Stella."

"Oh my *God*—that's so insulting," Stella snapped. "Maybe *you* are not real, Andy." She turned to MacAwen. "I'm sorry, MacAwen. He just isn't capable of letting himself believe—I mean, *not believe*," she frowned. "I guess he just doesn't want to see."

"What about me?" Patrick questioned Andy. "It's not just Stella; I see MacAwen."

"And so do I," Clarsah added.

Stella scooped up a small wad of mud and lobbed it at Andy, hitting him square on the forehead. "Hey!" Andy scolded as muddy water dripped into his eyes. He shut them tight, and tried to wipe the muddy water out, but it seemed to get worse as the whole wad of mud drooped down from his forehead.

141

MacAwen approached Andy with a gentle laugh. "Is not *dis*-believing the cause of this boy's blindness."

"Oh—yeah," Stella nodded. "Is not *dis*-believing the cause of this boy's blindness—"

"What!" Andy cut Stella off. "You hear the same voice I do?" he exclaimed, still striving to wipe the muck from his now closed eyes.

"Not in *not believing* is the cause of his blindness," MacAwen paraphrased as he reached Andy and wiped the mud clean from the boy's eyes, as though he had mud vacuums at his fingertips. "Is the cause of his blindness in *believing not*."

Andy opened his eyes wide now, and they were clean and clear. "You *are* real!" he gasped.

"Well, it's about time," David said. Stella had almost forgotten David was standing there all this time. "And as for me," David stood facing the little brown man, "I am truly honored, Sir MacAwen," David gave a formal bow.

Stella's jaw dropped—amazed that David, who believed in nothing, was so quickly and clearly able to see. He hadn't been joking at all when he claimed to have seen MacAwen—even before anyone else here—other than Stella herself, perhaps. But of course, now that she thought of it, David's *not believing* in things was not the same as *believing not*. And suddenly she saw David in a whole new light.

MacAwen cupped his hands together, forming the mud he had drawn from Andy's eyes into a ball. He withdrew his hands, and the ball of mud floated in the air before him. Moisture from the misty air was attracted to the floating ball, but the moisture condensed on certain areas of the clay while other areas dried up—and the ball began to expand. Stella was just imagining it to be the globe of the Earth when she noticed, it *was* a perfect replica—with continents, oceans, even mountains—and it started to spin. Then it began orbiting around them. But as she observed it, Stella began to realize that the center of its orbit…was her!

"Ah…" MacAwen's eyes brightened. "Hum…" he gazed suddenly at Stella. "Stella Childs," he whispered, nodding. Then with a little laugh and a clap of his hands, the orbiting ball of clay disappeared.

"A vast ocean—and a world of difference is there," MacAwen uttered softly, "between *believing not…*and *not believing*."

"Is seeing not necessarily believing," MacAwen said. "Is't the lesson of the day. Remember it well, and protected will ye be from the illusions that spins the Shadow Beast around ye."

"But now—" MacAwen's eyes lit up, his tone and expression suddenly very serious and intense, "is it great haste that must ye make. For imminent business have I elsewhere. And in dire need may be yer friends—if not counseled quick ta refrain from following blindly on *that* path of the Shadow Beast," he pointed up the trail Tom, Craig, and Robert had went. "May be it unfortunate that took our lesson so long. Tried I ta stop yer friends, but *see me* would they not," he shook his head. "Nor will see they the Shadow Beast. But see *will they* those possessed by it—if not warned. Must hurry ye and warn them—now!"

"But—" Stella's mind raced as she took in this sudden, shocking, disturbing, and mysterious news. "MacAwen—"

"*Terrible things*," MacAwen snipped, "are what The Shadow Beast is up ta in yer world—and beyond yer world." His eyes widened. "Great influence and control is it gaining over the powers that govern. Even in this moment—a great movement does it make!" He drew in a sudden breath. "Sense I my imminence growing ta burst!" His eyes flashed. His body twitched, his gaze snapping in the opposite direction from that which their friends had gone—*down* the path the Shadow Beast, or whatever it was, had come from. "Must un-do I quickly what has it done!"

Stella did not like this. She hated to see MacAwen looking distraught, yet she felt so distraught herself. If only there was no Shadow Beast and she could just spend time with MacAwen and learn from him. "We did our homework," she said meekly. "We identified all the tracks."

"Ahum, yes," MacAwen sighed, "did ye good Stella—and Patrick," he glanced at Patrick, then back to Stella. For a moment he closed his eyes. "So much more is there ta teach ye—so much more will need ye ta know. Time—" he sighed, studying Stella's face. "Time must we make." He grasped Stella by the hand, his great eyes staring straight up into hers. "Keep wide yer eyes," he whispered, "and be ever cautious. For great is yer destiny and purpose. Upon *ye*, Stella…."

143

MacAwen's eyes went wider than ever Stella had seen them. He seemed to hold back from saying more that was in his thoughts. He let go her hand, and his gaze snapped back in the direction of the trail from which the shadow beast had apparently come— where Tom, Craig, and Robert were now tracking it.

"Not yet ready were they ta face the form of The Shadow Beast lurking in that direction," he said quietly, as if to no one but himself. He turned his gaze back to Stella, Patrick, Andy, Clarsah, and David.

"Not wise would be it ta follow yet too far in that direction. A shadowed place is it—not yet prepared are ye ta see." He seemed to catch the whiff of something in the wind. He held his breath, his fingers feeling the air, searching. His eyes widened with a start. "Send ye aid will I if needs be," he stated with growing urgency. "But go now quick ta yer friends!" And without another word, MacAwen was gone.

Stella stood motionless—in shock. MacAwen disappeared so fast. They had barely got to see him. Now Tom, Craig, and Robert were in real danger. She could not even begin to fathom what MacAwen had whispered to her. She could not face it. She did not understand. Her mind was not capable of grasping it. And yet— somehow, some part of her sensed it clearly. And she was afraid. *"Keep wide yer eyes,"* he had whispered, *"and be ever cautious,"* he had warned. *"For great is yer destiny and purpose. Upon ye, Stella…"* Upon me, what? she wondered. There was more that he wouldn't tell her. "Uh…oh…wow—" she stared at her friends.

"Come on," Andy said, wide-eyed and intense, "we should run."

"Run?" David raised his brows.

"Better still, how about *I* do the running?" Andy suggested with a new found courage. "I'm the fastest. And I'll have a better chance of finding them before the Shadow Beast does if I can go alone and run my fastest."

"You shouldn't go alone," Clarsah said. "I'm the second fastest here, and I won't slow you down much. I'll be right behind you."

"Okay." Andy nodded to Clarsah. "No time to lose. Let's go," and he turned to the trail.

"You three stay together—and track us," Clarsah said, giving Stella a quick hug. Stella stared at her dumbly, her mouth open and her eyes wide. "We'll find those guys," Clarsah assured.

Stella nodded. "Good luck," she said as Clarsah turned to follow Andy. "Tread the word," she gave the piece sign with finger quotes.

"Tread the word," Clarsah returned the gesture with a quick smile. Then Stella watched her two friends run off as though it were a dream.

"Well, come on," Patrick beckoned. And shaking the dreaminess from her head, Stella joined Patrick and David— following the footprints of their friends—down a path none would ever have chosen if they had a choice—or knew better. Tom, Craig, and Robert had had no clue—and now, none of them had a choice. They were following where they did not wish to follow— down the dark path of the Shadow Beast. Their only hope—to find their friends before their friends found the thing that could not be known.

ᚠᛏᛝᛁᛞᚾᛞ·ᛞᚼᛁᛝᛞ·ᛞᛖ·ᛏᚠᚠY·ᛏᛖ·ᛝᛞ·ᛖᛝᛝᛁᚠᛖ

The terror lurking
in the forest's depths
that imagined out there—
way, way out there
comes from a place
a dark, dark place
closer than ever believed....

Chapter VII:
Forest Terror

Patrick had a wild-eyed, almost terrified look on his face as he hustled back to Stella and David from somewhere just ahead on the trail. "You need to look at these tracks," was all he said as they caught up to him. The three of them walked quietly and hurriedly together. Neither Stella nor David asked any questions. There was no point. They sensed right away—it was something no words could explain. They had to *see* the tracks. Whatever it was, they had to learn all they could of it. Yet they had to hurry. It was possible, the very lives of their friends depended on them.

In a few minutes they reached a wet, sandy area filled with tracks. Along either side of the trail were the footprints of their five friends who were now somewhere ahead. But it was the tracks running through the middle of the trail that caught their eyes. By the shuffling and by the angle of their friends' prints it was clear they had all observed the strange tracks running through the center of the path and had thoughtfully kept their own prints from destroying the weird sight. It was a very widely placed set of human-like prints embedded very deeply. Human-*like* because they showed the typical, long heal pad extending proportionately behind the ball of the foot—and whatever it was seemed to walk on two legs. The stride looked typical—of a very tall person. But the straddle of these foot prints was wider apart than a horse's, and whatever it was that left them appeared to be dragging a huge, heavy tail behind it—rather like a tyrannosaurus Rex. Of course they were smart enough to know that if they were ever so lucky to find T-Rex tracks, they'd not be quite as fresh as these. These strange prints were no fossils. They had fresh vegetation squashed into them. Besides, the toe appeared neither human nor dinosaur. It was quite clear in every track—there was one huge, long, pointed toe.

"Well, what do you think?" Patrick asked, turning to Stella.

A sense of dread came over her. She could feel her heart pounding in her chest. Her vision was losing focus. "What do *you* think?" she returned the question to Patrick.

"I dunno," he answered in an uncharacteristically stumped manner.

Stella breathed deep and strove to focus. She had to be alert. She had to find out all she could. "Well, obviously, it's the Shadow Beast," she stated. She continued breathing deep and slow. Patrick and David were silent. "It looks like it's dragging a

148

big tail—a very big tail." She knelt down—studying the long, unbroken track in the center between the foot prints. "It doesn't come off the ground like a mouse's does when it hops. I don't think this thing hops." She shook her head. "Look how deep its feet sink in," she eyed the human-like prints. "Do you know of any big animals that have one long, pointed toe?"

Patrick shook his head. "The only animal I know of with one toe is a horse," he spoke with his typical high-pitched and high knowing tone of voice. "But its toe isn't long and pointed—and it doesn't have *any* heal pad behind it, never mind a long, human-like heal print—as this one has. Of course, a horse walks on four legs," he continued as if they didn't know, "and its tail is rather light and doesn't reach—"

"OK, Patrick!" Stella shouted in his face. "We get the picture!"

"Uh, maybe it's wearing boots," David cut in, rather to distract Stella from strangling Patrick than to offer any plausible clues. Stella and Patrick both gave him very different looks, but neither replied to his statement. "Then I guess we better move on," he offered. At that they all returned to the trail.

They followed for about twenty more minutes, seeing no better clues—just the same occasional footprints and tail drags here and there in the softer ground, and lots of torn up and trampled vegetation. Then, "Bang!" They heard a gunshot—and then, another. Then they heard rapid fire—like that from a machine gun. The three of them froze in their tracks. The forest was silent. Then they heard a final shot—and all went silent again. Stella's heart again was pounding wildly.

"Must be the Cambulls," Patrick whispered, wide-eyed.

"Do you think they shot whatever it was that made these tracks," David questioned.

"Hopefully," Patrick answered. "Hopefully—" his voice failed. But his thoughts and concerns were obvious to Stella and David. For the Same thoughts and concerns were in their minds as well. Their friends had gone in that direction.

"Come on," Stella urged. "The Shadow Beast—" she paused. "We need to hurry." But she paused again. "However bad the Cambulls really are—it's not like they would go shooting kids or anything. They'd be in prison."

"Not if nobody found out," Patrick retorted. "They could bury the bodies way out in the forest and just say they never saw anybody."

"Get real, Patrick!" Stella glared at him. David shrugged and rolled his eyes, but offered no further comments. Stella felt a twinge of guilt for scolding Patrick, for she had the same fears—it just didn't seem logical, and she didn't want to dwell on illogical fears.

As they continued tracking their friends, and whatever it was their friends were tracking, they came upon a larger, open trail in the woods. It was well worn. And it was quite obvious who it must have been well worn by. For as Patrick, Stella, and David took a left onto this larger trail—as their friends, and whatever it was they were following, obviously had—they were heading straight in the direction from which they had heard the gunshots.

"It's too bad they had to go in this direction," Patrick stated, clearly disturbed and frightened.

"Well it just figures, doesn't it?" Stella added. David just sighed and shook his head. The three of them continued, cautiously.

It was more open and sunny on this larger trail. Stella was starting to feel overheated, as well as agitated. She could see that Patrick and David were sweating, too.

They came to a muddy place in the trail, and again they could see the clear tracks of whatever it was. Only now, the track of the tail appeared different. Rather than a dragging mark, Stella thought it had the appearance of being slammed down onto the mud and then lifted straight up. For here could be seen the square patterns, as of scales, in the long tail print. They all stopped and stared at this clear pattern in the tail print. But their thoughts on its appearance were not the same.

"It looks like the track of a bulldozer—or a tank, if you ask me," Patrick stated quietly.

"What?" Stella and David eyed him incredulously.

"Well—it is rather too narrow for a bulldozer or tank track," he admitted. "But it does have the look of a machine track of some sort."

"If it was a small tractor or something there would be two tracks, side by side," Stella raised her brows in a questioning

150

frown. "This thing has consistently shown one long track—in between two footprints." She looked into Patrick's face.

"I know," Patrick said. "But it just has that machine look about it—now that I can see it more clear. Snowmobiles have a single track," he eyed Stella, defensively—then looked to David.

"Don't look at me," David surrendered, glancing back and forth between Stella and Patrick. "I have no idea what this thing is."

"Well—*snow*mobile tracks are usually found in the winter...in *snow*," she added sarcastically, her brows raised. "Besides, they are much wider than this." Stella looked further up the trail. "Whatever it is, I'm afraid we *will* have to find out—soon."

"I'm afraid you *are* right about that," Patrick agreed, also looking ahead on the trail.

"Then I guess we all agree on one thing," David added, "We're all afraid." But not one of them knew exactly what it was they were afraid of.

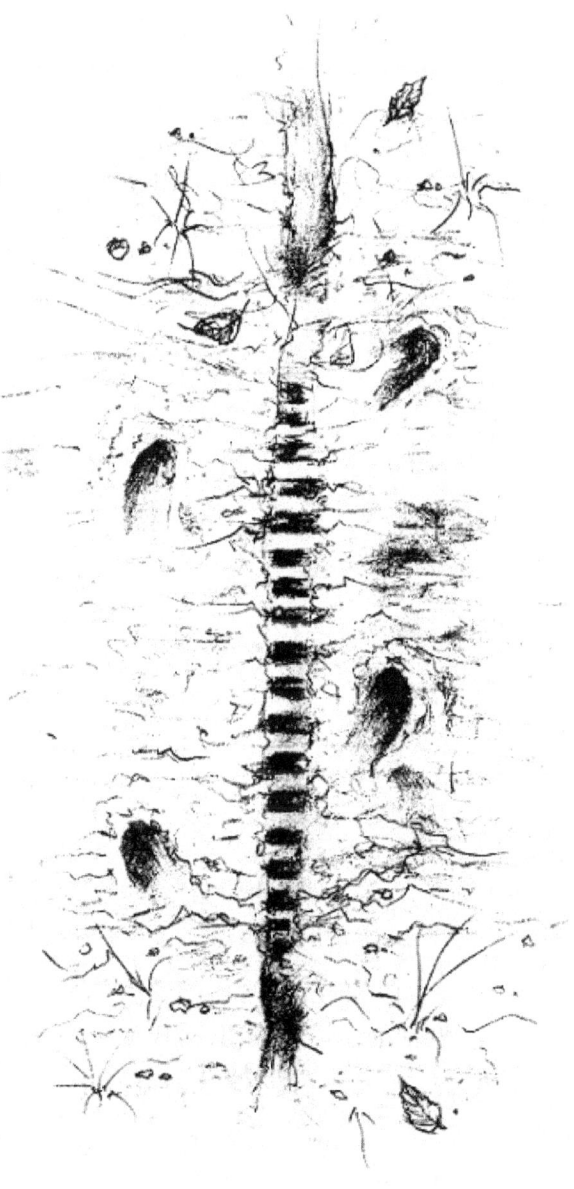

151

As they continued, the trail grew more and more worn. They started seeing dirt bike or ATV tracks, or both. Soon the tire tracks were all over—and big boot tracks. So they had a hard time telling if they were still on the tracks of whatever it was—except for an occasional *tail* or *machine* track. Whatever it was, they hadn't seen it turn off anywhere. And they could still see the occasional smaller footprints of their friends.

Hunks of metal and old tires started to appear here and there. And then there were broken beer bottles and other articles of trash. This trail most definitely was leading to the domain of the infamous Cambulls. A foul reek permeated the air. It grew worse as they walked.

The trail turned a ninety degree angle to the right. Just beyond that, they saw there was an intersection ahead on the trail. And just beyond the trail crossing, off to the left side of the path was a pile *of what looked like junk* stacked higher than Stella, Patrick, or David's heads. Beyond *the pile*, the trail entered a dark wood of tall pines.

At first it looked like the pile was a heap of old couches and coats and rugs or junk like that. But as they got closer, they began to realize; it was a pile of dead animals. Flies buzzed around it and the stench was overwhelming.

"Oh my *God*," Stella cried. "It's horrible." She squeezed her amulet tight in her pocket. As they approached they recognized the types of animals stacked near to the top of the heap. There was a bear, two raccoons, too many squirrels to count, three coyotes.... The further they looked down into the pile the individual animals became an indiscernible mass of fur and rotting flesh on a hill of bones.

Stella was overcome. She started to cry. "Who could do this? And keep doing this?" she shook her head, sobbing.

Patrick and David circled the pile on either side. "Those are domestic dogs!" Patrick exclaimed, pointing suddenly, to two dogs on the far side of the pile—a Labrador and a collie.

Stella closed her eyes, thinking she would turn her head in the other direction and continue walking. But there was one image in her head that haunted her—and she had to look again. On the top of the heap was a large, headless coyote, propped up purposely to look as though it stood there. Stella couldn't help but think of their guide from last week. "Sacrilege!" She didn't know exactly what that word meant, but it was the single word that came to her mind —and she knew it was the word that fit this horrible scene.

"Oh God," David shook his head in dismay. "Somebody's cat."

"Let's keep going," Patrick urged, turning his gaze from the pile to the ground. "I still see those guys' tracks. We've got to tell everybody to get the heck out of here!"

"Why did they keep coming this way, after they saw this?" David was still shaking his head.

"You know Tom and those guys," Stella folded her trembling arms with an angry and disgusted sigh. "I'm so worried about Clarsah," she added— "and all of them."

The path grew wider as they approached the Cambull's dwelling. It was cooler under the tall pine trees, and darker. Off to the left the woods opened to a huge swamp, which reminded Stella of the De Da Mua. She wished she could be there instead of here. She had thought she would be back in the De Da Mua today. If it wasn't for Tom and Robert and Craig....

There were junk cars and trucks and car parts strewn about all over the place—and trash—and bones. Beer bottles and cans and bones. Stella, Patrick, and David were straining their eyes to see what was ahead on the path—which is probably the reason they didn't see what was just off the trail to their right. It had just come into Stella's mind that she could smell cigarette smoke when they heard the sound of a car door opening—and they froze in their tracks.

It was a rusted old box truck with three flat tires and one wheel altogether gone. It looked like it had been parked here for thirty years. But the driver's side door was half opened—and with a rusty screech it jerked open all the way. At first they couldn't see who or what was in it. But in a moment a tall figure emerged. It was a very tall, thin man. He had on a loose, raggedy old coat. He was holding a sawed off shot gun in one hand, and he pointed it at the kids as he stood up. "Don't you try to run," he warned with a raspy voice. Then he reached into the truck with his other hand and pulled out a half drunk bottle of beer. Still aiming his shotgun at the three kids with his other hand, he swilled down the rest of what was in the bottle. He smashed the empty bottle on a rock, grabbed a smoldering stub of a cigarette from the truck, stuck it between his crusty lips, and started toward the three frozen kids. He was very dirty faced and scruffy, though he had not quite what you would call a true beard or mustache.

"We knew there was more of you vermin in our woods," he spat as he approached—a slimy wad of cigarette filter, burning ember, and brown saliva landing by the kids' feet. His mouth only had about half the teeth still in it. And of those, several were broken. "Now git you into single file," he ordered, "hands on yer little heads—and just you keep a walkin' the way you was goin'."

"We were only trying to find our friends," Stella pleaded, "and then go home. I promise we'll never come back—"

"Shut up, Toe Head!" the man yelled, "or I'll blow yer tiny brains out!" He extended his arm, the barrel of his rifle aimed straight at Stella's head. "Try any funny stuff—with me," he growled, "and you're dead meat." His eyes widened and squinted at the same time. The seventh graders had heard the expression, "you're dead meat," many times. But the true meaning had never dawned on them until this moment. Stella thought of the pile of dead animals—and she was pretty sure this man meant exactly what he said.

He walked them along the trail under the tall, dark pines—the swamp continuing on their left all the way to the run-down shack that was about five minutes further up the path from where they'd been captured. The Cambull dwelling was situated about a hundred yards from the swamp. The first thing Stella saw as they approached, mounted on a tree half-way between the Cambull house and the swamp, was the head of a coyote—positioned as though it was staring out into the swamp. No doubt it belonged to the headless body these horrible people had propped on top of the pile. Beneath the tree with the coyote head, Stella saw the rest of their friends—sitting on a log with their ankles tied and their hands tied behind their backs. Tom had a bloody nose and his face was covered with dirt. They all looked really scared. There were two men standing watch—a very tall, lanky one with a bent-crooked body and neck, rather dim looking eyes not quite level with one another, and a twisted smile—and a shorter, broad shouldered man with bulging muscles. They appeared to be in their early twenties.

"Yee-haw!" the tallest of the two jumped up excitedly when he saw them approach. "Looky what Ralphy bringed us!" he pointed.

"Shut the heck up, Flea Stack!" The muscular one turned on the lanky one and smacked him on the side of the face. "You—are the most irritatin' re-tread of a brother what anyone ever had!"

"You...calm...down, Billy Bob," Flea Stack pleaded, flinchingly.

Shaking his head, Billy Bob turned to Stella, Patrick, David—and the Cambull who was leading them in with the sawed off shot gun. "Put that dog-dang thing away— you idiot, Ralph! Them's just kids," he shook his head and chuckled.

"You got to tie yers up an' all that," Ralph argued. "Anyway, you ain't never been the boss of me, Billy Bob."

"I captured and bound these kids on *Buck's* orders," Billy Bob asserted. "He don't want none too hurt before he gets to inspect 'em—and interrogate 'em. Don't you remember what I telled ya?"

"I remember what *you* told me," Ralph spat, "but you never explained what Buck meant by *suspicious kids*. What's he up to anyway?"

A fourth Cambull emerged from the house, chomping on a hunk of some unknown type of meat. "Put that dang gun down, now!" he ordered.

"Okay, Charlie," Ralph lowered the gun. "I just ain't takin' no orders from this upstart," he glared at Billy Bob.

"I wouldn't be the first upstart to thrash *yer* butt now, would I?" Billy Bob smiled.

"You think you're like Buck." Ralph glared at Billy Bob.

"Maybe I am," Billy Bob retorted.

"You'll never be like Buck," Ralph snickered with his nose scrunched. "He's even younger than you—an' he's already thrashed you good, boy."

"Yeah, well, Buck thrashed my butt when I was three, an' he was one," Billy Bob answered. "Where you been all these years, Old Ralphy?"

Ralph didn't answer, but just snickered at Billy Bob with his nose scrunched again. "Every pack has a killer, Billy Bob. *Buck*...is ours," he nodded. Billy Bob nodded in agreement—a smile showing on his face. "Yeah," Ralph nodded again, "Buck could stare down a grizzly. But all you can stare down is Flea Stack," Ralph's mouth opened mockingly with his tooth impoverished grin.

"Oh yeah?" Billy Bob stepped toward Ralph.

"That's enough outa' both of you!" Charlie commanded as he approached. The other two reluctantly obeyed. Charlie looked to be in his early thirties, and his head seemed to be screwed on a bit straighter than was the case with the others. "Thank heaven there's only one Buck," he shouted, staring at the other two.

"Thank hell, more like it," Ralph added.

"Whatever!" Charlie shrugged, still chomping on his mystery meat. "You idiots captured a bunch of kids an' now we gotta figure what to do with 'em."

"We just want to go home," Stella pleaded. "We promise we won't say anything to anybody—and we'll never come back."

"Well—ain't that nice," Billy Bob smiled at her. He was only missing two teeth. "Problem is, see, this cursin' cuss of a rodent here already showed us what he's made out of," he smacked Tom on the head. "Threatened us with guns *and* cops, so he did."

Now Stella knew why Tom had the bloody nose and dirt all over his face. "Tom—you idiot." Stella felt bad saying it in the moment, but thought it was their only hope of being let free. "I can handle him, I promise," she pleaded. "Not one of us will ever say a word." She eyed her shocked and silent friends.

"Charlie senior don't want no more cops comin' round boys," Charlie, who was the oldest of the Cambull brothers warned. "It's a mess load of kids you got mixed up with here. I think you best let 'em go."

"Oh come on, Charlie," Billy Bob prodded. "Just a bit of fun is all I been after—not like Ralphy, with his sawed off shot gun."

"Not like Ralphy," Charlie agreed with a stern glance at Ralph. "But Billy Bob," he lectured, "don't you go bein' like Buck neither."

"What d'ya mean?" Billy Bob asked with a smile.

"What I mean, *boy,* is there's still hope for you to save your soul!" Charlie yelled.

"Ha-ha!" Ralph laughed. "Billy Bob ain't got no soul!"

"You—stay outta' this," Charlie glared at Ralph.

Ralph shrugged and shook his head—looking away until the heat of Charlie's glare was off him. Then he muttered to Billy Bob, "Charlie's been rememberin' our mama again."

"*Mama*—was a Christian, you slimy sinner!" Charlie snapped, turning and staring Ralph down once more.

"Oh, don't peddle that Christian bull, Charlie," Billy Bob retorted. "Christians have murdered more people—and each other as much as witches, Muslims, pagans, or Jews—"

"No true Christian ever burned no witch!" Charlie's glare fixed onto Billy Bob now.

"Well then—I guess there's been a heap load of *untrue* Christians," Billy Bob smiled.

"Then they wasn't Christians!" Charlie scolded. "Them's all was just liars what was callin' themselves Christian! Don't you mind what Mama told? No *true Christian* ever goed to no war over religion—nor was so zealous it brought them to hate."

"Oh, I get it," Billy Bob mocked. "The *true Christians* never hurt nobody; they just think they're better than everybody—and sit back while God or the *untrue* Christians do all the dirty work."

Charlie looked like he might explode for a moment. But he drew in a deep breath and sighed, his head shaking as his gaze went back and forth between Ralph and Billy Bob. "Obviously, you wouldn't remember; Mama said it was only twisted zealots what would condemn others for their beliefs—and it was only the most evil of all people ever that burned the witches."

"Obviously—*you* don't remember," Billy Bob retorted, now stepping up by Ralph's side. "Mama up and killed herself! How Christian was that?"

A *very* dangerous look came over Charlie. In a cold, quiet voice, he said, "that...is it. I'm gonna settle with Young Buck if I have to kill him."

Billy Bob and Ralph went silent. Charlie stared off, into the woods. "Buck and his *Pagan ways* have gotten away with murder," he half whispered, more to himself than anyone else. "And now he's controlling Billy Bob—and Flea Stack. It's show down time. *His* ways...or *mine*."

There was a moment of silence. Stella was hoping this older Cambull would control the others. Although they all seemed very crazy and dangerous to her—it seemed Charlie had a bit more sense about him.

"Ah, come on, Charlie," Billy Bob pleaded. "I'm a Christian —mostly," he grinned.

"No you ain't!" Ralph turned, suddenly, on Billy Bob. "Yer a dang heathen, just like Buck." He glared at Billy Bob now—as though he was suddenly as Christian as Charlie.

"Buck ain't no heathen," Billy Bob answered. "He ain't pagan —and he ain't an atheist. He worships, *you* know," his eyes lit up —"*something...*something what's alive and real," he nodded. "It gives him power," Billy Bob continued, a possessed look overcoming him. "And *yer* afraid of it," he goaded, raising his brows at Ralph.

"Yeah, well, I got a brain," Ralph answered. Then he turned toward Charlie. "I reckon these here trespassers," he gestured at the kids, "are just lucky our infamous, youngest brother—who ordered their capture, by the way—ain't around. Then again," he turned back to Billy Bob, "the way this here brother worships young Buck," Ralph spat in Billy Bob's direction. "It may as well be his clone."

"Billy Bob's his own person!" Charlie cut in.

"Oh, calm down, Charlie," Ralph soothed. "Billy Bob don't need no over protectin' big brother," Ralph gave his scrunched nose snicker, then turned back to Billy Bob. "You ought to be ashamed of yerself—worshippin' yer *younger* brother."

"Well," Billy Bob responded, "he is the youngest ever—State wide Mixed Martial Arts champion, ain't he? An' he's more proficient with fire arms an' war tactics than anyone I ever met. All his life he's been a mechanical genius...an' an inventor! Now all a sudden he's a computer wizard, too—" Billy Bob shook his head, smiling— "and an explosives expert! An' then..."

"Buck *ordered* the capture of these kids?" Charlie cut in—a disturbed look on his face and a violent fire blazing in his eyes as he scanned the forest.

But Billy Bob didn't notice, as he continued his praises of Buck. "Then there's just that *somethin'* else," Billy Bob's eyes lit up, "ye know—that he's got about him."

"Yeah, I know," Ralph rolled his eyes. "That's the part what scares me an' Charlie the most." He sighed. "But whatever it is," he gave Billy Bob a demeaning look, "you ain't got it."

"Maybe I got *some* of it," Billy Bob retorted defensively, a hopeful glint in his eye, "since I'm his closest kin in the whole wide world. A bit of what he's got must rub off on me."

Ralph snickered. "Maybe you ought to just lie down under him when he goes pee pee."

"Pipe off—you broken ole boozer!" Billy Bob advanced on his older brother, but was distracted by Flea Stack.

"Billy Bob! Billy Bob! Looky!" Flea Stack pulled on Billy Bob's arm, pointing up the path.

"*Goll...lee!* It's a coy dog," Billy Bob breathed as he grappled for his rifle and took aim. "The only good coy dog," he said with a smile as he locked on his sight, "is the one in the sight of my rif—"

"No!" Stella couldn't contain herself. "Please!" She reached for the barrel of the rifle just as Billy Bob shot. **Bang!** The gun fired off target. The coyote disappeared into the brush.

Billy Bob stared at her, astonished. A fire blazed up in his eyes. "Why, you filthy little toe-headed beagle!" He swung his rifle around—and whacked her on the side of the head with the butt end. Stella fell to the ground—stunned. She was more shocked than hurt. She stayed on the ground for fear he might hit her again.

"Now that's just cowardly!" Patrick shouted. "A grown man does not hit a girl!" Stella looked up. Patrick was staring straight into Billy Bob's unbelieving eyes. Stella was surprised by Patrick's courage, and felt appreciative, but really worried about what the consequences might be. She sensed it would cause more harm than good.

"Ooh…. A-*nother* feisty one, huh?" Billy Bob's eyes narrowed, his nostrils flaring.

"He's a brave one, ain't he?" Ralph snickered.

"*Brave*—has another name," Billy Bob growled—"*stupid.*" He glowered at Patrick. "How's this for cowardly?" He grabbed Patrick by the neck, lifted him into the air, and slammed him onto the ground.

"*No more!*" Stella screamed wildly, in a high pitched tone.

Billy Bob cupped his hands over his ears—a sudden pained look on his face. He turned on her, glaring wild-eyed.

"You cool it now, Billy Bob!" Charlie commanded, advancing upon him—a similar pained look on *his* face. But the real danger now was from Ralph. A sudden cloud of dust exploded from the impact where Ralph's boot slammed down next to her, covering Stella's body. With a start she looked up at him from her position on the ground. Ralph wore the most terrible, pained expression on his face—his hands gripped tight on the sides of his head as though the sound of Stella's scream was the worst torture imaginable.

"Dog dang, I hate screamin'!" Ralph cried. And he grabbed Stella from behind, very roughly, and lifted her over his shoulder. This man was very tall. It was a long way down. He started walking toward the swamp. Stella was terrified. She felt utterly helpless.

"What you gonna do with her, Ralphy?" Flea Stack asked—a dumb smile on his face and a most disturbing gleam in his eyes, as he ran along beside.

"You just drop her right there, Ralph!" Charlie ordered.

"OK, Charlie," Ralph agreed, "I'll drop her—but just a bit further here." And he carried her to the edge of the swamp. He clasped her by the ankles, holding her upside down.

This is going to be…interesting, she thought, though likely, not very pleasant. "You should listen to your older brother," she suggested, meek and desperately. Maybe this poor soul just wasn't nurtured enough as a child, she thought. "Ralph," she pleaded, "couldn't we talk this over a bit?"

In response, Ralph dunked her head, violently, into the mud—several times. So much for negotiations. It wasn't soft. There were hard branches or stones in that muck. The top of her head hurt at the first dunk. But then it was the impact that was worse. She felt a stabbing pain shoot from her neck down her spine. And her head just ached. When Ralph was done treating her like a jack hammer, he held her by the ankles so her head rested in the muck a few feet from where the swamp got deep. She was too numb and shocked now to think of how to talk her way out of this. There was no good running from, or fighting back against these Cambulls. She strove to remain passive—like a possum or a rag doll—hopefully he'd get bored and stop.

"We ain't gonna be able to return 'em if they're broken, you fool!" Charlie yelled.

Ralph lifted Stella once more—then dropped her, head first, into the muck on the swamp's edge. "I ain't breakin'," Ralph answered. "I'm fixin'. First, I got to get rid of the toed head." He scooped up two handfuls of muck and rubbed it all over her blond hair. "There, she looks a whole lot smarter now, don't she boys?" He grinned, then grabbed her by the shirt, ripping it in the process, and plopped her onto her knees. "She looks a whole load smarter —and kinda cute," he put his hand on her chin, smiling his almost toothless grin—breathing his foul breath right into her face. It seemed like he was going to try to kiss her. It was all Stella could stomach.

"Argh!" Stella growled at the top of her lungs, grasping one of Ralph's long fingers that had been digging into her chin and bending it back as hard as she could.

"Ouh!" he wailed. "You dirty, toe-headed cockroach!" He whacked her—hard, on the side of the head. She fell to the ground again, on the very edge of the swamp.

"Ralphy gone and done it now," Billy Bob shook his head with a sigh. Then smiling, "Well, well...what we gonna do with 'em now—eh Charlie?" Billy Bob turned to his eldest brother. "They's already too broken to return now."

"No thanks to you!" Charlie accused. "Dad is gonna have your hide if cops come a lookin' 'round here."

"It was Ralphy's doin' what made 'em not fit to return," Billy Bob answered. "But now—oh well then," Billy Bob smiled, "might as well have some sport with 'em before we get made to pay for our evil ways." Flea stack nodded hopefully, smiling at Billy Bob's side. But his smile vanished, and he shrunk back as Charlie approached.

"Before you burn in hell, Billy Bob, I'm gonna tan your hide," Charlie stated.

Billy Bob stood his ground. "It ain't fair—lettin' Ralphy have more fun than me."

"I'm gonna tan Ralphy's hide as red as yours if he makes me any more trouble," Charlie answered. But just as he was grabbing hold of Billy Bob, he was interrupted by the whine and the scream of a high revving two stroke engine—fast approaching. It sounded like a big, powerful dirt bike. Charlie hesitated, a worried look overcoming his face.

Billy Bob didn't try to fight back nor break free, but just smiled wide—the possessed look returning to him. "Too late to save my soul now, Charlie—unless you wanna try an' save Buck's as well," he dared. "It was on *Buck's orders* that we catch any snoopin' kids in our woods."

Charlie went quiet, his jaw clamped as his eyes searched in the direction of the sound. "What does our possessed little brother want with kids?" he demanded. But he released Billy Bob, and stood staring, rather concernedly, toward the sound of Buck's machine.

"Buck says there's been some little varmints gettin' too curious is all," Billy Bob answered, "and any caught snoopin' about the woods 'round here are to be held for questioning."

Charlie shook his head, but said nothing.

"Good enough then," Billy Bob added, "we'll just get back to our party—so as we can welcome Buck home proper like. Are you with us, Charlie?"

"I ain't no part of this!" Charlie snapped. "And Dad *will* hear about all of it—unless you release them kids quick, before Buck gets here. And either way, you better not leave no evidence lyin' about!" Charlie turned and marched toward the shack.

No! Stella thought. *Don't go!* Charlie had seemed like their only hope. Now he just turned and walked off. What did he mean —*don't leave no evidence lyin' about?*

162

"I promise," Billy Bob smiled, turning toward the kids. "I'll dispose of 'em proper."

"The pile?" Flea Stack asked with a hopeful smile. "The pile!" Flea Stack nodded vigorously. "The pile!" Flea Stack shouted with a deranged happiness. "The pile!" He started jumping up and down. "The pile!" he flailed about in a state of mad ecstasy. "Can we?" he nodded, pleadingly, "take 'em to the pile, Billy Bob?"

Billy Bob was not smiling. "Oh yeah, Flea Stack—you blasted idiot." Billy Bob rolled his eyes. "We'll just throw dead human bodies onto the pile, an' when the cops come investigatin' —we'll just say we don't know how they got there. Right?" He glared at Flea Stack. Flea Stack was still nodding, but slowly now, with his mouth hanging open. "I ought ta throw *you* on the pile instead," Billy Bob back-handed him on the face, "at least no cops would come a lookin' if *you* got killed. Only thing would come a lookin' for you'd be the maggots." Billy Bob shook his head. Flea Stack had the look of a slapped dog.

Suddenly, the whine from the engine of whatever it was Buck was driving died. No one seemed to notice, but Stella. Suddenly, there was a quiet—and in that quiet she heard a loud, all permeating sound of pure energy—like that she had first heard immediately following MacAwen's terrible scream that had awakened her and Patrick.

"But don't you be worryin', kids!" Billy Bob shouted with a wicked smile. "Me an' Ralphy knows where to dispose of dead bodies—an' y'all won't be the first." His eyes lit up. "Eh Ralphy?"

"Ye'll have plenty of company," Ralph nodded and laughed, "when ye lies a ways out there in that swamp." He pointed. "Loads of company...."

In a moment of absolute terror, Stella imagined corpses floating out there in the muck—and she and her friends becoming a few more of them. But worse, she imagined the torture they were likely about to endure. She was so scared. She could see that Clarsah and Patrick were crying—and Tom, Craig, Robert, and David were all silent, their eyes filled with dread. In that moment all felt hopeless.

From where she was lying on the ground, Stella could now see Flea Stack. He had his demented, hungry eyes fixed on Stella— and he was shuffling toward her. She squeezed the amulet in her pocket and prayed for this horror to end.

"You'll get your turn, Flea Stack," Billy Bob laughed, grabbing Flea Stack by the arm. "But I reckon Ralphy's got first dibs on that toe head. Eh Ralphy?"

Stella turned her attention to the tall man standing over her. But Ralph was still pointing out at the swamp, and now a worried look overcame his face. He stayed frozen, pointing and squinting. Then he started to tremble. He clamped his jaw. A mixture of fear, anger, and hatred took over his expression—possessing his body, his mind, and emotions. His lips started twitching—and his nose —and then his eyes, also. He opened his mouth. A wheezing sound came out of him—then a growl. Finally, he mastered his voice. "Cha—Charlie! Billy Bob!" he shouted, "it's *him*!"

Suddenly, it was like Stella had been awakened—but the world around her seemed like a dream. It was all slow motion and surreal.

Flea Stack and Billy Bob froze in their tracks. Billy Bob looked around wildly. Charlie had his back turned, and was just entering the house. He slowly turned back around, glaring madly into the swamp. "Are you sure, Ralphy?" he called with intense concern.

Before Ralphy could answer, something tore up out of the swamp in an explosion of mud, water, and rotten leaves. It went right over Stella without touching her. But whatever it was went over Ralph like he was a stalk of milkweed. In a moment Ralph was flat on his back, bleeding from the mouth, and covered with mud. And just as quickly, whatever it was had disappeared into the brush.

Billy Bob was fumbling around for his rifle, as well as for Ralph's sawed off shotgun. When he had them both he backed up against a tree and scanned the landscape. Charlie turned and ran into the house. In a moment he reemerged with an assault rifle. "Daddy's finest," he half whispered, stroking it like it was a pet. Stella shouldn't have been able to hear his soft words from this distance, but she was certain she had—as though she was right

164

before him. "Get to Ralphy, Billy Bob!" Charlie shouted. "Get him his gun! I got you covered!"

Billy Bob cautiously stalked toward Ralph. Charlie was covering carefully with his treasured AK 47 assault rifle. Nothing should have been able to hinder him. But something did. It happened so fast, Stella saw only a blur. It came swinging down on a rope or vine, and it knocked Billy Bob hard and fast to the ground. She heard the machine gun fire from Charlie's rifle. Bullets pelted the mud all over the place between Billy Bob's prone body and the swamp—where, once again, whatever it was had disappeared. But there was no sign of it. Ralphy got up and limped to Billy Bob. Billy Bob didn't move. Ralph looked at Charlie, then at Flea Stack, then off into the woods. "What happened to Buck?" he yelled. Flea Stack and Charlie glanced toward the wood where they had last heard Buck coming in on his machine. "The one time we could make good use of our *loose cannon*," Ralph squawked, "and he don't show up!" A strange look came over Ralph. "You don't reckon that swamp rat did somethin' to Buck, do ye?" Charlie shook his head unknowingly. Ralph took his gun and turned back toward the swamp. "You yellow bellied swamp rat!" he screamed, blood trickling from his mouth that was now minus one more tooth. "I'll blast you to smithereens!"

"Don't be stupid!" Charlie yelled to Ralph. "Not so close to the swamp!"

"I'm—I'm get outa here!" Flea Stack wailed stupidly, undisguised fear all over his expression as he turned to run.

"Turn your butt around or I'll shoot you myself!" Charlie warned. Flea Stack halted in his tracks. Charlie returned his gaze to the swamp. "Show yourself, you yeller bellied varmint!" he yelled.

"I got him! I got him! I got him!" Ralph roared excitedly. "I see the devil musk rat now!" He smiled, taking aim at some point just below the surface of the water. "Bang!" He fired, standing so close to Stella it was deafening. Then he stared into the swamp.

"Did ye get it?" Flea Stack asked.

"No. But I got him now," Ralphy assured. He fired into the swamp again—at a place just below the water, not five feet from where he stood. There was an explosion of leaves and muck.

"Did ye get him?" Charlie asked.

Ralphy nodded. "I got him that time for sure."

Charlie sighed a great relief and came excitedly from the house. Flea Stack was yelling yahoos and running toward Ralph. Ralph kept the barrel of his gun pointed into the mucky water just to be sure. Stella strained to see what it was, and if it truly was dead. "If ye thought we were bad," Ralph said to her, "you're just lucky we saved ye from this bloody swamp beast. He would of eaten ye raw, piece by piece—even before he killed ye."

That moment, a hand rose out of the swamp with lightening speed and grabbed the end of Ralph's gun barrel. Ralph fired. But the hand stayed clasped about the end of the barrel. Then it pulled the gun in under the water. Ralph had barely enough time to scream when a mucky, weedy figure arose and struck him with his own gun. Ralph fell and the mucky figure jumped right on top of him. It tied him hand and foot, incredibly fast, with some kind of thin, but apparently very strong cordage. Then it disappeared again, into the water. Charlie couldn't even get a shot at it.

Flea Stack, who had been running pell mell toward Ralph, now froze in his tracks. "Get Ralphy's gun, you idiot!" Charlie commanded. Flea Stack reluctantly did as he was told, then backed away slowly from the swamp. Stella saw something moving over by a clump of bushes and small trees—and apparently, so did Flea Stack. "I seen 'im!" he pointed to the trees. "He's over there, Charlie!"

"I got you covered, boy," Charlie assured. "Go check it out." Flea Stack approached slow, but shook his head when he got close. "He's gone Charlie," he lowered his rifle, turning to look at his brother.

At that moment the Swamp Man jumped up out of the weeds just behind Flea Stack's feet—now on the other side of Flea Stack, between him and Charlie. "Boo!" he yelled, raising his arms, just as Flea Stack looked over his shoulder. Flea Stack turned and ran as fast as he could—straight into a snare. A sapling tree sprang up from where the Swamp Man had apparently bent it over and secured it in readiness to spring—and now Flea Stack dangled upside down by one foot—a noose around his ankle, hanging from the small tree.

Once again, Charlie blew off a volley of rounds from his safe distance. But the Swamp Man had hit the dirt, or rather mud, exactly where the line of fire from Charlie to him would put Flea Stack, dangling as he was, in even greater risk of getting shot. Flea Stack was begging for Charlie to stop shooting, as he'd nearly been shot several times. And invisible as the Swamp Man had become again, Charlie was forced to hold his fire. But as soon as he did the Swamp Man sprang back up out of the mud, and whipped a golf ball sized stone at Charlie. It was incredibly fast. Yet it seemed ridiculous. In all the chaos and danger, Stella thought it was just amazing the swamp man could get the throw off, but it would be impossible for him to hit Charlie at such a distance. Yet to her double amazement, he did hit Charlie—right between the eyes. Charlie dropped his assault rifle—and fell unconscious.

In that moment the world went silent. Stella and her friends were in shock. Was it really over? Were they saved from these horrible Cambulls? Or about to be devoured by this dreaded swamp man?

They were stunned. It was too hard to process all the insanity they had just experienced. And who, or what, was this Swamp Man the Cambulls so reviled and feared? It seemed to Stella that the world was frozen. It may have been only ten seconds, but it seemed an unnatural length of time where nobody moved. Maybe it was an hour's worth of thoughts crammed into ten seconds that made it seem so long. Later she would find out that all her friends had that same experience at that time—which would inspire years of discussion about the relation of time and mind.

That moment ended most abruptly, however, when Billy Bob rolled over, leapt up, and ran for Charlie's assault rifle. When he got to it, he picked it up and spun about, taking aim. But there was no sign of his adversary. The Swamp Man had disappeared, again.

"Show yourself now, fish brain!" Billy Bob shouted desperately. There was no sound or sign of movement. "Then if yer too cowardly to face me like a real man, I'll just shoot these vermin!" He turned his rifle toward Tom, Craig, and Robert, with death in his eyes.

But before he could take aim a dart whizzed from the forest, striking his trigger hand. "Ouh!" he screamed, but quickly grasped the rifle with his other hand. The next moment a rock the size of a soccer ball smashed his other hand into his body, knocking him to his knees. The gun fell. The Swamp Man came bounding from his cover. Billy Bob jumped up, but had no time to go for the gun—so he plucked the dart from his right hand, and braced himself for hand to hand combat, in a karate stance.

When the swamp man got close, he slowed to a casual walk, straight toward Billy Bob. Billy Bob leaped to the air, throwing a spin around kick. The swamp man caught Billy Bob's foot with his left hand—then released him. Next, Billy Bob attacked with an impressive barrage of karate maneuvers—knuckle punches, jabs, chops, side thrusts, elbows….

Yet nothing Billy Bob could deliver had any chance. The swamp man blocked every attack with his left hand. *"Buck*—is gonna rip you apart," Billy Bob spattered, desperately, as he exhausted himself.

The Swamp Man smiled wide—and then he spoke: "Buck's machine broke down."

"What?" Billy Bob's arms dropped to his sides. "You *do* talk?"

"Enough for now," the Swamp Man nodded, extending his right hand to Billy Bob's face, just below the nose. He was holding some kind of puff ball mushroom. The Swamp man squeezed it, and a blast of powder shot up Billy Bob's nostrils—a small cloud hovering over his face. Billy Bob fell unconscious.

The mucky figure approached the bound kids, withdrew a large hunting knife from a sheath by his side, and cut the ropes that bound them.

"Whoa—" Tom stared in awe—as did his silent friends. "Who are you?" he asked—his voice all whispery, falling from his mouth—his eyes wide.

The muddy figure smiled. And from behind the mask and camouflage of fern, muck, and swamp debris there emerged a set of teeth—bright white, straight, even, and all intact. "My name is Faas," he answered. Then he walked back to the swamp's edge, where the water was deepest, and dove in.

168

ᚤᚦᚢ·ᚦ·ᚦ·ᚺᚦᚦ·ᚺᚦᚺᚦᚦᛘᛈ·ᚺᚢᚤᛏᛈᚺ·ᚤ·ᚦᚦᛈ·ᛈᚦᛏᚦᛈᚦᛏᚦᛈᛏᛈ

The twin of evil's stealthy agent
took to the trail to forge deceits.
Glancing back he saw the other
chasing reflections in water lands.
Yet he kenned not yet himself in the moment
So he did nae ken his kin...

Chapter VIII:

Faas

Faas emerged from the water—this time, amazingly, pretty much clean. For the first time, Stella and her friends saw him without his camouflage of mud, ferns, leaves, and swamp debris. They were surprised—and delighted, by what they saw. First and foremost, he was in fact a human being. Faas had a kind and pleasant looking face, and looked to be only about, maybe eighteen or nineteen years old. He was of about average height. Nothing else about this person was average—though he himself seemed oblivious to this obvious fact.

"Hi," he said, smiling brightly. "It's good to meet you," he sounded as though he was trying out the phrase for the first time in his life. "How are you doing?" he asked, looking around at the group. And it seemed the oddest question, Stella thought, given what they'd just been through.

When Faas's eyes met hers, Stella was struck by the look. It was a peculiar, almost startled or awestruck sort of expression—like he was as amazed and impressed to meet her as she was to meet him. He looked away quickly, eyeing the rest of the group.

Faas was very, very lean—not an ounce of fat apparent on any portion of his body. At first glance, he almost appeared to be scrawny. Yet every part of his body was absolutely ripped with muscle. Not a bit of the contrived, bulky, ballooned up type that bodybuilders get from pumping iron—Faas looked nothing like that. Besides, he would never have been able to move as fast as he did carrying that kind of excess. These were obviously the natural

169

kind of muscles, formed from a lifetime in the wild. Faas's physique reminded Stella of the mixture of sinew, muscle, and bone in the body of a deer or a wolf—and how, without being bulky, an animal can be so powerful, so fast—and yet so lean. Apart from the fringed and belted leather breeches that were his only garment of clothing, he was outfitted with an assortment of tightly belted pouches, knives, and what appeared to be quivers—though they were not long enough to hold typical arrows, and they were tied shut by leather thongs—probably to secure whatever was inside during his acrobats through water or air.

Wide-eyed, Stella studied his handsome, boyish features—his long, tangled hair—his bright, gleaming eyes—his amazing, feral body. All in all, Stella thought, Faas looked like about the coolest guy she had ever seen. And by the way her friends were all gathered around, staring in awe—in that moment, amongst this crowd, he was the coolest living person on the planet. Certainly, his timing was a miracle—for which Stella was most grateful. At that thought, she remembered what MacAwen had last said—that he would send aid if it was needed. She wanted to ask Faas if he knew MacAwen, and if MacAwen had sent him. But before she could, Faas spoke with a sudden urgency. "We need to leave this place!" No one in this crowd argued that point.

But just as he was turning to go, he hesitated and turned back, looking up into the tree upon which the coyote's head was mounted. Faas sighed. His eyes circled the group of kids gathered around him—and then his gaze rested on Stella, his eyes widening for a moment as he drew in a deep breath and sighed. He smiled as he looked away. It was a subtle thing, but Stella felt there was something very mysterious about that look. It startled her. And that was twice now.

She turned away from Faas and studied her friends. Clearly, no one else noticed any peculiar looks. It was just coincidence. Yet Stella felt so raw and shaken after all she'd been through, she could not calm herself. She breathed in deep, slowly and apprehensively returning her gaze to the wild man. But Faas was staring at the coyote head.

I must be imagining...fantasizing, Stella thought. A part of her felt that what Faas had given her appeared to be a look of something like...*reverence*—like...*awe*. Yet she was embarrassed by her own silliness. It was just the way *she* felt, looking at *him*. She must be projecting her own reflection in her dreamy mind—that was all. She was just a silly, little seventh grader that he had to rescue.

Faas walked to the tree and pulled down the coyote head. The way he looked at it—Stella saw that same look he had given to her. But the way he held it, and carried it—it made her want to cry. She thought she could see a welling of tears in his eyes, for a moment. But he started walking along the edge of the swamp, and he gestured for them to follow him.

Stella was struck by Faas's walk. He stealth walked, like MacAwen! Only Faas was human. He was tall—and he didn't have MacAwen's long toes. There *was* a flowing motion to his walk. And he moved like wind or water in and around the forest's undergrowth and over the terrain. Yet unlike MacAwen there was a youthful cockiness in Faas's motion—a bouncy sort of rhythm—a groove. And he *did* leave footprints.

"I don't know about this," Stella heard Craig's voice behind her.

"That's not exactly the way home," Robert added.

"Come on guys," Tom argued. "He just saved us from the nut cases."

Stella spun around, glaring at Craig and Robert. She didn't need a word to state her position. Her look spoke for itself.

"Are you sure he's any safer than them?" Craig pleaded. "He *did* just come out of a swamp," he raised his brows, "and even those crazies were scared of him."

"That's because *they*...are *evil*," she finalized the argument—as far as she was concerned anyway. It appeared Craig was about to say something more—but his thoughts sunk to the rising of a dreadful sound.

From somewhere beyond the Cambull's house came the terrible, wailing, screaming, revving noise of Buck Cambull's machine.

"Quick! Follow me!" Faas urged. "The Bad One is coming!"

"Bad *one*?" David and Tom asked in perfect unison with a heavy stress on the *one*. It seemed obvious to the whole group of seventh graders that *all* the Cambulls were bad ones.

"Buck is by far the worst and most dangerous one of them all," Faas asserted, "worse than all the rest together. Get down low —quick!" he commanded. "Do as I do!" And he hustled into the brush along the swamp's edge, bent double.

Stella had just a glimpse at Buck and his machine as it approached the Cambull domain. It looked like a motorcycle— only it wasn't on two wheels. It had a front tire, like a normal dirt bike. But instead of a back wheel, it was driven by a single, narrow track. It was like nothing she had ever seen. But as she saw the way Buck slammed his long, pointed-toed, steel boots to the ground on either side of the machine, to help it along as it obviously wasn't running correctly, she realized that she had seen its tracks. Patrick had been right. It was not a *tail,* but rather, a *machine track* between the two, long, *single-toed feet.*

If they had indeed been tracking the Shadow Beast, then *this* particular manifestation of the Shadow Beast was incarnated into the body of a machine. Well—half of it. It was not the machine alone that was possessed by the spirit of the Shadow Beast. For the machine, at this point, was still under the control of a rider. Suddenly, Stella was struck with the memory of MacAwen's cryptic words; *The beast who manipulates the shadow beast.* It must be Buck Cambull!

Faas led them through the brush and into a wood on the edge of the swamp. The noise of Buck's machine quieted to an idle— apparently stopped back at the scene of the crime. But in about two minutes it revved up again. It was clear by the approaching sound—it was in pursuit of them. Stella remembered; Flea Stack, though hanging by one foot, was still conscious. And though tied hand and foot, so was Ralph. One or both of them had no doubt seen them escaping with Faas. They must have alerted Buck to what direction Faas and the kids had fled.

To Stella, it now sounded like the machine was gaining on them—and she wondered why Faas didn't just hide and ambush it or something. "Hurry!" Faas urged, looking intensely concerned as he waited again for them all to catch up. "*This one* would be very dangerous to you all," he said, looking straight at Stella, as though he had read her thoughts. "This one," he explained with a rolling of his head, "can sense my presence—as I, his."

They ran as fast as they could, without getting separated. But the sound of the machine continued getting closer. Faas stopped, gazing studiously at the clear tracks they were leaving behind in the wet, muddy woods. Then his eyes went wide—searching about, back and forth and up and down through the trees while he waited yet again for all of them to catch up. It reminded Stella of REM; the Rapid Eye Movement that occurs when people are dreaming. It looked as though Faas was dreaming—but with his eyes wide open.

"I have a plan," Faas smiled suddenly, with a raise of his brows and a twinkle in his eyes, as they regrouped. "We're going to veer off to the left here," he nodded. "I want the fastest three kids to run right behind me. The rest of you will follow us as fast as you can. In about four hundred paces or so we'll come to a stream. I want all of you, except for the fastest three, to make your tracks look like you are going straight across the stream—as you will clearly see by our tracks—that your fastest three and I have done. But when you get into the middle of the stream, turn to your right—and walking in the middle of the stream, follow it until it empties into the swamp. We'll meet you there...after we leave some tracks to fool Buck into thinking we all went the other way. You got it?" He gazed at them searchingly. "Good." He nodded. "And while you're waiting for us—don't leave the water. I do not want to leave any tracks or signs for Buck to find later." He eyed them inquisitively. "Don't worry," he added. "It won't take us long to regroup with you. Now—fastest three," he gestured, "follow me." And he turned in a hurry, only stopping and looking back to make sure all were following his directions.

The fastest three—Andy, Craig, and Tom—followed on Faas's heels. Stella, Patrick, Clarsah, David, and Robert followed them as fast as they could without getting separated, until they got to the stream. By that time Faas and the three fastest kids were out of sight. On the other side of the stream, however, they could see clearly where Faas, Andy, Tom, and Craig's tracks crossed the stream and led into the woods. They did as Faas directed, taking a right turn in the middle of the stream. They walked quickly and quietly. After just about two minutes they heard Buck's machine come to a stop at the stream crossing. They froze, and listened. After a moment, Buck's machine tore off—obviously, and thankfully, following Faas and the others. The sound grew quickly more distant—and Stella and her friends continued downstream.

"The one whose tracks foretold all—" it had to be Faas! Stella thought. He used tracks to lead Buck away. *At the time of The Terrible War....* Would there be some great, *Singular* confrontation between Faas and Buck? It seemed to fit.

In a few more minutes they reached the swamp. Stella and Patrick were struck immediately by the similarities of this place to that of the De Da Mua—at least, that part of the De Da Mua they had experienced. They discussed this in hushed tones. The swamp here seemed rather deep—though they stayed at the edge as Faas had instructed. There were islands out there of varying sizes—some covered with grasses and small bushes, others with shrubs, and still others had medium-sized trees.

The sound of Buck's machine grew fainter, until they could barely hear it. After all they had been through, there was at last, quiet. And nothing to do but wait—and think.   They had a lot in their minds to digest. Stella's first and heaviest thought was, *How could anyone be so horrible as those Cambulls*—followed on a lighter tone by, *How absolutely amazing and awesome is Faas.*

A cloud of fog came from the depths of the swamp, rolling over them and up, into the woods. The air grew dead silent. They stood still, wondering how far Faas had led Buck on his goose chase, and when Faas and the others would return.

Robert gazed upstream, then turned to the others, standing like silent statues in the shallows of the swamp. "How would we ever know if Buck caught them?" Robert whispered.

"I don't think that's likely," Stella answered.

"We have no idea what's likely," Robert iterated, now in his typical monotone, shaking his head, "and no way of telling what's going on out there."

"Faas will lose him," Stella answered confidently. "I just know it. Isn't he so amazing?" she sighed.

"He might be amazing," Robert answered dryly. "Then again, he might be even more dangerous than the Cambulls. And how do you know he's going to lose Buck?"

Stella stared off into the tree branches. She had such a strong sense about Faas. Somehow, intuitively, she just knew he'd make it back with the rest of their friends—and that they'd all be safe.

She just couldn't think of any words to describe how or why she knew. She opened her mouth to try, but it was not necessary.

"Boo!" Faas was suddenly standing right there behind Robert in the middle of the stream—as though he had been there all along. Robert's eyes widened, and his body jolted. Faas had a very big smile on his face—though he was still cradling the coyote head.

"Whoa!" Robert whispered. "Where'd you come from?"

"Just a little roundabout loop," Faas answered, still smiling.

"Where's Andy and Craig and Tom?" Patrick asked.

"Coming right behind," Faas answered. "They'll be here in a minute." Sure enough, about a minute later, the three boys came puffing down the stream.

"How do you run like that," Craig asked in awe. Andy and Tom were also staring in awe at Faas.

"Been running my whole life," Faas answered nonchalantly.

"That's not normal running," Tom added. "That's…whew," he exhaled, staring in disbelief. "That's like a deer—I mean, not even an Olympic gold medalist could touch this dude," he looked at Robert. "You gotta see this guy leap." He stared, flabbergasted at Faas. "Faas—" he seemed to want to say or ask more, but just shook his head in amazement.

Faas shrugged, "My family were all great runners." Faas nodded. "I was always the slowest one when I was little."

"Who," Andy asked, "or should I say *what*," he blabbed, "were your family?" He caught two quick, stabbing glares—from Stella and from Clarsah. "Oh—sorry," he added with a sheepish smile.

Faas laughed. "I was raised by a pack of coy-wolves." They all stared at him, but nobody said anything. Faas shrugged. "Well, Buck is returning. He is still rather confused about how we all disappeared. And he is quite angry. I suggest we get moving." They all listened intently. Yes, Buck's high-pitched engine could be faintly heard once again.

"Where do we go?"

"Do you trust me?" Faas asked. Stella nodded—as did all her friends, except Robert. They heard Buck's engine revving up, as though picking up speed as it approached.

"I trust you!" Robert suddenly agreed, his eyes wide.

"Well, I guess you have little choice," Faas smiled. "Not to worry. You'll love the places I'm taking you."

"Places?" Patrick asked.

"First—my observation platform," Faas answered. "We'll want to hear what the Cambulls have to say. Then—" his eyes lit up brightly, "you can hear my band—doin' *De Da Mua at Sunset,*" he giggled, rocking his head and rolling it from side to side, his eyes almost shut, as though he was hearing the music now.

"Did you say *De Da Mua*—at sunset?" Craig asked—he, Tom, and Robert all looking as though they'd received a small shock.

Faas's head was still bobbing to the music within him. "I will explain after," Faas asserted, snapping out of it. "Now we must go —if you will follow me," he smiled wide, turning and wading out into the swamp. They all followed. The water was waste deep on Faas. Andy was over his chest. Soon it was up to Andy's neck and they started swimming. "No Splash!" Faas commanded with a harsh whisper— "dog paddle."

They dog paddled out to a shrub of witch hazel, bent over in an arch, growing out of a small clump of earth protruding from the water. Faas tapped the arch several times with his fingers, then went under, and beckoned them to follow. Stella thought of their birch keyboards, and shot Patrick a look. Patrick was already eyeing her with raised brows, as he had also noticed Faas's tapping. But neither said anything. In a little while the water got shallower. There were lots of tiny islands here and there, covered with shrubs and scrubby trees. It sure looked a lot like the De Da Mua. Tom attempted to climb up onto one of the small islands, but Faas stopped him. "No," he said. "We slurk."

"Slurk?" Tom asked.

"Slurking is how an adept Wetlander lurks about in a swamp," Faas explained. "It would be damaging to the flora—as well as to the soil above and below the water—if large creatures, as we are, went climbing over all these little islands. Also, it would be slow and cumbersome for us. But down in these waterways," he pointed to the places where the shallow waters ran between the islands, "we can move about like the otters, with nary a bit of damage to the wetlands."

The kids followed Faas's example, wading through the waterways rather than attempting to go over the islets. The waterways were like little roads of water—just wide enough for a person and about two feet deep. "That's better," Faas smiled, observing the troop coming along behind him.

"Are there any leeches in this water," Andy asked with a sudden concerned look on his face.

"Plenty," Faas smiled enthusiastically, "but we haven't got time to gather any now. Besides," he added, "I know of other places where they are much thicker."

Andy stared at him, dumbfounded. "Great," Tom spoke on Andy's behalf. "We'll be looking forward to gathering leeches where they're really thick...some other time." He smiled and nodded pretentiously to Faas.

"Ok," Faas announced, as he eyed the group approvingly, "you've graduated from *Slurking 101*. And now—onto the next level," he smiled wide. "For an even more efficient mode of travel," Faas explained, "you'll find this works much better." Faas got down on his belly, and began pulling himself along—his body floating horizontally, and moving, propelled along the waterway by his arms at an impressive rate of speed. "It's much faster and less tiring than swimming," he called back to his followers. "Try it."

There were varying looks on their faces—from Craig, whose jaw had dropped, but whose eyes were just beaming, most impressed—to Andy, who looked absolutely horrified. Stella tried it, and found it was indeed a very efficient mode of travel. The sides of the bottoms of the waterways had long, strong grasses upon which they could grab a hold and pull themselves along very quickly and easily. She didn't have to kick to keep her legs afloat because it was so shallow. And the bottom of the waterway was soft and smooth as silk. It was really fun—though a bit cold for this time of year.

It seemed like Faas had cleared open the waterways through this area because there were no logs or branches or anything to obstruct the water-paths anywhere. It was just perfect.

After slurking along on their bellies for about five to ten minutes, their waterway came to a larger island with an overland path leading up out of the water. They came up from the waterway like a pack of otters, now footing it along a path. The path crossed the island, and on the other side was a wide log, forming a nice bridge to the next island. On the other side of the next island was another bridge made of a log. Clearly, Faas had set these up, for there continued now to be great, wide logs connecting all the tiny islands. They could now move *over* the swamp without getting wet. Yet they could slurk, if they chose, for there continued to be exquisite waterways running all about. If it was summer, Stella thought, she'd rather enjoy the waterways. But for the moment it felt great to be once again, soaking up the sun.

They went on like that for a while. And as they did the underbrush grew thicker. It was all interlaced and tangled with vines. These vines eventually got so high and thick, they could neither see through nor over them. In fact the vines got so high and thick in spots that they grew over the path, forming tunnels.

One of these tunnels of vine seemed to go on forever. But eventually it came to a spot where there was an opening in one side. Faas led them through a short tunnel that forked off from the long tunnel they'd been traveling, and opened to what appeared to be a little pond surrounded by a high, thick wall of vines. Faas waded out into the middle of the pond where the water was to his chest. When all the kids had gathered, Faas pointed to a pair of witch hazels growing together on the far side, forming an arch. "You must pass beneath this doorway to reach my royal realm," he smiled wide, his eyes aglow. Then he dove under the water and did not reappear.

"Well, what are you waiting for?" they heard his voice from beyond the wall of vines behind the arching witch hazels. Tom dove in first, followed by Craig, then Robert. In a moment their voices could be heard also, from beyond the vines. It was amazing. It was fantastic. Stella was so overwhelmed with joy and intrigue she could not speak. She dove under the water, swam beneath the witch hazels, and came up into another tunnel, beyond the wall of vines. Faas was already leading them through this next tunnel, but it was very short. Then they came to a log that was leaning at about a forty-five degree angle and had steps carved into it, leading up through the tangled mass of vines. They climbed this stairway through the tunnel of vines, until it opened at the top, to a great wooden platform.

Upon the platform there were some very bright and sunny spots—though most of it was roofed with a canopy of vines trailing all over a lattice work of sapling poles. The platform was constructed of hundreds, maybe thousands of very narrow, straight saplings—each about an inch and a half in diameter, all smoothly de-barked, and lashed together with long, flat ribbons of the very bark that had been peeled from them.

On the far side of the platform was a dome shaped hut. There were several smaller shelters, or sheds, spread about. The main platform was about sixty feet long and forty feet wide—though there were several extensions protruding in various directions— some of them continuing beyond sight under the canopy of vines. This was a most dazzling sight to behold in the middle of a swamp.

Scanning the scene, Stella noticed what looked like the hide of a deer, stretched between two small, straight trees and two horizontal poles that were lashed to the two trees to form a square frame.

"You guys hungry?" Faas asked, as they stared about in amazement.

"I *am* hungry," Stella admitted. She eyed her friends, a bit sheepishly. They looked worried. There was no telling what Faas might have for lunch. Yet it was well after lunch and their stomachs groaned at the thought of it.

Faas smiled. "Come into my kitchen," he beckoned them. "We'll get a quick snack—then we'll have a peak down at my observation deck, to see what our Cambull friends are up to." He headed toward the largest round hut.

"Observation deck?" Patrick asked.

"First, a quick snack," Faas answered over his shoulder. "That should give Buck just enough time to get home. Then we'll have something to listen to."

"You can hear the Cambulls—from here?" Patrick asked.

"My observation deck is strategically set up—for visuals *and* acoustics," Faas answered, "so I can fix eyes *and* ears upon the Cambulls."

"Why all this trouble to observe the Cambulls?" Tom cut in.

"A bite to eat," Faas answered. "I promise, I'll explain it all to you after." Once inside the round hut, Faas urged them to take whatever they liked. They looked around. Clearly, this kitchen was packed with food. There were shelves set up with woven baskets and wood and bark containers of various designs. Herbs, roots, and dried meats and fruits of many varieties hung from poles. But none were of any variety familiar to these kids. They continued searching with their eyes, but nobody reached for anything. "We do need to hurry," Faas explained, "Buck will be back home in just a few minutes. I'm getting to know him pretty well. He will have tried fairly hard to find out where all our tracks disappeared to—especially mine. But by now he is quite frustrated and angry—and heading for home." Faas eyed his guests. Still, no one reached for his goods.

"Oh—" Faas sighed. "Much of nature's bounty would be foreign to you now, wouldn't it?" he frowned. They gave shrugs, nods, and various combinations of shrugs and nods. Faas shook his head, muttering something under his breath that to Stella sounded like, "another sign of…*the prophesy.*" Just as he said the phrase, *the prophesy,* he shot Stella a sudden glance—staring wide eyed at her for a moment, then quickly looking away.

The prophesy? Stella wondered. But Faas was staring at his food now, and no one else seemed to have heard him.

"Well, let me help you pick some things out," he offered in a lighter tone. And with a very big smile he opened a bark container and pulled out a rather thick, juicy, pickled worm. "Gourmet leeches, anyone?" he eyed the group of mortified kids while dangling the thing between his thumb and forefinger. "What? No takers?" They stared, but no one spoke. "Well—not quite yet," he laughed. No one else was laughing.

"Sorry—I couldn't resist," Faas eyed the stunned crowd curiously. "It was only a worm, really," he added, "and it *was* dead after all." He put that container away, and opened another—much larger. It was filled with rather small, but beautiful apples. There were great sighs of relief. Faas passed the container around, and opened two more—one filled with fat, moist raisins—the other with something like a trail mix of nuts, seeds, and chunks of dried fruits. They were a little hesitant at first, after Faas's worm trick. But once they tasted his wares, their taste buds were delighted and they were almost ravenous. "You might want to be careful with those apples," Faas teased, "it is possible they could be harboring little green worms."

"What I don't know won't hurt me," Tom smiled while chewing. "This apple tastes too good to waste."

"I'll try not to look too close," Robert added dryly, but squeamishly, as he did appear to be inspecting every bite.

"Alright," Faas nodded approvingly at the lot of them. "I thought you might need some sweet nourishment. I'll fix you something more substantial after our little peak and listen in on the Cambulls."

"Thank you." Stella looked upon Faas gratefully.

"Thank you," they all echoed at once. "And thank you so much for saving us," Clarsah added. They all echoed their gratefulness for that bit as well.

"Well, it was quite a bit of fun for me," Faas smiled. "I like playing with the Cambulls. But more than that," he added, now very seriously—"it was the greatest of honors to serve you." And when he said it, he turned directly toward Stella. And with a rush of adrenaline and a sudden mysterious pounding of her heart, Stella witnessed that same peculiar look.

Sitting on Faas's observation deck, Stella thought; *I...am just being stupid. I'm only fantasizing. I'm just a dreamy, A.D.D. girl. Everyone knows it.* Yet Faas had given her that look again. It was definitely directed at her. And maybe it was just a coincidence, but he gave the look exactly when he was saying, *it was the greatest of honors to serve you.*

If she was fantasizing, it wasn't like she wanted to. It made her feel terribly uncomfortable. She didn't know why, but it felt like something very big and mysterious was beginning to happen —not just with her and her friends, but with the whole world. And if she dwelt on it too much it scared the life out of her. So she tucked it away in the back of her mind. Like the time MacAwen had told her and Patrick that there was a war brewing. A *war for our minds,* she shuttered, remembering. And she felt all alone in her fear, remembering also that Patrick hadn't seemed to have heard MacAwen when he mentioned the brewing war. Stella had never brought it up since.

But Faas might know. If anyone in the whole world other than MacAwen would know—it would be Faas. And Faas *must* know MacAwen. Stella was about to ask him, but her thoughts were interrupted by the harsh sound of Buck's machine, roaring in the distance. And suddenly, as the machine reached the Cambull dwelling, the noise of it increased tenfold—due to the amazing acoustical positioning of this set up.

The machine shut off—and she could hear Buck and Ralph Cambull as though they were just fifty feet away. "Daaawg-dang it!" Buck swore. "Slippery frog slithered away somehow—with all of 'em. Tracks just disappeared."

"Dog-dangit," they heard Ralph answer.

"You guys ain't seen any sign of 'em?" Buck questioned.

The Cambull's door slammed. "No sign here," Billy Bob shouted.

"I'll get that filthy musk rat," Buck swore. "If it's the last thing I do, I'll get that slimy pollywog—and I'll rip him into small pieces." There was a short pause, and then Buck yelled, "No one sabotages my machine!" The Cambull dwelling went silent.

Faas assured the kids there was no way the Cambulls could hear them at this distance. They could speak in normal voices. It was only the strategic acoustical positioning of this deck in relation to the Cambull dwelling that amplified the sound from there to this spot. Stella and her friends were amazed by the ingeniousness of the set up. The observation deck was about fifteen by fifteen feet. As soon as they stepped off of it, and back onto the main platform of Faas's outpost, they could no longer hear the Cambulls. And sure enough, when they stepped back onto it again, they could hear the Cambulls again.

"Where do you reckon they got to?" they heard Billy Bob ask.

"Tracks went into a stream," Buck answered, "and never came out again."

"Ha!" Tom laughed. "It was totally awesome!" He turned to Stella and Clarsah, addressing them, Patrick, David, and Robert. "Okay—here's what happened," he clasped his hands as he started the tale. "After we crossed the stream, where you guys turned right—we ran through the woods, until we came to another stream. We entered *that stream* at an angle, so it would look like we must have gone *upstream,* to our right, since our tracks didn't go across. *Upstream* was close to the direction we had been running in, so it would have seemed logical. But we actually turned left, almost a hundred and eighty degrees, and ran *downstream*—until we got really close to the sound of Buck's machine. There we got down low, until he passed. Then we continued running downstream until that second stream emptied into the first stream that you guys had followed—only we were a little ways further up from the spot where *you all* turned right, and we had crossed. By now Buck was searching further up the upper stream, and getting further and further from us," Tom smiled. "It was so awesome."

They took turns looking from the one spot on the observation deck where they could actually see the Cambull dwelling. They had to sit on the very edge of the deck, facing the Cambull domain. There was a hole in the wall of vines surrounding them, just big enough to place one's face into. From that small hole the vines opened out in a cone shape—and the view, though distant, was clear all the way to the Cambull's.

When Stella sat on the edge of the platform, taking her turn to view the Cambull residence, she noticed Buck was staring out into the swamp as he paced back and forth, muttering something under his breath. "Could you quiet down guys," she begged, "I'm trying to hear what Buck is saying."

"Put on your wolf ears," Faas suggested—as he cupped his hands in the shape of wolf ears and held them behind his own ears, pushing his own ears forward. "This helps to amplify the vibrations on your eardrums."

Stella tried it—and was immediately astonished. She could hear the sounds of Buck's boots snapping twigs and scraping the ground as he walked. She could hear his panting breath. "It really works!" she gasped, removing her hands, then putting the *wolf ears* back on. Now she heard what Buck was saying.

"I know you're out there somewhere, Swamp Rat. One of these days I'll get my hands on you—it's just a matter of time. And as for them slimy, squirmin' pollywogs what's followin' you about—we'll find out where they live…every last one of 'em. Have no doubt about it, Pollywogs—we're comin' for you. All of you."

Well, Stella thought, *our lives most definitely are getting more interesting now.* Stella noticed she wasn't the only one using wolf ears. And there were some rather worried looks amongst her friends as the implications of Buck's mutterings sank in. A colorful discussion about what approaches they might take to deal with the Cambulls was heating up. Stella quietly listened to the various *solutions*, agreeing only on the arguments against each one, which ranged from *unthinkable*, to *unrealistic*, *ridiculous*, and finally, *downright stupid*, in exactly that order:

"I say we never set foot in these woods again," was Robert's solution, which Andy alone seemed to agree, *might* be a solution—until he heard David's reply.

"That's *unthinkable*," David replied on behalf of everyone else. "These woods are the most amazing and magical place we've ever found. We should simply notify the police—they can solve the whole problem and we can just stay out of it until it's all worked out," he added as a matter of fact, which a few of them seemed to think *might* be a solution—until they heard Robert's retort.

"That's probably *unrealistic*, David," Robert informed with his typical dry monotone, "since the police chief is an old war buddy of the Cambulls' father."

"I think we should tell all our parents," Clarsah added her two cents. "If they explained the whole thing to the Cambull's father, he might take their guns away and ground them for the whole summer."

"Hopefully, for more like a whole year," Patrick added, being the only one who didn't see right away how totally ridiculous Clarsah's idea was.

"I think they need to be grounded for the rest of their lives," Craig added. "But since that isn't going to happen," he glanced at Faas who was watching the whole debate with quiet amusement, "we'll have to learn how to camouflage ourselves, stalk about invisibly, and maybe have some snares and traps laid up in places."

Patrick and Tom were both nodding enthusiastically.

"Then we will need some weapons," Tom added brightly.

"*I* have my trusty old ash longbow," Patrick piped up, "*and,*" he added, raising a finger to the air, "a very nice, new re-curve." His eyes lit up. "Then there's my Dad's antique gun collection...."

"And that's just *totally stupid*, Patrick," Stella shook her head. "If you keep using your brain like that you'll end up being just like the Cambulls."

The group went silent. There *was* reason for concern, and the Cambull threat *would* have to be dealt with. But Stella had deeper questions. She was feeling really outraged and disgusted at the moment. And yet, she felt sadness.

"How could anyone be so terrible?" she looked to Faas, shaking her head. "Where do these people come from? I mean, why would a God create such evil?"

"I'm not exactly sure just yet," Faas answered. "Of course, it's not quite that simple—but questions like that are exactly what MacAwen sent me here to learn about."

"You *do* know MacAwen!" Stella's eyes widened in realization. "I knew it."

"Of course I *know* MacAwen," Faas returned. "Everyone *knows* MacAwen. But I don't just know him," Faas smiled. "I grew up knowing him. I've known him since before I could walk or talk." Faas looked dreamily into the sky. "MacAwen's the closest thing to a human that's been like a father to me."

Tom, Craig, and Robert were staring dumbfounded at Faas. The others didn't seem so surprised. It made perfect sense. They would all have expected Faas to know MacAwen. That is, if they believed in MacAwen's existence. Tom, Craig, and Robert had not yet subscribed to that belief. In fact they had believed very assuredly that MacAwen did not exist. Now their belief was shattered. For they could not shrug off Faas's word. *He* certainly wouldn't be a part of Stella and Patrick's hoax. Of course, if they had not met Faas in person, he would have been no more believable to them than the little brown man.

"MacAwen instructed me to set up here about a year ago, to keep a watch on the Cambulls, do some damage control—and to study," he smiled. "I'm learning about humanity."

"Unbelievable!" Tom jumped up from where he was sitting on the deck. "So Stella and Patrick's stories—" he stared at Faas, astounded. "The leprechaun is real!"

Faas shook his head, smiling. "He's more than just a leprechaun."

"MacAwen *did* send you to help us, didn't he?" Stella interrupted.

"MacAwen?" Patrick questioned, now interrupting Stella, "was like a *father* to you?"

"Yes," Faas smiled, nodding to Patrick.

"Then you really did grow up in the forest?" Patrick asked.

"Yeah," Faas answered. "I was raised by a clan of coyotes—and by MacAwen."

"By coyotes?" Stella stared in awe. "Wow—that is the coolest thing ever," she breathed reverently. Yet Tom, Robert and Craig were just staring at Faas incredulously.

"But what of your real parents?" Patrick asked, "I mean—your biological parents?"

"Don't know," Faas shrugged, "barely remember."

"Were they killed?" Andy blurted out. "Oh—sorry," he added, noticing the scowls from Stella, Clarsah, and David.

"No," Faas smiled. "It was just—I didn't like my family life." He shrugged. "Abusive home, I guess—ran away before I could walk."

Before you could walk?" Tom smiled incredulously. "Then how'd you get away?"

"I crawled," Faas answered as a matter of fact—as though it was ordinary. They stared at him with renewed awe. Faas smiled, then laughed. Faas's laugh was very odd—and funny—just about what you'd expect from someone raised by coyotes. Also, it was contagious. In a moment they were all laughing heartily—which Stella felt very healing to their spirits after all they'd been through. It was just the medicine they had needed. When they had almost quieted down, the sound of what would have been Faas's final little coyote chuckle caused another uproar. That got him howling again—and that caused the whole group to laugh even more.

When at last they got a hold of themselves, Faas cleared his throat. "Back to *your* questions—*Stella*," Faas gave her his odd look again, his voice almost halting when he said her name, "it *was* MacAwen," he nodded, "who sent me to your aid."

Stella nodded in return, but it dawned on her that she'd never yet told Faas her name. *How did he know?* she wondered. *It had to be MacAwen. MacAwen must have described us to Faas,* she reasoned.

Stella noticed Tom, Robert, and Craig all eyeing Faas with renewed suspicions, whispering quietly to one another and nodding wild eyed as they studied him. Finally, it was Tom who spoke. "On one hand, Faas, you *do* seem like you were raised by coyotes. But..." he faltered. "Like—how do you know—I mean, like, how come your English is so good?"

Faas nodded. "All my life," he answered, "I have been engaged in the most intensive education imaginable...in subjects and dimensions few modern people in all their lives will ever know exist. For few today are even capable of imagining the existence of many of the subjects I have studied in depth for years." That silenced Tom—at least, for the moment.

"How'd you know I was Stella?" she asked.

"Oh—*that*...is obvious," Faas smiled shyly—again, with that strange look. Clarsah eyed him, then Stella—then him, then Stella again. Stella gave her a puzzled nod. They'd talk about it later. No one else seemed to notice.

"Yeah," Tom cut in, "that *is* obvious," he smiled also, but with a rather sarcastic look. Stella rolled her eyes. *Returning to his good old self,* she thought.

"But how did MacAwen contact you?" Stella asked. "He was so far away—and he was in such a hurry—and he was going in the opposite direction—to undo some terrible thing the Shadow Beast —or Buck Cambull—had just done."

"That terrible thing—that MacAwen had to *undo*—" Faas shook his head, "it was beyond anything Buck Cambull, or any of his machines alone, could have done." Faas sighed, "Thank goodness for MacAwen. He has given the world time—time..." Faas eyed the circle of kids listening to him—as though suddenly aware that he was saying things they could not understand.

"Well, as for Buck," Faas shrugged, "he just gets totally possessed by the Shadow Beast sometimes. It's like a high for him —a demented sort of religious experience." Faas looked directly at Stella. "There is so much you do not yet know about the Shadow Beast—which is amazing to me," he raised his brows, "considering who you—" he cut his words suddenly, glancing into the canopy of vines above, "may be..." his last words faded into a whisper. He shot Stella that, now very familiar, yet still completely mysterious look, which she seemed to have been getting from him since their first meeting.

Faas sighed, looking away from her. "I'm sorry," he shook his head, staring off into the vines again. "We're getting side tracked. I know you must have new questions, rising from my ramblings. But you have already asked a couple of questions that I have not yet answered—and I would like to try." He turned his bright gaze back to Stella, and for once he did not give her any strange looks. "Didn't you ask me something else—about how the Cambulls could be so terrible?"

Stella shook her head. "Oh—I mean, yes." Her head was swimming. She felt relieved to have gotten a normal look from him this time, but also, disappointed. "I just was wondering," she stared into the canopy, "how could anybody be so horrible? And why—" she paused, looking at Faas. "What would possess God to make them so?"

"Oh yeah," Faas nodded. "I remember how you put. Like, if there was a god—why would *God* create such terrible beasts? Right?"

"Yeah," Stella answered. "I feel bad saying that about anyone, but—for like no reason at all—they would have killed us."

"Oh, I don't know about that," Faas shook his head. "And I'm not sure it's quite that simple," he raised and crinkled his brows. "If you like reasons, there are reasons for anything and everything." He looked about, this way and that. "If you want to discover what the reasons truly are, however, you may have to search." Faas's gaze went into the mists, then came back to Stella.

"First of all—to the *god* part of the question," he sighed. "To imagine a god—to be creating—from the very beginning—in a direct and purposeful way—these, or any human beings—to be exactly as they are…." Faas raised his brows, shaking his head. "Well, it just doesn't take into account any decision making or responsibility on the created. I mean, we do have a hand in creating ourselves—or at least, affecting the outcomes of what it is we are growing and evolving into. These Cambulls are people— like us. They're not just monsters."

"This is exactly why MacAwen had me set up here," Faas nodded, "to observe, to study, to ponder." His eyes flitted about the surrounding wetlands, onto each of his new friends, and toward the domain of the Cambulls. "We're all related—all part of each other." He smiled. "My work here is to study the cause and effect —to see how evolution happens within a snippet of time—maybe a human lifetime or two. Then I'll be searching back a few generations…and then many—to see how the past relates to the life evolving around this family. For ultimately, that relates to myself, to all of us—and to the whole universe." His eyes widened, gleaming—as usual, an intense yet somewhat impish expression.

"Wow," Stella stared at him in awe.

"Also," he smiled. "I'm here to keep an eye on them so they don't corrupt the natural world around them much more than they already have. Hopefully, with a deeper understanding—" his smile widened as he eyed two ravens, croaking suddenly in the air above them, "as MacAwen says, though I don't really understand it, *can remake we a lost harmony…*" he trailed off, staring at one of the two ravens which had perched in the thicket above the edge of the platform. It cocked its head, seeming to look straight down at them, and gave a short croak. Faas answered it with two very raven-like croaks—a short syllable and then a longer gurgling one. Then he cocked his head suddenly, first in one gesture, then in another. The raven appeared to gesture back at Faas. Then Faas continued his conversation with Stella and her friends as though all was completely normal.

"You know, the Cambulls are not as purely terrible as they appear to be." He received a circle of incredulous stares. "I know. They *are* terrible. But as for *killing* you—I really wouldn't have thought—" he sighed, shaking his head. "Well, something *is* changing for the worse with them lately. Especially Buck. He is unique, that one. It's like he's totally possessed. I suppose I should not put anything past *him*. And I suppose he can get Billy Bob to go along with anything. Flea Stack of course would do what any of the others tell him. But as to the *for no reason at all* part of your statement, Stella—" he shook his head, his brows raised. "Tom and Craig and Robert—" he glanced at the three, nodding, "well, they were not exactly respectful when they intruded upon the Cambull's domain."

"*We* tried to stop them," Clarsah added. "Andy and I—"

"And *we* tried to stop Tom," Robert added on behalf of Craig. "But he was dead set on trying to find trouble."

"What?" Stella squinted in Tom's direction with a piercing gaze. "Clarsah and Andy caught up to you? They warned you? We could have avoided all this trouble?"

"Yeah," Clarsah shot Tom an accusing look. "He argued with us and laughed at us," she shook her head, disgusted. "He was so insulting—to us—to MacAwen, *our little brown figment of*

189

imagination," she gave Tom a refreshed glare, "and then, to the Cambulls. He said he wasn't afraid of any *hillbilly hicks*—and if they really lived out there he was going to find their house, and walk right up, and throw rocks at their door. And that's exactly when Billy Bob appeared. He heard everything Tom said. He knew these guys were just there to snoop around and cause trouble on his land—and he probably thought we all were."

"Yeah, and he guessed there was more of us out there," Andy added, cause when Ralph came out, Billy Bob was like, *I got this, Ralphy. Back off. Anyway, there's probably more. Why don't you go and watch the trail.* And that's why Ralph was just waiting to catch you guys."

"Tom—you total, complete idiot!" Stella glared at him.

"I'm sorry," Tom admitted, defensively.

"Sorry?" Stella stared blankly at him. "You almost got us all killed! And now you've brought out the very worst in these people, and set them after us! *This*—is the stupidest thing you've ever done in your life!" she glared at him, shaking her head in disgust, "and you've done a lot of *really…really…stupid… stupid…things,*" Stella gave Tom a big nod with each of her last five words.

Tom turned beet red. And for the first time since Stella had met him, he did not return a scathing criticism with sarcasm or argument. "I know it was stupid," he shook his head, looking down at the platform. "I really…am sorry," he sighed heavily. "I just wanted…excitement. I—" he looked around at the vast wildness surrounding them. "I didn't know what I wanted, really," he admitted painfully. "It was like *I* was possessed. Not by any *thing*—just my own…stupidness," he shrugged—"just by an attitude I always put on that's not my true self." He looked sheepishly to the circle of friends around him, but no one said a word. "I've always been like that," he shrugged.

"Why can't you just be real?" Clarsah questioned him.

"*I am* being real!" Tom snapped back at her.

"Well, why can't you *always* be real?" Clarsah retorted both angrily and pleadingly.

"I don't know," Tom answered. "It isn't fun." He was staring down at the platform. "Sometimes, I just don't know what else to do with myself!" He looked at his friends. "Being real all the time is boring. I've always just—" he looked out into the bog land. "I wanted to be more than I was—but I didn't want to fantasize—like you guys do. I was after something…something intense, but real —something…" Tom's eyes searched the wetlands around them, "something *wild*." Tom raised his brows.

"But now I found something more intense, and way more wild than anything I ever imagined," he looked at Faas. "And I'm changed," he added with an air of conviction. "Cause now I know —*true wild* isn't senseless," he gleamed. "It's just the opposite of that. I know you won't believe me, but…I'm never going to be the same again. At least—I want to be better," he nodded. "I promise," he folded his arms, "I'll never be so stupid again."

Stella had never seen Tom apologize. She'd never even seen him admit he was wrong. Clearly—he was changed.

"I forgive you, Tom," Craig smiled, extending his hand— which Tom took gratefully and shook with thankfulness.

"I forgive you, too," Robert added without expression, extending his hand.

"Me too," Andy smiled. They were all extending Tom their hands in forgiveness, which he shook in turn.

Finally, Stella was the last one. "Well Tom," she added, "those *were* about the biggest words I ever heard you say," she smiled and extended her hand. Tom took it appreciatively, and shook her hand with a hearty nod and a smile.

"And now I've learned more about humanity than I expected." Faas added, extending his strong hand, "well done, Tom. I forgive you too." And Tom shook Faas's hand with the greatest reverence.

"Thanks, Faas," Tom looked up to the feral young man. "You —" he paused. "You've inspired me—to be better," he looked down by Faas's feet. "I do have some more questioning for *you* though," he looked back up into Faas's face with a hesitant bit of a grin. "There's one thing I still don't quite get—about you."

Faas nodded—in invitation for Tom to continue.

"Well," Tom began, "we have all heard of human children being raised by wolves. I've read a little bit about it. It's not that uncommon in India. I mean—it's not unheard of. But those kids grow up pure wild. They can never adjust. Most can't even learn to talk. I mean, well, you are wild, but you're like… *educated*—"

"Yeah," David cut in, wide eyed and brightly, "you're like—*totally cultured*, Faas."

"Yeah, *cultured*," Tom nodded. "Like, I mean, most of those feral kids I've read about can't even relate to other people—or learn to talk. If you were raised by coyotes…"

"I was adopted by a coyote family," Faas nodded. "And they raised me like one of their own—sort of," he smiled. "It was obvious I was different. But MacAwen has always watched over. And as I said, I had other teachers. And I *have* other teachers."

"Did you go to school?" Andy asked.

"School? What's school?" Faas asked innocently.

"It's a place where you learn," Andy answered, smiling.

"I learn everywhere—all the time," Faas replied very seriously.

"Yeah, but school is a specific place you have to go a certain number of hours each day," Craig answered, also smiling incredulously at the naivety of this feral young man.

"*And* a certain number of days each year," David added, "to learn *specific* subjects—like math, English, and science—at *specific* times," he lectured.

"But I can learn all those subjects," Faas answered, almost child-like, "and many, many more—any time I want to—any where I want to."

"We know," Clarsah cut in, "but school is required by law for us—"

"I'm so sorry," Faas said, shaking his head, "terrible laws." He frowned. "School sounds like a bad place—like a prison."

"It's not prison," Clarsah smiled, almost laughing. "School—"

"Faas is right!" Stella cut in. "School *is* like prison. Well," she hesitated, "our school isn't *so* bad."

Faas broke out laughing. "I was just kidding," he giggled. "I know what school is."

They all stared at him in sudden silence. Faas's sense of humor *was* a bit off.

"Oh—" Stella crinkled her brows, "have you ever gone?"

"Never," Faas smiled. "And yet," he paused, nodding to the wildness all about them, "I'm always in school."

"What about books?" David asked. "Do you know what books are?"

"Yeah—I can read books," Faas shrugged. "And I've read plenty of good ones. But they're nothing compared to the great texts and tales I get from *the Primal Inscriptions*—and *the Ancient Literature....*" He nodded to the raven, still watching them from his perch. "Whether it be epic sagas—" Faas's eyes went wide to the wisps of clouds, wafting by on winds far, far over the seventh graders' heads— "or straight information—" his gaze sharpened suddenly, and fixed on a clear trail of coyote tracks, which he pointed to, printed on the platform by muddy paws—"straight *and voluminous* information," he continued, "on behavioral science, physics, geometry, chemistry, biology, botany, geology, evolution, zoology, anthropology, or whatever I happen to be gleaning from the primal text...." Faas went quiet as he noticed the blank stares, confused looks, and looks of awe on the faces of his young friends.

"Well," he smiled, "what I was coming to was the fact that *the Primal Inscriptions* and *the Ancient Literature* are simply superior to the modern *textbooks* and *novels*—when it comes to depth, that is. Admittedly, the modern texts are easier and quicker to learn to decipher."

"You mean tracking!" Stella exclaimed. Her head spun, thinking of all she had learned in so short a time—from MacAwen, from the two tracking field guides she had been studying, and from their experiences following trails. "By *Primal Inscriptions* and *Ancient Literature,* what you mean is *tracking!* Right? Is there a difference between the two? Have you been learning all this all your life, from MacAwen?"

"As I was saying, not all my learning comes direct from MacAwen. There is a whole society of the most amazing and inspiring teachers who I have known all my life."

"Like a University?" Clarsah asked, very much impressed.

"Beyond that," Faas answered. "More like a Multi-Versity. Each of my teachers are as independent as a college of their own. Together they make up a college of colleges. MacAwen is mentor to all, to the degree that each college member wishes."

"Wow," Clarsah sighed. "It must be such an intense, rigorous, competitive—"

"No, no," Faas shook his head. "Not at all like that. That style of teaching *destroys* so many aspects of the mind. I have been blessed with *Natural Education*. Along with the necessities

193

of life which come at one by way of hunger, cold, thirst, and other basic needs—I only ever study what I want—when I want—and however I want to study it. I follow the divine inspiration—the pure love of learning—however I will to imagine each moment."

Stella stared dumbly at Faas. *Natural Education.* It made so much sense. She was so impressed by this *young man.* Yet a part of her–a wounded part of her that had always longed for Natural Education, without consciously knowing what it was—could only wonder; *why couldn't I have had that sort of education? Why can't we all?*

"Though I have not attended, I *have* studied the effects of modern schooling—on those who *have* been institutionalized," Faas stated. "The Cambulls of course are all graduates of the public school system. Buck, in fact, graduated early—with high honors! The military recruiters did pull a few strings; they were gleaning him for a career in the *special forces* of a secret agency they strangely call *Intelligence.*"

"Sorry," Faas smiled, "I'll try not to confuse you with too much information. And I'll *try* to answer as directly as I can.

"Often times," his eyes lit up, "the answer to a single question will birth several new questions. And it gets difficult to stay on track—or on a single set of tracks, crisscrossed by seemingly unfathomable sets of others. Still, I have not lost any of *your* tracks. Trust, we will come around to them all. And more and more, you will understand how they all connect."

Stella was blown away by the way Faas's mind worked. He was a little hard to follow, but he was amazing. And she just wanted to hear more.

"Stella, you have asked one question that I have not yet answered." He looked directly at Stella. "That question…was a trail of thoughts—like a set of tracks that seemingly was not followed. Yet it has remained in the back of my mind—even as I've followed other thought trails through our back and forth conversations. And I have come around to it now."

Stella raised her brows questioningly, in a rather perplexed sort of look. Faas giggled. "Trace your own thoughts backwards," he said. "Track yourself back to the unanswered question—and you will see how the answer now has greater meaning than it would have had before you trekked this far." He looked at her intently. "Do you follow?"

Stella's eyes were wide and her mouth hung open. But she was nodding. She *had* followed. There was confusion—and there was amazement in the minds of these seventh graders. But also, there were realizations. Connections were beginning to be made...from many *trails of thoughts*. Not everyone could follow the abstract footprints of Faas's *mental trails*, but Stella now remembered exactly what the question was that Faas had not yet answered.

"How did MacAwen contact you?" she asked.

"Web alert," Faas answered.

She stared at him, questioningly—almost stunned. It was a rather short answer, coming from Faas. "Web alert?" she asked.

"I'm almost always hooked up," Faas nodded. "And MacAwen is a master at setting off alerts."

"You're always hooked up to what?" Stella asked.

"To the World Wide Web," Faas answered.

"The world wide web?" she stared at him incredulously. They were all staring at him—all dumbfounded.

"Yeah," he nodded, scrunching his brows, "the world wide web—of tracks and trails," he nodded, again, now raising his brows—as though anyone should know.

"The world wide web—of tracks and trails?" Stella questioned again. "So—do you have a computer, or..."

Faas laughed. "I've been trying not to say too much—so as not to confuse you. There *are* many different forms of computers in the natural world. But I don't need any of them to log on. I just get onto a set of tracks," his gaze intensified, his speech accelerating, "and it intersects with another set—and each is connected to many others, crisscrossing," his eyes flicked about in rapid movements, "and all hold bits of information—and all are connected to the web that covers the whole world—" Faas halted, eyeing the kids. Then he sighed and smiled.

"When you become proficient at reading tracks you can just plug in subconsciously and find out anything you need to, almost instantly—or, as in MacAwen's case, send any message you want to, to any where you want to."

"Wow..." Stella stared at him. Everyone was staring at him.

"Yeah," Faas nodded. "Digest the possibilities. But," he raised a finger to the air, "first you must master the ABC's of tracking—and learn how to read some simple stories, poetry, and the daily news. Only then may you really begin to understand how the world wide web of tracks and trails works, and how to use it." Faas smiled. "I did say the word *digest,* though, didn't I? So, who's hungry?"

"Starved!" Tom answered. "Uh…what do you have in mind?" he added hesitantly, "to eat?"

"Have you ever heard the term, *Entomophagy,*" Faas asked in return. They all shook their head*s*. Faas nodded very seriously. "It pertains to the consumption of insects." Faas began a rambling discourse on *entomophagy*—with graphic descriptions of all kinds of bugs and methods of preparing them—as though he was an eccentric professor who designed to educate by shocking. "If that doesn't suit you, perhaps geophagy would be more to your liking."

"And geophagy pertains to...?" Tom questioned.

"The consumption of soil," Faas answered. He was given some rather odd looks. "A small amount of soil can provide a tremendous nutritional supplement," he defended his case. "Good, clean, healthy soil, that is," he added, "soil that is alive and writhing with healthy microorganisms. But come," he eyed the group. "You are starting to shiver in your wet clothes. We will have fire." He turned and headed toward the dome shaped hut.

"What about the Cambulls?" Tom questioned as they followed Faas. "Won't they smell the smoke?"

"They sometimes smell my smoke," Faas answered over his shoulder. "And Buck at least is sometimes curious about its source. But I have no worries of him finding it."

"How do you make fire?" Patrick asked. "Do you have flint and steel?"

"I like to use a hand drill," Faas answered, as they got to the stone fireplace just outside the door of his hut. He stepped into the doorway and grabbed his fire making apparatus.

"The drill—" he held up a wooden spindle, about a foot and a half long. "The fire board—" he held up a tiny, flat board with several notched burn holes drilled into it. "And some tinder—" he held up a fistful of plant fibers rendered nearly as fine as a cotton ball. Before anyone could ask another question, Faas had placed his fire board onto the tinder bundle, stuck the wooden spindle into one of the burn holes in the fire board, and was spinning it rapidly between his palms. Within seconds there was smoke, then a tiny spark which Faas blew into flame. Within a minute he had a crackling campfire.

They were speechless. It was awesome...wonderful—almost magic! Instantly warm...and...thankfully, as it turned out, Faas was the master of a good many recipes that did *not* include any insects or raw dirt. And his cooking was wonderful. Though most of the dishes were raw: fruits, berries, leaves, sliced roots, and a variety of odd vegetables. The very best was the stew—wild turkey, cattail tubers, tiny white carrots, grain from some sort of swamp grass, and various herbs and spices.

"Absolutely...delicious!" Stella exclaimed, even though she usually was a vegetarian. No one disagreed. They all felt nourished and in good cheer as they relaxed around Faas's campfire with various crude but artistic wood and clay mugs and bowls of steaming tea.

The sun was getting quite low in the sky, however, and most of them had to be back home in time for supper. "Won't you stay to hear my band?" Faas asked. "We start kicking' in just after sunset."

"You have a band?" Tom raised his brows in disbelief. They all stared at Faas inquisitively.

"Oh yeah," Faas answered excitedly. "*OmniVerse*. We jam just about every night—"

"What *kind* of music?" Craig asked with his usual monotone broken and an expression on his face that revealed layers upon layers of beliefs and dis-beliefs peeling and falling away.

"Indigenous," Faas nodded, with an expression that fully conveyed his feeling that this was the very coolest style of music ever. "We can play anything," he added, "rock, metal, wood, hop, roll, hip, thrash, bound, classical, thunder, folk, jungle, swamp, grunge, jazz, buzz, flap, rag, rap, scrape, reggae, you name it..."

"Wow...we'd love to stay," Clarsah stared at him wide eyed and dreamily, yet shaking her head with regret. "But we'll have to take a rain check."

"*Rain check?*" Faas glanced to the sky, frowning. Then he put a hand to the ground, gazing intensely—first at his finger tips, then off into the surrounding wildness. Stella noticed: Faas's thumb and fingertips were embedded in a footprint left by her or one of her friends. Faas lifted his fingers from the track, holding his thumb and fingertips together, and placed them to his nostrils. He sniffed vigorously, still gazing intensely, somewhere out of focus from the world around them.

"Oh…yeah," he smiled, "*rain check*," he raised his brows. "Alright then," he nodded, "after tea I'll get you all back to your familiar trails."

Stella was giving Faas the odd look now. "Did you know what *rain check* meant?"

Faas gazed wide eyed at Stella, for just a split second, then gave the subtlest wink—as though he was a magician and she'd spotted his trick. He smiled. "There are so many words and phrases to learn—so many tracks to follow…." He sighed. "Although I am well read, I've not had much contact with folk outside the De Da Mua. I was not familiar with *rain check*—but I am familiar with *plug in*—and *download*," he nodded with his impish smile. "But since we're out of time, those explanations will have to wait."

That reply certainly didn't answer her question. Clearly, it was only meant to create new questions and intrigue in her mind. All Stella could imagine was that somehow, Faas was trained to use his nose like a USB plug in—and he could download information directly to his brain from a smell. She could hardly wait until *next time* she met Faas.

It would have been a long, and wet, hike. But Faas had a stash of coracles—tiny, lightweight boats—rather like skin covered baskets. They floated very high on the water, and were quite effective for navigating the shallow waterways. On the way he carved Ogham Keys for Tom, Robert, Craig, David, Clarsah, and Andy.

"Could you carve one for our friend, Jessie?" Clarsah asked. "She wanted to come so badly, but gave—"

"I can't give her a code until she has visited the De Da Mua," Faas answered. "You have to be brought in for the first time by someone who's been in. Only then may you be granted a code— by a key master, like me," he smiled proudly. "I've got authority from MacAwen to mint keys."

They all would have just loved to stay longer. And they would have loved to come back and visit him again the following day. He was so amazing. There was so much to learn. But their homework was stacked ridiculously high—and they'd already made arrangements with each other and various parents, to get the assignments done together. So they agreed to meet Faas again in one week.

As Stella and her friends parted ways with Faas, on the edge of the old railroad path, Stella turned to him and said, "We *will* meet again—next week?"

Faas looked at her. And once more, it was that peculiar look. Only this time his gaze was sustained and penetrating. It hit Stella like a shock of electricity, pulsating through her body. Or so she reacted to it.

"We *will* meet again," he nodded, staring solely at her, then down into the footprints leading to her position, "sooner," he whispered. He glanced at Clarsah, then David, then Patrick—then at the whole group. He breathed in deep, and then sighed. "All my life...time, I have had in abundance. Now," he breathed in deep again, his eyes wide to something moving in the air. "I feel it spinning so very, very fast." He shook his head, and then smiled.

Stella's heart raced. Her head swam. She stood mystified, wondering what was wrong with her. Was there more Faas wanted to say, but was reluctant to? Why? What was it? She felt the pulsation growing stronger in her brain. Then she saw the Awen, wild energy, pulsating in the air exactly in sync with the sensation in her head.

Faas nodded, then turned and disappeared into the shadows of the woods as though he had been but a daydream—leaving the kids to their seemingly ordinary lives.

Yet never in their lives had things been further from what they seemed. And never again would they be. This, Stella sensed with all her heart—as her heart raced with excitement and dread at once. Sooner than she or her friends could ever have dreamed, Stella sensed, every comfortable illusion would be gone—especially for her.

≡╫╪╪≡╠╪ . . .

Plug ye in
an' log ye on
an' down ye load—
re-boot!
Sniff an' see an' dream
an' ken anew!

Chapter IX:
The World Wide Web

Stella stared blankly at her math workbook. She was striving to focus, but her head was in a fog. Her eyes were opened, and there was nothing wrong with her vision, but she was not seeing the problems on the page. Her mind was elsewhere—*anywhere* elsewhere. It was just so hard to force her entire consciousness into the tiny boxes that it just hated to be stuck in. Her mind desired *so strongly* to wander free.

There was so much purpose to the *wandering* desires of her mind. There was so much adventure *out there*—so much mystery —so much to learn that was alive and connected to everything else in life.

But these stupid math problems had no meaning for her. There was no life in them—no mystery. When she solved them it was just obvious—just numbers. It could all be broken down to adding, subtracting, multiplying, dividing…small numbers, more numbers, big numbers. So what?

She was mentally capable of doing the work, but it was *just excruciating* to force the grand, lively, flowing, dreaming, and complex mind into such tiny lifeless, square bits of thought. The pain Stella experienced was physical, spiritual, and emotional. It felt absolutely *wrong* to force herself to concentrate when it was her nature to expand. There was no reason.

Actually, there was *one reason.* And that was *to get it done—* so she could be free. The wide world was awaiting—and that was inspiration. She had to get back out there. Faas was out there. MacAwen was out there. There was so much to find out. They had not yet even learned the ABC's of tracking. And there was something mysterious that MacAwen wasn't telling her…yet. And those weird looks Faas kept giving her….

"Stella—" Clarsah stared pleadingly at her friend. "We've got to get this done."

"Oh…yeah…I know," Stella frowned hard. "I'm…*striving*."

"What number are you on?" Clarsah peered at the worksheet Stella was working on.

"Um…" *How could anybody just be **on a number**,* Stella thought.

"Stella?" Clarsah eyed her friend concernedly.

"Oh—yeah—number—" Stella's mind shrunk down to the problems on the page. "Thirteen," she said, focusing once more on number thirteen. *Oh yeah,* she remembered this problem. She had tried to focus on it five minutes ago—*or was it ten minutes?* The problem was easy, really—*painfully easy*—if she could just concentrate on it! But that was so, so hard.

"You're pretty far," Clarsah encouraged. "We could be out of here in like—fifteen more minutes—if you just focus on them," Clarsah pleaded sympathetically. She knew what it was like— though she didn't have the same magnitude of struggle that Stella had.

"I know—you're right," Stella focused on the redundant, meaningless drudgery—and went through the motions. It was painful. It was limiting. But there *was* a reason—she had to *get it done.*

Clarsah had slept over. She and Stella had made plans to study together. They had worked the night before until they were exhausted. And then, this morning, they had gotten up at the crack of dawn—and had gotten right to work. They had incentive—to get back to the De Da Mua. They had convinced their parents to let them return to a *magical place they'd found in the forest,* where they could observe *the most amazing sunset—if* they finished all their homework. Without that inspiring her, Stella could never have gotten through it. But she did. And to the surprise of her mother, Stella had all her homework done by ten O'clock AM. They were free….

Stella and Clarsah were racing along the path. "Wait," Stella called ahead to her friend.

Clarsah stopped, looked back, smiled. "What?"

"I was just thinking," Stella panted as she caught up. "You know how sometimes less is more?"

"Less? Is more?" Clarsah crinkled her brows in confusion.

"Yeah, like if somebody had something really important to say —and people were like, gathered to listen—and then the speaker just like, went on and on, using way too many words. It would be like less of the important stuff ever got heard because the people would be so bored. But if less was said, more would be heard and remembered."

"Oh yeah—I get it," Clarsah nodded. "But what does that have to do with us now?"

"Well," Stella looked this way and that, into the woods—up, into the sky—and ahead, along the path, "I was just thinking, "sometimes slower is faster."

"Slower is faster?" Clarsah had a puzzled look on her face. "Wait," she smiled. "What do you mean?"

"Well, the De Da Mua is not just what it seems. We enter it from somewhere in the wet wood lands we're heading for—which of course is *in* our town. But the De Da Mua is *not* contained within our town—not even within our state." Stella put her hands on Clarsah's shoulders and looked intensely into her eyes. "I'm sure it's not even contained within our world."

"Wow..." Clarsah whispered wide eyed and reverently—a sparkle of inspiration in her gaze and a smile of anticipation on her face. She looked ahead, deeper into the woods, searching. For a moment they stood quiet. Then Clarsah's mind snapped back to their conversation. "That is so awesome, Stella. But what does that have to do with slower being faster?" she smiled.

"Um..." Stella stared off, into the woods. "Everything!" she answered suddenly, her focus snapping back to Clarsah. "The borders of the De Da Mua are always moving and changing. To find it, you have to have wide eyes and ears—and all your senses on full alert. And I just think—like, if you go slow—you see more and hear more...and sense more. So, we'll probably get into the De Da Mua faster if we move slower."

Oh," Clarsah nodded, "Yeah," she smiled, and they continued, slowly now—though they both knew there was no way they were going to enter the De Da Mua yet. They were still on the old railroad path. They would have to leave the trail first, and then get into the wooded wetlands. Yet it was good they slowed down, for no sooner had they, when they spied a set of coyote tracks trotting along on the pathway.

"Our guide!" Stella whispered excitedly, as she got to her knees to study the tracks.

"Couldn't they be from a dog?" Clarsah asked.

"You see how the middle two toe pads are spaced pretty far ahead of the outer toe pads?" Stella pointed.

"Yeah," Clarsah answered.

"Well, that's more indicative of a coyote," Stella continued. "Also, see how the hind feet are just about direct registering?" she pointed to where the hind foot prints landed on the fronts. "And the gait pattern is so consistent here, and has such a purpose about it —I can just *sense* that it's a coyote."

Stella got down on her knees, and studied the tracks very closely. "Look, Clarsah!" she pointed. "See how the hind feet prints are consistently registering slightly to the outsides of the front prints?"

Clarsah dropped to her knees, also, to observe the tracks more closely. "Yeah. What does it mean?" Clarsah asked.

Stella was on her belly now, her head moving from side to side —her eyes, practically in the prints. "It means, this coyote is probably female. And look—" she pointed out how the inner part of the back of the heal pads were usually imprinted deeper than the outsides—with some exceptions of course for the varying hardness of the ground and placement of stones in the mostly muddy earth.

"That's another indicator. She is a female," Stella informed. "Not the same coyote guide we had last week."

"Wow..." Clarsah stared at Stella in amazement.

It reminded Stella of the strange looks Faas had given her, and she felt uneasy. There was something in Faas's looks that frightened Stella. Yet mostly, it intrigued her.
It wasn't that Faas frightened her. But he knew something—something about her. She could sense it. But then—that was just stupid. She was just fantasizing. But, then again...Faas definitely did keep giving her those odd looks.

"Stella?" Clarsah was staring at her. "What are you thinking?"

"Oh...just...about the looks. *You* know."

"Maybe he likes you," Clarsah giggled.

"That *definitely* is ridiculous." Stella snapped. "Faas is like, nineteen, and the most awesome and amazing guy ever. And he's so thoughtful...and good. It would just be *wrong* if he liked a seventh grader."

"I was just kidding," Clarsah said. "But maybe," she added, "since he grew up in the woods, without people..."

"He's not like that!" Stella burst out. "He's totally educated. And like, cultured."

"Yeah, you're right," Clarsah conceded. He *is* cultured. And well adjusted. And just way too cool to be confused like that."

Stella sighed relief that Clarsah agreed with her. Yet she would have been disappointed if she hadn't felt *something* was going on with Faas's looks. Stella never told Clarsah about what MacAwen had said, right before he disappeared to go undo whatever the Shadow Beast had done. *"great is yer destiny and purpose. Upon ye, Stella...."* What had he meant? Or did he really *mean* anything? She felt too embarrassed to admit she'd been thinking there might be something...*special* about her. *Special?* Actually, she'd heard that description of herself many times in her life, though the meaning of it had rather changed to a negative over the last couple of years.

"You're sure? No one else noticed the looks?" Stella asked.

What?" Clarsah looked confused for a moment. "Oh—the *looks*," she smiled. "No," Clarsah answered. "Well—like I told you before, David noticed once—"

"David—" Stella rolled her eyes. "Well—he *is* different than most boys. I mean—he *does* notice *some* things. Well—he does *notice* a lot of things, for a boy, but he doesn't have that greater sense, you know? Only girls do." She eyed Clarsah inquisitively. "So, you *are* sure? He *did* notice once?"

"I've told you six times already," Clarsah sighed, exasperated. "but after, when I tried to talk to him about it, David just said: *it did **appear** to be a strange look, but we shouldn't assume anything we don't really know.* You know how he puts on his *sophisticated air*," she rolled and batted her eyes. "When I told him I thought there was something more to it, he just rolled his eyes and shook his head like he always does. And he said, *You girls read into things **way** too much.*"

"He's probably right," Clarsah concluded. And you're right, too. There's no way Faas would *like* you."

"Of course not." Stella said. And the true emotion hidden inside her was betrayed.

Clarsah shot her an alarmed look. "You like him!"

Stella turned away quick and said nothing. Her heart pounded. She had not actually realized it before. Now there was no denying it. And it was frightening. She had never really liked anyone. Well—David. But that was like nothing now. This was...dangerous. She could not face it. She turned her attention to the tracks and and blocked her feelings from her mind.

Stella and Clarsah followed the coyote tracks along the old railroad path until they turned left—at exactly the place where Stella and Patrick had first left the path to follow MacAwen—where Stella, Patrick, and Andy had followed the tracks of their first coyote guide—where just yesterday, eight friends had an unforgettable adventure. They were not *without* fear—for it was down this path they had met the Cambulls. But they were not held back by fear—only made cautious. For it was down this same path they had followed MacAwen, also. And though it had not yet appeared to be a path when she had first followed MacAwen, Stella now saw that it was turning into a rather busy highway. For here were the worn imprints of coyote, deer, rabbit, fisher, fox, bobcat, chipmunk, squirrel, mole, mouse—and now human.

They followed the coyote tracks—even as the cotyote tracks veered off from the tracks they themselves had left the day before.

Soon they were in a deep, dark, muddy area. The girls had their Ogham key boards out, and were tapping them as they searched the forest.

In a short time they came to a conspicuous shrub of alder. The main trunk had grown straight up. Four horizontal branches, evenly spaced, all protruded in the same direction. It reminded Stella of the letter "F." It did have two extra branches-- compared to the typical "F." But...this was a tree letter.

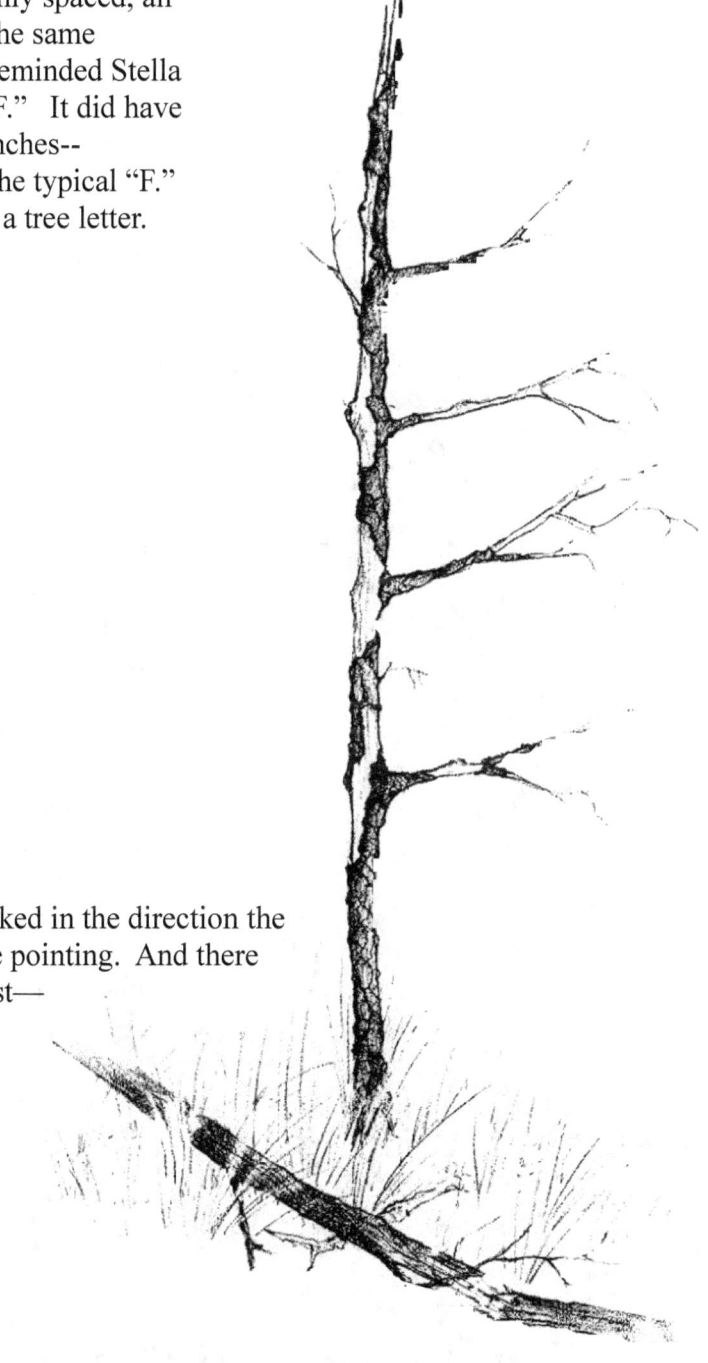

Stella looked in the direction the branches were pointing. And there was a sign post—

the stump of an old tree. It had the distinct claw marks of a bear scratched onto it, leaving it with a semblance of the same "F" symbol as that which the alder had grown into: four horizontal lines on one vertical.

"Faas," Stella said aloud, as she approached the stump. "This symbol represents his name—I'm sure of it."

Clarsah smiled wide at her friend. "Are you *sure* you're sure of it?" She glanced at Stella, then back at the stump. It did look like a stump with claw marks on it, which was exciting. But to Clarsah, it did not resemble the little alder shrub—and the shrub had not appeared to be a letter "F" —unless a very imaginative person, like her best friend, Stella, looked at it.

"I think I'm sure that I'm sure," Stella answered, as she approached the stump. Clarsah followed, good natured. Whether they were on target or not, Stella's inspirations always turned into some sort of adventure.

When they reached the stump they noticed a fresh set of human tracks—barefoot—quite large. It had to be Faas! They followed excitedly.

The tracks led to another stump. This one was very large around, and hollow. On the north side there was an opening. The tracks disappeared within.

Stella and Clarsah peered into the great hollow stump. It was empty. The tracks had gone in, and just ended. They never came out. Stella looked within again. There *was* a tunnel leading deep down into invisible depths. She peered in, imagining worlds below the rotted roots of this ancient tree. But only with imagination could she or any human descend those depths. It was much too small an opening for her physical body to actually squeeze into— much less Faas's. *Where had he got to?* Stella wondered. *How had he disappeared? Tracks don't just end...unless they belong to a bird.*

A trilling and melodic whistle sounded from above and behind them—like that of a mocking bird. They looked up, and there sat Faas, lounging on a great limb of an ash tree.

"Faas!" Stella cried. And she almost laughed, seeing his silly, lazy demeanor. "But how'd you get up there—" she shook her head, smiling. "I mean, how'd your footprints get inside this hollow stump?" she pointed, "and not come back out? And you're up there?"

"I am an Aspiring Duirken," Faas smiled. "I go some places where no footprints follow. And some places my footprints go…" his grin widened, his eyebrows dancing, "are only meant for others to follow."

"Oh—so you left a little trail to trick us?" Stella asked. "What's an Aspiring Duirken?"

"The trail of the trickster is a text typed to teach," Faas smiled. "I knew you'd be back today!" he added excitedly. "I read it in your tracks yesterday! And MacAwen gave me instruction on how best to teach you," he said proudly. "So, you've been following the path of coyote."

Stella thought of their guide. Then she thought of the coyote the Cambulls had murdered. Then she thought of MacAwen—and how he had said they would have another lesson after they completed their homework. "MacAwen said coyote would be our guide," she said, with mixed emotions.

"Yes. Coyote *is* your guide," Faas answered soothingly, apparently sensing her emotions. "He—and sometimes she—is the guide of all aspiring duirkens. But so wise and tricky are coyote's lessons that we don't always fully get them right away. Often, we don't even know when we *are* getting coyote's lessons."

"But as for your other question," Faas raised his brows with an impish gleam, "*you are.*"

Stella gave him a puzzled look. "I am what?"

"An Aspiring duirken…."

Stella and Clarsah stared at him, stumped, waiting to hear more.

Faas stared down at them, as though he was some sort of overgrown tree dwelling ape-elf, Stella thought, conversing mockingly with two members of a related, but Earth-bound species. "You asked me; what's an aspiring duirken?" he smiled. "I answered; you are. And so is Clarsah—as are several of your friends." Faas rolled from his lounging position, and in one amazing leap, stood casually before them.

Clarsah and Stella stared in awe. Clarsah seemed to have lost all words, but there was something like a smile in her amazed expression. Stella was a bit more expressive. "Wow," she gawked at Faas—then her eyes swam around the surrounding woodland. There were a number of large rotting stumps in this area—as though it had been drier land at one time, but was perhaps flooded. *Probably by beavers,* Stella thought. "Yeah," she said out loud, "Beavers." Faas gave her a funny, inquisitive look. She turned to Clarsah. Clarsah was giving her a similar look. "Oh, well— I didn't know I was *an aspiring duirken.*" She smiled at Faas. "Beavers," she exclaimed, "What's a duirken?"

Faas crinkled and raised his brows. He looked at her sideways. He looked into the branches above, then over his right shoulder, then over his left. Sighing, he folded his arms. "One who knows the roots of oak and can open the forest doors...and work magic, commune with non-physical beings, see things from afar, the future, the past, read minds—stuff like that. You know. Don't you?"

"Uhh...wow...yeah—I guess so," Stella answered. "And so the coyote... is the guide of all aspiring duirkens?"
Faas nodded, and was silent—*as if remembering someone*, Stella thought.

"Faas," Stella asked, "The coyote head...that you took from that tree—at the Cambull's," she grimaced sympathetically, "did you know that coyote?"

Faas nodded. "I did," he answered, still nodding—then sighing. "He was one of my great nephews." For a while nobody said anything. "You must understand," Faas said, "in the coyote world death is a constant, and very often, part of our life. My immediate family—my adoptive parents and siblings—they are *all* gone now. It is always sad. Yet we take death for granted. Their spirits are always with me—and they live on in all the descendants of our pack. There are many," he smiled. "My pack was blessed with resourcefulness. And I am now blessed with affiliation to over twelve packs roaming throughout New England, New York, and Southern Canada."

"That's amazing," Stella stared wide eyed into the trees.
"It's wonderful," Clarsah added shyly.

211

"You said MacAwen gave you instructions?" Stella blurted suddenly. "On how to instruct *us*? I miss MacAwen," she sighed. "Is he around? Did you see him? Did he undo whatever that terrible thing was that he had to undo?"

"I didn't see him," Faas answered. "He sent me a message. He's in Washington."

"Washington?" Clarsah exclaimed—so amazed that for once all the shyness was gone from her.

"D.C.," Faas answered. "He's whispering in somebody's ear."

"I can't imagine MacAwen being in Washington D.C.," Clarsah shook her head.

"Oh, yeah," Faas laughed. "Well, they've got some small patches of wetland that haven't been filled in—and myriads of secret tunnels. There are some grand old trees down there," he added, as though remembering from trips he himself had taken. "Anyway, the De Da Mua has portals to anywhere—especially for MacAwen."

Stella and Clarsah stared at him in silence. Everything about Faas, MacAwen, and the De Da Mua seemed to be getting weirder and more amazing by the moment—the more you found out. "Good," Faas nodded. "I see your wonder has achieved new levels." He smiled. "You've barely seen anything yet."

Faas walked to the stump where his footprints had disappeared within, and gestured for them to follow. "Observe my footprints closely," he instructed, as they approached the stump. "Careful you don't trample on them—we'll be back to study them again later...*and to follow them!*" he added excitedly.

Faas instructed the girls to study on their own. Meanwhile he lied down on his belly in front of another hollow stump nearby—his face inside the opening, resting on his hands.

The girls studied Faas's footprints for about five minutes. "OK—" Stella called to Faas. "We've studied them. Now what?"

"What have you learned?" Faas called back to them, without moving from his position.

"Uhh...well—you went into the stump—"

"Study them more thoroughly," Faas instructed. "See how each track relates to the next within the trail."

The girls studied for a bit longer this time. They noticed the subtle variations in the angles of the individual tracks—and how each print, and its exact angle to the prints before and behind it, related to the essence of the trail in general.

Satisfied—in fact, growing bored and impatient—Stella called to Faas again. And again, without pulling his face from within the hollow stump where he had planted himself, he asked her to explain what they had learned. The girls explained what they had now observed. When Stella said the phrase, "essence of the trail," Faas pulled his nose from the stump at last.

"Now you're beginning to get on track," he said.

"Beginning?" Stella reacted with an incredulous look.

"Yes—in the *essence* of the trail," Faas nodded, still lying on his belly. "This is where you *begin* to follow. Now—*within* each individual print, notice where the impact was most forceful. And, as importantly, how the pressure released into the earth as the foot impacted, moved within the Earth, and then left the track." He put his face back into the stump and said no more.

Again, the girls studied. As well as on the trail in general, they now followed the essence inside each track. Where had the greatest impact been when the foot came down? And just as importantly, where and how was pressure released as the foot moved within and then left the track.

Looking again, with new eyes, they now saw varied and complex *movements*...inside each and every track that they had not seen before at all. They had just never thought to look for such minute

213

details *inside* a track. Now these markings appeared like magic—inside each and every track. And they were not just minute details, really—at least, no more minute than a mountain is on a map. The closer the girls looked, the greater the features inside each track appeared. There were features within the features. It was amazing. They were on their knees, bent over low, noticing the way the dirt within each track was thrust, thrown, or spun as the foot impacted the Earth and then left the print.

Stella lowered herself to her belly—her eyes almost level to the ground. From this position the features seemed to grow larger still—and even more detailed. She was simply mesmerized. Her imagination took hold. And all she imagined, she relayed to Clarsah—how the results of Faas's foot-pressure releasing had left explosions, hills, plateaus, and craters inside each track. She was so enthralled that she forgot all about how much time she was spending on this study—or whether or not she needed assistance from Faas. Clarsah was also amazed by what *she* found inside each track—but more amazed by Stella's sudden and growing inspiration.

"Look," Stella pointed into the side wall of one of the tracks, "a cave—and there," she pointed to a feature in another track, "a tectonic plate." Clarsah laughed at that one. But Faas heard some of what Stella was saying, and he sprang to his feet and ran to them. He stared down at them—but *he* was not laughing. He was amazed.

"I think this one is an Earthquake crumble," Stella continued her findings—not

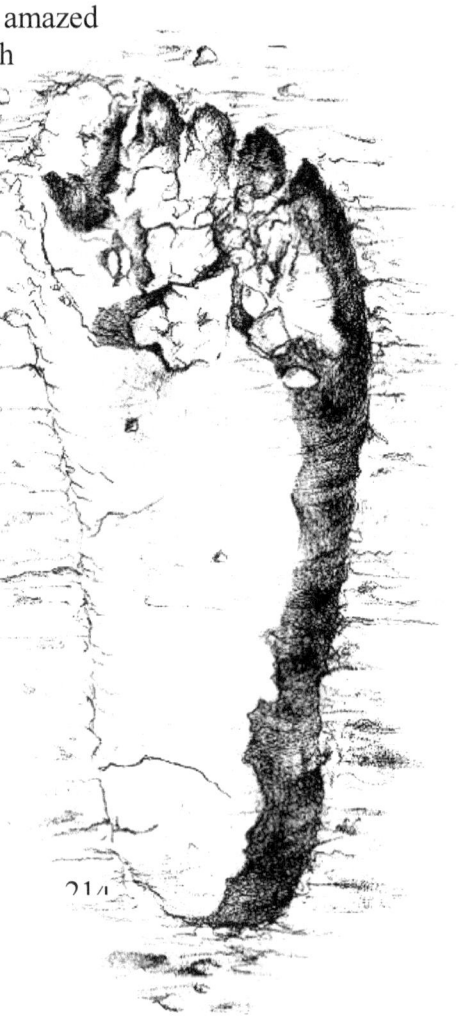

even noticing Faas standing over them. "Oh…wow…" she whispered. "Look at all these ridges and peaks," she pointed, "on the outsides—not actually *in* the tracks."

But just like the features within the tracks, those formed outside the tracks were caused by the impact, the reverberating impulses releasing pressure from Faas's feet while they were moving within each track, and the pressure releasing from his feet as they left each track.

"Maybe this is how some of our *real* mountains got made," Stella pondered, "only—" she looked suddenly upon Clarsah— "only the real mountains were created by something—or some *things*—with much bigger feet than Faas's!"

"Like giants?" Clarsah smiled.

"*You*—are in the essence," Faas half whispered. Stella looked up at him, and there was that look again—awe, amazement. "You are on track," he nodded. "Those *things*—with the big feet," he nodded again, "were glaciers. And on a grand scale—they leave exactly the same kinds of impacts and Impaction Reverberation Symbols that small objects do." He glanced at Clarsah. "So you were on track too," he nodded; "Ice Giants."

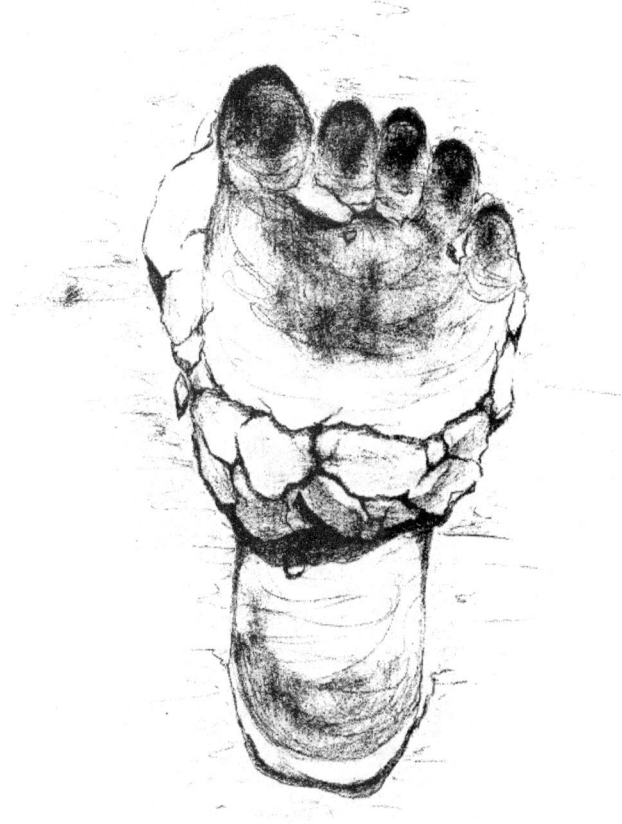

"This is just the beginning," Faas smiled wide, "but you are naturally gifted." His attention, again, was focused on Stella. He seemed to hesitate for a moment, then asked, "Do you have memories...of tracking—like...long ago?"

It was an odd question, Stella thought. "Uh...I don't think so," she answered.

Faas sighed. "Listen," he looked at her intently. "This is ancient knowledge. Few people, in the modern world, remember—or even have the faculties left to remember.... Yet—it is in you," he gazed wide eyed upon her. "It is in us all," he added, glancing at Clarsah. "All you have to do is remember. I will help you as far as I can." He was obviously focusing on Stella, and looking at her very strangely.

Stella looked at Clarsah. Clarsah looked nervously at her—then at Faas—then back to Stella.

"I'm sorry," Faas sighed, shaking his head—a smile returning to his face. "This is very exciting to me. It is very important work. In fact—" he nodded slowly, "it will spell the future of the world."

Stella and Clarsah were still staring at him, questioningly. Stella *was* excited by her findings, but this reaction from Faas was kind of weird. Then again, from Faas, maybe weird was kind of normal.

"Let me explain something," he nodded, then knelt down close to the tracks. "You see these hills, valleys, cliffs, canyons..." he pointed to the miniature formations, both inside and around the edges of the tracks, that looked like the larger geological features he was naming.

"Hills, valleys, cliffs, and canyons, etcetera are exactly what master trackers have been naming these features inside , and around the edges of tracks—for thousands of generations. Because they are created by the same types of forces that create their larger counterparts—only on a much tinier scale. When you learn to read what is within the tiniest tracks, then you may read the large features of the Earth even easier. You have begun to see the basic —that is, *the major Impaction Reverberation Symbols*."

"Wow..." Stella whispered.

"Listen," Faas said. "To my eyes, in a single human footprint there are hundreds of different Impaction Reverberation Symbols. Each one has a specific meaning. They will describe the way an animal was moving—whether it was male, female, hungry, frightened, looking to the left—or even thinking about turning," he smiled. "But here is an example of the impaction and reverberation in some prints that do make a turn."

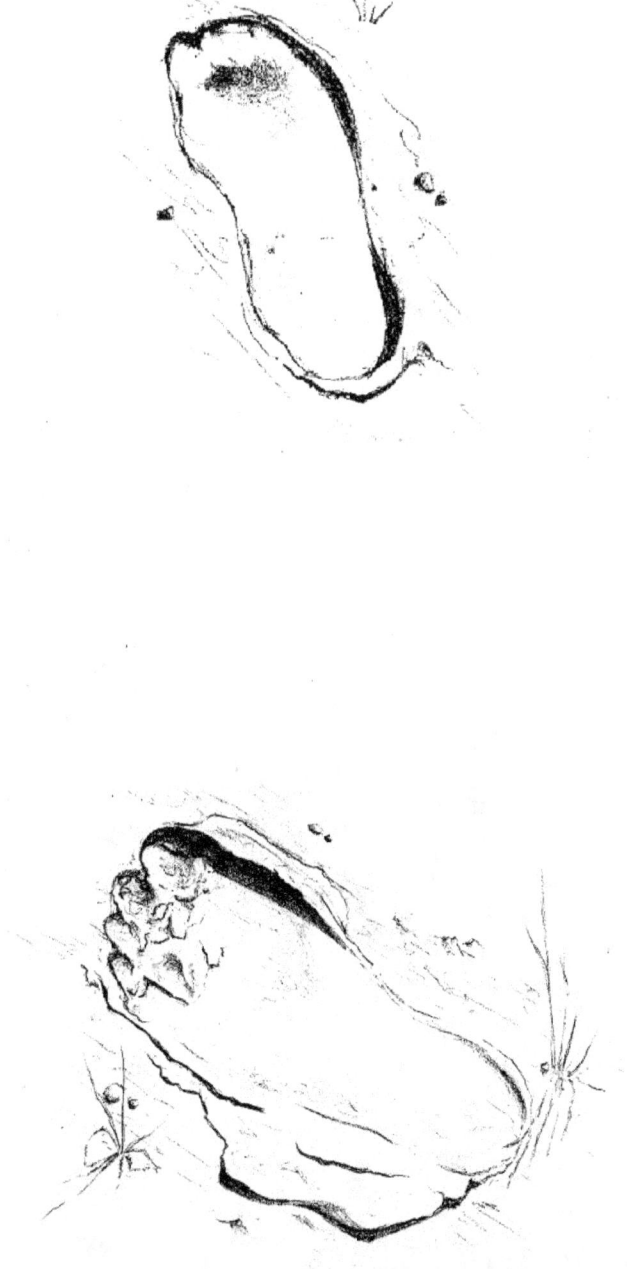

"Look here," he pointed to the heal of a track, "see how my heal impacted deeply as I was looking up, into the sky? Yet I can see by the rolling motion toward the toes, and the rolling up of these bits of earth," he pointed to a tiny hill at the ball of the footprint, behind the outer toes, "that my head was already rolling downward."

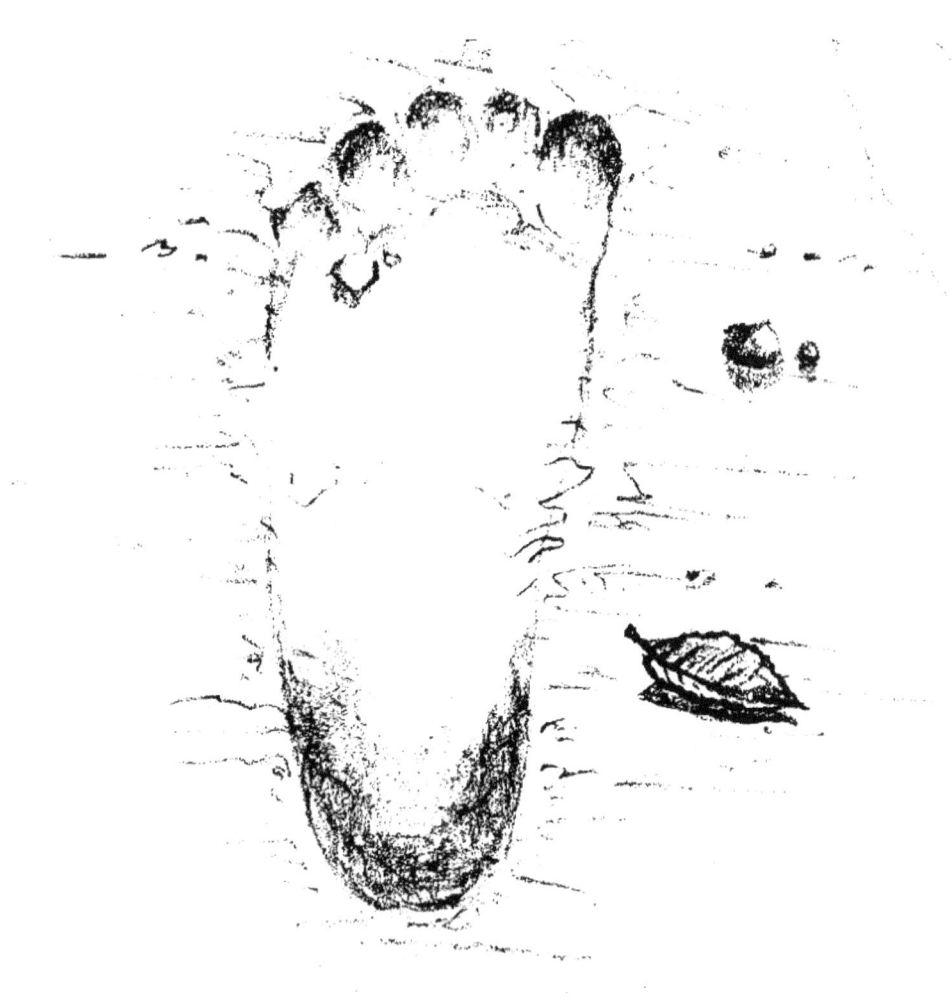

"And here, in the next print, my head rolled further forward, thrusting up a larger mountain at the ball of the foot as I walked. See how there was less pressure impacting the heal and caves are forming in the toes?"

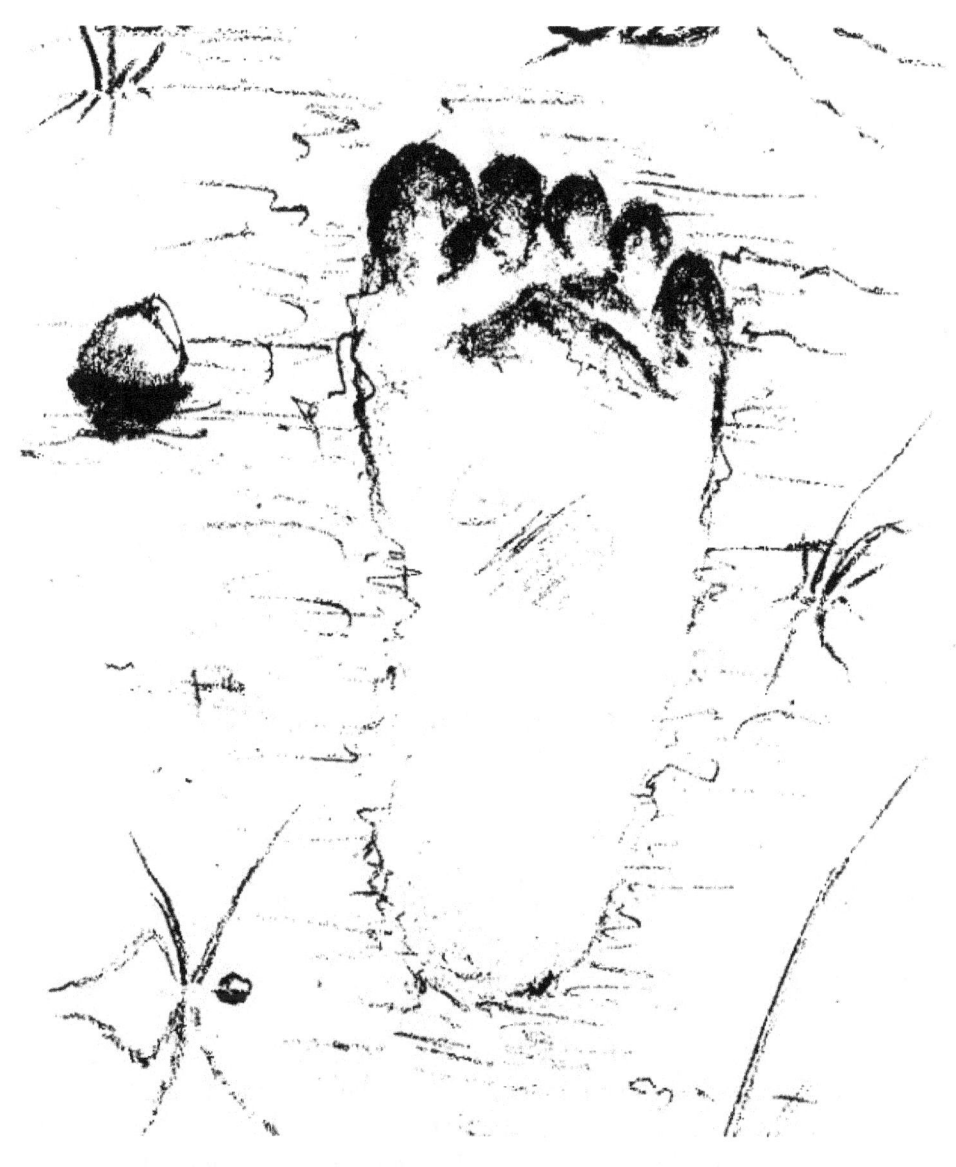

And finally," he pointed ahead to the next track, "here I was looking down to the ground. See how there is virtually no pressure on the heal now and the toe caves are so deep some are caving in? and there is a whole mountain range type formation rolling up at the ball of the print from the movement."

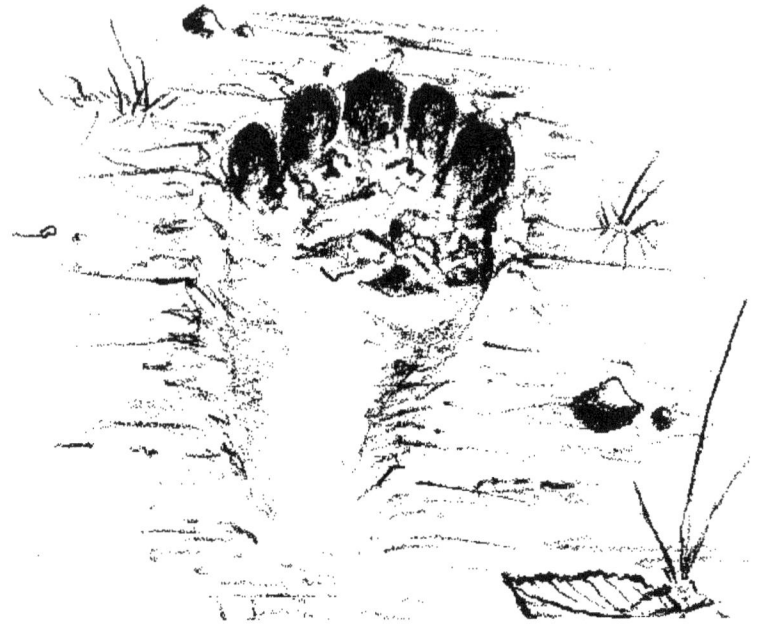

" And this is just the very beginning. It is through this essence of the tracks that I access the Primal Inscriptions...*and* the Ancient Literature."

"This is *so* amazing," Stella looked at Faas. "Are these *Impaction Reverberation Symbols* the ABC's of tracking?"

Faas's eyes flashed, but then he sighed and rolled his head. "You must understand," he continued, "to start with, at least, this is not an alphabetic system. It's not a logographic system. It's not a syllabary. It's not hieroglyphic. It's not pictographic—"

"I don't know *what* you are talking about," Stella interrupted, wide eyed, a confused smile on her face. Clarsah had a similar look, and gave a sigh of relief when Stella interrupted.

"Oh—sorry," Faas shrugged. "I've recently been studying the evolution of *all types* of reading and writing," he smiled. "What I'm trying to point out is Tracking is older and more universal than any other system of reading and writing. And it tells much, much more. The whole story. Every bit of the ever continuing creation and re-creation of the universe."

"That is just—" Stella sighed. "It's just so amazing." Her head rolled. "Wow. I just want so much to learn how to read tracks like that." Stella's dreamy eyes drifted into the tangles of branches in the scrubby trees and shrubs about them. "Why did we even invent letters in the first place?" But even as she asked, she started perceiving *tree letters* all throughout the branches and twigs —like the ones on the keyboards that MacAwen had made for them. But also, a different type, growing in the living branches and twigs. And the thought occurred to her that neither humans nor even MacAwen had invented the tree letters. Rather, some wise, wide-eyed person, or people, simply discovered what was already there. Their metaphorical meanings already existed— natural communications from the trees. That must have later inspired someone to make alphabets.

"Because—" Faas smiled, realizing Stella's mind had drifted off. "The reason people invented their own symbols and alphabets is because Tracking is much more complex—and requires far more study than any of the other systems to master. That is why, for convenience, humans have continuously evolved new types. From tracks, to pictures that represent words, to symbols that represent words, to symbols that represent syllables—and finally, to letters that represent the tiniest fragments of sounds. The alphabetic is the easiest system to master—tracking is the most complex."

"But the good news is, you don't need to be a master to read tracks. Look at me," he shrugged. "I'm not a master...yet. But I can read the great texts to my own level of understanding, which is always expanding...like—"

"Like the universe," Stella interrupted, still staring mesmerized into the labyrinth of living tree letters she imagined growing purposely from the forest.

"Yeah—or maybe like the growing emptiness inside my stomach," Faas sighed—his eyes suddenly wide. "Perhaps we should come back to these tracks and tree stumps after a bit of lunch."

"Yeah...good idea," Stella replied dreamily, her eyes fixed on the bent branches of a birch tree. "I think they invented themselves," she said. "Humans—really wise humans—or human-like creatures, like MacAwen, just figured out what was already there."

Clarsah and Faas eyed her peculiarly. "What are you talking about?" Clarsah asked, smiling as she tried to see what it was Stella was staring at.

"Umm...oh—" Stella snapped out of the branches and twigs, noticing Clarsah and Faas staring questioningly at her. "What?" she smiled.

"Who invented themselves?" Clarsah asked.

"Who?" Stella looked confusedly at Clarsah and Faas.

"You said, *they invented themselves*," Clarsah laughed.

"Oh," Stella smiled. "Yeah. The tree letters," she explained. "They're just an expression of the trees. I was just imagining that, like some wise people from long ago just sort of figured out what the trees meant by the way they grew."

And there was the weird look on Faas's face again. He was nodding his head subtly as he stared wide eyed at Stella. "Let's get some lunch," he sighed. "This way—" he gestured.

When they reached Faas's platform, he led them into one of the shelters they had not been in before. This hut was filled with smoked meats, bones, and antlers.

"Oh...no—" Stella hid her head in her hands for a moment— then looked again, aghast and saddened by the sight of all these deer remains that were clearly the result of killing.

"This deer *asked me* to take him," Faas explained, sensitive to Stella's feelings. "I *was* reluctant," he nodded and sighed. "So beautiful, he was—so graceful...." Faas stared through the roof of the hut as though he could see the deer in its life.

"He ran from me as hard and fast as he could—and fought fiercely for his life," Faas's eyes lit up, "as is meant to be!" Faas breathed and sighed dreamily. "It was our sacred dance," he explained. "His spirit and mine had agreed to participate in it— fully. And when I hesitated, his spirit came to me and said, *what's the matter, man? You said you would free me from this body—that we would be one.*"

"But you run in fear from me, I answered, and strive to live."

"Ah, man—don't you remember our sacred dance? The sacred hunt? The fear and the pain is ours together—as is the glory of transformation and new life. I know you will not disappoint me."

"After that communion with his spirit I strove with all my speed and strength—and I did not disappoint him. I ran him to near exhaustion. And then I leapt upon his back, grasping his antlers tight so as not to be impaled by them. I wrestled him to the ground—and then, I slit his throat with my knife!" There were tears in Faas's eyes now, as he recalled the final moment. "I cried then," Faas almost cried now, "as I felt the life go out of him. But just before he left, our eyes met. *I am so sorry, dear brother,* I thought. But his eyes communicated to me that it was all right now—our spirits became one."

"He will always live on within me—and I, within his essence...." Faas went quiet, breathing deep and reverently. There were no more tears in his eyes.

For a while no one said anything. Finally, Faas sighed. "I am *mostly* vegetarian," he raised his long, thick light brown eyebrows, "other than the delicious variety of nourishing worms and insects I eat," he offered a smile. Stella and Clarsah returned him some looks, but neither could quite eek out a smile. "But one should not be so prejudice towards plants and animals," Faas added.

"What do you mean—*prejudice* towards plants and animals?" Clarsah asked.

"There are many sentient beings I know," Faas began, "who are plant rather than animal—whose consciousness is beyond the knowledge of animals." Stella and Clarsah stared at him in silence. "Plants are our relatives as well as animals," he continued. "Some wish to be eaten. Some really small ones continue to live within us. Some even change our neuro-structure —as their consciousness enters into ours."

"Plants are really smart," Stella nodded, smiling.

"I *have* heard that plants can feel," Clarsah smiled shyly, "but they don't have brains, so they can't actually be smart, right?"

Faas nodded. "I can walk with that thought, Clarsah. But imagine for a moment that there are different types of intelligence. You don't need a brain to have awareness. Plants *feel*—which is more than the most advanced computers can do. Some plants can feel even more than people. But without a brain to organize their senses into thought, plants don't have the ability to think like us. Computers have no sense of pain or love, as plants do, but they have equipment more organized like brains than what you'd find in *almost* any plant. Does that make computers more sentient than plants?"

"Definitely not!" Stella cut in. "Plants are totally alive and like, *full* of feeling. Computers are just—like electronic storage of billions of digital numbers that people can light up or turn off. They have no sense."

"I know," Clarsah agreed, "computers have no sense like living things, but computers are so complex—and they hold so much memory—and can recall anything so quickly."

Faas giggled. "Computers don't recall anything on their own. You have to have a will to recall. People use computers as an extension of themselves, as a tool, to recall information—just like they used to do with markings on the ground, scratches on trees, stumps, stones, and bones—and more recently paper files, books, pictures, and movies—only now it's all contained in one machine. Still, the most highly evolved computer is not yet as complex as the brain of an earthworm," Faas smiled wide, pulling an earthworm from a container and sucking it into his mouth the way a bad mannered boy would do with spaghetti.

Clarsah and Stella stared incredulously at Faas, but said nothing.

"But there is a type of plant life that does have brain," Faas added while chewing with his mouth opened. "Mycelium."

"Mushrooms!" Stella lit up. "I love mushrooms. I've been reading about them for years. I think I might be a mycologist when I grow up. They're so magical—" she paused suddenly, eyeing Faas questioningly. "Did you say they have brains?"

"There are few things you could find in nature," Faas answered, "more closely resembling the structure of neuron networks making up human brain tissue than that which you find in the growth patterns of certain types of mycelium. And it *is* aware. Mycelium even moves through the ground by its own will —which is a capability modern science attributes only to animals. But further, mycelium learns. It scouts out new territories. It consciously adjusts itself to changing environments. It is smart— very smart."

"Wow! That is so awesome!" Stella glowed. "I always knew there was something amazing about mushrooms—but that...." she sighed, shaking her head and went silent.

Faas nodded. "I have studied many, many types of fungus— extensively. And many times, I have had profound communications with various types. But all types of plants communicate with other plants—and with animals. Plants do talk to each other," Faas nodded. "This has been known by primitive people since long before we evolved into people—or even into mammals. Yet it has been forgotten. So long has it been since most people retained their primal senses. Yet some modern scientists are, through their own methods of observation, beginning to re-learn that plants talk to each other. And that plants have their own internets."

"Internets?" Clarsah laughed.

"It's true," Faas answered. "I know it may sound amazing to you, but computer technology and internets didn't just spring out of nowhere in a couple of human generations. There are worldwide webs beyond your imagining. Some have been in use for thousands of generations. Others are as old as evolution. This awareness is built into us. It's in our DNA. And it's in the DNA of plants." *

"Take strawberries," Faas continued, very excitedly, "they have a network of shoots above and below the ground. It is through this internet they communicate to one another. If a chomping insect attacks one plant—that plant warns all the others. The other plants then put their armor on; they release chemicals that quickly harden their leaves, and make them taste bad. They even release toxins to ward off the attacking insect. But they not only communicate with their own species—they talk to birds also, and ally insects who prey upon those who eat their leaves. They attract allies by colors and scents. There are many ways of communicating."

The girls said nothing, but quietly digested the bunches of new information they'd been fed. "Here," Faas took a basket from a shelf and handed it to them, "While you're digesting those thoughts, bite into a few of these." The basket was filled with wild strawberries. They melted in their mouths, and dazzled their taste buds—far more flavorful than domestic strawberries. After that Stella even ventured to take some venison jerky. And it too, was wonderful and nourishing. She imagined the spirit of the deer running through her own veins. "This is good," Faas nodded. "You will need your strength."

After they finished their lunch, Faas led them back to his footprints that led into the stump. "You're going places today," he said. "*And…*" he smiled, "you're going to meet someone very special."

"I'd like you to look a little deeper into this old stump," Faas said, as he pulled a hardwood stick from one of his pouches and began tapping it on the hollow stump. "Oh, I almost forgot," he paused. "Before we proceed…some very simple techniques of self defense—"

226

"Self defense?" Clarsah interrupted, a concerned look on her face. "Against what?"

"The dark forces," Faas answered.

"Dark forces?" Clarsah took a step backward, her concerns increasing by the second.

"Nothing to worry about," Faas assured— "just to be aware of."

"Defense Against The Dark Arts!" Stella stated excitedly. "And this is the real thing!" she turned to Clarsah. "How cool is that?"

"Oh…wow…yeah!" Clarsah's eyes lit up. "Let's do it," she turned to Faas eagerly.

Faas eyed them confusedly.

"You know—from *Harry Potter*?" Stella stared at Faas incredulously. "You *don't* know? But you *have* read books," she raised her brows.

"Is this *Harry Potter* a famous author?" Faas asked. They both stared at him, bewildered.

"How can you be so *educated*," Stella asked, "and not know about *Harry Potter*?"

"I'll gazil it—later," Faas said.

"*Gazil* it?" Stella raised her hands, a questioning look on her face.

"Later," Faas nodded. "Now let's get on with *this*," his eyes widened. "As I was saying—techniques for protection. Not necessarily *against* the dark forces. For most of the forces of darkness—at least those you're likely to meet at this level—come from within ourselves."

"Within ourselves?" Clarsah looked perplexed.

Faas nodded. "Now, this may not *appear* to be the case—but as it is with the Shadow Beast, it is not what it *appears* to be. We must concern ourselves with what does *not* appear to be—that which we are unaware of."

Stella and Clarsah stood spellbound, giving Faas their undivided attention.

"Your techniques, at this level, are threefold," he informed. "These three are the basics. Everything else in defense, no matter how complex and evolved, is built from these three: *Sensing— Illuminating—Transforming*."

Faas drew three symbols on the earth:

A hand, with an aura emanating from the fingertips, representing *sense.*

A sun, with shining rays, representing *illumination.*

*A*nd something like a *Yin/Yang* symbol, only it was surrounded by a double spiral instead of the typical circle, representing *transformation.*

"Of course, to understand what it is you are defending, first you must know—*All* spring from the *One*." Faas eyed them seriously. "*You* start with yourself. You are one—one with the Great Spirit moving in all things—one with Awen."

"Second, your *self*, you must realize, is a sphere of dualities. There is the part that we are aware of—our conscious personality. And there is the part we are unaware of—our shadow self."

"When something frightening, aggressive, or disturbing comes into our experience, the first thing we must do is *sense*. Without sensing, we would never know we were attacked—*especially* when we are attacked by our own selves." He studied Stella and Clarsah to make sure they were following.

"When it is our own shadow that attacks us, it is termed; *an inside job,*" he said gravely. "There are many *inside jobs* that go undetected by our conscious selves. Therefore, it is vital that we *sense*. Many are senseless because they are afraid of the truth. They do not want to know their own shadow—or even that they have one. *They* will never be duirkens. In fact, *they* will never be whole functioning human beings."

"Once we feel, the next course of action is *illuminating!*" Faas lit up—his eyes wide, his excitement growing. "We must shed light on that which we sense. The light of awareness! Awareness is the next phase of evolution, growing from its root, *sense*. There are thousands of sub-techniques for shining the light of awareness," he spoke very quickly. "Searching, finding, re-searching—looking, seeing, reflecting—listening, hearing, echoing. There is lifting veils, curtains, blinds, shades. There is digging, exposing, tracking, reading. There is shining light into dark caves, dark thoughts, unconscious plots. We must be *really* looking, *really* seeing, hearing, feeling, understanding—and revealing. For true awareness does not belong to any *one*. This is all about learning *and* teaching as one. *This...is enlightenment.*"

Faas paused, studying the girls carefully, but only for a moment. Then he continued. "From enlightenment comes *transformation*. With awareness, we can change. Light transforms the darkness. The shadows melt before the light. And that which was hidden within shadow now can be transformed. Or," Faas smiled, "perhaps it is we who are transformed when we see things in a new light."

"Sometimes it is not the dark force that needs transforming, but our relationship with it. For Dark does not necessarily equate to evil. Both light and dark are part of the whole balance."

"Like Yin and Yang," Stella interrupted.

"Yes," Faas nodded, "like yin and yang. But there must be a constant revolution between these opposing forces—a constant exchange of information and energy–a constant transformation of each into the other. Like day and night. It is when energy—exchange—information is withheld we come to imbalance. Interaction between our consciousness and our shadow must happen."

"Wow," Stella sighed. "That is just...*amazing* stuff. But what does gazil mean?" Stella asked again, smiling.

"Ehh...later," Faas answered her shortly.

"Oh...okay," Stella shrugged. "I didn't know you could be so stubborn," she added nonchalantly, with an impish gleam in her eyes.

"Stella!" Clarsah stared at her friend, flabbergasted.

"It's okay," Faas smiled. "I didn't know *she* could be so pushy —but this actually backs up my other theory about her," he nodded with a wink to Clarsah.

"Theory? About me?" Stella stared wide eyed and open mouthed. "What is it?" she asked, completely transfixed.

"Later," Faas answered with *his* typical impish grin.

Stella drew in a quick rush of air, then sighed with a subtle shrug. It was time to get down to business. Faas instructed Stella to follow his tracks as far as she could into the stump. Clarsah, he instructed to do the same in the adjacent hollow stump where they now noticed another set of his tracks—only these tracks seemed to be coming *out* from this stump—apparently, without ever having gone in. Faas refused to comment on this, but resumed his drumming on the side of the stump Stella was entering.

Stella peered into her stump from the opening—focusing her vision deeper than she had before—as deep as she could perceive, down into the darkness of the depths. Yet, as she concentrated, her vision filled the darkness. In fact, there was light—the swirling energy that MacAwen had taught her and Patrick to see illuminated a descending passageway.

The tapping of Faas's hardwood stick on the outside of the hollow stump reverberated like a mesmerizing drum. It seemed to clear her mind instantly of all distracting thought. It inspired her. The passageway was opening. Stella's vision followed further down.

She found herself, actually entering the tree stump— descending the passageway. It spiraled down, under the ground.

Deeper and deeper, Stella spiraled around—deeper and deeper down....

For a strange moment, as though she had been dreaming, it seemed she had floated, spiraling down. But now she came to a different state of consciousness, she was wide awake, and she felt hardwood steps beneath her feet—a spiraling stairway. She came to a new realization: the rotted stump she had entered was only one branching limb of a great tree that she was now within. The wood all about her now was solid. There were no signs of rot. And here, as she descended, the opening grew much larger around. The wood of these stairs was almost like rock—carved apparently from some ancient, gnarled inner roots of this mighty oak.

The drumming intensified to a rapid pulse. It was enchanting. And it was vibrating in perfect sync with the brightening Awen energy pulsating all around her. The air in the stairway grew lighter as she descended. Now she could see the bottom. There was a great oak door within a huge, thick wooden frame. The drumming grew louder as Stella approached. The pulsating Awen brightened further. Stella reached for the door knob. It was large and round, hard and smooth—*a burl from the root of this ancient oak,* she imagined as she turned it to the left. She felt the door unlatching, yet so smoothly, it made no sound—not even a click. And though very thick and heavy, when she pushed the door it swung open with ease.

The drumming ceased at once, and she found herself stepping into a fair, green country. There were great, tall trees here—unlike anything she had ever seen—and beneath them, lush, green grass. It was a wild, forested place, yet it had an amazing, gentle, calm feeling about it. Wildflowers of all sorts were blooming before her. Fat, furry bumble bees droned and bumbled about—blissfully engrossed in the gathering and gorging of sweet nectar. It was so peaceful. And it was so very, very ancient. Stella could tell it had been just like this for a long, long time. She looked back at the doorway. It opened out of the trunk of a giant, *living* oak.

A music came into Stella's consciousness. A gentle, beautiful melody. She swayed within the sound. It held her, and as she relaxed into it, it felt like the music actually lifted her, physically, and rocked her—like the gentle, yet powerful, secure arms of a mother, swaddled around an infant. Stella floated blissfully in the sound, losing all sense of time or space.

Gradually, Stella realized that this beautiful sound in fact was the humming, singing voice of a woman. She hadn't realized her eyes had shut until she re-opened them—and found herself staring up into the familiar, yet wonderful and unfathomably adoring eyes of her mother. Strangely, she was not surprised. It was just what she would have expected to see—if she had expected anything at all. For all her life she had been held by this woman. It both was, and wasn't, Stella's human mother. It was the living, loving Goddess, Mother Earth herself.

In that moment, Stella *was* an infant, floating, swaddled in perfect bliss, seeing the world as though she had just opened her eyes for the first time in her life….

The singing voice soothed her so—and those loving eyes, so wonderful… She was mesmerized. And she drifted into blissful sleep….

Stella opened her eyes once more. Now she was lying in the lush, green grass. There was a warmth—as of sunshine, wafting upon her. And there was a brightness, but not from any fiery orb in this sky. No. There was no sun to be seen here, but light emanating from everywhere. Awen. It was all radiant, pulsating from everywhere—and from everything! The trees, the sky, the flowers, the bees—even from her own breath, the light emanated. Also, it emanated from her very thoughts. As she imagined, she saw the imaginations vividly before her. And now she remembered what she at first had only felt; she had known this place all her life—and that beautiful, beautiful, *powerful* woman.

Yes, She was very, *very* powerful….

Stella felt a rumbling from somewhere deep under the ground. Her heart too, she now felt quickening within her chest. Something great beyond her imagining was moving—rock, ancient and solid, stretching hundreds and thousands of miles in all directions—and more than a thousand miles thick.

Stella could feel the rock of the Earth as though she was one with it in body and mind. She could feel all the way through the dense, hard depths of the Earth—all the way to the core. Stella sensed the molten heart at the center of all the rock—the yoke of the Earth. She felt the intense heat of the gigantic swirling globe of liquid iron that is the Earth's core. But it was more than that… so much more. It was alive—pulsing, vibrating. A Central Sun. She felt the magnetism, the gravity. And suddenly—it was frightening.

Stella's heart pounded. Her vision blacked out. All, suddenly, was darkness. The darkness grew red. And then, Stella had a vision:

Across a turbulent ocean...there arose a distant volcano. It was gigantic, rising from a mountain range that spanned a continent, North to South. Her vision zoomed in on the volcano.

Sulfur and steam plumed from its spout as rivers of lava flowed down its sides.

Someone was walking upon the fiery cone, spiraling toward the summit, leaving a trail of footprints behind. Stella's vision took her closer. Every footprint had secret symbols embedded within them—as if this person was writing a great, esoteric saga.

Her vision zoomed in closer. Now she was there. No longer observing someone else. She *was* that person, walking the pattern that left the great story, written in tracks. Cataclysmic earthquakes ripped the land all about her and beneath her. Tidal waves like she had never imagined rumbled inland from every shore. The whole Earth shook. Mountains fell, crumbling. Great floods of ocean rose up and devoured the sinking land—until the great volcano was but an island in the sea. And still she walked upon it, striving toward the summit....

Plumes of dust and ash rose skyward, forming a cloud so thick the day turned at once to night. She was close to the crater at the mountain's summit when something came out of the shadows and seized her—a terrible, many tentacled beast! In a moment of terror she struggled, but could not move.

Then she remembered: *the threefold initiative.* First, *sensing.* She relaxed her frozen breath with a sigh, and sensed. This was *her* vision, *her* imagination. She felt it, from a quiet place deep inside her.

She slowly closed her eyes—then opened them suddenly wide. The sun burst through the clouds and she beheld the tentacles wrapped tightly about her—her own arms. *Illuminating.* There was no Shadow Beast here, but herself.

In fact, she was not even there; it was only a vision. *Transforming.* Stella sat up in the soft green grass. The volcano had been only a vision—thank goodness. But this place was real! She looked gratefully upon the fair, green country with its giant trees and warm, gentle light. She ran her fingers through the lush, silky grasses. It was so calm here—so peaceful, she thought, *I could stay forever.* But a voice inside her head said, "I've got to go back up." It was her own voice—and yet it was someone else's at the same time. And Stella knew that *that someone else,* for some reason, had to go back up, onto the volcano she had seen in her vision. But *she* had to get back up to Clarsah and Faas.

233

Then she heard another voice, singing: *"It is time, Stella Childs, time to receive..."* It was the gentle, powerful voice of the ancient mother.

The Mother Goddess was standing next to a sheer wall of stone. There was a groove in the great wall of rock, carved by a gentle trickling of water that must have been flowing for untold thousands of years to have made such an imprint. A stream of lava flowed by the Goddess's feet. She beckoned Stella toward her.

As Stella approached, the Goddess bent down, cupped her left hand, and scooped up a palm full of lava. She circled her right hand over it—three times. Then she dipped the thumb and forefinger of her right hand into the liquid stone. She raised it to her lips and tasted it, with an expression as though it was honey, then let it drip from her fingers, back to the stream.

When Stella stood before Her, She took Stella by the hands and knelt, guiding Stella to kneel with Her. First, She placed Stella's hands in the moist, rich clay where the water trickled from its groove at the base of the sheer rock wall. It was cool, yet it tingled with life energy. She turned Stella's hands over, and with Her fingertips, swirled the cool, wet clay in a circular motion around Stella's palm. She reached into the lava stream again and plucked a molten drop, which She placed in Stella's palm. Then She breathed upon it, and closed Stella's hand about it.

Steam issued from Stella's hand, but it did not burn. For a moment she felt something solid in her grasp. Then she felt it absorbing into her. When she opened her hand it appeared empty —there was only a round, clay stain in the center of her palm. But from it there emanated a golden aura.

The Goddess took her by the hands again and stood. Stella stood up with her, facing her. The Mother smiled and embraced Stella. As she did, she transformed into a mist, swirled about Stella, absorbed into her, and disappeared.

Then again, Stella heard the singing: *"It is time, Stella Childs, time to return..."* A gentle breeze came to her and swirled around her, holding her. And the arms of the mother lifted her… up…up…up….

Stella could hear Faas's drumming again, as she rose up through the dark tunnel. At first it seemed she was floating—

lifted, carried. Then she was climbing on her own, back up the spiral stairway. She could see the light above, at the end of the tunnel, and she wondered how long she had been down. She remembered the volcano, and suddenly, she faltered. Her feet grew weary. They felt heavy.

Somewhere in the world above, she thought, *that volcano is getting ready to blow.* For one vivid moment, again, she saw the trail of her footprints on the volcano's slope—each print embedded with symbols. Faas's drumming grew intense. She had to climb. She forced herself, though she now felt feint and thought she might collapse.

The drumming ceased suddenly, and she opened her eyes. She was lying on her stomach, her arms folded, her chin resting on her hands. Her head was in the opening of the old tree stump. She rolled over, and sat up. Faas was putting his drumstick back into its leather pouch. Clarsah was just emerging from the other tree stump, adjacent to Stella's. Only, somehow, it seemed to Stella that they had swapped tree stumps.

Stella's palm was tingling. She looked at it—and there was the clay stain—a golden aura emanating from it. She felt the tingling sensation moving up her arm. She placed her hands together, over her heart—and she felt the energy from that deep place—of the clay, the lava, the droplet of water, and the Goddess's breath—all combined, moving throughout her body, recharging her. With excitement she looked to Faas and Clarsah.

"Let us not speak now of your personal journeys," Faas said.

"What?" Stella raised her brows, shaking her head. How could she not speak of this most incredible experience she had just had? But then, another thought came to her. "Okay," she said, sighing. "But you've got to tell us what Gazil means." She looked Faas in the eye. "You promised you'd tell us later." She looked into the sky, then back at Faas. "Well—it's later."

Faas nodded. "Ok." He eyed the two girls studiously. "If you need to find out something," he asked, "what do you do?"

"Well," Clarsah rolled her eyes, "they teach us how to use dictionaries, encyclopedias, research bulletins—stuff like that. But when we just want to find out about something—fast—we google it."

"Precisely!" Faas nodded. "And when I want to find out something fast—I gazil it."

They stared at him, questioningly.

"Well—gazil is a rather large and complicated verb. It may help if I first describe its relative noun; a gazillion." He eyed the girls for a response. Aside from some crinkled and raised brows, there was none. "A gazillion is basically the same as a zillion," Faas continued, "only it has more pizzazz. It is not exactly a number. That is, it's not an exact number. You can't count to it— or even program a computer to count to it, like you can with a googol. A gazillion can be far, far larger than a googol, or a googolplex, or any number anybody can conjure. But also, it can be smaller. It's a matter of perspective. A gazillion is not a fixed number. It's just a way, way lot...more than we can count at a given moment. It changes with our perspectives and with our imagination. To a little kid, in an intense moment, twenty could be a gazillion."

"Wow...Faas," Stella interrupted, "that is an amazing description—but we do already know what a gazillion is. Can you just tell us what it means though, when you gazil something?"

"I *am* getting there," Faas smiled. "I just wanted to make sure you understood the noun before we got into the verb." He paused, drawing a heightened sense of attention from his listeners, his face glowing like one who is about to reveal a great secret. "*Gazil* is a word I made up myself, to describe how truly adept trackers, since ancient times, have *tuned in*—or, as you might better understand, *logged on* to the world wide web...of tracks and trails."

"Wow! I knew it was something like that," Stella exclaimed. "I knew there was a way—I knew you could do something like that! But how? Does it really work? I mean, can I learn how to like...surf it? Is it even better than the internet?"

Faas smiled. "It *is* an internet." His eyes widened to the heavens—then scanned about intensely over the ground. "It is as old as the planet—and even connected to internets spanning the stars. So, in a sense, you may perceive that it is much greater than modern humans' electronic internet. Yet even your little electronic internet is connected to the world wide web of tracks and trails. When I'm really, really tuned in, I can access almost anything. MacAwen—" Faas shook his head. "Whew—" he whispered, smiling wide eyed. "Well, someone like that can know anything, anytime, anywhere...." His expression went all dreamy. "That's why I call it gazilling!" he snapped back to the moment.

"Whew!" Stella whispered, echoing Faas's expression of awe. Clarsah just stood amazed, overcome by the possibilities. "But what does it matter, what you call it?" Stella asked.

"Everything," Faas answered. "All words have power. Names are especially important words. Google is a play on the word, googol—which is the largest defined number, other than googol*plex*, etcetera. That makes it a fairly good analogy of the modern electronic internet, which is obviously huge, but not infinite—in fact, barely a blip within the infinite. Gazil, on the other hand, is a play on the word, gazillion—which is potentially infinite, limited only by the universe—or by how much you are willing to expand your imagination. That makes it a good analogy to the world wide web of tracks and trails. But as to your other questions—it takes a great deal of skill in tracking to access the *World Wide Web* of tracks and trails. When one's tracking skills achieve a certain level—with so much practice and experience, intuition takes over—like walking or reading or riding a bike. You no longer need to think about what you're doing. You no longer need to study single tracks. Nor even track patterns. Yet in one single track—or with a single glance at a trail—the whole story streams through intuition into your consciousness, from thousands, mils, and gazills of pathways at once."

"How do you log in?" Clarsah asked.

"You log in, tune in, hook up, or link up—however you wish to perceive it," Faas answered, "by using your natural senses and intuition. You might start by reading animal track and sign, tree letters, wind—star tracks, wisps of mist and fog—soundtracks, scent-trails—"

"Soundtracks?" Stella interrupted. "Scent-trails? You mean like...like whale song—and like, how coyotes follow trails with their noses?"

Faas gave her a more subtle version of one of the odd looks he'd been giving her ever since they met—followed by a smile. "That's exactly what I'm talking about," he nodded. "Whales have an internet of song that spans the globe—only on a much deeper and broader bandwidth than that which most humans can connect with. But yes, even coyotes have incredible USB capabilities."

"USB?" Clarsah smiled wide.

"Universal Serial Bus," Faas answered. "Universal means it can connect to any available data by way of all data having USB interface. In modern computer technology it's a bit of an exaggeration. For instance, it doesn't take into account the information that can stream from one entity to another by way of scent. A coyote's nose is a *powerful* USB device. Now, *I* have an incredible, keen sense of smell by modern standards—but growing up I could never match my adoptive siblings. As good as I got at reading tracks with my eyes—my brothers and sisters could just plug their noses into a footprint—and whiff—they knew things about that animal that could fill a library of textbooks—things modern humans cannot even imagine. Sure, they could tell exactly what the animal had been eating its whole life—especially recently —and exactly where the animal got that food—and of course they could tell whether the animal was male or female—and exactly its size and weight—and what it was thinking and feeling—but also, so much more." Faas eyed his young friends. "Maybe this is a bit heavy for you—all at once, I mean. Perhaps you'd rather relax and listen to some music?"

The girls stared at him in silence. "Uh...we'd love to listen to your band, if that's what you mean," Stella responded. "But isn't that like—another way of possibly...*tuning in?*"

"I suppose it is," Faas nodded. "But it's much more than just that. To the extent one is willing to expand into the universal imagination—there are all sorts of USB terminals. But I think it's more fun, and wholesome, to shift through various different modes."

"I can *totally* sense how all this *infinite* consciousness can like, just *flow* into us and out of us from like *everything* else in the universe—and back to everything again," Stella's body moved with her emotions, as was her way, *feeling* to the depths of the meanings of every word she spoke. "But could you like—give us an example—how you might find out about some *specific* thing— like, an eighteenth century recipe for apple pie, or something like that?"

Faas stared at her open mouthed for a moment, then smiled. "Okay. I'll gazil it. And the perfect place to start surfing for a piece of information like that," he smiled, "is right here," he pointed to one of Stella's footprints. "A rare breed to be sure," he half whispered.

"Eighteenth century recipe for apple pie?" Clarsah shook her head, smiling. But she didn't bother asking where Stella came up with that one. She was used to it.

Faas got down low, studying intensely. He sniffed Stella's footprint. Then he touched it. Then he tasted it. His eyes turned up to the sky—wide and seemingly blank for a moment. Then he followed her tracks backward, fairly quick. He stood and stared about as though in a dream—his body swaying as though he were Stella himself for a moment—or one of her great, great, or even greater grandmothers. And then he snapped out of it. "I like it," he nodded. "The old world apples were so rich in flavor and pectin back then. Even the wheat was hardier." Faas looked at the girls. They eyed him questioningly. "First, the filling," and he rattled off the recipe: "seven to ten sliced apples, two tablespoons of flour, one cup of sugar, one loot of cinnamon, two tablespoons of butter." Faas took a quick breath and continued, "Then the pastry: three cups flour, one teaspoon salt, one cup butter, one egg, and one half cup water." He drew in another breath. "Combine the flour and salt—"

"Okay Faas!" Stella interrupted, rolling her eyes. "We get the picture," she laughed. "I mean, we get the recipe. But how'd you come to it?"

"Well—one thing connects to another," Faas began. "All things connect to everything else. If I look closely enough at a dog print, a fisher print, a coyote print, a sparrow print—even a mouse print, or whatever—" Faas eyed the ground. "See this squirrel track," Faas pointed to some marks the girls could not discern. "Well, they were left here just over a month ago. I can read from the Impaction Reverberation Symbols that this squirrel was pretty hungry—and not very fat. Of course, at the mere thought of any trail, I also am triggering gazillions of neuro-paths in my brain." Faas drew in a quick, deep breath, then continued speaking, very rapidly. "I know this squirrel—and his family. He took a scrape from a Red-tailed hawk last fall—barely got into his nest alive. I can hear the scream in my memory. It connects with more memories in an instant than you could imagine. That hawk hung around this squirrel's nest for a week. It had flown in from the West where its ancestors used to hunt. Those lands were filled with beeches, oaks, ashes, spruces, pines, and countless rodents who found shelters and forage amongst those trees. In that land, great stands were cut recently, for human habitations and businesses." Faas paused only for another quick breath.

"My words could never keep up with a millionth of what is racing through my subconscious," he laughed. "The tracks and trails I speak of are but a couple of strands of the gazillions streaming through my mind—like rushing water. That hawk hunted Norway rats imported from England on a ship that left ripples through Bermuda waters that...sending shoals of fish flitting South to the mouths of dolphins whose songs have told the tales of the sea.... I can tell by the Impaction Reverberation Symbols in this squirrel's tracks that it was afraid of something from above. I know who was watching. I have seen the tracks of this hawk—and the tracks of many other creatures who had this hawk in their consciousness—as I remember from *their* Impaction Reverberation Symbols. Only a gazillionth of what I'm surfing through is in my consciousness. Yet the more I am conscious of, the faster my surfing speeds become."

Faas's eyes shifted back to Stella's footprints. He placed a finger into a toe print, then placed the tip of his finger under one of his nostrils. He blocked the other nostril, and drew in the scent— his eyes going up and out of focus as though he was in a trance— or as though he was a computer, temporarily reduced from other functions while a large download occurred. His eyes flashed opened suddenly, and a wide smile appeared on his face. "Your tracks, Stella, tell everything about you—and of your ancestors. For a tracker like MacAwen—your entire genome could be decoded in a glance. I can only discern a fraction of the strands— yet enough to tap into that which I'm specifically searching for. The recipe was in your walk, Stella. It's in your own unconscious memory. I could just as well have gotten it from Clarsah's tracks— or from my own. Or even this squirrel's, though it would have taken longer. Apple pie is pretty basic—and there are certainly gazillions and gazillions of pathways to many recipes."

"As for reading your own tracks," Faas's eyes widened, "another time I can show you techniques for walking backwards in time—to retrieve memories...or even to re-program past memories —that is, the past as you knew it, in order to change future destinies by cause and effect. In essence, you can re-run and change past experiences to transform the present—and thus the future."

Stella shook her head—intrigued, but overwhelmed. "Let's go listen to your band," she sighed.

Faas nodded, smiling. And again, he led them back to his platform.

When they arrived, Stella noticed, someone else was already there. On a wicker chair, there sat a large woman—blacker skinned than anyone Stella had ever seen—yet she had bright, fiery, copper hair—very curly. Several bumble bees hovered about her. Stella turned to Faas, questioningly. He looked surprised, and was smiling like a giddy, child.

"NeeGaia!" he shouted, and ran to her unabashedly—like a five year old might run to his favorite grandmother. The woman smiled and stood up, her arms outstretched. She was considerably taller than Faas—big, round, and warm. Faas sank into her massiveness, embracing her lovingly. Clearly, he had known her all his life.

Yet Stella was also attracted to her—like *she* had known her all *her* life as well. NeeGaia made several interesting sighing, humming sounds, then looked at Stella and Clarsah.

"Ahh..." she opened her arms in an inviting gesture. while still embracing Faas. Stella gravitated straight away into NeeGaia's encompassing hug. Clarsah did, too. Somehow, Stella felt a familiarity with NeeGaia that she could not fathom.

NeeGaia released their embrace and stepped back to look at the three of them. "Ahh....heard I yer summons, Faas, hum..." she smiled pleasantly. "Came I ta meet yer friends—ah...and ta hear yer music—hum...."

Stella was stunned. This beautiful woman had a voice so like the Mother Goddess Stella had communed with, in that deeper place she had visited beneath this level of the De Da Mua. Yet the way NeeGaia formed her sentences was like MacAwen! Only NeeGaia seemed a bit less accustomed to forming sentences. She seemed rather to do most of her communicating by empathic sensing—and by sound. A style of hums, tones, and even grunts that were beautiful.

NeeGaia's arms seemed...extra great—even for her height. Her brow ridge was strong, like MacAwen's, but her forehead sloped back and her head was rather large. As Stella studied NeeGaia's face, she realized—she could not tell how old NeeGaia was. In moments she perceived someone who was like, maybe Faas's age—but then, the next moment, she looked more like she could be Faas's grandmother—then again, she wasn't *that* old looking. And yet, in various moments, NeeGaia's eyes had the look about them of someone older than Stella could imagine. She seemed ageless—or rather, all ages, always changing. *And always beautiful, in all her aspects,* Stella thought—thinking, also, about the goddess. The bees hovering about NeeGaia reminded Stella of those fat bees she had seen in the world below.

Stella was startled by a sudden, loud machine gun-like drumming overhead. She looked up. And there, on the side of a towering stump, was the hugest, red-headed woodpecker she had ever seen. Faas nodded to the bird, and withdrew two drumsticks from one of the pouches strapped to his side. The woodpecker went silent. The sun was near approaching the horizon. The whole world went silent—as though for a moment, holding its breath. Stella looked slowly around—and then up. Even the clouds were still. And then—a gentle wind rustled through the De Da Mua. The orb of the sun dipped over the horizon—red and brilliant. From it, rainbows of light emanated over the heavens. And the band, OmniVerse, began to play....

It started with crickets—quiet at first, then gradually loudening. Then the peepers kicked in. A distant bird chortled—and Faas tapped a drum stick to the side of a tree. A bullfrog croaked. Something like a katydid buzzed. Peep, peep—croak. The woodpecker drummed. Peep, peep, croak. Faas hammered the tree. A coyote howled in the distance. And Faas howled back. Splash, splash, went a beaver's tail. Several coyotes took to yipping. And Faas howled again. It all had a rhythm—an amazing groove. Stella was spellbound—and Clarsah, too. An owl hooted. A fisher cat screamed. All the music got louder. And the tempo grew. Faas strummed his sticks—over the poles of his platform's floor. NeeGaia hummed gently in the background. The music rose up—like a rising tidal wave. There was a crashing. And all around, Stella saw flocks of birds approaching—ravens, geese, blue jays.... Then out of the water there leapt a creature—followed by another, and another, and another. Otters! Though Stella didn't realize it until they all had splashed back under.

The tempo and volume of the music receded. Again, they could hear the crickets and peepers and songbirds. Again they could hear NeeGaia. The coyotes were very close now, and all around them—their tempo and pitch again arose. Suddenly, in the distance, from the direction of the setting sun came the singular howl of a wolf—deep, long and slow. And then from the east there came another. From north and south came a third and fourth wolf howl, followed by the primal sound of a hunting horn. Faas was beating out a fast rhythm now. But abruptly, he stopped. A didgeridoo could now be heard, droning...not far off, and getting closer. From the shadows, the source of the sound approached—a man moving slow towards them with his face buried into his instrument. Then the sound of the horn rose again—and behind it...some mysterious sound that Stella could only imagine coming from some ancient form of bagpipes. As the sound grew nearer, her imagination was confirmed. From the darkening shadows of one of the waterways came a coracle carrying the piper.

The music grew louder and louder—and faster and faster—until a great climax. And then, again, NeeGaia's humming, crickets, peepers, and now...the plucking of some sort of strings. And then more strings, droning by way of bows or slides or both.

All and all, it was the most awesome music Stella and Clarsah had ever heard. They listened, mesmerized, until the sky grew dark. Then Faas took a break from the band, and came to them. "Now I've got to get you girls home!" he exclaimed, his voice elated.

"That was the most awesome concert I ever heard!" Stella blurted.

"Me too!" Clarsah added. "Omniverse...rocks!" she exclaimed, overcoming her shyness.

"Ominiverse—" Stella looked excitedly to the sky, "is going to be the new Rage!"

"Is that a prophesy?" Faas asked, smiling.

"Ah...." NeeGaia rose up, wide eyed. "Hum..." she smiled, rolling her eyes. She gave Clarsah and Stella a farewell hug. "I *will* be seeing you again, dears."

The rest of the band continued the music—except for the piper, whom they now saw had two coracles in waiting to shuttle them back towards home. He was a short, swarthy man who spoke no English. Clarsah went in the coracle with him—and Stella, with Faas. They moved quickly along the waterway, and Stella realized—not only was this most amazing day coming to its end, but also, it could be a long time before she had another chance to ask Faas the burning question.

"Faas—" Stella faced the wild, young man nervously.

"Yeah?" Faas looked at her closely, apparently sensing the emotion in her voice.

"Um—" Stella's heart pounded in her chest. Why was she so nervous? It was stupid. It was nothing. "Well—I was just wondering—" she dug up the courage to ask. But why should it take courage to ask a simple question? What was the big deal? What was wrong with her? "Well—why do you sometimes look at me... strangely?" She looked away from him, then back again. "I mean—I don't know if I just imagine it. But—especially when we first met—it seemed like you— you gave me these looks—like—I don't know. But I never saw you look at the others like that."

"Oh...yeah," Faas nodded and shook his head. He sighed. "Well, I didn't know I was so obvious," he smiled. "It was just some things MacAwen had told me."

Stella stared at him, waiting for more.

Faas sighed again—with something that sounded like a nervous laugh. "We've known about—well, we sense certain presences moving about in the world. Sometimes people, and other creatures, are sensed before we meet them. You were predicted before we met you, that's all. And, well—I've seen your footprints. So, I've actually known about you for...some time." Faas sighed. "But I didn't know if I would, for certain, be meeting you. And then, I wasn't sure it was you—"

"Me? What about the others?"

"The others—oh, well—yes..." his voice trailed off.

She raised her brows, again waiting for more.

"MacAwen should have warned me about you," Faas added on a lighter tone. "You are of course very perceptive, persistent—and likely have the ability to pry information from the rocks of the earth. But MacAwen *has* warned me against saying too much, too soon. Too much new knowledge is like too much food—without the time to digest, to process—it can be dangerous—poison."

"So that gets you off the hook?" Stella asked.

Faas laughed. "Actually, it gets me across the water, and out of the boat," he answered as they were reaching the shore. "Thank goodness—for now, I mean. But I promise, soon...."

"Thanks for the most wonderful concert ever," Clarsah said to Faas and the piper. "And for teaching us so much, today," she added.

Stella nodded vigorously. "Tread the word," she smiled, holding up the peace sign and scrunching her fingers twice—making her signature "quotation sign" as she said "tread" and "word."

Faas stared at her—as though stunned—his jaw hanging opened.

"What?" Stella asked. "What is it?"

"It *is* you," Faas nodded, staring at her like she was the second coming of Christ—or the ghost of the greatest prophet from the ancient world. "It *is* you."

"*What*—is me?" Stella asked.

"You…" Faas shook himself out of his trance, his eyes lighting up, "you are the one who treads the word!" he broke into one of his odd coyote giggles.

"Oh my God!" Stella sighed heavily. "Why did you do that to me? You are like, freaking me out."

"I'm sorry," Faas smiled. "It's just…a really great saying," he nodded and winked. "Tread the word," he returned the gesture, complete with the finger quotes as he repeated Stella's signature phrase. Then he turned—but just before he vanished into the trees, he froze.

Faas was staring at Stella's tracks—his eyes glued to the ground. He slowly turned around, following them toward her. Just in front of her, he stopped—and Stella now saw what it was he was staring at. There was another set of tracks, crossing hers—boot tracks. Whoever it was had passed this way twice—once in each direction along the edge of the wetland. Faas shot her an alarmed look. And this time there was no hiding the seriousness in Faas's expression.

"It's Buck Cambull," Faas informed. "You unknowingly just crossed his path—*twice,*" Faas added, as though it was somehow significant. "First he was traveling in this direction," Faas pointed, "searching for *our* tracks or signs. On his way back," Faas pointed at the trail going in the opposite direction, "he *had* seen the tracks you girls left this morning—on your way to the De Da Mua." Faas looked at them very seriously. "Be careful," he said, "things are changing more quickly, I fear, than has been imagined." He gave the piece sign again. "Tread the word," he said, "but tread carefully." They nodded agreement. Then Faas turned and disappeared into the wood.

Stella and Clarsah stared at each other. "I love that guy," Stella sighed, "he is really, really wise—and yet...he *is...really* strange." She shook her head.

Clarsah raised her brows, nodding her head in complete agreement. And the two of them started for home on the old railroad path. What Stella didn't say that was on her mind was that Faas definitely was hiding something. She more than sensed it now—he admitted it! And for some reason she sensed he would only reveal the truth if she had time alone with him. She didn't know why, but whatever mystery it was that he had promised to tell her soon—he did not intend to tell the others. If she wanted to find out—she would have to approach him alone.

As childhood simplicity
complicates to its own ending....

Tentacles all around you
Tentacles within
In the bodies that bind you
as in the net-brain.
The hopeless hope listless
The helpless refuse
Yet a savior awakens
restoring lost views

Chapter X:

Memories, Madness, and Dreams

Stella had been tracking a large creature through a wood that had seemed familiar, at first. But now she did not know where she was. It was getting dark. Then she stumbled upon her own tracks —following those of this large creature. Now she realized, this was no mere creature. It was the Shadow Beast. It had led her in a circle. This had happened before. What this meant, of course, was *it* was following her. And suddenly, she felt it. Silently, it was closing in from behind.

Stella turned around, searched the darkening woods. Everywhere, shadows loomed—growing shadows. She could not see the Shadow Beast's form, but sensed it very close. Alone in the dark, she listened intently. She heard a breath—a large, raspy breathing. And then—a terrifying whisper....

"No." Stella said out loud. "I'm only imagining. This is just a dream!"

"You *are* waking up," the voice of the Shadow Beast answered her. "But when you awaken, *fully,* you will realize that your whole life is no less a dream than this."

Stella opened her eyes, her heart pounding. She lay in her bed. It was Monday morning. *Perhaps the Shadow Beast was right*, she pondered. But there was little time for pondering, much less meaningful contemplation. She had to get up for school....

The next two weeks...were the worst and the weirdest Stella ever had—at least since coming to her new school. Reflecting back on this time, two weeks later, it seemed more like a long series of strange dreams than any cohesive chain of memories—a series of strange dreams from which she could never return, not even by awakening.

First of all, time constraints and unlucky *co-incidents* had prevented her from getting back to the De Da Mua—or even very far into the forest. Ever since Faas pointed out that she had *double crossed* Buck Cambull's path—or that Buck had double crossed her path—it seemed their paths kept crossing and re-crossing again. He was stalking her. Once, at least, Buck had actually stalked her all the way back to her yard. This was more than a little unnerving because now there was little doubt, Buck Cambull knew where she lived. Still, she would have risked crossing his path again, to get into the De Da Mua.

It was a series of events at her school, however, that eventually made it impossible for her to even try....

To be fair—at her old school they had tried to force her onto ridacull—and two other drugs she couldn't even remember the names of, while at her new school they had said at first that she just needed fresh air, a few special exercises, some tutoring—and to be allowed to be a child.

She had almost believed she actually *liked* the Spruce Hill Goethean School. It had its draw backs. Teachers, and certain parents, were always quoting Goethe: *"Goethe said this,* and *Goethe said that—*and *Goethe did this,* and *Goethe that...."* Stella could hardly stomach it. But she did seem happier in the school program Mr. Goethe had designed—until the infamous last two weeks of seventh grade, and life, as she knew it.

Certainly, Spruce Hill had not been as bad as the public school she had attended previously. But to be clear, *not as bad* does not mean good. And more and more, as this year progressed, *not as bad* had become the most common phrase used to describe Stella's new school. Oh, there were variants, like *not as harsh*, when

248

describing punishments, *not as much,* when discussing homework, and so on. But Stella *always* could read between the lines—even if she did have trouble staying *on* the right lines. She felt she was not as easily fooled as the average student. Contrary to popular belief —especially amongst teachers who only saw the lack of attention she had for their (in Stella's humble opinion) *pathetic* subjects— Stella had a broad and deep awareness about nature, people, politics—and the order of the universe in general...as she imagined it. This gift—or curse, as it usually was perceived, even by Stella herself—is precisely what caused Stella to be singled out by a certain member of the visiting team of expert teachers and psychiatrists; *Dr. Warburger*....

Stella's feet pounded the Earth as she recalled how this... *person* had been invited into her life. *The bearer of the sign of the Double Cross,* she thought to herself, as she ran through a pitch black forest—fear and confusion swimming through her consciousness with the memory; *Dr. Warburger*....

Memories, madness, and dreams all intertwined in a mass of confusion as Stella ran. Two weeks of memories, madness, and dreams....

There were those placed in charge of the school's politics who suffered from the incredulous belief that it would be a benefit to the school's credibility if it were visited, analyzed, and scrutinized by a team of *experts*, who would hopefully write a positive summary to the long report that the Spruce Hill teachers had written on the school's practices—and ultimately give the school their *official stamp of accreditation.*

What absolute nonsense, Stella thought from the moment Mrs. Caledon first told them about it. They're going to come in here and observe us, and study us, and interview us, for one week—and then our school gets its little stamp that says; "we are what we say we are." And Stella hardly gave it another thought, having more important matters on her plate.

But there was more to it than that, much more. Now she knew —all too well. Yes, there were other reasons for accreditation procedures. And they were not all good reasons. But since there were so many stated reasons—and since they all *seemed* to be good reasons—and since they were *almost* all good reasons—the ones that were bad could be easily hidden.

There was one reason, at least, that *was* bad—very, very bad—in fact, diabolical. Which of course means evil. If Stella had only known the reasons, she could have protected herself. Unfortunately, she had thought the whole thing to be nonsensical—until it was over.

On Monday morning they had pulled her from her ordinary class. Not that she really missed the ordinary class—it was just that she rather despised the little set up they had waiting for her. And she despised the inhuman being who was waiting to observe her: *Dr. Warburger*—as if Stella needed a doctor. She wasn't sick. On the other hand, they *were* making her sick.

Dr. Warburger was a tall, broad, fierce looking woman with pure white, shoulder length hair—straight and stiff. She had piercing blue eyes, a very long nose—and breath, so nasty, Stella thought, if she got too close it would knock her unconscious. This menacing psychiatrist was dressed in a rather masculine black suit. A white collar and black tie were all that could be seen beneath Dr. Warburger's perfectly fitted, wrinkle free blazer. But of everything Dr. Warburger wore, that which made the greatest impression upon Stella was the silver pendant, pinned to the front of her jacket. On it was a symbol of a Double Cross. And Stella had an immediate prejudice against this woman which no logic could shake.

Warburger's voice was quite deep—*more like a man's than a woman's*, Stella thought. And she had a foreign accent so peculiar, Stella wasn't sure if it was a speech impediment. Stella had to take some tests—and play a few stupid little games, while *"Dr."* Warburger observed—like Stella was some kind of test rat finding her way through a maze.

When she told her mother about it that night, Ms. Childs' eyes took on the momentary appearance of two smoldering volcanoes. She made a phone call to Stella's teacher. There were some words —fireworks, almost. Stella's Mom had pulled her from public school precisely because of...*psychiatric politics* remarkably similar to what Stella seemed to be describing.

Miraculously, Tuesday was free from anomalies—until Stella got home. Her mom informed her that Dr. Warburger herself had called. "She seems like she *really is* a smart—and a thoughtful woman. This wasn't about promoting drugs after all," her mom had said with a relieved smile.

Oh no. Of course not. Dr. Warburger was a strong advocate of natural remedies, like physical and mental exercises, vitamins, talk therapy etc., etc....

Dr. Warburger had promised: *"Ve can make Stella's school life more comfortable, more easy...more normal...."* Dr. Warburger, as it turned out, was far more clever than Stella had at first imagined—but no less diabolical. On the other hand, Stella felt a growing, painful sense that her Mom was not as clever and on top of things as Stella had always believed.

Wednesday the testing resumed; "Stella, I vould like you to lie down on zis couch and make yourself comfortable. Have you ever heard of hypnotism? I vill take you on a guided journey. Really, I am just going to tell you a story. It is your job to use your imagination, to see ze ssings I descvibe to you...."

Stella had pretended to cooperate. It really could have been fascinating, even fun—under different circumstances.

There was more of the same on Thursday. Then Friday, the meeting happened. The result was shared with Stella's mother—which she in turn shared with Stella. Stella now remembered it as though she herself had heard Dr. Warburger's voice: *"In litewally tens of ssousands of cases much less sewious zan zis, dwugs awe pwe-scwibed after a mere tventy minute assessment. I have gone to all zis extva twouble to examine all ozer possibilities. To wespect yo desires to not give dvugs to yo child—and yet somessing clearly must be done for zis poor girl. She must be suffering terribly. She is literally off ze charts in terms of normalcy—in bvain function zat is. I'm not saying she isn't smart. She is in fact a very bvight girl. But her pvocesses are all backvards and mixed up. Her methods of ssinking and solving pvoblems are peculiar. Vhat I am vecommending is a series of neurological tests. Ze sooner ze better...."*

Stella was forced to spend, what turned out to be six excruciating hours that Saturday—one on one—with just her and Dr. Warburger.

Stella's mother had asked Dr. Warburger many questions during their long dialog that evening. Stella herself only heard what her mother relayed to her. But in her mind, now, Stella heard only the voice of Dr. Warburger:

"Vizout dvug intervention, I view zis case almost as an emergency. Ma'am, can you not see ze pain your daughter is in? Does she not speak to you?"

"Vell, she confided in me over ze course of zis veek. For v'one ssing, she has made up a delusional story about a little bvown man who lives in ze forest—and a vild man who vas vaised by volves."

"Yes, volves! And she is suicidal. She has a plan all vorked out—how she vill jump fvom a certain cliff, smash her skull, and zen fall into ze vater of a gveat bog—a bog zat she and her fviends have been svimming in by ze vay. She vill surely dwown—if ze impact does not kill her! I hate to ssink how zose awful cveatures vill tveat her remains."

"I am sorry ma'am. I just cannot bear ze responsibility if you do not act immediately. I am compelled by ze law."

"Boston Youth Hospital, psychiatric vard. I can get you in, v'one veek fvom tomorrow. 10:30 AM."

"You ask your daughter about zis little bvown man and zis vild, feral man. You vill find out...."

This was the most confusing and disturbing part, because Stella had never told Dr. Warburger about Faas, MacAwen, or the De Da Mua. She would never.... Could Stella really have been hypnotized? And revealed all this to Dr. Warburger while in a trance? But it seemed so ridiculous. That fool of a psychiatrist could never hypnotize Stella, without Stella letting her—certainly not without Stella knowing about it.

Yet how else could that psycho-woman have known so much? Maybe Stella *had* been hypnotized. And if she had, then maybe...Stella *was* crazy. Because she had no memory of being suicidal. *Well, I guess I am depressed sometimes*, Stella had thought. *And I do sort of check out—wander into other worlds or whatever, during math classes...and lots of other times when mundane stuff can't hold my attention. Everyone tells me it's like I'm not there.*

It seemed, at times, that Stella was a natural—gifted with insight and imagination. She could glimpse order in chaos—make logic out of nonsense—coherence out of meaningless. Intuitively, she could see through the chaos in natural law and order. She could translate the deeper meanings of apparently random cause and effect. She was a leader with unique intelligence. But in school—as a student—she was a failure....

Stella was in the forest, following the trail of a strange, unknown animal. Clarsah was with her. She was studying the tiny Impaction Reverberation Symbols within the tracks—and suddenly she knew! It was the greatest revelation of all time...

"Stella..." Mrs. Caledon called her back from dreamland, "you need to be on the right page now...."

"On the right page now...on the right page now..." It echoed inside her mind.

"Nice going in math class, Stella," David smiled. "But you do have your lines memorized, don't you? The play is in one week."

Stella eyed him the way a doe would eye a lone coyote that was too bold—maybe too close to her fawn. David was comfortable in crowds, and on stages, but it was unwise of him to offend her, she thought, when there was no one present but themselves.

"Unlike when in a surrounding horde," she said, glancing at the unpopulated space on the playground around them, "when a coyote is all alone, a doe might just slam her hoof through the side of his skull," she smiled at him.

"Whoa...easy...." David gave her a horrified though rather humored look. "Sorry if I offended," he offered, casually. "I just wanted to offer you my help practicing the lines," he gave her a quick version of his puppy dog look. "Besides, I thought the *coyote* was your *guide*," he added cleverly, with a *let's be friends now* sort of smile. Stella was reminded of her newly changed perception of David—since he had met MacAwen. Yet for some reason, the smallest of jabs from this boy roused from within her the greatest complexity of emotion.

"It's a metaphor." She rolled her eyes and shook her head, thinking how obsessed he was with his *glamorous plays* and *grand performances,* how smug he seemed—and so frustratingly sophisticated. She strove within to conjure a metaphorical hoof to slam through the side of his ego-centric head. *He thinks he's so perfect*, she thought, but she could think of no further metaphors, so she cut straight to the chase; "I think this school has way too many performing arts in comparison to the things that build *real* character," she said, "like the more *contemplative*—and *meditative* arts and crafts," she added with an air—"like woodworking," she eyed him with raised brows.

Woodworking was one subject that *she* excelled in, but David...well, he *would* be good at it, *maybe—if he wasn't so lazy. Maybe, if an audience was in the shop watching and cheering for him,* Stella thought. The seventh graders at Spruce Hill were growing more conscious of *self esteem,* and how their teachers were trying to build them up—or some of them—mostly through performing arts.

"I think being comfortable with oneself, *on stage,*" David retorted with his own air, "requires a higher degree of self esteem."

"A higher degree?" Stella was struck dumb for a moment, by his *clueless-ness.* But the boy knew how to push the right buttons. "A higher degree—of shallow ego, more like it," Stella struck back.

"Ouch," David placed a hand on his heart.

"Just because actors and, like, *public* people, know how to *act* like they have the highest self esteem," she gave him a penetrating gaze, "I bet most of them can barely stand it when a deeper, quiet type really looks them in the eye." Stella continued staring into his eyes.

David rolled his eyes, but Stella felt confident she had hit the nail right on the head. Not that David was really just one of those shallow types; *he* was complicated—which was why she felt mixed about attacking him further. But with the perfect sentence forming in her head, she could not resist banging the nail home; "A deeper...*inner* self esteem can only develop where one must work on oneself, constantly—*without* an audience looking on and clapping for you."

David raised his brows, then looked about, nodding. "I suppose you're right," he offered casually. Then, spotting Patrick in a group of their friends standing next to the school building, he shouted, "Hey, Patrick! How are *your* lines coming?"

"They're coming," Patrick stepped forward with a nod and a smile. "I think our teachers are just a *little bit* extra edgy," he said, raising the pitch of his already high voice, "with all these visiting teachers *observing them*." He smiled with wide eyes.

Stella noticed how David, like a crafty coyote, could trot carefully, yet casually, away from the sharp hooves of a doe, toward the comfort of his crowd. But there was so much more to David; Stella thought further about how easily David had seen MacAwen, when others had had to strive or had simply not seen....

Stella's attention had shifted then, to something much more disturbing to this doe than any coyotes—or wolves, even. She thought of the Lyme Disease epidemic she kept hearing about from teachers and parents. It was spread by *deer ticks,* which suddenly seemed to be everywhere in the fields and forests around their homes and school. It was the perfect metaphor for the visiting accreditation team. Like an intentionally implanted infestation of ticks, they quietly crept around the campus, barely noticed. Most of them were harmless. But Dr. Warburger was a tick that carried the virus—and it seemed like somehow she was latching on to everyone in the whole school. All the teachers listened to her— like she was some kind of god. And strangely, *co incidentally*, it was Dr. Warburger who heightened the actual *tick scare:*

"Zis is a wery visky pvactice," Dr. Warburger commented, loud enough for all to hear, as she observed Stella and her friends on the playground, "allowing ze childven to play outdoors, vith ticks all avound. You do not even have paved gvounds."

The Spruce Hill teachers were very quiet. But at least Mrs. Caledon said *something*: "The parents who send their children to *this* school feel strongly about children's needs to have a connection to the natural world."

"Zese parents are *poorly* educated," Dr. Warburger snipped. *"Zey* should not have ze aussority *here*. Zere should be *laws,"* she eyed the teachers, aghast. "I vill advise ze aussorities on *ziz* matter."

"How can *our school* let itself be influenced by this group?" Stella shook her head. "I thought *Spruce Hill* was *supposed* to be different."

"According to Mr. Gregg," Iona quoted, mocking his English accent, "the teachers at Spruce Hill follow the inspirations of Goethe, not the dogma of modernism."

Stella looked around the grounds. "It's looking more and more like...like we're following along—" she eyed her friends gravely, "like, maybe on a *slightly* different path than public schools, but still ending up in basically the same place. We're all getting *infected,*" she raised her brows, "by the same—"

"Would you *please* shut up, Stella!" Gretchen cut her off, shaking her head and eyeing Stella distastefully. "You're just *freaky.* Our school is nothing like public school. Anyway—public school isn't that bad—"

"*You* don't know what it's like!" Stella cut Gretchen off. "*You* never had to go!" She glared wildly at Gretchen; and for once, Gretchen was silenced. "First, they force you to get vaccinations, which everyone knows are full of all kinds of poisons—most of them much worse than the diseases they supposedly protect you from. Then they have this program called like, *No Child Left Unique*, that they force all the teachers to follow, even though most of them know it's really horrible for kids. It's a method, designed to turn us all into IRZ's. Then, if you still don't quite fit in, they have forced drugging, for like, total mind control. That was the final reason why my mom took me out of public school—"

"What are IRZs?" Patrick interrupted.

"Idiot Robot Zombies," Stella continued, with a sideways glance at Gretchen. "Just look around you. They're everywhere." She shook her head.

"If you ask me," Iona stepped in, "Spruce Hill *is* getting more and more like a public school. My dad has studied Goethe's writings—and he says Goethe was totally opposed to any forced homework assignments—ever. He believed forced homework assignments were the greatest destroyer of kids' will to learn."

Stella stared at Iona, dumbfounded. This was incredible. Maybe Goethe really was great. But what happened? Why didn't the school follow his teachings anymore? She glanced at Jessie—just as Jessie glanced at her. "Isn't Iona so wise?" Jessie exclaimed, wide-eyed, then looked back up at their tall friend.

Iona gave Jessie a quick smile, then continued. "Goethe believed kids naturally learn much more when they have free time—and most importantly, they learn how to think for themselves. That was the main reason why he created Goethean Schools. Because he saw what was happening to kids in state run schools.

256

They were trained to memorize facts and follow directions. But they were losing their ability to think for themselves or be inventive."

"Wow..." Jessie whispered. "That's like...*amazing*, Iona."

"It's incredible!" Stella cut in. "But what's happened to our school then, is like...*evil*."

"Ah—*dear* me!" Tom interrupted, placing both hands over his heart. "How did our *wonderful,* little school ever succumb to all this evil?"

"Pressures from parents who want higher standards," David cut in smugly—ignoring Craig who bent double laughing at Tom's antics.

"Higher?" Stella turned on David, almost in a rage. "What's higher? What's lower?" she threw up her arms. "Sometimes higher is lower. Who are they to judge?"

"Uhh...they're the people with all the money," David answered, as though *she* was clueless, "the ones who pay for all the school's expenses."

"Oh—I get it," Stella nodded angrily. "Our curriculum is *now* decided by those with the most money. Maybe it's getting *worse* than public school around here," Stella fumed.

"Then maybe you should just go back there," Gretchen retorted, having regained her composure and seeking revenge. Stella felt a volcano blazing up inside her, but when she turned her fiery gaze to Gretchen she was met with a glare so cold it stunned her. "I wish you would," Gretchen stood, facing her, "go back to public school, I mean," she folded her arms. There was an uncomfortable silence.

"I don't feel safe here," Craig smiled, looking around at his buddies.

"Our school is getting very dangerous," Robert added dryly.

"Our school is turning into a prison camp," Tom piped in with a smile.

"Actually, it *is* a prison," Stella added her two cents worth.

Gretchen rolled her eyes. "If this is a prison, Stella, tell me, where are the bars?"

"We live in time as well as space," Stella answered.

"Uhh...what's that supposed to mean?" Gretchen placed her hands on her hips, eyeing Stella as though she was some inferior, sub-human, sort of creature.

"Well..." Stella's head cocked back, her eyes looking dreamily about as she gathered her thoughts.

Gretchen shook her head in disgust when it appeared to her Stella *had* no thoughts. But Stella was gathering broad and deep thoughts from afar and wide. Not the type of thoughts that reside on the tip of one's tongue.

"*Bars,*" she continued at last, "constrain a prisoner's freedom to designated bits of space. *Schedules* contain a prisoner's freedom to designated bits of time. If you were in a concrete and barred prison you'd not be able to leave the walls. But within those walls you might have more freedom to do what you wished in your *time* than what you have at this school—*locked within your schedule.*"

Gretchen frowned, shaking her head, rolling her eyes, and sighing. "Freaky answer, Stella. But at least, *maybe* you're not just *totally* stupid after all. Maybe you're just weird and crazy...."

Coming from Gretchen, Stella had taken that as a compliment. Sometimes it seemed, maybe she *was* just a weird, spaced out girl.... Yet other times, there was a part of her that just knew things. Not normal things like math or any of the subjects you're *supposed* to know about. But weird things....

Stella was running as hard and fast as she could, through a pitch black forest, as she thought of these *weird things* and strove to remember all she could of the past two weeks. Everything had just kept getting worse and worse, and stranger and stranger, as the two weeks progressed. It was not until the series of events culminated in a real life nightmare that Stella tried to put it all together and make some sort of sense out of it. But a part of her felt she was trapped in a time loop—and now there was little time to think. For Stella was running for her life—her mind drifting through unconsciousness, and subconsciousness as she ran.

Another playground image re-played in Stella's memory:

She was standing with a circle of her friends. "All we see in the physical world is limited to two eyes," Stella said, "and we see only out of one spot on the lens of each eye."

"Yeah, so?" Tom laughed.

"Imagine if we were all eye lens—like, our whole body, seeing in every direction all the time," she searched around, wide-eyed, her body swaying as she spoke. "Or better yet, imagine if our vision was unlimited by any single physical place—seeing in all directions from everywhere...."

"I think you should go talk to that visiting psychiatrist," Tom suggested with his typical smile. Craig was smiling very wide, but said nothing.

"Where do you come up with all this crazy stuff, Stella?" Gretchen asked in her usual demeaning tone, but with a bit more interest.

"I don't know," Stella sighed, dreamily. "It just comes to me."

"Like, out of thin air?" Gretchen smiled disrespectfully.

"Yeah—" Stella answered. "But the air is not so thin—nor empty."

"Yeah," Gretchen nodded, smiling, "and your skull is not so thin either—but it *is* rather empty."

Stella rolled her eyes and smiled back, sarcastically. "Not everyone is able to understand all that they think they understand."

"Wow, Stella, you make so much sense," Gretchen retorted.

"Actually," Patrick's high voice cut in, "to quote Richard Feynman, one of the foremost minds in modern physics, *if you think you understand quantum mechanics, you don't understand quantum mechanics.*"

"That's totally dumb, Patrick," Tom laughed.

"Patrick, that does not make any sense at all." Robert put in his dry monotone.

"Actually, I think that's a good one, Patrick," Craig added, with some sincerity. "It doesn't make any sense, but it is a pretty good saying." He smiled.

Stella did appreciate Patrick coming to her defense—though as usual, his choice of words was only vaguely helpful in an argument against your more normal type seventh graders.

"Oh..." Stella looked up suddenly with a glowing smile. "Another raven." She had been seeing ravens everywhere she went, lately—at school, at home, while out shopping....

"Certain sign of death," Tom assured her with a smile. But Stella rather felt she was being watched over by benevolent spirits....

Of course, not all spirits are benevolent. Some are ambivalent...like the *elementals*. And like all ambivalent spirits, the elements can be manipulated....

Stella thought of the *Stealth Clouds,* which Uncle Ken had told her about.

"Stealth Clouds are not natural clouds," Uncle Ken explained as he pointed to the sky from her back yard. "They're man-made. And in fact, they are partly metallic."

"Metallic?" Stella looked questioningly into Uncle Ken's care worn face. His piercing eyes stayed fixed on the sky.

"You see that one, there?" he pointed to a long, narrow cloud that covered an eighth of the visible sky from north to south, but stretched beyond the east and westward horizons.

"Yeah," Stella answered, a shiver coming over her and a sense of dread. Yet she was intrigued. Of course, Stella had already noticed such clouds.

"I watched that being created," Uncle Ken continued, "only half an hour ago." He turned and lowered his gaze to Stella. "Stealth Clouds first appear as long, thin clouds—like ordinary contrails from jets, only much bigger and longer lasting. They are made from *aerosols*: tiny airborne particles—or rather, *particulates*, which form the nuclei upon which water vapor condenses."

Stella stared dumbly at Uncle Ken.

"The nuclei are the center pieces upon which invisible vapor condenses into either ice or water clouds," he explained. "This is how all clouds are formed. Don't they teach you this stuff in school? No, I guess they wouldn't," he shook his head. "Well, there are naturally occurring particles in our atmosphere—from salt, dust, volcanic ash, and all kinds of soot. Of course there are man made pollutants of many kinds, from industries. But I'm not talking about accidental by-products. I'm talking about a very intentional effort." Ken turned his gaze back to the sky. Stella did, too, just in time to witness another Stealth Cloud being created above them.

"There are several theories on the methods of putting particulates into the stratosphere," Ken went on. "Some say they are sprayed ahead of time, from far above, to begin attracting moisture from the atmosphere as they fall into the flight paths of commercial airliners, which then add more moisture and particulates from their exhaust emissions. But the really huge Stealth Clouds are initially formed—or should I say, sprayed—from pressurized aerosol containers in very large jet tankers. These are military tankers, carrying cargoes of aerosols, including metal particulates...and other elements."

Stella stood shocked. She said nothing. Of course, she had been noticing Stealth Clouds in the sky before Uncle Ken told her about them—and she had been having nightmares. But her conditioned logic had told her it was just her own imagination...and paranoia. Now the reality could no longer be logically denied.

"Who is spraying these? What kind of metals? Why?" Stella was filled with questions.

"They're mostly made of barium and aluminum particulates," Uncle Ken informed her. "It's part of a top secret conspiracy being carried out by the Triple Leverage Corporation—in tandem with the military's deceptive *High Frequency Active Auroral Research Program,* or *HAARP*, as they call it," Ken smiled sardonically, "which among other things is microwaving our atmosphere. It's all about controlling the weather—possibly to ionize the atmosphere for their global communications and control grid. Definitely for shadow warfare. And ultimately, just for control—total control. It's clear these Stealth Clouds are the big contributor to the greenhouse effect, which they say causes global warming; yet soon they will tell us the spraying is needed to combat global warming. This is how big, secretive, and very deceptive organizations operate."

Uncle Ken smiled, as he often did after saying something controversial. It wasn't like he was a total fruit cake who expected your typical IRZs to comprehend what he was saying or think it was sane; he just liked to try to get people to think. But Stella could hardly tell when he was joking or serious—and she didn't understand many of the words her uncle used, so she just focused on one; Barium.

"What's Barium?" she asked.

"It's a radio-active, heavy metal," he replied. "Nothing you ever want to be breathing when it falls toward the ground." And she almost wished she hadn't asked. Everyone knew Uncle Ken was really smart, but also, quite odd...and more than willing to speak about things normal people would rather not even know about.

Stella was not sure if it was Uncle Ken's stories that had initially given her a bit of paranoia and some bad dreams about toxic, mind numbing Clouds; she might have heard him in the background, talking about Stealth Clouds to her mother, or to Ari. But now Stella was seeing the *Stealth Clouds* forming with her own eyes—almost every day. Instead of dissipating in a few seconds, like normal contrails, the *Stealth Clouds* stayed in the sky —often for hours. They remained visible as they slowly spread out and changed shape. If there were enough of them made over several hours they would connect with one another, forming a total cloud cover—even on what would have otherwise been a beautiful, clear day.

Though she had not seen much of her Uncle Ken since he had informed her of the existence of Stealth Clouds, Stella began her own intensive study of these wispy clouds of strange and bizarre formations. When sunlight reflected from them rainbow colors appeared. *Not the pretty type*, she thought, *but a chemical type, rather like those seen in an oil slick.*

They mostly formed into cirrus clouds, but also dropped into cumulo-stratus, stratus, and even cumulus cloud forms when conditions were right. They seemed to make her feel ill—and cause the worst confusion and lack of focus she could ever remember experiencing. Total head fog. Could the barium be affecting her brain waves? She would have to ask Uncle Ken.

Of course, she had experienced the bouncing back and forth between varied moments of head fog and total clarity all her life. But once she became aware of the Stealth Clouds—whenever she noticed the head fog, she'd look up, and there would be Stealth Clouds. And whenever she noticed a moment of great clarity—she would look up and the sky would be totally clear of Stealth type clouds.

Stella grew quite concerned—even scared. She started to talk about the Stealth Clouds with her friends. Clarsah pretty much believed anything Stella said. Patrick wasn't quite so sure. "Well —I'll have to get verification from my Dad on that one," he responded.

Then there were the others:

"Oh, yeah—right," Tom laughed. "And aliens have taken over our government—and they're planning to eat our brains. And first they want your brains, because you're special—right Stella? Say— shouldn't you be wearing one of those tin foil hats?"

"Ha!" Gretchen burst out laughing.

"Whoops!" Tom said. "Crap—" he sighed.

Stella glared at him. She had started thinking Tom was a friend. Now she felt like slapping him in the face.

"It sounds like you've been listening to your insane uncle again," Gretchen added.

"Okay—that's enough now." Tom stepped between Stella and Gretchen. "Actually, you never know." He looked at Gretchen."Stranger things *have* happened." He turned to Stella. "I was just kidding about the tin foil hat."

Stella sighed, relieved that she had not slapped him in the face.

Later, some of Stella's friends told their parents about Stealth Clouds. Amazingly, most of the parents either believed, automatically, that the whole theory of Stealth Clouds was a hoax, made up by crazy conspiracy theorists like Uncle Ken—or it was just too overwhelming and scary for them or their children to have to think about. Some of these parents told Mrs. Caledon about it. This was during the week after Stella had been evaluated by Dr. Warburger. Now Stella was *talked to* not only by Mrs. Caledon, but also, by the *psycho-psychiatrist* herself, as Stella now referred to Dr. Warburger.

In her "therapy session" with Stella, Dr. Warburger lectured Stella about Conspiracy Theorists, Hate Groups, and White Supremacists. Stella simply could not fathom any connection between those who simply wonder about things—and people who are hateful and racist.

"What does questioning our government have to do with hate groups or racists?" she asked. But then she realized, she was asking the wrong person. Anyway, the true answer came into her thoughts; *the conspirators embedded in our government are a hateful group—of not merely white supremacists, but world supremacists.*

"Be careful, Stella," Dr. Warburger warned. "You may end up in pvison..or vorse...."

Stella finally survived that little meeting—by pretending she believed the "official story":   Stealth Clouds are nothing more than ordinary clouds—and the so-called chaff-trails, that Stealth Clouds allegedly emanate from, are nothing more than ordinary contrails, from ordinary jets.

This *official story* was totally ridiculous. Stealth Clouds looked *nothing* like ordinary clouds—at least, *not to anyone who studied clouds*, as Stella did. Nor did the so called *chaff-trails* being sprayed upon the sleepwalking population look anything like ordinary contrails. At least not to anyone with a bit of sense. Certainly not to anyone who observed the sky on a regular basis. It wasn't like Stella was an IRZ who never looked closely at the sky —or believed every obvious lie the *official experts* tried to feed her.

On the other hand, the *official psycho expert* probably didn't believe Stella's lie either. For with a vengeance, Dr. Warburger, and her team, stepped up the campaign of interrogations which they had been engaged in all week.

None of Stella's friends were spared—nor were any of her not so friendly acquaintances. Of these, Stella was sure Gretchen had been the one most willing to relay stories that backed up Warburger's theories about Stella's delusional mind.

Though Stella could only imagine what Gretchen might have said, she was convinced that Gretchen had first leaked the stories about Faas and MacAwen. Stella was the first to be interrogated— the week before. She had determined not to tell Warburger much of anything. She asked her friends also, to not cooperate with the psycho-lady. But once the leak was made by one kid, the others were pressed hard.

Tom, Robert, and Craig—during their little interrogations— had denied ever seeing any little brown man—but admitted to meeting Faas. This raised new concerns—for Dr. Warburger now determined that *Faas*, in fact, *was* a real person—and the entire school was forbidden from entering the forest.

David, Clarsah, Andy, and Patrick—during their respective interrogations, had not only backed up the story about Faas, but also, stuck by all accounts of *the little brown man*. After that, under pressure, Stella also admitted to the validity of the stories. But Dr. Warburger was far from done. She kept working on them

—now, with a whole team of psychiatrists she had brought in to work under her—always against one kid at a time.

"Zis," she said, "is a very serious case of delusional ssinking. Ze ozers, at zis stage, are mainly just protecting zeir fvend. *Communicable Delusional Protectionism* is a natural first wesponse amongst some childven when a fviend zat zey love, is suffering fvom hallucinations. I see zis type of behavior fvom time to time—it has been extensively studied, and it is wery vell documented."

Eventually, the team of psychiatrists got all the others to believe that the little brown man had only been a fantasy, a figment of their imaginations, and that they had unconsciously deluded themselves into believing it as a way of embracing and protecting their more deeply afflicted friend, Stella.

Finally, Stella had even pretended that she now believed it *was* all just illusion—to get the psychos off her back. But Dr. Warburger was still concerned about her. And about *zis vild man:*

"Ze childven all vitnessed zis vild man dvugging young Billy Bob Cambull wiss some sort of poisonous dust vhich he actually blew into ze young man's nostvils. I contacted ze aussorities—and zey tell me zey believe zis man is a vanted terrorist zey have been searching for. Intelligence sources say he is part of a terror organization zat pvactices vilderness survival and has hideouts in ze forests. Ze name of zis terror group is *Clan Taluv.* Zey are extvemely dangerous—and known to use various mind contvol techniques. He probably has dvugged all ze childven to confuse zem and get zem to believe his vild stories. It seems he has used zem as guinea pigs for his mind contvol experiments. Stella, I'm afraid vas exceptionally susceptible, as she alveady vas depvessed —afvaid and vesisting ze vealities of gvowing up—and genetically pvone, I believe, to delusional ssinking."

In the days that followed, Stella grew more and more confused —and depressed. The sky, constantly, was filled with Stealth Clouds. Sometimes they were layered so thick the sky turned dark gray with their ugliness. Also, Stella began noticing *black lines* that emanated from the noses of the Stealth Sprayers, sometimes traversing the whole visible sky in the pathways in front of the jets. No one else thought it was unusual or unnatural—and no one would talk about it. Not even Stella's sister, Ari. And Uncle Ken was never around anymore. And anyway, everyone else thought Uncle Ken was crazy. Maybe it ran in the family, as Dr. Warburger had implied. There *was* something wrong with her. I guess I *am* abnormal, she started admitting to herself. Maybe they *could* help her. Maybe her attention *would* get better. Maybe school *would* be easier. Maybe Faas *was* part of a terrorist group. No. She would *not* believe *that*. He was the coolest guy—and he had rescued them from the Cambulls. Dr. Warburger had it backwards:

"Zis Billy Bob is one of ze Cambulls. Zey awe a family of mis fortunates whose only hopes of education and success awe by vay of ze military. Intelligence sources believe zis vild man's terrorist group, zis Clan Taluv, have been experimenting on ze poor Cambulls."

When at last Dr. Warburger perceived that Stella was having doubts about herself, she seemed suddenly to have another side to her. Was it compassion? Or trickery? Stella did not want to let her guard down. Dr. Warburger's voice had grown more soothing. "You veally awe not all zat unique, Stella. Alzough your ssought pvocesses *awe* far fvom normal, I have seen ssousands of cases zat at first appeared to be just as stvange. Yet we have cured zem all. It is as simple as reconfiguring a computer zat has its pvocesses mixed up. You do play with computers, yes? Vell—sometimes a computer's *vegistry* has errors vhich must be scvubbed, so to speak —to improve ze vay it boots and operates."

Dr. Warburger seemed to make more and more sense. Maybe she really was compassionate. Maybe she was not at all what she had seemed to Stella.

"Stella," Dr. Warburger said to her one day, in a very quiet and serious voice. "You may not be so delusional after all. I vill tell you a secvet zat may help you—even zough ze MIF vill be upset vith me. Do you know vhat ze MIF is?"

"Yes," Stella answered. "It stands for the Middle Information Front, a secret part of our government."

"Wery good, Stella. But it is not a secvet part of government," Dr. Warburger smiled. "It is a part of government that gathers secvets. As you know, I am in contact vith intelligence officials. Ze ozer day, as I discussed zis case with a colleague fvom ze MIF it vas leaked to me zat ze terrorist gvoup know as Clan Taluv awe using hologvaphic pvogections to confuse, manipulate, and ensnare zeir victims. Do you know vhat a hologvaphic pvojection is?"

"A holographic projection?" Stella raised her brows. "You mean like in Science Fiction? Like when someone or something is made to appear—but isn't really there?"

"Zat is correct. But somessing *is* zere. An energy field zat may even feel solid and veal to ze touch. Clan Taluv has zis technology. And Stella...zis, I believe, is how zey got you, and even some of your fviends, to see zis little bvown man."

There was a silence following Dr. Warburger's statement—like that which occurs after a bomb goes off—when the deafening explosion has passed and all that is left shock. Then comes the return of consciousness—but changed by the realization, the integration of new information. It was like Stella's brain had crashed and rebooted.

"I am very sorry, Stella. I know zis must be most difficult for you. Vhen ve are young and innocent ve tend to believe vhat ve vish to believe. You, vith your dveam-like vays, were the most vulnerable to this awe-vull tvick.. But vith the correct tveatment and re-education pvogvam I am fully confident you vill become the visest, most vell adjusted, and un-tvickable person. You vill excel in school and you vill become a highly successvul person."

Stella stared in disturbed confusion. A part of Stella hated Dr. Warburger more than ever—because another part of her knew that Dr. Warburger actually cared about her, was trying to help her, and was incredibly smart.

Stella said nothing to Dr. Warburger, but got up and left. She repeated nothing of Dr. Warburger's words to anyone, but remained quiet and detached—in confusion, in contemplation, or both.

None of her friends now believed in *the little brown man*. MacAwen himself had said, "to not believe." Could that all be part of some twisted trick? Mind control? Stella had so thoroughly *sensed* that MacAwen was so real and so good. Now she could no longer trust her own senses. She felt so weak....so tired...so confused—*depvessed*.

Dr. Warburger *had* been all over the world. On top of being a psychiatrist, she was one of the top scientists in the world—probably *the* top scientist in her field of study. And she *had* seen so many cases—and of course she really must know how to help. She was the top expert in the whole world....

Stella's destiny, it seemed, was etched in stone; the following morning she would be checking in at Boston Youth Hospital's *Psychiatric Ward....*

Once more, Stella was following the trail of the Shadow Beast; Buck's machine for certain, but now she was connecting the dots. This thing was not *just* what it appeared to be. And yet, it *was* what it appeared to be—only, also—much, much more. *And this time it's not just a dream*, Stella thought. *I'm awake now.*

The full moon was high in a cloudless sky, making the tracking conditions quite good on the trail to the Cambull's. Stella had sneaked out her window earlier, hoping beyond hope to get back into the De Da Mua—and get some questions answered. There was so much she needed cleared up. She *had* become afraid now—to meet Faas alone. But her desire for truth was stronger than her fears. And she could *not* believe that Faas was a terrorist. Yet she had to find out for sure.

On her way to the De Da Mua, however, she once again crossed paths with Buck Cambull. Fortunately, this time, he was not aware of her. She heard the noise of his approaching machine and hid off the side of the path. He drove past without event. *But what was he doing out at this hour*? Stella was compelled to track him. He was not heading toward the Cambull home, but toward the town of Mason.

She had a long way to go that night. And along the way, strangely, the tracks of Buck's machine changed—several times. It appeared they transformed—from the single, narrow ski mobile like track, which she and her friends had once mistaken for a tail— to a pattern like that she and her friends had observed; there were boot tracks to either side of the center track. But these boot tracks were much, much bigger. And then, the center track disappeared altogether—so it appeared Buck's machine was walking on two legs!

There was no way he could pick the machine up. It was way too heavy. Anyway, the straddle of these huge feet were placed much too far apart, and the stride was much too long to be Buck's. *What was going on here*? Stella wondered. *Buck must have modified his machine*. Again, she remembered what MacAwen had said; *The Singular Confrontation—between the beast who manipulates the Shadow Beast—and the one whose tracks have foretold all*. She could no longer hear it ahead on the trail, as it had gone too fast before her. But she continued tracking—eventually at a slow run.

Stella jogged all the way to the end of the trail. It came out at the rear parking lot of an old warehouse on Route 31. The parking lot was dimly lit, by a single spot light on the rear of the building; and there were three cars parked in it, near the back entrance. Two of these cars were very odd looking to Stella—very large, black, and...*like the kind you see on TV, driving important people—not the kind of cars you see in Mason, New Hampshire*. There was no sign of Buck's machine.

Stella crept up to the building and peered into the window on the back door. The back room was empty, and very dimly lit. She tried the door, but it was locked. Not that she would have entered; she was just checking. She circled the building, trying to get a peek inside from somewhere. But all the windows were totally dark, other than the one in the back of the building. The front door also, had been locked.

But just as Stella had gotten almost all the way around to the back of the building again, she found an opened window. Like all the rest, it led into a dark room. But when Stella stuck her head inside, and her eyes adjusted to the darkness within, she noticed a thin line of light on the floor; this light, she figured, must be coming through a crack under a door on the opposite wall.

She glanced at the space behind her, and into the sky. The full moon had tracked far toward the western sky. *It must be like two O'clock in the morning,* she thought. *And this is crazy.* But she could not stop herself. She had to see.

She climbed silently through the window. Carefully, she crossed the room. She found the door knob above the crack of light. Slowly, she turned it. Even slower, she opened the door a crack and peered out.

This door led into an empty hallway. The lights were not on, but the hallway was dimly lit by light emanating from under the cracks of every doorway on the opposite side of the hall—and from somewhere around the corner, toward the back of the building. Stella opened the door wider and slipped through.

Once in the hallway, she could hear voices. She reached for her amulet. She was scared. But she had to see what was going on here. She followed the hallway toward the front of the building, where the hallway was darker. She rounded a corner. Then she approached one of the doors leading into what she was guessing must be one very large room in the center of the building—the room with the lights on.

Her heart was pounding as she reached for this doorknob—and her hand was shaking. She squeezed tightly, and turned. Carefully, slowly, she opened the door and peaked within.

It was a very large room indeed, with a very high ceiling. On the far side was what looked like an altar. Twelve men were facing it, kneeling. Their backs were turned to Stella, so she could not see their faces.

Above and before the twelve men, suspended over the center of the altar, was a great, white pyramid that shone like polished alabaster. At the apex of the pyramid was the orb of light which illuminated the pyramid, and all the space around, above, and below—except for that which was directly beneath the shadow cast by the pyramid itself.

As her eyes adjusted to this light, there, in the shadow of the pyramid—directly beneath it—she beheld a giant, black effigy; it was a figure, standing almost invisible before an equally dark backdrop in the center of the altar—and frighteningly similar in appearance to the Shadow Beast she had seen in her dreams. The top of its hooded head was against the bottom of the pyramid suspended above it.

The men were chanting quietly. Looking quickly up and around, Stella noticed a sky light through which she could see a helicopter parked on a pad on the roof. *This is pretty high tech for an old warehouse*, she thought, *and very, very strange—and creepier than anything....*

A great base drum sounded sudden and rapidly. A stunning, but very weird, scary woman appeared from behind the dark effigy, dancing erotically—her arms flailing over her head—a large snake held in each of her hands. The twelve men stood and cheered.

Three of them approached the altar. "Oh! Oh! Oh!" they each chanted once, as they dropped to their knees before her.

Oh my God, Stella thought, that is just...disturbing.

The woman disappeared behind the dark effigy—as a sudden shower of money rained down—apparently, from the top of the pyramid. The other nine men now rushed forward, clamoring for the falling bills. "Fifties, hundreds, thousands," they chanted. "Fifties, hundreds, thousands..."

"Fools!" a sudden loud and booming voice silenced the chanting men. "Fools! Heathens! Worshipers of dust and lust!" A man in black robes appeared, wielding a great spear high over all the others. They all went silent, cowering before him. "The New Dawn arises!" he shouted. "And with it a new power...for those who will be *illuminated!*" he pointed his spear to the top of the pyramid.

And in that moment, the light from the orb at the top of the pyramid intensified. The twelve men arose from the floor and formed a circle around their leader. He stood unmoving, his spear still pointing to the orb at the top of the pyramid. The spear point was jet black. The shaft was silver. And from the butt end of it their trailed a thick bundle of long, wavy threads that started out white, fading to gray and finally red at the tail end.

"I now bring to you," the leader boomed, "**Ur...Jah... Bull...Fom...ev...sed!**"

The rapid base drum sounded again. The light at the top of the pyramid turned into a beam, scanning the great room. Stella ducked down, horrified, as it passed over the doorway she had been peering through. But none noticed the cracked door. The light beam continued turning until it rested on a strangely familiar object, also at the back of the great room, but opposite the side where Stella was; *Buck's machine.*

Buck's machine started up. It moved toward the front of the great room—no one driving it. Stella looked back at the circle of men. She now noticed that Buck Cambull was amongst them— and looking very proud. But there was another familiar face, also. An older man—she had seen him on television! He was a senator! What on Earth was he doing here?

She looked back at Buck's machine—and it did the strangest thing. It stood up and began walking toward the altar on two legs.

Arms protruded from its sides. Buck's face was ecstatic as he watched. As it reached the altar, the machine's arms closed around the dark effigy, squeezing it, compressing it, and stuffing it into a compartment within the body of the machine. The drum rolled. The men cheered.

Now the machine stood beneath the pyramid—in the form of a man, but faceless. The pyramid descended onto the head of Buck's machine. There were a few clicking sounds. And then the pyramid arose, revealing a transformed head—and face—upon the machine. This face was so strikingly like the face of the Shadow Beast Stella had seen in her nightmare that she just froze in terror. It's eyes ignited. And behold; the machine could see. In a sudden voice like thunder, it spoke:

"The Dawn has arisen! The eye of the one, again, sees all!" The men cheered. **"Yet—"** the Beast-Machine silenced them— **"*She*...is amongst us:"** A beam of light from the eyes of the Shadow Beast Machine shot straight to Stella's position—and fixed upon her! She stood frozen—in terror—as the circle of men stared in amazement at her face, illuminated in the doorway....

Stella's heart pounded so hard it jolted her to full consciousness. She sat bolt upright in her bed, her eyes wide. One booming heartbeat, she felt. Then...another. Finally...a third heartbeat. Finally, she let out a stifled breath. The dawn had just arisen.

What a horrible dream, she shivered, her heart still racing. *I can't believe that dream came out of my own mind. I guess I really do need this evaluation.* She only wished she could have *really* sneaked out, and gotten to talk to Faas. Now she wondered if she ever would even see him again.

Yet she could not help imagining; her dream might have been more than just a dream. Perhaps she'd had an out of body experience and had witnessed something that actually happened. If that was true, *they* were aware of *her.*

On the other hand, that was just the kind of thinking that had gotten her singled out—ever since she was a young child.

On the highway to Boston Youth Hospital Stella had looked up at the sky and observed three jets spraying their metal particulate contrails in the exact form of a "Double Cross."

She had a sinking feeling she had stepped into a snare. In all, she counted thirteen Stealth Sprayers during the two hour trip. By the time she arrived in Boston the entire sky was obscured under Stealth Clouds. Her mother would not talk to her about the subject. And not another soul in the city seemed to notice—even though, to Stella, it seemed impossible not to notice. How could the whole population be so unaware? So senseless?

The next thing Stella knew, she was checked into the *Psyche-Ward* at Boston Youth Hospital. She had to remove her own clothes and wear their ridiculous gown. The only thing of her own that she was allowed to keep on her person was her amulet. Not that they wanted her too, but she vehemently insisted that she had to keep it in the pocket of her hospital gown, for so long as she had to wear the thing. Thankfully, her mother backed her up on that one. She would only have to remove it for the CT Scan and the MRI.

Of course, no one would ever have allowed her to carry her Survivalist Knife into the Psyche Ward—if they knew. But Stella had carefully bundled it in her clothes—and miraculously it came in undiscovered. She didn't know why the knife was so important to her. But it was a gift from Uncle Ken. It was hers. And it belonged with the backpack.

They had her lie down in a bed—as though she was sick. *"It's just to make you comfortable,* they had assured. They offered her television, junk food, popular magazines, video games...all the stupid stuff to take her mind away from what they assured her were just a whole lot of boring procedures.

"Now, we're just going to put an I.V. into your arm," the nurse informed, as she approached Stella with the equipment.

"An I.V.? But I'm not having an operation. I haven't lost any blood. And I don't need any medicine," Stella responded, concernedly.

"Oh no," the nurse laughed. "It's nothing like that. This is just normal procedure. It's the universal protocol these days. We just need to make sure your electrolytes are in balance—and be able to monitor your signs while you're being tested, that's all. Trust me," the nurse added, "it's a whole lot better than getting a hundred different needles for every type of blood test they'll be running on you."

That sounded logical enough. And so it began. And it really wasn't too bad for the first few hours. Stella did watch a dumb movie—and some even dumber TV. It got so boring, eventually she even flicked through the dumb magazines.

On the TV news there were reports of a conglomeration of mega electric storms, raging from Texas and the Southwest to the Midwest. There were tornadoes, power outages, flash floods, and general chaos. For Stella, that news had been the most exciting event at the hospital—up until the moment she overheard Dr. Warburger's conversation with the neuro-surgeon. From that point on, never again in her life was there a dull moment.....

First, Stella had been strapped down, and placed inside a machine. There were strange lights blinking all around her. She imagined she'd been abducted by aliens—and they were doing strange experiments on her to see how the human being functioned —or maybe they were experimenting to see how they might alter the human being—change her brain wave patterns, alter her DNA. The fantasies helped pass the time during the weird, and long, boring tests that the doctors really were performing on her.

But then there was *the helmet*. Stella came close to the limit of her toleration when they made her wear this totally freaky helmet on her head, with weird wires attached to it.
"We need to monitor your brain functions," they told her.

She tried to keep it together—to remain calm. But she was feeling worse than a little edgy. She felt like an experiment, like a freak. It was bad enough just wearing it. But then they even made her keep the helmet on when she went to the bathroom. She felt she had lost all her privacy and control over herself. She was just a case—a head case.

Stella's fate changed drastically when she came out of the bathroom, disoriented, and took a wrong turn. Or was it a subconscious choice? She walked the length of the hallway and rounded the corner. There, emanating from a cracked door with a sign on it reading; "PRIVATE," she heard the distinct voice of Dr. Warburger.

Stella put her ear to the opening and listened. Now she heard the voice of the neuro-surgeon whom she had met earlier, while undergoing tests: "If you advise, then G-6 will be the adjusted placement of the micro chip in this patient's head."

"I do." Dr. Warburger answered. *"Ze most vonderful ssing for zis girl,"* Warburger continued, *"is zat she von't ever need to even know zat she has zis chip—and viss our constant monitoring and contvol, she can live a normal, happy life."*

And that was when Stella reached her breaking point. She realized she had taken a wrong turn. In this place, wrong was right. Suddenly, it all became very clear to her.

She returned to the bathroom, removed the insidious helmet with all its wires, and all the other wires they had taped to her head, stamped on it until it was good and flat—then plopped it into the toilet, and gave it a royal flush!

Shaking, she returned to her room, went straight for the backpack that was stashed in the corner, and removed the small bundle of Tee shirts strategically packed in the center of her clothes. She didn't know why she was taking it. It was just instinct. But she knew she would look suspicious walking the halls of the psyche ward with her backpack, so she had to leave that behind.

As Stella walked down the hallway, away from her room, she saw a *white shirt* walking toward her. She nonchalantly stepped into the nearest room. But almost subconsciously, her right hand worked its way through the bundle she was holding, and grasped the handle of her knife—her left hand still holding the bundle of Tee shirts over the blade.

The sight she beheld in that room shocked her. There was a girl, about her age, strapped flat to a bed. On her head was a helmet exactly like the one Stella had just removed. But clearly, this girl already had her microchip implanted.

Her eyes were wide and her head twitched. She looked exhausted, but seemed pretty much relaxed now. In the bed next to her was another girl—also with a helmet, but without the bed straps over her. She was sitting up with a portable desk in front of her. "I would like some more drills, please," she asked.

"More fractions, decimals, or algebra?" a woman's voice answered from behind a curtain on the far side of the room.

"I don't mind," the girl replied.

"Well, *you've* come a long way," the woman answered. "I'll bring some more work sheets to you in just a moment." Stella noticed how every time this girl's eyes started to wander from the desk on her lap, they darted back onto it. It was a subtle movement, but it was unnatural. The girl never even noticed Stella standing inside the doorway. Stella imagined this girl having been very much like herself only days before. Perhaps the one who was still strapped down would be just like this one in another day or two.

The nurse strolled through the curtain, pushing a cart in front of her. For that moment, as the curtain was pushed forward, Stella saw a third girl in a bed behind the curtain. This girl also had the helmet on, and was strapped to her bed—but her expression was frozen in terror.

An ancient, wizened man with bright, terrible eyes stood over the girl. He reminded Stella at once of "the Emperor" from "Star Wars." He raised a lever on a hand held control device—and the girl's head turned upward. The man glanced at Stella—and she was struck, as if by an electric shock. In his eyes was something absolutely horrible—an intelligence so cold and calculating it was not human, at least not as she had believed human to be. For a moment she imagined him a reptile, or an alien. He hardly regarded her, turning back to his work with a subtle smile. But Stella stood frozen, as if thrown into a sudden trance....

The curtain had closed behind the nurse and had reopened. As Stella snapped back to her senses she realized, the nurse was staring at her! Fortunately, the nurse, also, was momentarily shocked to see an uninvited visitor. But unfortunately, the nurse also, was coming back to her senses. The nurse turned suddenly, and opened her mouth—as if to alert the man behind the curtain. "Uh... Uh—" the nurse seemed to stutter.

Stella never again wanted to see that man with those terrible eyes.... *He is a Nazi scientist*, she thought. She didn't know how she knew, but she was sure of it.

Seizing the moment, acting purely on instinct and intuition, Stella drew her knife from the bundle of Tee shirts—and like a knight about to charge into battle, raised it high over her head.

The nurse stared, frozen in shock. With her other hand, Stella grasped for the amulet in her pocket. Then she turned and ran out of there.

Stella knew that running would attract attention. She knew also, that the doors to the ward were locked. She knew they'd have already noticed she was missing. And in moments, the nurse she had frightened would recover from her shock. Stella's surface personality would likely have panicked, but something from deep in her soul took over. Stella needed to be cool. She needed a lot of luck. And her timing had to be perfect.

She wrapped her knife back up in her Tee shirts, squeezed her amulet, prayed, and followed her intuition. It was like she was in a trance. Everything around her moved in slow motion. And she moved, strangely relaxed.

She carefully rounded a corner. She saw the door at the end of the hallway—the door out of the Psyche Ward. It opened, and a janitor came through, pushing a mop and bucket. She ran for the door.

"Close that door—quick!" a commanding voice shouted to the janitor. Stella looked to her left and saw a tall white-shirted figure approaching fast from another hallway. It was the neuro-surgeon! Dr. Warburger was right behind him, her arm raised in commanding gesture, pointing to the door and practically pushing the neuro-surgeon forward.

It would be a close race. Stella looked back toward the door— and at the janitor standing frozen in the opened doorway. The janitor eyed Stella dumbly—as though *he* was in a trance. Stella looked prayerfully into his eyes. The janitor smiled.

"Close the damn door—now!" the doctor shouted, desperately, as he realized Stella might actually escape. It would be close, but the doctor had to get around the janitor's bucket. The janitor looked at him, confused. "Now—moron! Close it!" the doctor yelled, losing his cool, as he and Stella closed in on the door. Stella glanced at the doctor one last time. She would reach the door before him, but would be within his arm's reach. The janitor stood, blocking the doorway; but Stella could dive and roll by him if need be—if the janitor didn't lunge at her. "Grab her— now!" the doctor raged, "or *you* are in huge trouble!"

The janitor, suddenly shaking, let go of his mop and bucket, raising his arms like an angry bear—but not in the direction of Stella. "Go girl, go!" he whispered—as Stella bolted past him.

The doctor was right on her heals, reaching for her. But *he* was not cheered on by the janitor. Stella felt a desperate hand, grabbing her by the hair and cuff of her gown, but then it let go. She glanced over her shoulder, and saw the janitor slam the doctor against the wall. She could hardly believe it; *help un-looked for*. She paused for a moment, staring back at him gratitude and amazement.

"I been in *huge trouble* all my life, Doc!" he shouted in the doctor's face. "You know why?" he smiled. The doctor did not respond, but stared, frozen. He had the doctor by the collar and was shaking him. "Cause—every time...some pompous... demeanin'... white collar bastard... like you...pushed me to the edge —I pummeled 'em! And stamped on their faces!" He widened his eyes in a crazed and threatening gesture.

"But not this time," the janitor smiled. "I don't get paid enough for this crap!" He glanced at Stella, gave her a nod, then shooed her off with a hand gesture.

She lip-synced a *thank you*, then turned and bolted down the stairway, hoping the janitor didn't get himself into trouble as she heard the last of his fading shouts. "So—I'm a moron, am I? And you want me to grapple with little girls, do you? Well, we'll just see who gets in *huge* trouble this time! When that girl's parents sue your ass!" Stella pushed open the door at the bottom of the stairs and hit the pavement. She was on the street and running free.

Stella found an entrance to the subway system less than a block away. She ducked under the gate and hopped on the first train that stopped. At that point she didn't care what direction she was headed in—as long as she made some distance from the hospital. She was a country girl, stuck in the city with no money, no phone, and wearing only a hospital gown. But she was free! And being Stella, she was resourceful. She'd visited the city enough times to basically know how to get around on the subway system. Anyway, she didn't care if she was lost. She was free! She felt exuberant.

After she got a comfortable distance from the hospital, Stella got off the train to study a map of the rail system, so she could take the proper trains to get as close to home as possible. After all she'd been through, ducking under the gates to steal a free ride was a piece of cake.

While on the train heading North, toward home—after studying a middle aged man, and determining that he was a good sort, she asked to borrow the cell phone he had clipped to his side. She called her older sister, Ariana. Hearing her story, Ari drove straight down from New Hampshire, and in less than an hour, met

279

Stella at the Train Station in Fitchburg, Massachusetts. It was 12:10 AM.

Ari pulled up just in time—less than a minute after the train. Two men in black suits were standing near the turnstile, holding some kind of palm devices. They looked at Stella, nodded to each other, and one of them had just started to approach when Ari's car pulled up. Stella ran for it, and jumped in.

"Go! Go! Go now!" Stella screamed. Ari looked at her like she was crazy, especially as she noticed the knife in Stella's hand that once again was unwrapped. But Ari took off just the same, to appease her frightened little sister.

"I'm not crazy! I'm being chased," Stella told her.

Clearly, Ari didn't believe Stella was actually being chased. But she none the less went along with her disturbed little sister's desires, for the moment. Obviously, Stella had been through a horrible ordeal—even if she *had* misunderstood what was *really* going on—and in her panic, had imagined the worst. "Don't worry, Stella," Ari soothed. "I've talked to Mom. You're coming home now—and she won't make you go back to that place if you don't want to."

"*Want* to?" Stella thought of the girls who had RFID chips implanted in their brains. "Never--" she half whimpered.

When they got near home, Stella and Ari stopped at a 24 Hour Coffee Shop, to get some hot chocolate. Stella stashed her knife in Ari's glove compartment. On the television in the coffee shop were more reports of the coming mega electrical storms. They had reached Pennsylvania and Western New York—and would be in New Hampshire by daybreak. People were warned against going outside. They all looked so scared and concerned on the news. But Stella was excited. She looked at the clock. It was 12:50 AM.

Back on the road, they had driven almost all the way home when flashing blue lights came on, from an unmarked car tailing behind them. They were being pulled over! And for no good reason, as far as Stella could imagine. "You weren't speeding, Ari!" Stella panicked. "There's no reason for them to pull you over! They're after *me*!"

"Calm down, Stella!" Ariana rebuked her little sister. "They just get a little extra nosy when it's like, one o'clock in the morning. All they're going to do is run a check on my license and registration," she explained.

But Stella was shaking in her hospital gown. On impulse, she popped open the glove compartment. "They're going to try to take me!" she cried. "I have to get out of here!"

"Stella!" Ariana eyed her as though she had gone crazy. "Calm down. Nobody can take you!"

"Don't look at me like that!" Stella cried. "You're the one who is always talking about corruption and conspiracies!"

A stunned sigh issued from Ari's mouth, her eyes wide. "I'm sorry," she said softly. "Mom was right. Uncle Ken and I shouldn't say all that in front of you."

You don't understand, Stella thought, staring silently at her sister. Of course, not even Stella herself could comprehend what was taking place—only what her instincts told her. She grabbed her knife, and a little flashlight that she saw, stashed in the glove compartment—then carefully snapped the little door shut, breathing deep. As soon as the car stopped, Stella opened the passenger door and bolted. *I have to find Faas,* she thought.

Stella had gotten into her woods, no problem. But somehow, *they* had tracked her. Stella did not know who *they* were. Stella was not absolutely sure *if* they were. Perhaps she had truly gone mad and had dreamed it all up. Either way—her worst nightmares had become real. And somehow they all merged into one great, terrifying confusion of madness....

And in that madness, Stella was running—running, running...running for her life.

Part III:

Toward The Awakening

ᚦᚾᚦ·ᚦᚥᚾᚠᛒᚠᛏᚦ ᚦᚥ

In the wild heart
Terror rings
Runs for life
Poison Stings
The evil beast
The man machine
Birds of prey
Closing in...closing in....

Chapter XI:
The Flight

It was dark—in the thickness of the forest—the utmost dark; pitch black. Yet darker still were Stella's thoughts, her emotions, her suspicions, her fears. A confusion of memories raced through her mind. She was beyond simple fear.

"The worst sort of nightmare is the sort you wake up in the middle of, and realize, to your horror—it is real!" The words of the Shadow Beast echoed in her mind. A part of her felt she was trapped in a time loop. *But perhaps it is actually a spiral,* she thought. *Perhaps there is a way out.*

Stella was running for her life. Her bare feet were bruised and bludgeoned, but she barely felt them. Her pursuers were many. Their tracking devices were of a technology whose invention most people had not yet even imagined.

Death—in a free world, she thought, would be far better than what will happen if they catch me.

If only she could wake from this terrifying nightmare. But there was no waking, because Stella wasn't sleeping. This *was* real....

She would have cried if she had a moment. *How did it change so fast?* Her life had been good. Sure, there was school and homework and all that—but she'd take it all back in a heartbeat if she could only lose the horrible nightmare her reality had become.

Stella remembered: Blinding beams of light—strange doctors examining her, prodding her with alien-like instruments—and those terrible eyes....

This pitch black forest had been comforting compared with the memories racing through her mind as she ran through the darkness —at first. But any sense of comfort, and even the memories, were driven from her by the rising sounds of engines and the terrifying vision of flashing lights. *They* were closing in—and not only from behind her now, but from ahead and all around!

Stella stopped short—almost in a panic. She had to get off the trail! Trembling, she left the path and felt her way into the brush.

But if she had been afraid while she was running, it was nothing to the fear that came over her now. The sudden pounding, clattering vibration of a helicopter came raging out of nowhere, and hovered—barely over her head! A sonic weapon discharged.

Stella's mouth opened—and all breath left her lungs. But she did not know if she actually screamed. For what may have been the loudest outpouring of emotion ever to come out of her was like silence under the all consuming and terrifying sound of the helicopter's deafening clatter.

Yet it was the highly focused sonic beam that ravaged her nervous system. Her face turned up in pure shock and awe—her head tilting back. The knife dropped from her hand. All terrain vehicles and foot soldiers closed in from every direction. It was over. They had caught her. Frozen, and completely overcome with horror, Stella fell.

She did not feel the ground. She felt nothing. She neither saw nor heard anything. She lay on her back, her eyes and mouth open, as though dead. No thoughts. No dreams.

When the soldiers closed in, it was apparent their quarry was unconscious. Their leader, Commander Grey, shone his flashlight beam onto her face. The second in command, Lieutenant Green, was standing right over her. He removed his goggles, shaking his head at the sight of the young girl, then looked questioningly at Commander Grey.

"I know. It's hard to believe," Commander Grey answered the lieutenant's questioning look. "But terrorists come in all shapes and sizes. And *this one*, as I have been *most clearly* informed, is extremely dangerous— and...*of the utmost importance*."

Lieutenant Green shrugged. Whatever she supposedly was, it was all over for her now. But she, *most clearly*, was not looking so impressive. He signaled to his troops. They turned on their flash lights and approached.

Yet even in unconsciousness, through closed eyes, and the cover of clouds—even through *Stealth Clouds*—the light of distant stars pierced the veil about her and entered Stella's vision. Through her subconscious came an awareness of dancing, swirling sparks of light; they were all about her and upon her, touching her skin, absorbing into her—dancing, swirling sparks of *life; Awen*.

Awen—the force that moves through all things, the inspiration of life. It entered her heart, coursed through her blood and nerves, and into her brain. And from this living energy there came a voice, whispering into her ears:

"If wants ta see ye *really* something horrible, then just keep ye lying unconscious, right where are ye!" The Awen exploded, suddenly, throughout her body.

"*MacAwen!*" With a bolt of energy, Stella leapt to her feet and ran like she had never run before. There was a gap in the circle of flashlights closing in on her. Maybe she could make it through.

For her pursuers, there would be a moment of confusion. She had fallen and lain unconscious. They must have been confident she was captured. Perhaps they were wrong. They had underestimated her. Perhaps they weren't as efficient and all powerful as they believed. And in their overconfidence they had revealed *their* positions by turning on their lights. Now she could see where *they* all were—and now *she* was not so foolish as to turn on her own flashlight.

Stella charged between the widest gap in the circle of flashlights—and she was no longer surrounded. She ran with new strength.

But the helicopter tore after her—and the lights of her pursuers, again, went dark. She could no longer see where they were. *Oh no,* she remembered. *Infrared...thermal! They can see me in the dark!* Of course they'd be tracking her by her thermal emissions. If only she was a snake, or even a turtle, maybe she could escape. But all warm blooded animals emit heat—and no matter how dark it was, *they* could see her heat signature.

Still, there might be a way. She would rather die trying than be taken. She would *not* fall victim to fear again. She would follow all her senses. She slowed down a little, that she might hear or smell or some other way *sense them.*

All sound, however, was overwhelmed by the helicopter hovering above her. *Taller trees,* she thought. *Maybe I can lose it if I get under some taller trees.* But even as she paused to search through the darkness around her, she became aware of an unnatural mist descending upon her. She was being sprayed! By exactly what, she could only imagine. But it was obviously coming from the helicopter—and it wasn't vitamin water. She had to run. Fast!

Stella stumbled from the thicket into an opening. She recognized this place at once. She was on the old railroad path! Here she could more clearly see. And heartened to have navigated so well through the dark woods, she ran with all her might.

But the helicopter stayed on her, and now sprayed her even more intensely, almost knocking her down. It was disgusting. Whatever poison it was, she thought....

She hardly got to complete the thought when the poison took effect. Suddenly, she was confused. Her head was in a fog. She was stunned—as though she had been sledge-hammered on the side of the head.

She staggered, stopped running, and walked—almost in a full circle. Fear came over her once more—not intense as before, but with a confusion now that grew worse each moment. Where was she trying to get to? Her head ached. Then it throbbed. In moments the pain in her skull grew almost crippling. *Why was I running?* she wondered, the pain and disorientation worsening each moment. *Where am I? And what is this horrible banging over my head—or is it in my head?* She put her hands on her face —and noticed sweat and saliva all over her hands. She wiped her hands on her pants and felt for her face again. Liquid was dripping, oozing, secreting from her mouth, her nose, her eyes, her ears, the pores of her skin....

The circle of foot soldiers was closing right in upon her now. Stella saw one of them. In the darkness, with his protective clothing, helmet, gas mask, and infrared goggles, he looked like an alien. For all she knew, perhaps he was. Staggering, she ran in the opposite direction.

She was on the old railroad path, though at the moment did not know it. Her memory was almost completely gone. She knew only that she was chased—that her pursuers were more terrible than any nightmares she had ever conjured from her own unconscious—and that she was confused. She knew she was confused. And that in spite of her pain, she had to keep running—running with all her might.

A huge, dark shape lunged suddenly onto the path—right in front of her! Stella froze in her tracks. This enormous, dark figure could be no mere human. *But what?*

She'd been afraid to turn on her flashlight. But now she had no choice. For whether or not her light revealed *her* position, *she* had to see....

The beam of her flashlight was almost blinding. But more blinding was the shock of what she saw that moment—the Shadow Beast! It stood, manifested in the real world, standing before her, face to face—as it once had in a nightmare.

As in a bolt of lightning—a seeming eternity of thoughts, perceptions, and emotions blast upon the mind, then vanish—Stella's eyes adjusted. Then, so did her mind. Her flashlight was shining—not onto the Shadow Beast, but directly into the face of a black bear, standing upright, inches from her. It let out a great roar; Stella let out a scream. It ran in one direction, and she in the other.

"We've got her in range!" she heard a man's voice shouting.

"Fire tasers!" another man commanded.

"We've hit her—but she's still moving!"

"Stun again! Until she freezes!"

"We hit her full force, commander! She's still moving! Toward *you*!"

Stella saw flashlight beams turning on. "It's a damn bear, you idiots! Kill it! And get back on the damn subject!"

Stella heard gunshots. The image of the bear's face, illuminated for that instant by her flashlight, was emblazoned in her mind. In its eyes was the same terror Stella imagined in her own eyes at the thought of the lights of her pursuers. It was a girl—Stella sensed it. And whether it wanted to or not, it had given its life to save her. She felt for it. It was just like her—a reflection of her—a parallel self. If she truly had been trapped in a time loop, then this bear's and Stella's paths crossing—and the shining of light on the Shadow beast—had opened the way out. She had to make its death worthy. She had to get away!

"I've got her signal," another voice called, "twelve degrees south of west—48 meters—move it!"

"She's been sprayed, for Christ's sake," a different voice responded. "She's not going far now—or fast."

The flashlights turned off again. They were coming. In the dark, they could see her. She remembered that. Little else was in her memory. She stumbled along the path. But the sound of ATVs behind her made her realize she had to get in somewhere thick.

The loud revving sound of something different came suddenly from the opposite direction. Stella remembered the helicopter. But this was not the helicopter. What happened to the helicopter? As this new sound got closer, she recognized it. It was not an ATV. But where had she heard this sound before?

"Well, well!" the commander's voice shouted suddenly, from much closer than Stella had known. "If it isn't Sergeant Cambull!"

"*Sergeant* Cambull?" another voice responded questioningly —this one, on the other side of Stella. She was once again surrounded, and she hadn't even known it.

"I raised young Buck's rank, Lieutenant," Commander Grey answered. "It was recommended by Mr. Horus, whose wishes, always, are my commands—as you know."

"Oh, yes—hail Horus," the voice of the lieutenant responded. "So— I suspect you will be giving your young sergeant the honors?"

"My plan exactly," the commander answered—just as Buck's machine came to a halt.

Buck's machine. The memories flooded back into Stella's mind. But with them came a great pounding in her head.

"Sergeant Cambull," the Commander greeted, "the subject is yours—if you can locate her."

"*If?*" Buck replied

"How do you like the new implant, Buck?" the Commander asked.

"I had a positive ID on the subject, a black bear, and all sixteen of her pursuers, from three point two kilometers out," Buck answered. "The subject will be delivered in fifty seconds, sir." And then there was silence.

Stella crept away as quick and silent as she could. *The subject will be delivered in fifty seconds?* A renewed fear came over Stella. It hurt her head to think or remember—but Buck Cambull, driving on his machine was something from a different nightmare she had had another time.

She heard the snapping of twigs—not ten feet from her position! She remembered her knife—but it was lost. Twenty five seconds had probably passed already. Her heart raced. She backed up, stumbled. Buck could see in the dark. *New implant?* Fear consumed her and tears poured out of her at once. Never before had seconds ticked away so certain and so fast.

A strong hand came swiftly out of the darkness and covered her mouth—as her assailant's other arm wrapped around her body from behind, pinning her arms to her sides. She struggled with all her might, but the hold was like that of a python, tightening every time she tensed. She could not scream. She could not struggle. She was captured.

She felt her flashlight forced from her grip. Her body was spun around, to face her captor. She cringed and held her eyes tight shut. She did not want to look at Buck's face. She *would* not.

She prayed in that moment to awaken—and for the nightmare to go away. As if in answer, the hand over her mouth let go, moved up to her eyes, and gently forced them open—just as he shone the flashlight onto his own face. He was so familiar, for a moment it made no sense. Then he blew a cloud of dust into her face, from some object he had clutched in his hand—just as she had seen Faas do once before. Her head cleared immediately—and her vision. She recognized him. She couldn't believe it. But it was true. With her mouth wide open, she stared into her captor's face. It was Faas!

"Fifty seconds, Sergeant!" the Commander shouted.

"I have the subject," Faas answered with a hard, deep voice—remarkably like Buck's. "But she came with a little surprise—so I'll need fifty more seconds for the delivery."

"You got it, Buck," the Commander answered.

Faas shone her flashlight onto the ground next to them—and there lay Buck Cambull, flat on his back, barely conscious. There was a crazed, angry look on his face. His breathing was stifled— but he jerked suddenly and his eyes flashed open—fixed on Stella. She jumped, and almost screamed.

"He won't move for a while," Faas assured with a whisper. But Stella had an awful premonition; *there would be vengeance for this.*

"Sh—" Faas held a finger to his lips, and held up a very sharp knife. "You have a tracking device implanted in your arm," he whispered, "I'll have it out in nine point two seconds—" He offered a quick smile, then gripped her forearm tightly with one hand and punctured her with his knife. Stella screamed, but Faas held her tight, withdrawing the knife and "shushing" her, pleadingly.

"What the hell are you doing to her, Buck?" the Commander called.

"It's okay now," Faas answered with his Buck voice. "She was more of a fighter than I thought. I'm just binding her, and we'll be on our way." He quickly poked Stella's opened wound with a narrow, hollow reed—which he began sucking on at once, very vigorously. It was quite painful. But then it was over. He shone the flashlight to show her the tiny microchip. Then, without a moment to cover her wound, Faas led her fast and furiously, away from her pursuers.

"There's something moving in there!" the Commander called. "Buck—what's going on?"

"It's just a couple of deer," Faas shouted back. Clearly, they had picked up on the thermal movement from Stella and Faas—but Buck and Stella's RFID chips remained still at the spot where Buck was.

"Deer?" There was a pause. "Buck, get that damn subject out here—now!" There was another pause. "Why aren't you moving, Sergeant?" the Commander shouted angrily.

But Faas did not answer him again. He led Stella through the dark, pathless woods until they came to water. They waded in, up to Stella's thighs. Faas gave her a large, hollow reed. "You have to breathe through this," he informed her. "Lie on your back, and hold your body stiff. I'll push you by your feet." Stella eyed him questioningly. "Infrared tracking," he spoke quiet, but intensely. "Submerged under water, we won't give them much of a thermal signal."

She did as he said. Faas took a great breath, submerged himself, and from beneath, pushed her very swiftly along a waterway. She did not remember much more of that journey—only that she was shivering terribly for what seemed like a long time. And for part of the journey she was vaguely aware of being carried further—in a coracle. But it was all so dream like.

The next thing she knew, she was in a soft, warm bed. It smelled of fresh leaves. It was in a hut. On Faas's outpost, she imagined—a thick, soft bed made of leaves, held in place by logs. There were soft blankets of fur and of woven plant fibers above and below her. Stella's shivering body was warmed and made comfortable. But then there came fever. In her head, she felt very ill—dizzy, dismayed, aching, and confused. For an amount of time she could not fathom, she was only vaguely conscious—and that, only for moments of wakefulness in a sea of dreams. She knew that Faas was by her side, caring for her. At times, she heard him chanting, softly. But her eyes never opened. She was drifting—in and out of memories and dreams....

*In and out of dreams, wanders,
searching for sweet peace of mind.
Yet though a thousand times, ponders—
in oblivion only for some moments finds....*

Chapter XII:
Between

Stella, Patrick, and Clarsah stealth walked eagerly, yet very slow and carefully, towards a great pile of sticks, leaves, and debris that was stacked against the uprooted base of a fallen spruce tree. This pack rat *nest* (or rather, *palace*) was enormous. MacAwen was already at the entrance. At long last, he was fulfilling his promise to introduce them to the infamous *Pat*.

MacAwen motioned for them to be still, while he gently tapped on the front door. In his extended hand, he held a peanut and a very shiny gemstone. After several minutes there emerged a very fat, whiskered face. "Ah...um..." MacAwen hummed soothingly. "Gifts have I brought ye...and *friends,*" he added with a tone as soothing as his hum. "Even *more* peanuts...and *more* jewels do have they for ye." He signaled for Stella, Patrick, and Clarsah to extend their offerings.

Pat sniffed and looked about—nervously, but greedily. He stood up on his hind legs and observed the three kids, suspicious and scrutinizing. Then he turned back to MacAwen, took the peanut and the jewel from his outstretched hand, and stuffed them in his cheek.

This was undoubtedly the biggest, fattest, cutest, and most amazing rat Stella had ever beheld or even imagined. On his hind legs he stood about half the height of MacAwen, but no doubt weighed much more. "My friends—" MacAwen gestured toward Stella, Patrick, and Clarsah. "*More,*" he said enchantingly. Pat

293

turned to the three, his whiskers twitching as he sniffed. As slowly and carefully as they had stealth walked to his den, he now approached them.

"Say; *well met* ta Pat," MacAwen smiled at them—as one by one Pat took the gifts from their outstretched hands.

"*Well met*, Pat," they each said in turn as he stuffed his cheeks with their offerings.

Stella never did get a peek *inside* Pat's nest. And though it was wonderful to meet him, a part of her felt disappointed. She had sort of imagined him to be more human-like—maybe even able to talk. But after all, he was only a *fairly* extraordinary pack rat. In other words, he was fairly ordinary....

Now Stella stood talking to Faas. She was back on his outpost. The sun was shining. Clarsah and Patrick stood next to her. David, Andy, Tom, Craig, and Robert were there, too. She wished Iona could be there, too—and Jessie...and Brighid...and Jasmine.

A great raven peered down at them from his perch atop the lattice work above the platform. It had a seemingly intelligent look in its eyes as it observed the conversation between she and Faas. But, much to her disappointment, Stella knew better now. In fact, this creature wasn't even a mammal like Pat. It was only a bird— with a bird brain. Even Pat, in fact, was more closely related to a human than he was to a bird.

"Pat was really...*something*," she said to Faas. "But he wasn't *as* extraordinary as I had imagined him to be."

Faas laughed out loud—in his bizarre coyote giggle. "Pat is as *extraordinary* as I ever hope to meet in a *Common* Pack Rat," he replied. "Like what did you expect?"

"Oh...I don't know," Stella answered. "Like—maybe an animal that could talk or something like that."

"Ha, hoi, ho," Faas giggled, "a talking Pack Rat! What do you think of that, Ravi?" he asked in a sudden high pitched tone as he eyed the raven watching them from above.

"Logical enough," the raven answered in an even higher and a very croaky voice, "for a naive human—uneducated in either zoology or rodent anatomy."

Stella stared up at the raven, open mouthed and amazed....

One dream faded from her mind, followed by another. But the next dream was more of a memory replaying in her mind:

"Of course! Even a parrot can repeat a phrase! But can they paraphrase?" Uncle Ken debated Stella's mother with his typical passion, absurdity, and brilliance. "Exposing kids to this *big, terrible stuff*, as you say, may cause a few nightmares. But they'll be better equipped to deal with the devils they know than the ones we hide from them. Besides, no one else is going to do a damn thing about it."

"Ken—please!" Stella's Mom begged. "The school feels children should be protected."

"Protected?" Ken eyed her aghast. "Psychopathic predators are systematically trying to destroy us—*and* our children—but we don't want to risk this knowledge *upsetting our children? S*o we'll just send them out amongst these predators? Unknowing? And unprepared! And these people think that is *protecting* them?"

"*We* never had to deal with anything like this," Stella's Mom pleaded, "Why should our children?"

"Because *we*...and our parents...*and* our *grandparents* allowed *them* to creep in and take over." Uncle Ken shook his head. "No —we didn't have to deal with these issues when we were kids. Nor did our parents *or* grandparents—at least not on this scale. But now—everyone has to—or perish without a fight. Kid and adult alike." He eyed Stella's Mom, but she was just shaking her head, looking at the floor.

Uncle Ken frowned and shook *his* head. "I think *kids* can handle this stuff better than most adults. Just look at the way these parents and teachers stick their heads under the sand, like a bunch of ostriches—and then ostracize the ones who are brave enough to open their eyes and look around."

"I know," Stella's Mom sighed, now trembling, her eyes closing. "They're accusing you of being an alarmist, and..." she eyed him apologetically, "a *conspiracy theorist.*"

"Yeah?" Ken eyed her incredulously, his mouth hanging open in a smile. "A *conspiracy theorist?*" he raised his hands. "And that's supposed to be an accusation? A dirty, shameful label?" He shook his head.

"Mary, *Conspiracy Theorist* is simply a label invented by conspirators to discredit those who question—and propagated by the programmed sheep who can't comprehend what free thinkers dare say. Anyone who even thinks for themselves a little bit gets labeled, *Conspiracy Theorist.*"

"Dead right, I'm a conspiracy theorist!" Uncle Ken shouted. "And damn proud of it," he smiled. "Where do you think we would we be without conspiracy theorists? Who would ever have even questioned, much less investigated, the likes of Richard Nixon...or Adolf Hitler...or Adam Weishaupt?" He glanced at Stella, then continued.

"*John Lennon...*was a conspiracy theorist. *Martin Luther King* was a conspiracy theorist. *John F. Kennedy* was a conspiracy theorist. Albert Einstein was. George Washington, John Adams, Thomas Jefferson, and Ben Franklin were all conspiracy theorists. There would never have even been a United States of America without conspiracy theorists. Of course Chief Seattle, Geronimo, Crazy Horse, Sitting Bull, and Chief Joseph all became conspiracy theorists—too late. If only *their* people weren't so naive and trusting they might not have been the first known victims in the history of the world to be decimated by biological warfare."

"Ken—" Stella's Mom tried to interrupt.

"*Gandhi...*was a conspiracy theorist," Ken continued. "William Wallace was a conspiracy theorist. Joan of Arc was a conspiracy theorist. Joseph—" he paused, for once, respecting the look of alarm in the eyes of Stella's Mom. "I am sorry, Mary." Ken shook his head. "But if it wasn't for Stella's Dad...I would never have become the conspiracy theorist I am. And one more, Mary—*Jesus...*of Nazareth—" he raised his brows, nodding. "He was the epitome of a conspiracy theorist."

Stella's mom sighed heavily, but did not interrupt further.

"So," Ken continued, "if I stand *accused* of being something these great people were—the real question is; what kind of *accusers* believe this greatest of honors to be a shame?"

Stella's Mom looked reverently, but worriedly, at her older brother. Ken stood tall—a gaunt and wiry man with sandy hair that was rarely combed. His face was scruffy and his voice raspy, but his eyes, as always, were piercing and bright.

"You're a good man, Ken," Mary sighed. "I just don't want you, or my daughter, to have the kind of endings that most of your heroes have had. If there is a global conspiracy—let the MIF worry about it. That's what they're there for."

Uncle Ken shook his head with restrained disappointment, looking at Stella's Mom like she was still just his baby sister. "Jesus—" he sighed. "Mary—look at me. And listen—carefully. The greatest threat to *we the people* comes not from any foreign government or terrorist organization—but from the very agencies that are *supposedly* put in place to *protect us*. When congress allowed the shareholders of the Triple Leverage Corporation to set up the MIF, supposedly to alert us of any possible foreign threats— it was like hiring foxes to design and install the security system on a hen house. And those same foxes have installed the security systems for every hen house in the world."

"Ken—" Stella's Mom interjected. "Please—" she frowned, "not in front of Stella."

Ken looked at Stella. "Don't let them clip this little bird's wings."

"Ken! That's enough," Stella's Mom demanded.

"Uh...I've got to go outside—" Stella cut in— "to feed the ferrets." And she ran outside. Not to feed her ferrets, but to get out of sight so Uncle Ken and her Mom could continue their conversation. And hopefully, she could catch some more of it through a window.

"It's this whole *Geo-Engineering* monstrosity—" Ken's voice boomed through the window as Stella approached. "It's the last straw. It's the worst crime they've ever committed—and it's the biggest mistake they've ever made. 'Cause mark my words; when enough people look to the sky and ask questions," Ken nodded, smiling—a wild fire blazing in his eyes, *"The Revolution* will begin."

"Revolution—" Stella's Mom gasped.

"Not like 1776!" Ken smiled, rolling his eyes at her ignorance while trying to reassure her. *"The World Freedom Revolution,* remember?"

Mary Childs sighed. "I do remember what Joseph said."

"He said it will be worldwide," Ken nodded.

"He said it would be peaceful!" Mary snipped.

"He did," Ken nodded. "Let us pray he was right."

Mary closed her eyes, sighing and shaking her head. "He was the kindest, most compassionate soul," her voice strained, "but some of the things he said...it was like he was from another planet. And in retrospect, I think he was paranoid."

"Paranoid?" Ken shook his head. "Mary...any fears *Joseph* had were legitimate."

Stella's Mom sighed very heavily. "I loved him so much, Ken," she spoke with a sadness that she never exhibited in front of Stella. "I still do. But he was a dreamer!" she raised her voice. "All that talk of *the World Freedom Revolution*...." She shook her head. "Then he just disappeared! He's gone, Ken," she said, tears in her eyes. "And his dreams are gone with him. So please...let the fears be gone, too."

"Mary—"

"All he left us with is Stella!" Mary cut Ken off. "We have to protect her...from the kind of thinking..." her voice began to break, "that gets some people..." Her voice failed. The room went quiet. Stella put her head up to the window for a closer listen.

Ken seemed to spot Stella outside the window. But he looked away, as though he didn't see her. "I know how you feel, Mary," he said soothingly. "But the *World Freedom Revolution* was an idea, Mary. A man can disappear—or be killed. But an idea cannot. It lives on. The World Freedom Revolution is all I know of that the next generation will have left to hope for. And soon, the only ones left to carry it forth will be that next generation. We have to have faith in them. We have to trust them. For certain— we can't let these...

conspiring control freaks train our young to be chickens when they're meant to grow up and be eagles!" Ken smiled and gave Stella a wink through the window.

That was the last time she had seen Uncle Ken. She hardly understood half of what Uncle Ken said. But he clearly knew his stuff. And...he had known her Dad. He counted her Dad amongst his great conspiracy theorist heroes. Ken knew Joseph Childs even longer than Stella's Mom had. *World Freedom Revolution?* Stella had never heard that one. What did it mean? And what else did Ken know about her father? If only she could ask him....

On the other hand, the things Uncle Ken talked about probably *had* instigated some of her paranoia and troubling dreams....

Memories of images of MacAwen swam through Stella's subconscious. *Was it all just imagination?* She wanted to believe in him, but he himself had warned against believing. *What was it he had said about believing not or not believing?* She strove to remember, but her question was washed into an ocean of unconsciousness by wave after wave of inner dialogs, repeating monotonously—over and over again in her mind; *Zis girl is delusional—literally off ze charts in terms of normalcy... off ze charts in terms of normalcy....*

Why would *anyone* be after Stella, anyway? She was just a seventh grade girl. It was absurd. And a whole squadron of special forces? With a helicopter? And *Buck Cambull*—with an implant? *...off ze charts in terms of normalcy.*

And she is suicidal. She has a plan all vorked out—she vill jump fvom a cliff, smash her skull, and 'zen fall into 'ze vater of a gveat bog.... Perhaps Stella had already smashed her skull—and even now was dreaming her last dreams, as her body floated in that great bog. She remembered the bog near the Cambull's house—and how Ralph had promised she would have lots of company. She remembered the corpses floating out there, in that bog.... *But that was just a memory of something,* she thought, *of something I only imagined. What's wrong with me? What am I?*

With all her will, she drove those thoughts from her subconscious, searching instead for happier dreams...of the De Da Mua. This was no mere bog. It was a living labyrinth of labyrinths. She had barely begun to explore it. She remembered NeeGaia—and the Mother Goddess in that peaceful place, deep within. She remembered Faas's band. It was still playing when she and Clarsah had had to leave—and more creatures and mysterious people had been arriving. Faas had so many amazing friends. He was not just a loner after all. *Zis vild man is a known terrorist—part of a tvaining cell zat pvactices vilderness survival....*

Standing on the edge of Faas's outpost, Stella saw the tail of a giant whale, rising from the water—then splashing down again. But how could a whale be in fresh water? Anyway, the waters around Faas's outpost were only thigh deep—maybe neck deep at their very deepest. Or were they?

299

Stella stepped into the water—and very swiftly, she sank. Now Stella was under water, floating. She could see the whale. She was with the whale. She had been shivering for so long. But now she felt warm and peaceful. Stella put her hands on the whale's face. She caressed it, gently. Its skin was soft and smooth —and had a feel like—like *gentle electricity*. She could sense its emotions—almost, its thoughts. It was so loving, and yet…sad.

Her hands, still on the whale's skin, she drifted to its large and wondrous eye. It slowly closed. Stella put her face right up to it. She closed her eyes, also. The world went dark.

At last, all other dreams, images, and maddening inner dialogs went silent. There were no more thoughts. In her mind—only one, vague image: the great, dark eye of the whale, opening before her.

Into that one image, she was drawn—the final focus of a wild imagination. Stella penetrated deep, into the dark eye—and it penetrated her—as if she had been a swirling galaxy, now vacuumed into the gravity of a black hole. She was drawn through a long, dark tunnel. Somewhere ahead…there was light. Or so she imagined. *And so it was.* Though it could have been light years way. Then again, she might be there in an instant—if so she imagined. *And so she did….*

Ten thousand years solidified,
yet it speaks of the now.
What will be was laid out before us;
The Pathways...

And yet....

Forks in trails written in stone;
our choices,
however unconscious,
are in the footprints...of this moment...

Chapter XIII:
The Prophesy

Stella opened her eyes. She lay in a tiny hut. It was dark within, but a campfire sparkled just outside the doorway—and there was a dim glow in the atmosphere, as of early morning. She was warm. She was safe. She could see Faas's silhouette through the doorway, sitting by the fire. He noticed her stirring, and came to her.

For a moment, he didn't speak. He just looked at her. He looked sad. "It is a hard pathway...upon which you tread," he nodded and sighed. "But not every step," he smiled. "Would you like some hot tea?"

Stella nodded. Faas rummaged through a rustic, make shift sort of cabinet near the head of her bed. A sudden flight of ravens just outside the doorway startled Faas. He dropped the cup from his hand and spun around—his knife at ready in hand, pointing toward the door. So fast was his movement—Stella knew not how the knife, from the pouch, to the hand, was drawn. And all for nothing. She eyed him with alarm, questioningly. This reaction was disturbingly unlike Faas.

301

"I'm sorry," Faas sighed heavily. He put the knife away, then picked up the cup and a bowl of something he had stashed near the door. He flung the contents of the bowl to a suddenly raucous and ravenous gathering of dark, feathered friends as he went out by the fire. In another moment he returned with the cup, filled.

She hadn't realized how dry her throat had been until she tried to say, thank you. The tea was immediately soothing. But Faas's reaction to the flight of the ravens was not. "Why are you so jumpy?" she asked in a raspy voice.

"It's okay now," he sighed. "And you need to stay calm," he added with a nod. "But I will hold no more truth from you. Not after all you have been through." He shook his head. Faas took a long, slow sip from his tea. "The Guardians of the De Da Mua are beings of great wisdom and power—but they are not invincible."

Stella raised her brows questioningly.

"For thousands of years *they* had no way of getting past the Guardians," Faas said. "But truth be told, *they* have frightening new technology—and now," he sighed, "*they* are trying to break into the De Da Mua."

"What?" Stella looked at him aghast. "Who are *they*? Why?"

Faas sighed. "*They* are after somebody—and for their part, they will stop at no end until that somebody is captured—and destroyed."

A quick rush of air entered Stella's lungs—her eyes and her mouth frozen wide, her mind racing as she recalled something Dr. Warburger had said: '*Zis vild man is a vanted terrorist.*

Now Stella remembered some of the other details of her nightmares—or of her nightmarish memories. She glanced nervously at her arm—and it *was* bandaged! Trembling, she lifted the bandage—and there was a fresh scar...from which Faas had removed a Radio Frequency Identification chip!

She stared back up at Faas in horror. The worst of all her nightmares came back to her now—and it was no mere nightmare —unless she was still in it. But she was wide awake. She could feel her body. Her mind was clearing. This was very real. At least she wasn't crazy. But—that meant they had actually implanted an RFID chip into her arm!

"Oh my God," she half-whispered in horror. "It was real!" she gasped, looking at Faas in terror and dismay. "Why? How? I don't even remember anyone..." Then it dawned on her—at least one small piece; "The I.V...." she breathed—amazed, horrified, and disgusted all at once. "They implanted that chip through the I.V.—without me even realizing it!"

"I'm sorry," Faas shook his head.

"But why?" Stella asked. "Why— and why are they trying to get in? Why do they think you're a terrorist? How do they even know about the De Da Mua?" Then she remembered; *Sergeant* Cambull. "Buck!"

"Actually, they have known about the De Da Mua for a long time," Faas sighed, "long before they had Buck." Faas breathed in very deeply and sighed. "They have known that we have a secret place—and that we have ways of getting places—and ways of communicating. They've been trying for a long time to infiltrate our sanctum—" he nodded, "since long before Buck or I were even born. But now they are close. Now—"

"But—who are they?" Stella interrupted. "What do they want? None of this makes sense. I—" She strained to sort out her memories. "I was getting tested. This crazy psychiatrist...." Abstract pieces of an ever more complex puzzle were floating into Stella's consciousness. "Dr. Warburger told our parents and teachers that *you..."* she stared at Faas apologetically, *"are a terrorist!* Part of a secret training cell! We haven't been allowed to come here. Not even into the woods. That's why you haven't seen me."

"I know," Faas sighed, glancing out the doorway and nodding. *"She* is an agent...of *The It Animal."*

"The what?" Stella followed his gaze through the doorway. A raven stood at the entrance, peering in at them.

"Actually, she works for an organization that works for The It Animal." Faas nodded to the raven again, then jerked his head twice to the left. The raven returned Faas a similar gesture, then walked out of Stella's view.

Stella tried to force herself into a sitting position, but her head swam in dizziness. She felt very weak. Faas grabbed two large, fur cushions and propped them up behind her. "Thank you," she sighed. "Please, keep talking. Tell me—who are *they*? And what is this *thing*?"

"The *It Animal* is a beast described in an ancient prophesy. Those who pursued you, and assaulted you, three nights ago, are agents of a secret organization that was founded by, and is under the control of, *The It Animal*."

Stella stared at him, dumbfounded. "What? Three nights ago?" She looked about in awe, then sighed and closed her eyes. "I had no idea," she whispered, "I slept and dreamed so long." Faas did not speak until she opened her eyes and questioned him further. "How did you find me?"

"*Concentric rings*," he answered. "In the forest there is a constant harmony of sound. It rises and falls, *rhythmically*, through the course of each day. All the forest's sounds make their own waves, which blend into *The Harmony*. But bring in a foreign disturbance, from outside—and it's like throwing a rock into a serene pond." He paused, his eyes turning up to his left, wide and out of focus, as he listened intently—as he often did.

"The ripples that go out from a disturbance can be detected from all over the pond," he whispered, "or in this case, the forest." He looked at Stella. "You remember my band; we play with nature's harmony—adding to it, our own. Each typical day there are four main climaxes—the dawn chorus, the dusk chorus, the midday chorus, and the midnight chorus. Without any disturbances from any creatures that instigate emotional alarm amongst the singers—or any weather that affects the same—the chorus has a perfectly predictable tempo. But bring in a feared predator—or wind or rain or snow—and an interruption is sounded in the harmony's typical rise and fall. A coyote, for instance, will alarm the nearby mice, rabbits, and deer. The movements of the mice, rabbits, and deer will affect the snakes, crickets, and frogs. Each of these creatures has subtle rippling influences on further creatures around them. And all these movements can be heard, *and understood*, by one who listens to the music every day."

"I am not like MacAwen, who could tell you exactly what a particular deer is doing many miles away." Faas sighed. "But the disturbance made three nights ago," he widened his eyes, nodding, "was enough to alarm me from deep in my dreams."

Stella sat back on the cushions and thought deeply about all that Faas revealed. And she understood—the part about the forest's Harmony and the Concentric Rings. It was amazing—and wonderful. But there was so much more—*all* amazing, but *not* all wonderful.

"What about the microchip?" she questioned, her eyes suddenly widening. "How did you know it was in me? How did you know where?"

"It *is* strange," Faas looked up, into the thatched ceiling. "It *has* disturbed me. And I do *not* understand. But I *have* been aware for some time, that of *all* people, I am *most* easily able to sense the presence of *Buck Cambull*. At first I thought it was only because his energy made so profound a disturbance in nature's harmony. But later I realized that *he too*, can sense *me*. Of all the people I have ever encountered, Buck Cambull is the most difficult for me to hide from, or to stalk up on unknown."

"Now he has an implant that enhances and amplifies some functions of his brain. And it amplifies our connection—his and mine—which disturbs me very deeply," he shook his head. "And yet, on that night, it likely saved our lives," he sighed, "yours and mine. For had that chip remained within you—" Faas shook his head. "I doubt even the Guardians could have turned them away. It was through *Buck's* senses that *I sensed* and pinpointed the microchip within your arm."

Stella digested that bit until it instigated another question. "But how could *you* approach that spot, without *him* or any of the others detecting *you*?"

"That was easy," Faas shrugged with a bit of a laugh. "A human being's natural sensory apparatus is vastly more broad and harmonious than any of the shoddy junk these modern hacks concoct—if one simply learns how to tune in and turn on what the Great Spirit has endowed us with through our grand and divine evolution."

"I don't know if you recall Buck Cambull boasting to his commander that he was able to detect *the subject, a black bear, and all sixteen of her pursuers, from three point two kilometers out,*" Faas rolled his eyes. "But through the *many* disturbances I felt moving through the harmony *that* night—I was able not only to detect all that Buck detected, and much more—but also, to detect it much sooner."

"I had time to read all the movements, and to predict the outcome of everyone's intersecting trails, well ahead of Buck's radar. So by the time he was getting positive identifications on everyone involved in the action, I was already molded into the ground—waiting in the very spot where I knew Buck's path and yours would intersect. He was so intent upon capturing you, he never saw me until I sprang from the ground. He was sniffing puffball before he even knew what I was," Faas smiled. "But then, as I was quietly laying him on the ground, while our bodies were in close contact, I sensed what he was sensing. And I knew, that chip had to come out fast, before we escaped."

"That is *so* amazing," Stella stared up at Faas with renewed awe. "I owe you my life—two times now!"

"We are part of one life," Faas smiled, "for which my part owes the greater debt to you."

"What?" Stella gave him a puzzled look. "What do you mean?"

"Oh," Faas sighed, "where do I begin?" He shook his head, his eyes wide and rolling.

And out of thin air snapped the answer, in a familiar, raspy whisper, "Is the best place ta begin, *usually*, at the beginning."

"MacAwen!" Stella sat bolt upright. But she did not see any little brown man. "Where are you?" she searched about.

"*Always near ye, Stella Childs—and all around ye,*" MacAwen's voice answered. But as had happened once before, MacAwen's voice was *in* her thoughts. Or was it just *her thoughts* in MacAwen's voice?

"Do you hear him?" she looked at Faas.

"Not exactly. But I did pick up a vibration," Faas answered, as though it was perfectly normal.

"Where is he?"

"All around you, Stella," Faas smiled, "but also, very busy in many places. I promise, I will explain everything explainable, but MacAwen has prompted me to start from the beginning. And thus I must. But first, let me finish explaining The It Animal. It is the beast described in *the prophesy*."

Stella shook her head and sighed. "Uh...The Shadow Beast?"

"Not exactly," Faas shook his head, "but it is connected. The Shadow Beast is *unconscious*. And," Faas looked up, into the thatch of the roof, "the shadow beast actually lurks within us all to varying degrees, at various times. It is still debated, but the most common hypothesis, backed by years of gathered knowledge *and* intuition, states that this thing we call the Shadow Beast also lurks within The It Animal. But The It Animal is a *conscious* entity. And somehow, it has attained a conscious mastery over the Shadow Beast. It *uses* the Shadow Beast to carry out its deeds."

"The Shadow Beast works for somebody? The *It*-thing?" Stella asked.

"It *is* written," Faas answered, "*fairly* clear in the prophesy:

"The It-Animal-I will employ the Shadow Beast to its service," Faas recited a piece of the prophesy.

"That is how we know The It Animal is separate from, but connected to, the Shadow Beast. There are many allusions in the prophesy to this interconnection between the Shadow Beast and The It Animal."

"That's a freaky name," Stella shook her head. "Why is it called The It Animal?"

"We don't know," Faas answered. "There has been much speculation about the name—for as certainly as the name is odd and cumbersome, we all agree that it must have great significance."

"*We?*" Stella searched Faas questioningly. "Who's we?"

"*We* are Clann Taluv," Faas answered, "the *children of the Earth*. Our mission—is to keep alive the knowledge of the prophesy—and to guard it, and all who read it, from The It Animal. We, Clann Taluv, also, were spoken of in The Prophesy," he smiled proudly.

Clann Taluv; Stella had heard this name—from Dr. Warburger: Intelligence sources say he is part of a terror organization zat pvactices vilderness survival and has hideouts in ze forests. Ze name of zis terror gvoup is Clan Taluv. Zey are extvemely dangerous—and known to use various mind contvol techniques.

"The *It Animal*," Faas continued, "is actually short for The It Animal *I*."

"Eye?" Stella raised an eyebrow?

"Not *eye*, as in *eye* ball," Faas pointed to one of his eyes. "*I*, as in me, myself, and *I*," he pointed to himself. "Let me explain. In the old languages, from which the prophesy was handed down, the word *'the'* usually had a masculine or feminine connotation. But prefixing the name with the word, *It*, suggests that this *animal* was neither male nor female. And yet the *Animal* suggests that it is alive—that it moves—and that it is a physical rather than a spiritual being. The *I*, it has most often been suggested, refers to an ego consciousness. The physical body that is neither male nor female, but has a conscious ego. Further, it is said to be a many tentacled beast—an animal or a thing that has a body with many parts—or *members*."

"From what we have gathered, from the strands of the prophesy we've been able to study, it seems that *parts* of The It Animal are able to separate from the main body, and walk about independently. But the "*I*," the ego-central power knows and sees all, and controls all its *parts*. It sees and acts through the many eyes, ears, and arms of all its members. Thus, *The It Animal I* is never seen in action—only its parts, its members, which are all dispensable. For it is always growing new appendages. And the "I" is protected by its invisibility. Ever, it remains in dark places. For light, it is said, would destroy it—if ever the light could reach it."

"That's…*disgusting*," Stella cut in, "*and* scary. Is it really… *real*?" she gave Faas a fearful, disgusted and yet unbelieving look. "I mean, *literally*?"

"Yes," Faas answered flatly. "No one, but The It Animal itself, knows what it actually looks like. But for those who can read its footprints the evidence of its deeds throughout history are over whelming. And never has it had more power than it does at this moment. For it uses technology, in every way imaginable, to its great advantage. In fact, much of modern technology has been invented by, or instigated to be invented by, The It Animal's agents."

"I suppose I should mention," Faas added, "The It Animal is also referred to as *the Lie*. There are some in Clann Taluv who speculate the true name of the beast is *The It Animal—Lie,* rather than The It Animal—*I*. The Prophesy was not written, nor preserved, in perfect clarity."

"Who wrote this…*Prophesy?*" Stella asked.

Faas's eyes widened. "Good question," he smiled. "We'll get to that in a bit. But back to describing the name of the beast. If the third word was meant to be *Lie*, as some suggest, it would describe the reality that The It Animal is the all time master of *conscious* deceit—a devil far more terrible than the Shadow Beast. Not to underestimate the Shadow Beast—but as I said, The It Animal is conscious of what it does."

The tea seemed to have cleared Stella's head, and strengthened her. She sat up now, and the dizziness was gone. She felt like she wanted to get out of bed—and she was suddenly starving.

"Could I please have some food," she asked, pushing the blankets from her—but halting, and quickly pulling them back over her with the sudden realization that she had no clothes on. After an awkward moment, memories came back to her—the hospital gown had gotten soaked. She'd been shivering. Faas had instructed her to remove it before she got under the covers, so as not to get hypothermia.

"I have venison stew by the fire," Faas answered her food request. "I'll go serve you a bowl. And your gown is hanging from the ceiling," he pointed. "But here—if you like, I made these for you—" he tossed her a pile of leather garments, and left the hut.

Stella got out of bed, and realized, as her body trembled, she still was not very strong or steady. She unfolded the garments Faas had tossed her—and immediately was stunned by the care that had gone into his work. The first piece she unfolded was a doe skin shirt. It was soft and beautiful. When she put it on it felt like the most comfortable shirt she'd ever worn in her life. It fit perfectly. On either side were pockets with fold over tops, buttoned shut. Stella unbuttoned them and slipped her hands into the pockets. To her astonishment—and great relief, there in the right pocket was her amulet. She pulled it out and stared at it. The design was strange and mesmerizing...and yet comforting to look at—just as it always had been. This amulet—aside from her own body—was the only physical evidence she had to verify that her father had ever existed. How it had stayed in her hospital gown through all her ordeals was a wonder. But Faas must have found it when he washed the gown. Stella was so grateful. She prayerfully placed the amulet back into her pocket. Her knife, she knew, was gone. Probably, *they* had it now.

The next piece she unfolded turned out to be a pair of leather breaches—like Faas's. *Boy's clothes*, Stella shook her head—a bit disappointed, but laughing inwardly at Faas. She had expected it to be a leather skirt, but it was just like Faas to make her something more rugged.

As it turned out, the breeches were pretty nice—loose and comfortable, with soft leather belts on either sides of the hips to snug them just right. Then, there were the moccasins. These also fit perfectly, and were an absolute luxury. Stella felt like a real wild woman. *Well, not quite like a woman*, *with the breeches*, she thought. But in spite of Faas being rather clueless about feminine garments, she felt a gratitude for his care, like she had never felt in her life.

Yet in those moments of thoughtfulness, her mother came to her mind; Stella was struck suddenly, by how little she had ever appreciated all that her mom had given to her…her whole life. For a few moments she stood still, missing her mom terribly—and wondering when, and how, she could see her again.

There were so many fears and questions in her mind. But after three days without eating, hunger was number one. Before she left the hut, her eyes were drawn to the hospital gown. *I want to burn it.*

"Hey—not bad," Faas greeted her with a smile—and a bowl of stew, as she emerged from the hut.

"Would it be okay—if I through this in the fire?" she asked, holding up the hospital gown. Faas nodded. And Stella placed it on the highest flames. In spite of her hunger, she waited until it was completely gone before she ate. The stew was the most delicious thing she had ever eaten in her life. She felt the goodness and the strength of it coursing through her veins.

Although it was morning, it was still quite dark. For there was a heavy mist in the De Da Mua's atmosphere—thicker than any fog she could ever remember seeing. It was magical. Stella loved misty weather. She remembered the mega electric storms that had been predicted. She must have slept through them all. But she could feel the effect they had left in their wake. The air around the campfire was charged and cleansed. She breathed it in deeply, feeling invigorated and comfortable—in just the right mood for listening, as Faas began the tale...of *The Prophesy.*

"First, some advice," Faas sighed. "In case anything happens —tell no one what I tell you about the prophesy—at least for the time being. This knowledge is vital—and yet, very dangerous.

For long, it has been suppressed—forbidden. Those who carry it must do so with the utmost care—until the destined time of mass revelation."

"Now," he said, resting his tea cup on a flat stone by the fire, "to the beginning...."

"Every step we ever take...every one of us—it is recorded," he tapped a foot to the earth. "We're telling our story. The history of the world...is written in tracks."

"In fact, the entire history of the universe...the very story of space time itself—it is written all around us, here and now," Faas's eyes darted all about, glowing brightly in the light of the campfire.

"Yet what I am about to tell you of stretches beyond histories passed." Faas smiled. "It is a common saying that the future is *not* written in stone. In fact—*it is*."

"There is a prophesy so ancient, yet so great, that remnants of it have survived in oral traditions from all corners and curves of the world. Also, parts of it have been transcribed in pictographs, hieroglyphs, cuneiform, tree letters, and various other early writings. Yet none of these transcriptions or re-tellings do you truly need to discern the prophesy, Stella," he smiled. "For the original *was* written in stone—and it is perfectly preserved to this day."

Mesmerized, Stella stared across the fire at Faas, sipping her tea in eagerness to hear more.

"Now, I must tell you of *the Prophet Walker*," Faas continued, "the greatest prophet ever to walk upon this earth. A duirken so great—he walked in full consciousness of his every step. To fully understand what that even means, you have to be a master reader of the Impaction Reverberation Symbols. For only one who knows the exact meanings of the hundreds of possible Impaction Reverberation Symbols created in a single footprint could consciously know of every subtle nuance the Prophet Walker was writing into his tracks. And, as a *master walker*, he could write stories at will as he walked. For the Prophet Walker was much more than just a prophet. He was the most skilled of all the ancient Walkers."

"*Skilled*...walkers?" Stella asked. She remembered her vision of the volcano—and the secret symbols embedded in her footprints.

"Oh yes," Faas answered. "Walking was considered one the most important of all ancient skills. Tens of thousands of years ago, the most amazing arts and sciences were wholly devoted to walking. You have to understand," Faas explained, "a culture that so deeply revered the track—must also revere the walk. For it is the walk that creates the track."

"Of course, *the track* and *the walk*—at least those directly related to *physical* human beings—both owe their existence to *the Earth*; physical embodiment of the Mother Goddess. One of many reasons the Mother Goddess was connected to, worshiped, and loved to the depths of human compassion in ancient times—as well as now, by all Clann Taluv."

"You worship a goddess?" Stella raised her brows with enthusiasm.

"Ah, the Goddess..." Faas's eyes lit up. "Worship? Well—by the right definition, yes. This Earth—" Faas reached down and reverently rubbed his two palms into the dirt, then rubbed the dust and essence all over his face and head, finally resting his palms on his heart. "She is the feminine aspect of the Great Spirit; of the Infinite Energy of the Universe. As in essence, all things in nature are aspects...of the divine that is moving everywhere. This Earth is the embodiment of Her spirit."

"I know," Stella nodded. "I met Her," she smiled enthusiastically, "on the day you had Clarsah and I explore into the lower levels. Clarsah met her too. Yet..." Stella remembered the deep sense of familiarity she felt at that *meeting*, "we both realized that we had known Her all our lives."

Faas nodded. "As we explore the various levels of the De Da Mua, different layers of *sub*-consciousness awaken in our minds—and in our hearts. But we're getting side tracked—which of course always happens with The Prophesy!" He smiled.

"You see, so great and detailed is The Prophesy, it is connected around the world through many of its fragments that have been found and translated by the great shamans. These prophesies are inter tribal, inter species, and they all go back to the one. There are those who have studied it from afar, by way of the world wide web of tracks and trails—and there are those who have made the physical sojourn to *Ben Bel Teine:* the Mountain of the Fire of Belial."

"It was nine thousand, nine hundred, and ninety one years ago —during a most remarkable snowstorm on the side of *Ben Bel Tienne*—while the volcanic mountain oozed, that the Prophet Walker left his tracks, written in the still soft and pliable, but rapidly cooling lava flows."

Stella was awestruck and mesmerized, as she listened to Faas describe this ancient scenario which seemed almost identical to the vision she'd had.

"Even while he walked The Prophesy, spiraling upwards around the cone of the mountain, he could see far and wide beneath him—the once great land of his people was sinking beneath the sea. For the vengeance of their own attack on the harmony of nature had backfired. Those who worshiped only the fire, and not the oneness of all—those who strove above all else for power and dominion—those who isolated fragmented sciences, void of the wisdom of the spirit of the one that encompasses all— those who sent fire to destroy others…unwittingly brought up the Belial fires onto their own land. Many years of destruction followed. But compared to the grand scope of human life on Earth, it all happened in the twinkling of an eye."

"Shortly thereafter, throughout almost the entirety of that land, the molten fires of the earth retreated—fast and deep, beneath the earth—and far deeper even than the *seemingly* rising ocean. The plates shifted and separated, opening gigantic voids. And thus the land fell. An entire continent disappeared, except for a few tiny islands—on one of which The Prophesy is yet preserved."

"It was from that land, before its destruction, that The It Animal had arisen. There *It* had grown so mighty and powerful, *It* took over the ruler ship of the continent. In the end *It* had enslaved most of the people—not only of Atlantis, but of the entire world."

"Atlantis? Wow!" Stella gazed this way and that through the mists. "I just knew Atlantis was real!"

"Yeah," Faas nodded. "Though I didn't intend to name it yet, so I might stay more focused on The Prophesy. I suppose," he sighed, "without some fragments of the stories that go with it, The Prophesy could hardly be spoken of."

"What is now China," Faas continued, "was the last of the great countries that was completely independent of *It* which ruled Atlantis. The It Animal had designs on total control—world domination. It created a terrible weapon to destroy the resistance in China. But the weapon was tested improperly. It backfired on Atlantis. In the fires and floods that followed, The It Animal itself was broken, diminished, scattered—and almost totally destroyed."

"Yet pieces of it endured. They fled to Egypt, the Americas, and Europe with their secrets. But so too, did Clann Taluv. And Clann Taluv carried the secrets that The It Animal, to its folly, had ignored: the wisdom of the tracks, of the holy walk, of the world wide web, and most of all—of The Prophesy. Clann Taluv loved their land and did not forsake it for fear of fires or floods. They stayed on the remaining islands, guarding the secret of The Prophesy. Over time it grew camouflaged in obscurity. So none needed guard it physically—only to keep it secret."

"Secret, Clan Taluv has kept it—and passed on the sacred wisdom of the tracks and the Walker for all these thousands of years." Faas's eyes glowed, as he gazed deep into the embers of the fire. "I myself have sojourned to Ben Bel Tienne," Faas sighed heavily, "just over a year ago. I have read The Prophesy—to the best of my abilities. And as such, I will relay what is most pertinent of it to you and I right now."

"The first thing you should understand is that The Prophesy is written from the base to the summit, in a pattern reminiscent of a gigantic, myriad branching vine. This pattern describes *time lines,* from the moment The Prophesy was written, through the myriad *futures* that now are histories, stretching just beyond ten thousand years. So you see, we're coming very close now, to the Prophecy's end. Yet every branch in The Prophesy represented a choice. Thus, although written in stone, there were many possible futures written in those tracks ten thousand years ago."

"Now, however, the vast majority of The Prophesy is either history, or *might have beens*, if humanity had chosen alternative paths through different time lines' causes and effects—alternate realities, if you like. But let us now stay focused here!"

"Basically, there are three major parts to The Prophesy: *The Prehistoric Era*—that is, the long, slowly evolving time lines before the creation of alphabets—from ten thousand years ago to around four thousand years ago. *The Quickening Era*—that is, the time lines from the beginning of alphabetically recorded history, about four thousand years ago, up until about three hundred years ago. And finally, *Beo gun meidh*—these are the time lines from about three hundred years ago, up until..." Faas paused, eyeing Stella with uncertainty. "Until sometime in the very near future from now."

"Beo Gun Meidh are the time lines we are most concerned with, because we are now in the thick of them. It is described as the era of the most rapid changes—but the beginning of it will be like sleep compared to the end—for the increase in the velocity of changes in this era was predicted to be exponential."

"Sorry—" Stella cut in. "What does exponential mean?"

"It's when the growth rate of something—in this case, technological development—advances proportionately from what it was each time it has a growth spurt. So like, if the number one grew to two, two grew to four, four grew to eight, and eight grew to sixteen, etcetera—you would see the growth expanding faster and faster. Although proportionately, it's only doubling over and over—what it's doubling from is twice as big each time it doubles."

"But we're not exactly speaking of numbers. We're speaking of cultural and technological changes. Beo Gun Meidh is an era when the world is living without any single balance—but rather in a constant and reckless evolution."

"There were several choices of paths laid out in this era of The Prophesy—some of which represent choices yet to come in humanity's pathway. We could have taken some very divergent ways, recently, that would have lead us on pathways to very different futures. But here we are. And now there are few choices left. We are at a fork, even while I speak, but it seems almost certain we are heading down the path that leads to *The Singularity.*"

"The Singularity will be the most chaotic and fast changing branch of time *within Beo Gun Meidh.* It is the explosive culmination of Beo Gun Meigh—the climactic transformation.

The Prophet Walker foresaw that at the beginning of The Singularity, many human beings will be able to fly all over the world at will, and some even to the stars. An amazing, wireless internet was described, that would provide instantaneous virtual travel anywhere on Earth. People could fully interact with one another from opposite sides of the world—not only with live voice and inter-spacial three dimensional imagery—but also, with touch. *But*...this amazing *internet* will be taken over by The It Animal. And then, through it, The It Animal will control the people—many of whom, by that time, will have gotten implants in their bodies and brains—as we now have already seen with Buck Cambull. Along with these human/machine hybrids, the cloning of animals, human beings, and the blending of human beings with many other species was described for this period."

"The majority of the world's population, it was prophesied, will already be living under slavery to varying degrees at the time of this divergence. Yet the peoples' minds will be so hypnotized, they will not even realize they have become slaves. The It Animal will have multiplied and sent out great numbers of its dismembered parts to carry out the grand plot that was deceivingly designed and redesigned over millennia. All will be under constant surveillance."

"During *The Singularity,* it was prophesied that ninety percent of the Earth's gigantic population would perish. Unless, this hypnotized population somehow, awakens—and regains the free will to stop their mindless progress in its tracks. This could only happen if they become aware of The It Animal, and the Shadow Beast it is using to control them. The one thing that can bring that about is *the Return of the Prophet Walker.*" Faas paused, sighing deeply—then lifted his cup for a long, slow sip while staring intensely at Stella. Stella mirrored his gaze, waiting eagerly to hear more.

"*The Return of the Prophet Walker* was spoken of extensively in The Prophesy—and the exact time of this *return* is nigh upon us." A great raven swooped down and perched upon one of the sapling poles that made up the lattice work supporting the canopy of vines over head. It cocked its head, staring straight down at them. Faas returned it a head jerking gesture. Stella thought of the ravens she had been seeing lately, everywhere she went. And she suspected Faas had sent them to watch over her, but didn't ask. She was captivated now, and had to hear first, all she could of The Prophesy.

"It is very difficult to follow the trails of the Prophet Walker," Faas nodded. "Only the most skilled of walkers—and only one possessed of the greatest of prophetic minds—and of the highest abilities to read and translate tracks…could follow in his footsteps exactly." Faas sighed heavily. "I saw much, but it became more and more difficult to understand as I ventured further along the pathway representing the time line of *The Singularity* "

"The Singularity is the greatest and most awesome of all events foretold in The Prophesy—and the most complex. The It Animal, having spread its members all over the globe, into every power structure they could infiltrate, then begin creating the master power structure—a planetary grid-work...." Faas sighed, shaking his head. "It is almost complete," he whispered, as if only to himself. "Always in secret, and yet...in plain sight," he sighed, "if only people would look."

"Yet though it has gained almost total control, The It Animal fears this time. For it is prophesied that *The Return* of the Prophet Walker could be its undoing. Towards the end of the time line representing *The Singularity*, the Prophet Walker left The Prophesy unfinished—intentionally. For in real life it will be a time of great choices—the most profound choices in ten thousand years. And, at the end of the prophecy, the Prophet Walker wrote that before humanity comes to this actual time, he will return, to finish The Prophesy: *Look for me, toward the end of Beo Gun Meigh—just before The Singularity*."

"In fact, there were several alternative futures that all had *the return* written into their time lines. Depending on which path humanity had chosen to take, at the time of *the return*, the Prophet Walker would either be advising the masses of humanity on our possible choices—or, if the masses had gone beyond choice—he would be advising Clann Taluv alone on ways that we might survive the *Decade of Decimation*." Faas looked searchingly at Stella, as if to see how she was following his words. She said nothing, but nodded, wide eyed, to show that she was following.

"*The Decade of Decimation* coincides with The Singularity. It is just a term that came into use a few hundred years ago, after a member of Clan Taluv returned from reading The Prophesy, and revealed that The Singularity is a ten year period when ninety percent of the Earth's population is destroyed."

"How?" she shook her head. "And how could the Prophet Walker have known all this?"

Faas eyed her gravely. *"There will be the rounding of the mountains, the rising of the waves, the shifting of the poles..."* he recited. "But none of these planetary events will compare to those directly brought about by humanity's choices," he paused, sighed heavily. *"The air from the Earth to the sky will be filled with poisons. The Death Clouds will thicken, turning from grey to red. There will be fires that blaze to the sky and set the clouds aglow from East to West."* Faas shook his head. "Yet if we go down that path, it will be disease and starvation that take the greatest toll— and both will be created by our own doing."

"As to *how he knew,*" Faas continued, "the Prophet Walker was an amazing tracker. He could surf the world wide web of tracks and trails like very few others, even in prehistoric times. Of course, to the Prophet Walker, there were no prehistoric times. Everything, from the beginning of creation, was written, and remains recorded, in tracks. But as to the future—remember what I told you, about how I foresaw where your path and Buck's would intersect? And thus I knew exactly where to lay in wait? It was simple cause and effect—with educated guessing on what choices would be made at various points of intersecting trails. I knew the landscape intimately. I knew the people well enough to predict their choices. It is a very predictable science, really."

"Yet I was searching less than an hour into the future. The Prophet Walker was so skilled, and so much at one with the Harmony—not only was he consciously hooked up with what is today defined as the *collective unconscious*—but further, he was in direct communion with *Awen*—the force that moves in all things, all places, all times. Intricate and far reaching visions—future, past and present—moved through the Prophet Walker's super conscious mind as he walked. His walk translated those visions, leaving his message imprinted in the rock of the Earth for future scholars of tracking to translate for generations to come."

"And The Prophesy does have many translations," Faas nodded. "For it has been translated innumerable times over millennia—"

"Sorry—" Stella interrupted, raising her brows with a smile. "What does *millennia* mean?"

"Thousands of years," Faas replied, as he continued. "No two translations are identical, yet most agree on the majority of details.

And all agree on the main themes I'm presenting now." Faas took a deep breath and sighed. "At the summit of Ben Bel Tienne—"

"Wait—" Stella sighed. "This is *so* amazing. But, it's like—getting so big, and spread out—I mean—it's *so...incredible*. But I'm not sure I'm getting it all clear now. And I don't want to miss anything. I think I just need to digest a little."

"I am so sorry," Faas sighed. "But very soon now, it will all become clear to you. I promise." He started to form a smile, but it vanished with a sigh. "You do not yet need to learn even the whole of the main theme of The Prophesy. But it is vital that you learn the basic story of the Prophet Walker."

"Just imagine the pieces of a jigsaw puzzle—all within your view, but scattered all around you. Or more accurately, imagine yourself following a set of tracks on the side of a mountain. But these tracks are interwoven with so many other branching and interweaving sets of tracks that it appears as a maze of confusion. That is how it now is for you. But when you are able to follow the exact tracks humanity has walked—when you read the whole story —all the pieces will be brought together into one clear image. And in that image, you will see exactly how you...and I...Dr. Warburger... Buck Cambull...and everything and everybody in all of history fits."

"Not all of this could I even tell you," Faas said. "But what you need to understand—"

Faas paused, sniffing, his eyes drifting into the surrounding mists. He stood up, cupped his hands into *wolf ears*, behind his own ears, listening intently. The nearby ravens broke into a sudden frenzy, scattering in all directions.

"What is it?" Stella whispered, searching the mists and cupping her own hands into wolf ears, behind *her* ears.

For a while, Faas said nothing and did not move. At last, he sighed, slowly shaking his head. "It is a small thing...yet it is a disturbance unlike anything I have ever sensed before."

Stella felt the hair on the back of her neck standing up. A tingling sensation circled her head and body. "I...I feel like we're being watched!" She looked to Faas. "Sorry—" she cut herself short. "I guess after all you just told me—"

"No—" Faas silenced her. "Do not undermine your better senses." He nodded, whispering, "You are right." "Something alien to the De Da Mua is probing this area."

"Caw! Caw! Caw!" the ravens reappeared out of nowhere, erupting again in sudden complaint—apparently in reaction to whatever was causing the mysterious disturbance in the Harmony.

"Ravi!" Faas shrieked. And one great raven looped back toward them.

Stella remembered meeting this raven—but that was only in a dream!

"Ravi—" Faas repeated in a squeaky voice— "get…it!"

The raven reeled about on its wings—and suddenly was trailing some large sort of beetle or dragonfly. The bug had very large wings and made a loud, droning buzz. The raven grabbed it mid flight in his beak and returned toward Faas. The great raven landed before them and dropped the thing on the ground. Stella had not realized how big the raven was until he stood before them. He was awesome…and beautiful! Not really black, when seen up close—but brilliant with iridescent blues, greens, and violets. *But how had she known—in her dream—that his name was Ravi?*

But there was no time for analyzing dreams, for Ravi took off in a hurry, perching on one of the poles making up the framework of the canopy over Faas's platform—and she and Faas were left staring at a most peculiar…and disturbing…*bug*.

Rather than having typical insect guts spewing out its sides where the raven had crushed its shell, this *bug* had wires and electronic hardware. Stella looked questioningly at Faas. He was staring—as though in shock.

"It says in The Prophesy," Faas whispered, still staring at the *bug,* "that during The Singularity, Clann Taluv would be stalked by insects carrying the eyes and ears of The It Animal." He shook his head very slowly. "It seems certain now—we are entering that time line."

Stella eyed the bug again. *A remote viewer—a flying video camera and recording device.* Faas stepped on it, crushing it almost flat. He picked it up and placed it under the pole where the raven was perched. "Ravi," Faas squawked. "Take…away…." In a moment, Ravi swooped down, picked up the bug, and flew away….

320

Faas stood silent for some time, listening, looking, sniffing… sensing. At last he sighed. "Our time is shorter even than I thought. But let us warm our cups back up while we can—and let me finish telling what you must hear." They refilled their teacups and returned to their seats by the fire.

"After days of walking on the snow and ashes of the still pliable, but hardening molten rock of the volcanic mountain's side," Faas continued, "the Prophet Walker apparently had a revelation at the peak. In his steps it is written—explaining that his tracks, in that lifetime, could not finish The Prophesy—that another must come to complete it." Faas paused, staring trance-like at Stella.

"Many have tried," he continued, "including myself, but the one who completes it, it is said, will do so without conscious effort—and will be able to translate it whole. In time, it is hoped—to save humanity from the near total annihilation that will otherwise be brought about by the beast The Prophesy says will have arisen and enslaved, through deception, the people, who know not even that they are enslaved." Faas sighed heavily, then tossed several more logs onto the fire from the pile he had stacked beside him.

"It says further," Faas added gravely, "if the people cannot be awakened—then Clann Taluv will be instructed in what *we* must do. We know, basically. But the final part of those instructions is not yet written. For that missing piece, Clann Taluv has waited these thousands of years."

"What you must know also, is that The It Animal I has, over thousands of years, gathered many pieces of The Prophesy. It knows about the Prophet Walker. And It knows about his prophesied return. Now you will begin to see why It wants The Prophesy buried…forever. The Prophesy holds secrets about The It Animal's plans, and about The It Animal itself, that could destroy those plans, or even destroy The It Animal—if it was revealed to the masses at the right moment. Ever since It put this much together, It has wanted The Prophesy obliterated. Only, It has not been able to find The Prophesy—in spite of the many manipulations and tortures its members have carried out against indigenous peoples throughout history."

"What do its *members* look like?" Stella asked.

321

"They are disguised to appear as ordinary people," Faas answered. "It is said, the dismembered parts of The It Animal do not carry the full central consciousness of It. Compared to The It Animal itself, some of these members are barely aware of what they are—much like an arm, a leg, or perhaps just a finger, is barely aware of the whole body—or the brain that controls the body."

"It—" Stella sighed. "And *they?*" she questioned, "these *members* of The It Animal—they have lived all these years? Dismembered from It?"

"The It Animal, yes, certainly. It has survived many thousands of years. As for its Separate parts—maybe." Faas shrugged. "But there are always new parts of The It Animal, new members—*and...human* agents. Most of these human agents are completely unaware of The It Animal itself. Manipulated by the Shadow Beast that is manipulated by The It Animal—these agents in turn use the Shadow Beast to manipulate and control others. To varying degrees they think they are working for a greater good in spite of the evils they commit. They do not realize the true nature of what it is they are a part of."

"But The It Animal, and the circle of members immediately attached to it, who are most conscious of it, believe—even if they can't find The Prophesy—that they *can* stop the Prophet Walker. For it has been leaked to them that it says somewhere in The Prophesy—*if* the Prophet Walker returns...."

"If?" Stella questioned.

"Yes," Faas nodded, "*if.*" He sighed heavily, staring at Stella very gravely. "The It Animal believes the Prophet Walker either will, or already has, reincarnated. But It is striving, with all Its forces, to find the Prophet Walker—and to destroy the Prophet Walker—before the Prophet Walker returns to Ben Bel Tienne to translate the full prophesy—and finish it."

Now Stella was beginning to put the pieces together in her mind—and her heart pounded. *Faas* must be the reincarnation of the Prophet Walker! She remembered the clues MacAwen had given her; *At the height of The Terrible War will come The Singular Confrontation—between the Shadow Beast's manipulators...and... The One whose tracks have foretold all.*

No wonder Faas looked so grave. No wonder *Its* agents were striving to break into the De Da Mua. And that must be why they put the RFID chip into her—as a tracking device—to use her to find Faas. And that chip they had intended to implant in her brain…. Sure, it would have *normalized* her—and stupefied her—and put her under their control. But also, it would have turned her into a walking video camera and audio recorder. It was a nightmare. And though *she* may have escaped it—thanks to Faas —*he* would still be hunted—relentlessly. She felt so bad for him— and so worried. No wonder he had to grow up in the forest.

"Faas—" She didn't know what to say. "I'm so sorry," she shook her head, "about The Prophesy and everything. Like, what it means. I'll do anything to help. Everything in my power."

Faas stared at her. And there was *the look*—but with it, confusion. "Do you know?" he gazed at her, bewildered. "Or do you sense—who?" his eyes widened. "Who the Prophet Walker is?"

"It's kind of obvious," she answered. "After everything you've shown us, and taught us—and how you can track and everything. And how you were raised in the wild."

Faas's mouth dropped open. He shook his head. "Oh no," he sighed. "Oh no. You do not understand." He no longer tried hiding the look. It was blatant now—but there also was grave concern, and sadness, in his look.

"Why do you give me that *look*?" Stella asked. "What *is* it?" she demanded. Neither was she, any longer hiding her burning question.

Faas sighed deeply, his head nodding *and* shaking. "I did find myself in those tracks," he spoke with the utmost intensity. "But *I* am *not* the Prophet Walker." He shook his head. "For long, we have known—as have agents of The It Animal—that the Prophet Walker would be born a child of a very special mind—*a very, very dreamy mind*," his look intensified. "One so dreamy—he...or *she*," his voice trembled, "would be able to see into other times and places—thus it would appear, to those unknowing, that he, or *she*, wandered in other worlds."

Faas rose from his seat across the fire from Stella and approached her. "The Prophet Walker could be identified by an ability to *just know things*—one whose focus would drift far beyond the here and now—one who could see MacAwen when he was invisible to others…" Faas knelt down before her. "This Stella, is why I have looked at you so."

Stella shook her head. Fear and confusion came over her. Her heart pounded in her chest. She thought she knew what he might be saying. But it didn't make any sense at all. He was wrong.

Faas looked very close and straight into her eyes. "*You*, Stella," he nodded, "*you*…are the Prophet Walker."

Stella shook her head. "No," she whispered. "It can't be. You're *not* serious!" She shook her head. But she could see plain enough that he was serious. Faas had thought this about her since the first moment he saw her—and even before that. "*You*…are the perfect person…."

She stood up, stepped backwards, toward the entrance of the hut. "I—" she exclaimed— "am just an ordin—" she swallowed hard "—ary..." she breathed heavily, "seventh grade...girl." Stella was struck immediately by the untruth of her own statement. She searched within—for something more reasonable.

"*I*...could *never* track like you. I'm not a…*skilled walker!* I don't even know anything about it!" Fear gripped her—and confusion. This simply could not be.

"Why do you say, *Tread the Word*?" Faas asked, pressing her further.

"*That*...doesn't mean anything!" she answered, defensively, almost in a panic. "I just liked the sound of it when I heard it. *I* didn't even think it up. It totally came about by accident—pure coincidence!" She looked into the doorway of the hut, as if searching for some dark place to hide in. "I overheard two eighth graders' conversation about a certain tee shirt their teacher wouldn't let one of them wear—and when he said *wear the shirt,* I mistook it for *tread the word.* It was just a mistake!" She looked back at Faas from the doorway.

Faas nodded—but in a manner as though she had only verified what he had known all along—as though he was reassured—as though that finalized it. "It came directly from your subconscious," he said. "I know this is hard to hear, Stella. But you are a genetic, direct descendant—and, *the* spiritual reincarnation…of the Prophet Walker."

Stella stepped into the doorway of the hut and stared into the darkness within. If Faas was right, what that meant was—*they* were hunting Stella. And suddenly, in a moment of horror, the pieces all fit. It was obvious. They *had* tried to destroy her. She remembered the poor girls she had seen in the Psyche Ward at Boston Youth Hospital. She felt so bad for them. Then she thought of how she was tracked and hunted. It wasn't Faas they were after. It was her. And finally, there was her own vision; she had seen herself, climbing Ben Bel Tienne--leaving tracks embedded with secret symbols.

Stella stood motionless in the dark, her inner eye focused on visions in places far beyond the back wall of the hut where her physical eyes stared. She saw the mountain—upon it, The Prophesy, written in symbols she could not comprehend. She saw those girls who were just like her, in the hospital, deformed in mind and emotion by RFID chips implanted in their brains. Why destroy them, too, if she was actually the *one*? She felt so sad, so scared, and deep within her, contained for the safety of her own sanity—a growing sense of rage.

"Stella—" Faas stood in the doorway behind her. "There is no place dark enough to hide your brilliance. Yet, when you return to the light—there will be no darkness that can assail you. And when you shine...there will be no shadow that can endure you."

Stella turned—and there stood Faas in the doorway, like a warrior from heaven, the fire blazing behind him. "Remember," he said, "*they* are afraid of *you*." He nodded, smiled, turned, and returned to the campfire. Stella was compelled to follow. Whatever her destiny was, she felt she had no choice but to face it.

It is many tentacled.
It is ancient. It is Invisible.
It encompasses the whole world,
whispering untruths and poisonous vapors.
As it comes into view...
See the jaws open, waiting.
See the claws poised to clench.
And Yet a wrench...in the works is
A thorn in Its side;
Spirits in the machinery
that none shadows can hide....

Chapter XIV:
The Beast's Monster Conspiracy

Stella sat, staring into the fire, cradling her third cup of tea. Faas stoked the fire up high, and threw more food to the ravens—*as if to lighten the mood,* Stella thought. *Create a party atmosphere.*

"It isn't working," she scolded him. Faas looked questioningly at her. Stella shook her head, closed her eyes. *It's not his fault,* she reminded herself. "I'm sorry," she said. "You can just...keep talking—if you want," she shrugged. "Tell me more about the Prophet Walker—about *me,*" she shook her head. "Or how you think you know...whatever," she sighed. "Like, as if I have no choice in this, just tell me whatever you want."

Faas raised his brows. "You do have choice! You have always had choice. All your life, Stella, you have made your own choices—to walk the paths you have walked, to become what you have become. Before you were born, your spirit, no doubt, made its choices. And even now, of course, you continue from free will, to do and be what you will. But that does not mean your choices cannot be guessed ahead of time by others. Especially those who read the signs and symbols clearly, with unfettered intuition. It is by your choices that we know you."

"What about the girls I saw in the Psyche Ward at Boston Youth Hospital?" Stella questioned. "What choice did they have?"

Faas sighed. "I do not know about any of them, individually —only that The It Animal has thrown a wide net. Others, I'm sure, have tracked them. We are all tracked, Stella. But as I was saying, the choices you make in your walk inspire or deter different trackers from staying on your path. Thus we have stayed on yours."

"We have known about you since...well, *some of us,* since before you were born," he smiled, but it faded fast. "MacAwen would not, or maybe could not, tell us for sure," Faas continued. "For it is the way of MacAwen to let us find out things on our own." Stella did not bother asking who *us* was. At the moment she was more concerned about her own fate than who *us* might be, aside from Faas. Clann Taluv, obviously. But at the moment she had too much else weighing on her to be curious about who the individuals might be, that made up Clann Taluv.

"Clann Taluv has been tracking you all your life," Faas stated. "Me, personally, for the past year—though *I* was not permitted to follow fresh tracks forward, until the day we met. I could only follow *old tracks* in the direction you were heading. Fresh track, I had to follow backwards, in the direction you had come from. *We* strove not to interfere with your life. But we had to learn about you—and watch over you. For we were not the only ones out to track you."

Stella got a shiver thinking about The It Animal and its agents trying to track her down...on top of the Shadow Beast. "I never knew I was so popular," she batted her eyes sarcastically, then shook her head. "But...I guess that's because they never knew exactly who it was they were looking for. Thank goodness!" she sighed with a fright. But then she shrugged, rolling her eyes with a sinking feeling. "Well, I guess they *do* know now."

"You might be comforted to know," Faas said, "The It Animal was hunting the Prophet Walker ten thousand years ago; and as far as I know, It hasn't caught up yet." Faas looked her in the eyes, "the Prophet Walker has many good friends, wise *and* powerful— including the greatest of all possible allies; MacAwen."

Stella eyed him with uncertainty. Faas closed his eyes, shaking his head, "You can only imagine...." Faas looked her in the eyes again; "he was there, Stella, ten thousand years ago."

That got Stella's attention. Her eyes widened. Her brows crinkled in confusion—then she raised them questioningly. "MacAwen," Faas nodded, "was the Prophet Walker's mentor."

Stella's head swam. She actually smiled. Ten thousand years old? It was outrageous. But MacAwen was a mysterious creature —perhaps more mysterious than she'd imagined. She recalled Warburger's absurd statement that MacAwen was a mere holograph. But what *was* MacAwen? She did feel like she'd known MacAwen all her life. Though she'd only actually known him for about a month—in *this* lifetime.

But no—she could not actually believe all this! "No!" She shook her head, suddenly overcome by the part of her that had been trained to *believe not*. "I'm like...*stupid*. I'm in my own world—" she stopped herself. Being in her own world only verified what Faas was saying. "It can't be." She shook her head —smiling one moment, in awe or terror the next. "I'm like— *terrible* in school. Like—the *opposite* of a genius. No teachers— not even the nice ones—have ever thought I was even smart!"

Faas's jaw dropped. "Hasn't *anyone* even taught you the most basic of the basics?" He stared at her, amazed. "First of all, have you never heard that genius is usually not visible to the eyes of the ordinary?"

"No," Stella answered. "They just think I'm an ADD, Attention Deficit Disordered girl—lost in another world."

"And you believe that?" Faas looked incredulous. "You've been surrounded by a non-sensing crowd!" Faas sighed. "It seems that everything you've been trained to believe are your weaknesses...those are your greatest strengths; gifts beyond the understanding of those who have tried to teach—or rather, to train you. Those teachers obviously are not capable of *educating* you— because they have no clue as to what it is they're trying to educate. It's way over their heads! It's like...*IRZ*'s trying to educate Einstein."

Stella's eyes jerked wide. "Did I tell you about IRZ's?"

"You talked in your sleep quite a bit during the fever," Faas answered, "mostly incoherent, but some quite humorous statements, and one articulate description of *Idiot Robot Zombies*," he smiled. "But staying on track with what I was saying," he held up his hands, "this is why you are in fact in another world— *from your teachers*. Because *you* are an absolute genius. And absolute genius is out of *their* world. Yes, *in another world*—from *them*— and obviously beyond their ability to see!"

"And as for your Attention Deficit—it's *not* a Disorder!" Faas asserted, shaking his head. "They just haven't offered much that's worthy of a free thinking genius's attention. If anything, it shows brilliance—and super tenacity on your part, for being able to project your attention *out* of their tiny, limited world—even when they're trying their darned hardest to capture and contain you within it—even under threat of psychological torture."

Faas stared at her, sympathetic and disbelieving—then nodded. "You *do* get the picture," he sighed, forcing a smile. "You just are having a hard time admitting it, because they've been telling you so much less for so long. But you must know," he shook his head, "your so called ADD Psychological Type is a gift, not a disorder. Primitive people have always known this. And throughout history this gift has been bestowed to various degrees on all poets, prophets, artistic geniuses, and inventors." He then stood up. "If you'll excuse me a moment, Stella. I just need to check on something. Are you okay?"

Stella nodded, wide eyed. Faas left the fire, and in a moment had disappeared into the fog. It was dead quiet, but for the sound of the fire—and even that was muffled and absorbed by the fog. Stella was alone with her thoughts and emotions. They moved through her mind and body with an intensity and a ferocity that seemed unnaturally *loud* in this quiet place—like, a passing animal could surely sense her vibrations.

But her body was frozen. Not from cold. And not exactly from fear, but rather—shock. Everything she ever knew or believed about herself, and her world, was swirling upside down and round and round. She was overwhelmed—and frightened. And yet she felt enlightened—trapped and yet freed—confused and yet clarified—happy and sad. It was wonderful to receive such compliments, especially from Faas. Maybe—*maybe...*she really could be the Prophet Walker.... And maybe that could be okay.

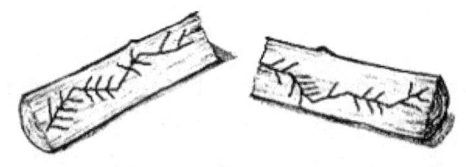

A part of her just knew it to be true—as soon as he told her. To one part of her it was simply logical. Yet the very idea was so mind blowing, she was just torn to pieces thinking about it—and about all she had so recently been through.

In another time and place, *maybe*, she *could have* been someone great. In fact, in another lifetime, she *was*—if Faas was right. But no—she couldn't let herself think such thoughts! But the thoughts were inescapable—and the more she thought about it, more and more of what Faas said made sense—even to the part of her that believed not.

Under the typical rigid thinking of modern society, anyone like Stella could be regarded as a *less than normal, ADD type* in need of remedy—either by chemicals, special training, or both.

Yet long ago—those very same qualities that made her unique would have been regarded as a gift—and in the extreme case, could have elevated her to the status of the world's greatest prophet.

What, she wondered, could have caused modern society to change its views so extremely from those of ancient society?

The answer to that question, like so many answers to so many questions, just came to her; *modern society was designed this way—intentionally!*

Suddenly, she could see it—crystal clear. Though she could not quite believe it. And *why* modern society was designed this way.... Stella expanded her mind in her typical way—a process of streaming imagination—not making believe or fantasizing, but somehow channeling consciousness from beyond herself. Or, maybe, she actually was that consciousness—and it was infinite— and a little bit of that infinite consciousness that she actually was channeled into the little person who she had believed herself to be.

In a moment came the answer to her next question; *Why* society was designed this way was **to stop her in her tracks**—and anyone like her. Because *It* was afraid of her qualities. And somehow, *It* was the architect of modern society's power structures. *But how?*

A phrase she had never heard came suddenly into her mind: *The Hierarchical System.* And somehow, she understood how it worked. At least, for a moment.

Faas reappeared at the fire—without a word or even a sound. He sat and let out a sigh, looking rather grave for Faas. He closed his eyes, then shook his head quickly, as if to shake off some other burden and force himself to focus.

"I doubt I now need to tell you," he half-whispered, studying Stella's face, "much of what *we* have known—so also, The It Animal has known." He lifted his teacup and stared into its depth. "It knew *the reincarnation* would begin life as a child of a unique type of mind." He glanced at Stella, then back into his cup. "It would be a mind so free...so independent..." he looked to the mists about them, "the *system* The It Animal created might not be able to ensnare or contain *this child*," he glanced at Stella, "not even in the intricately devised webs of distraction and mental entanglement *Its* unknowing agents had spun for all the normal types."

"The It Animal knew enough about The Prophesy to know—at all costs, It would have to identify this *reincarnation* of the Prophet Walker—and somehow destroy him. Or *her*," Faas smiled. Stella nodded—for now Faas's words only clarified what, intuitively, she already knew. A part of her, she realized, had *always* known—only, subconsciously.

"Finding the Prophet Walker," Faas continued, "might have seemed a task near impossible—considering how many people are born into the world. *It* knew it had to greatly enhance the system it had in place. *It* needed more oversight, more accounting, more control. Thus The It Animal devised a plan—and the side effects of this terrible plan would serve multiple purposes. *It* desires to keep track of everyone born, to analyze them—and to control them, completely. Not just in body, but also—in mind."

"In mind..." Stella sighed, repeating Faas's last words. "Oh...wow...yeah...like—a part of me has always sensed this. But...like, I could never—I mean, no one would believe this. How could *It* possibly do all that?" Stella shook her head, her eyes wide.

"It was a complex strategy," Faas answered. "So complex you likely will find this part difficult to accept," Faas added. Yet the core of this *big idea* is really simple—which I will explain after, to the best of my abilities. Of course, I am not the best one to explain it," he sighed. "Soon you will meet the full council of Clann Taluv," he nodded, a gleam returning to his eyes.

"Part of the *big idea* was to institute, world wide, a system of regimented mental training—mandatory for all people other than the elite agents of The It Animal and their children." Faas sighed. "The It Animal designed to turn the mass of the world's population into a slave army/work force of mind controlled...what you would call IRZ's."

"The first mandatory public school system was designed to this very end. To dumb down and make obedient all who could easily be molded—and, to varying degrees, depending on each individual's resistance, torture and even drive to madness all those who would not be easily molded, so they could then be remedied, normalized." Faas studied Stella, as if to see her reaction—as though she might find it difficult to accept this information.

Stella gave him a look—like, this was amazing, all this information he had. And yet, he was kind of clueless, about her. Or rather—about the life she had been living.

"*I...*have been through all *that*! And I have sensed something like this all along." Stella shrugged. "I just never thought...it was really made this way...on purpose—consciously."

"Oh, yeah, well—" Faas nodded, smiling, "let me explain. That type of *school system* was first initiated in Prussia, hundreds of years ago—supposedly, to train their soldiers to become perfect, unquestioning parts of a machine, rather than free thinking warriors who might *not* blindly follow orders."

"Yet the modern public school system *is* a direct offshoot from the *Prussian Experiment*. And in spite of the countless well intentioned and smart teachers, literacy rates in your country have gone down, consistent with increased school days and school years. Home schooled students consistently outscore schooled children in all subjects. The system is teacher proof. Of course, really good teachers do make a difference, but the schools they work for all serve the next level of the plan. If The It Animal could somehow *normalize* the minds of all potential initiates to Clann Taluv, all rebels and free thinkers—*especially* the Prophet Walker...."

Stella's jaw dropped in realization. Faas nodded, then shook his head, sighing. He opened his mouth—as if to say more. But suddenly, he froze—his eyes wide.

334

Faas gestured for Stella to be still. Carefully, slowly, he stood, peering this way and that, into the mists. They both listened, while —as well as his eyes—Faas's nose, ears, and fingers scanned the mists.

The De Da Mua was abnormally hushed—as though every bird and beast in the wild was reacting to some disturbance, exactly as Faas was. Even the insects...even the trees...somehow, even the winds seemed to be paused—as though suddenly conscious and scanning the inner atmosphere for some alien presence that had penetrated, or was trying to penetrate.

After an uncomfortable stretch of silence and stillness, Stella slowly raised her brows, looking at Faas, questioningly.

"I don't know what it was," Faas half whispered. Then he shrugged with a frown. At last, he sighed and continued talking, though now in a hushed tone.

"Over the years," he half whispered, "agents of The It Animal have experimented with various harsh and cruel techniques in their *school systems*. But eventually *they* found the covert to be more effective than the overt."

"What does that mean?" Stella interrupted. "Covert, I mean."

"Covert means hidden," Faas explained. "Opposed to *overt* which means *out in the open, obvious, in your face,*" he thrust his face in front of hers, just as MacAwen sometimes did when making a point.

"I think I get it," Stella responded.

"Okay," Faas nodded. "You see, brute force was met with opposition from common people. But seduction, deceit, and subtle mind control techniques went unnoticed by most. And the best slaves, they discovered, are those who do not know that they are slaves."

"That...is *so* horrible," Stella cut in. "How could all these agents who are human beings contribute to this?"

"You have to remember—the agents of The It Animal are under total mind control. They do not know what *it* is that they work for. They actually believe they are carrying out the greatest works for the benefit of all humanity. *They* are merely servants— for the *greatest good*, most believe."

"But let me finish," Faas sighed. "Back to the *covert:* near the beginning of Beo Gun Meidh, agents of The It Animal created

The International Psychiatric Research Foundation. This organization created to some degrees, and infiltrated in others, the various emerging sciences of psychiatry and pharmacology, influencing the movement to study, analyze, and categorize all types of minds. Any *unusual* or *undesirable* personality types were to be given labels—as diseases, or disorders. Specialized treatments and drugs were designed and prescribed to *normalize* each and every personality type that might be *extraordinary.*"

"It's really easy to see how the best intentioned, and many of the brightest of doctors and scientists, could work in this organization. For they did help thousands of people with real mental and emotional disorders. Yet—*through their work*—The It Animal, also, was accomplishing *its* goals. Brutal experiments were carried out—on thousands of innocent, unknowing people— so-called *treatments* using surgery, radiation, electric shock, chemical, viral, fungal, and bacterial experimentation—"

"I think *I* get the picture!" Stella held up her hands.

"Sorry," Faas sighed. "I know you've experienced some of this stuff first hand. But it's important for you to understand what is going on—what is behind it all."

"It's unbelievable," Stella shook her head. "At least, I wish it was," she sighed. "It would have been—before...." They both went silent. "I *thought* psychiatry was *supposed* to *help* people— even if it didn't *actually* work most of the time. *God*! Is it *all* really that bad?"

Faas shook his head. "It is not *all* bad. But the modern organizations have all been co-opted. Indigenous shamans have always had powerful methods of helping people in their tribes to overcome psychological and emotional troubles. Sure—some individuals were devious—but shamans were closely connected to the people in the tribe whom they helped—unlike the world of modern psychiatry where individual doctors are much more enmeshed with the association that *trains* them, *licenses* them, and *monitors* them than they are with real people."

"Let me tell you just one extreme example of how experts and authorities in an association like this can define a mental disorder and its corresponding cure: *Drapetomania* was a real psychiatric term from the 1850's. It was a label defining the *disorder* that caused slaves to have *an uncontrollable urge to run away.* Their official *cure* for this *disorder* was *whipping.*"

Stella stared at him in a moment of disbelief. "Oh my *God!*" she expressed her growing anger and incredulity. "That can't be true!"

"It is true—dead true. Research it yourself," he nodded. "Just gazil—" he paused, shrugged— "just *google* Drapetomania," Faas sighed. "But that's not all. Over the years *many* disorders like drapetomania have been conjured, as well as the gradual initiation of mass drugging. One of their latest inventions is a mental illness called *Oppositional Defiance Disorder—or ODD* for short. At this point, ODD is a term mainly used to label young children who really are overly defiant and disruptive. But as time goes by, and people grow accustomed to it, it may be used to describe anyone who questions authority and refuses to follow orders."

"You see, The It Animal would no longer need to *find* the Prophet Walker if, instead, all personality types who *might become* Prophet Walkers were labeled and suppressed through various means. With the school system—"

"Wait a minute!" Stella interrupted, her head shaking. "Are you saying...agents of The It Animal...have done all this...all these years? And..." she sighed, her eyes wide," they've done it all for me?"

"It cannot allow the Prophet Walker—" Faas paused, looking very grave— "to fully reincarnate." He looked away quickly. But before she had time to ask what he meant by *fully reincarnate*, he continued talking. Now, with a strained look and not facing her— "No Stella. It's not all about you. It's everybody.... But especially certain types," his eyed her again, his expression lightening.

"It is not all *just* for the Prophet Walker," Faas smiled. "This *hierarchical system* is designed, also, to stop the growing members of Clann Taluv; because free thinking individuals—potential members and allies to *The Children of the Earth*—are incarnating now by the thousands."

"But you still do *not* yet understand," he shook his head, sighing, "the importance of the Prophet Walker." He paused, staring at her. "There is vital information—not even the elders of Clan Taluv yet know."

337

"This scheme, this web," he continued, "does serve also, to keep in place the millions of what you call, IRZs. They are good people, Stella. Although they fit in and work very well within the system, like tools, and though the system seems to work well for them, it is suppressing their divine potential, also. You must know, we are all IRZs at times, and we all have the potential to awaken and become so much more. And just as surely, even an awakened member of Clann Taluv could be drugged or lulled into an IRZ. Certainly, any potential *Prophet Walkers* or rebels who might be drawn to Clann Taluv could be caught in The It Animal's great web."

"Oh my God," Stella repeated, shaking her head, "that is *so* horrible." With great pain and empathy, she thought of the girls she had seen in the psyche ward who had micro-chips implanted inside them. "It has taken over the whole world—even America. How? How did it ever—"

"It has had thousands of years to infiltrate the world's power structures," Faas smiled lightly," kingdoms, religions, governments, corporations…everything—"

"The Triple Leverage Corporation!" Stella interrupted, whispering intensely. "Uncle Ken was right!"

Faas nodded. "But there is so much your Uncle does not know."

"How do *you* know what my Uncle knows?" Stella asked, defensively.

"I told you," Faas sighed, "we've been tracking you…and your friends…and your family."

"What?" Stella asked, once again amazed and indignant on different levels as she searched through her thoughts of her friends…her sister…her uncle…her mother….

"I told you," Faas answered, "we had to—"

"My father!" Stella gazed at Faas, suddenly intense. "What do you know of my father?"

"Very little," Faas answered shortly—clearly sensing Stella's emotions, and yet trying to stay on focus. "All I know is Clann Taluv lost track of Joseph Childs before you were born, and we've not found a trace of him since. Of course, I was just a small child and knew nothing. Others in Clann Taluv do know more. And I promise, you will get to meet them," he nodded. "But for now, we must stay on track so I can inform you to all that you need to know now."

Stella went silent. There was new hope. She would soon get to meet members of Clan Taluv who might know more about her father than even her mother or Uncle Ken. She was overwhelmed with intrigue. But Faas was right. She had to focus and listen now —learn all that she could.

Faas sighed heavily. "Now, more than ever before, The It Animal has pawns in positions of power...in multinational corporations, in governments, in the medical associations, in education, and in the media.... Don't get me wrong. These organizations are mostly filled with good, innocent—even smart people. Yet they are deceived, and unwittingly carry out the work of The It Animal."

Faas looked very closely at Stella, and sighed. "You're probably wondering; how can The It Animal do all this? How can it have so much power—even to manipulate and control opposing governments and their armies to carry out its will—which often leads to them destroying themselves—and how it can do all this without anyone *knowing* about it?"

"No," Stella stated flatly. "That's obvious."

Faas went silent, staring at her in confusion.

"I *saw* Star Wars," she shrugged, her hands extended as though it should be totally obvious to anyone. Then she remembered that Faas had probably never seen a movie.

"Oh—well...there was just this *movie*," she raised her brows, "that like, everybody has seen. Well—almost everybody," she shot him a look. "Anyway, there was like, this senator who pretended to be really good and caring—but he was also some kind of like..." she frowned, shook her head. "Do you even know what a Jedi is?"

Faas let out a one syllable laugh, shaking his head. "I've read the story. And there *is* much truth in it," he nodded, "like any good story. But I'm not talking about *a galaxy far, far away*—nor of an evil that was destroyed *a long time ago*." He smiled. "Of course, you must know—that's not really what science fiction or fantasy writers are talking about either." He raised his brows.

"I know *that*," Stella shrugged. "I'm not an IRZ. But—" she closed her eyes, shaking her head. "In the real world—everything is so complicated, and...confusing," she shook her head.

339

"I know," Faas nodded. "The It Animal's power structure, and it's whole system, are made to appear that way. But as complex and confusing as it seems—in truth it is very simple," Faas answered. "There are circles of power in the world—"

"*Circles* of power?" Stella cut him off, raising her brows thoughtfully. "Wow, yeah—well...I know all that," Stella lit up.

"You do?" Faas looked puzzled, then amazed.

"Of course," Stella shrugged. "I read *The Lord of The Rings*."

Faas nodded slowly, open mouthed, a growing smile on his face.

"I suppose everyone knows this—at least, subconsciously." Faas sighed. "Yet consciously, most people have scarcely any awareness to what is all around them. These circles, or *rings*, of power appear in many different forms and have many types of names attached to them: *Associations, Agencies, Religions, Secret Societies, Foundations, Think Tanks, Councils, Commissions, Groups*—whatever they might be called, there are hundreds of these circles of power. They each have their own agendas. Some may even be opposed, or appear to be opposed to one another. Yet in truth, they are all interconnected."

"But—Clann Taluv is a secret society," Stella interjected.

"Yes." Faas answered. "By necessity—a matter of life and death—for many innocent and even unknowing souls. But unlike most other *Secret Societie*s, Clann Taluv was not forged by The It Animal. We *do* have to be vigilant—make sure we are not infiltrated—and that our members are neither seduced nor coerced by The It Animal or *its* agents. And if our members move about in other circles, we must be ever aware of what is tracking us. Unlike those circles of power that are controlled or manipulated by The It Animal, it is our aspiration to share all we know—to empower rather than to control individuals. Yes, we have had to keep safe, the secret of the prophecy's location, lest it be destroyed—and keep secret the membership of the Clann, lest *we* be destroyed—until The Prophesy is walked. But then, if we are successful, all the secrets will be revealed."

"Back on focus," Faas sighed. "First, you must fully understand The It Animal's power structure. Yes, it is based on circles within circles," Faas nodded. "The rings of power—starting with *the one,* ultra secret, central circle, or ring, built around The It

Animal itself and its separable members. Obviously, not a tiny ring one wears around a finger—but a body of persons, corporations, agencies, etcetera."

"When The It Animal's members separate from the main body, they go out in the world disguised as ordinary people, and create circles around each of themselves. Those further circles are made up of agents who know not even of The It Animal's existence. Yet they also carry out its will. They each go out and create larger circles—or infiltrate existing circles."

"Each greater circle or group knows little of the inner circle that formed it—or is *co-opting* it. But The It Animal knows and sees all—and controls all. Perhaps not every single detail. Yet there is a system of communication and command through the core of each circle. It is an idea that has risen and fallen since the first civilization created money, thousands of years ago. Yet now it is entrenched in the societies of the world like never before."

"Money?" Stella questioned.

Faas shrugged. "We could get seriously side tracked on the subject of money. It is a worthy study all on its own. In fact, money is The It Animal's main source of power." Faas sighed. "We have all heard it said, *money is the root to all evil.* I think it more accurate to say; *fiat* money is the root to *the organization* of all evil. Money is created by people. In the beginning, it was purely out of convenience." Faas sighed, shaking his head. "As MacAwen says; *Aware be of convenience.*"

"Long ago, The It Animal became aware of how the Shadow Beast grows out of the unconscious of the masses—how the Shadow Beast operates—and how it affects the masses in turn. *Convenience,* The It Animal discovered, *inevitably* evolves into *unconsciousness.*"

"The It Animal realized, it could exploit the Shadow Beast—employ it—feed it—use it toward its own ends, to control the world. It sent out its members to accomplish just that—wherever the Shadow Beast could be made to manifest. Thus, the Shadow Beast has grown—out of The It Animal's intentional cultivation—as never before—nor never otherwise would be possible. Now it is gigantic, many armed, many tentacled. It works for The It Animal. And—" Faas sighed deeply, "it is growing more rapid than ever before."

"And yet, we in Clann Taluv have long been aware that the *members* of The It Animal, unknowingly, are actually possessed themselves, by the very Shadow Beast they employ. The *human agents* of the inner circles are seduced by their desires to rule the world. *They* are the super wealthy elite. They were made that way by The It Animal's *system*. Most of them don't consciously know that much—or care to know that much about the true nature of the beast. They are seduced by greed. *The system,* they believe, works for them—and is good for *their* families. They hardly notice how horrible the struggles of the less fortunate are. So they who could have some power to change things simply uphold *the system.* They practically worship it. Yet in the end, sadly, it will lead to their own slavery—*and* to that of their families. No one is out of this loop."

Faas eyed Stella carefully. "In the country you've grown up in, The It Animal has spawned a most terrible offspring. Perhaps the most powerful of all the *E-Vampires*—"

"Vampires?" Stella shot him a look.

"Not like ones you read about or see in movies," Faas shrugged."

"I don't waste my time," Stella rolled her eyes.

"But there are real vampires," Faas nodded. "They do not suck blood, of course. That is, at best, just an old metaphor. What they do in reality is steal energy. Yet the E-Vampires spoken of in The Prophesy don't just suck energy out of individual persons. We're not talking about little vampires that walk around and look like people themselves. We're talking about gigantic creatures. They are part flesh and blood, part machine, electronic—and like The It Animal, they are not all in one place; they have separable members moving about in society. They have human agents working for them. They are embedded in the infrastructure. They work through computers, through the internet—"

"Infrastructure?" Stella interrupted. "I don't get it."

Faas sighed. "It does seem complex," he nodded. "In the simplest terms, an infrastructure is that which is within and underneath a structure's surface. But we're not simply talking about physical structures. We're talking social and economic structures." Faas paused, sighing. "I'll spare you the technical explanation for now. But once one of these creatures is successfully embedded and latches on," Faas shook his head, "they suck the energy from an entire population."

"As I was saying," Faas continued, "in your country, because of the wealth of energy, The It Animal spawned its most terrible and powerful offspring. It is known as *The Creature From Jekyll Island*," he half whispered, with feigned hesitation, but a gleam in his eyes. Then he sighed. "Do you know what money is?"

"Uh..." she studied his expression to see if his question was serious. It seemed a bit off focus. But then, sometimes Faas was focused on an awful lot at the same time. And somehow, in his mind, he could grasp the working inter-relationships of so many things. "It represents gold?" Stella shrugged. "So we can buy stuff without carrying heavy metals around?" She looked at Faas for an answer, but he was quiet. "Uh...it represents a value—like an amount of energy—like, from somebody's work?"

"Those are really good explanations," Faas nodded. "And that is what money was intended to be, by those who simply wished for convenience. But the money you carry today is not backed by gold, silver, grain, a set amount of labor, or any tangible thing—not even beans. And it does not represent a set amount of energy. It has no stable value. What you carry today is *fiat money*."

"*Fiat money*?" Stella crinkled her brow. "I *think* I've heard my uncle say something about that, but I have no idea what he was talking about."

"Fiat money is a vital part of The It Animal's *system*. It is money based on, and backed by—*nothing*. It is not backed by gold nor silver...nor even beans. In actuality—nothing but debt. It is loaned into existence. And the people who use it are unwittingly forced to pay interest on nothing. When a government wants to spend money it doesn't have, it simply borrows however much it wishes to spend—from the *Central Banking System* the government has authorized to print its money."

"Wow—" Stella frowned, then smiled. "This is amazing. So, like, the government can have all it wants—like, access to infinite money?"

"Yes," Faas answered. "But by printing more money with no set value, and putting it into the circulation of the economy, what the System sort of does is pour water into the soup. It dilutes the value of the money that common people work so hard to earn."

"Wait!" Stella exclaimed. "Isn't that like counterfeit?"

"You *are* sharp on economics," Faas smiled. "But this is much worse than petty counterfeiting," he answered, shaking his head. "Because, since the government has to pay back *interest* on the money it borrows from this *Central Banking System*—and since the government raises its revenue from taxing the people, other than what it borrows, it is the poor people who have to pay *interest* on money the government borrows—money that is printed out of thin air! It is through this mechanism that the E-Vampire, embedded in the Central Banking Infrastructure, sucks energy from the people. The E-Vampire then funnels this energy directly to The It Animal, shares it with other E-Vampires, or uses it itself, to carry out the will of The It Animal I."

"In your country today, the debt is so great that interest paid on that debt equals all the income tax collected each year. People think they're paying taxes for services—roads, schools, hospitals, armies—but it's a trick. They work and work to pay *interest* on the debt."

"You mean—this actually happens? For real? In the real world? I mean—like, in America?"

"This year alone, in your country alone," Faas answered, "*the system* collected Four hundred fifty one *billion,* one hundred fifty four *million*, forty-nine *thousand*, nine *hundred* and fifty dollars...and sixty-three cents, to be exact," he smiled, "from interest *it* collected on money *it* simply printed out of thin air."

"Wow..." Stella's head swam about in the atmosphere for a moment. Then she shook it hard. "I never knew economics could be so interesting! I always thought it was like the most boring and confusing thing we ever had to study in math class. But they never taught us about these... *creatures*. What a scam! What a rip off! How evil? How much money did you say this... *E-Vampire?*" she crinkled her brow, "stole from the people? Just this year?"

"It was four hundred fifty-one billion, one hundred fifty-four million, forty-nine thousand, nine hundred fifty dollars, and sixty-three cents," Faas answered. He picked up a small parchment of birch bark and wrote the numerical figure with a sharp piece of charcoal: **$451,154,049,950.63.**

"A lot of beans," he said, as he passed the parchment to Stella. "And this is just in your country—which is just one of so many countries where the *E-Vampire Infrastructure* operates. Almost every country in the world now has a *Creature* embedded in its infrastructure. And every year—even though the people of the world work so hard and pay so much of their money to their systems—their debt grows."

"But—" Stella stared in disbelief at the figure on the birch bark. "That's enough money to feed and clothe everyone in the whole world! That's enough money to like—end hunger... house the homeless...heal the whole planet!"

"*They* have other plans," Faas silenced her. "*It* has other plans. Unfortunately, these plans are well laid. They've had thousands of years—"

"God!" Stella shook her head. "How can it be stopped?"

"*I* ...am not sure if it can be," Faas sighed. "At least, not in time to prevent The Singularity. But if the people of the world stopped feeding the beast...then it would simply starve," he nodded. "Without the energy it steals from people—it would simply shrivel up," he smiled.

"But the masses would have to be awakened." He shook his head. "I doubt that is possible—I mean, probable —soon enough." He shrugged. "One thing is for sure; The Prophesy must be walked."

Faas paused, as though something suddenly disturbed him. He glanced around, listened, sniffed, probed the air with his fingers. A breeze moved through the area. Stella heard a far off croak of a raven. She thought she might sense something, maybe. But the De Da Mua was no longer hushed. Rather, there was a quickening to the energy in the atmosphere.

Faas took a few deep breaths, then continued, only now speaking more quickly. "It was not *they* who first invented money —nor banking, nor lending, nor borrowing. But it was *they* who first invented interest; *usury*. And that goes all the way back to Atlantis."

Faas paused again, listening very intently and sniffing vigorously—his eyes wide. He was dead quiet for several minutes —his hands outstretched, his fingers moving in a subtle motion. At last, he let out a heavy sigh and turned back to Stella.

"After Atlantis's destruction," he continued again, "the whole idea of money, banking, and the manipulation and control of individuals' economic power became obscure, almost obsolete. But it took hold once more—about five thousand years ago, in what is now Egypt, where The It Animal had begun to rebuild its power structure."

"Now, operating this way, The It Animal's offspring are like —" Faas studied Stella for a moment, "like *alien super ticks* that burrow into all of humanity. Now you can understand how, what they are in truth is *Energy-Vampires*. Known as *E-Vampires* for short. "

"But E-Vampires not only suck the life-blood and energy from their hosts. Through the infrastructure they build into an economy they actually burrow right into the brain and central nervous system of a society. They take over—controlling not only economic policy and government, but economic thought and belief as well."

Stella was getting a bit overwhelmed and her mind started to wander. She envisioned The Prophesy, written in tracks on the slopes of Ben Bel Tienne—as Faas finished his discourse on E-Vampires and the history of usury:

"Of course, for much of history, it was difficult for members of Clann Taluv to understand E-Vampires. For they could only imagine what the Prophet Walker meant by part *machine...electronic...computer...* etc.. But The It Animal had all this in place before Atlantis's destruction. Now, it has long been working to rebuild its infrastructure. These E-Vampires are maintained by the same ring of banking dynasties, directly descended from the ancient money changers, who *consciously* follow their ancient predecessors' initiative—to control the world by the creation and control of all the world's money. But *unconsciously*, they in turn are controlled by The It Animal."

"How do you write The It Animal?" Stella interrupted. "I mean—how did the Prophet Walker write it, in tracks?"

Faas gave her *the odd look* again, but now with a smile, shaking his head. "It is fitting *you* would ask—and vital that you know," Faas raised his brows.

"The Prophet Walker invented a secret alphabet—thousands of years before alphabets are thought to have been invented. It is called *Bal-Onu-Fes*. Or just *the BAL*, for short. His visions into the future were so clear, with such depth, that he actually learned the world language that would be spoken at the time of *Beo Gun Meidh*. Thus, the Prophet Walker's secret alphabet is based on that world language which he perceived in his distant future—modern English!" Faas smiled.

"Much of The Prophesy, as I said before, was handed down, orally, from ancient languages—but not all. Parts of it were laid out in universal symbols that any skilled tracker could read, regardless of the language they spoke. Other parts, written with this secret alphabet, could only be discerned by the most learned members of Clann Taluv."

"*The Sacred Alphabet—Bal-Onu-Fes*—is written in twenty-seven symbols; these symbols not only represent the sounds of the English language—but also, some of the most common *Impaction Reverberation Symbols* that occur in a human footprint. So, as well as being written by hand, this alphabet can be encoded into the footprints of a highly skilled walker! That is how, from the Prophet Walker's footprints, *modern* members of Clann Taluv have translated the exact spelling of The It Animal *I*."

"As I mentioned," Faas added, "The It Animal is also referred to as *the Lie*. This does describe The It Animal quite well. But the reason some in Clann Taluv speculate that the true name of the beast is *The It Animal—Lie,* rather than The It Animal—*I,* is because the Prophet Walker's prints do not make it perfectly clear. The ancient spelling either used two L's at the end of the word, *Animall*—as most of us have discerned. Or, the second *L* is the beginning of the third word in the name, *Lie*— as others have discerned. The Prophet Walker certainly did not use an *E* at the end of the word, *Li*. But he also used a *U* rather than an *A* for the third vowel in Animal. Some words he seemed to sound out, or simply write in short hand. Or rather, short foot," Faas smiled. So he actually spelled it like this—" Faas printed each letter in the earth while saying it out loud:

"*I–T* for **It**. *A-N-I-M-U-L-L*—for **Animal**. And *I*—for **I**.
Or:
I-T–for **It**. *A-N-I-M-U-L*—for **Animal**. And *L-I*—for **Lie**."

"It is really hard to know for certain, because BAL ONU FES has no upper or lower case letters. And, while there are spaces between separate words, represented by a silent *tip-toe* symbol, there are also silent symbols between some letters *within* words. This is necessary when a walker is printing BAL ONU FES symbols because each symbol represents two different *sounding letters*, depending on whether it is in the right or left footprint. And it would not be physically possible to print the intended Impaction Reverberation Symbols, when two or more symbols in a row need to be printed by the same foot, unless the walker steps on the opposite foot, making the silent symbol between sounding letters."

"So, whichever meaning is correct, from BAL ONU FES to modern letters, keeping the spaces where the Prophet Walker placed them, it translates looking exactly like this:" Again, Faas printed the name in the ground:

THE I T ANIMUL L I.

"Take your pick," he concluded, "The It Animal I or The It Animal Lie."

"Another oddity was that the Prophet Walker always walked backwards when writing The It Animal. To signify the deceitfulness of this beast, it is supposed."

"Of course, for all these thousands of years, modern English was not a language known or spoken...or even in existence, outside the inner circle of the most learned members of Clann Taluv who had learned this *future language*. So of course, even those most learned were not able to master the future language as easily and naturally as we can now. Many translations have long been open for debate, but most are clear to us now."

Faas silenced himself suddenly—his gaze intense, piercing the mists toward some distant mystery.

Stella followed his gaze, and saw nothing. But in a moment she heard a distant raucous of ravens. And in another moment, saw two ravens flying out of the mists toward them. In response, the flock that was hanging around close by commenced squawking and taking to the air. Stella glanced at Faas—then did a double take. There was a look of shock on Faas's face—not something she was accustomed to seeing in the likes of Faas.

"What is it?" she asked nervously.

For a while Faas did not answer. He just stared wide eyed into the mist. Finally, he sighed, very heavily. "It is Buck Cambull," Faas answered, "on his machine."

Faas looked at Stella—and there was a disturbed, saddened look in his eyes. "His machine—it now has *amphibian* capabilities." he shook his head. "The waterways…." He closed his eyes, his head still shaking. "It is no longer safe here," he sighed heavily again. "*Sergeant* Cambull has penetrated the De Da Mua."

Stella froze in terror—and even as she did, she could hear the approaching sound—the whining, revving, and thrashing of Buck's machine! In a blur, Faas dashed into the hut, but Stella stayed frozen. All she could think of was *the final showdown* between *the beast who controls the shadow beast and the one whose tracks have foretold all.* That *one*, she now knew, was *her*. But the Beast who manipulates the Shadow Beast…it was not just Buck Cambull after all. It was The It Animal itself.

To her absolute horror, the noise of Buck's machine was suddenly overcome by the thunderous clattering of a helicopter! But of course—he would lead them *all* here. The last refuge and sanctuary—infiltrated!

"Follow me!" Faas took her by the arm suddenly, and shook her. She hadn't seen him reemerge from the hut. He had a bow in his hand and an extra quiver strapped to his back.

A flock of ravens, the size of which she had never before seen, was gathering in the air and heading in the direction of the helicopter. Then there arose a disturbed honking of geese. Stella paused, eyeing the great birds. "Canadians," she said dreamily as Faas pulled her away by the arm.

"Newfoundlanders," Faas nodded, smiling. "They're known for taking down jets."

A small cloud of what appeared to be mosquitoes flew past them as Stella followed Faas to the far side of the platform—near where she and her friends had observed the Cambulls weeks before.

"We have some swimming to do," Faas informed. "And some slurking," he smiled with a quick raise of his brows and a nod. Stella shook her head. When it came right down to the most dangerous action, Faas seemed to get a strange sort of thrill. Stella

349

trusted Faas more than anyone—other than MacAwen. But she neither shared nor appreciated this wild sense of adventure. She was feeling she had had quite enough.

At last the beast appeared—and was seen.
At last as an ending came to the dream
And the hero awoke.
No one knew how she lived on the run,
nor imagined she witnessed the Central Sun
whirling molten fiery orb.
None knew ever what she went through
nor imagined in fact it all was true
Yet in the end they will.
In the end we will...

Chapter XV:
The Journey Begins

Stella followed Faas as though she was in a trance. They swam across a deep area, then slurked along some waterways. The sound of the helicopter rose and fell...then rose again. A sudden, then continuous machine gun fire issued from it. Were they now trying to kill her? She looked up in the direction of the noise.

But the copter was maneuvering—spinning, rising...striving to avoid a black cloud that pursued it—a black cloud that, she realized, was a flock of ravens. With a sudden splattering, then a sputtering of the rotor—the copter went down! She didn't hear a crash, but all sign of it was gone.

Yet the whining of Buck's machine grew closer. "Come on!" Faas urged her, "Quicker!"

Yet amazingly, as she followed Faas, it seemed to Stella they were circling around—and actually moving nearer to the sound of Buck's machine.

Stella grabbed Faas by the quiver strapped to his back. "Why are we getting closer?" she asked with a growing sense of desperation and confusion.

He turned around with an impish grin. "Buck is trying to track us," he answered, "so we're going to make some tracks for him to follow."

Stella did not like the sound of this. "Is this really necessary?" she eyed him fearfully.

"I *am* having fun," Faas admitted, "but I would never lead you into unnecessary risk. It's important to lead Buck back toward the perimeter. But you can relax now—for I've led Buck around many times over the past year. And now..." he glanced up and around the abounding tangles of vines and thickets, "I am not working alone," he smiled. Stella gave him a questioning look. "The Guardians," he answered, excitedly. "Come on!"

Faas led Stella toward the sound of Buck's machine until she could barely take it. They were so close—she was sure, any moment Buck would come tearing into them. Finally, Faas turned and led her in the opposite direction—very quickly, but now rising from the waterways to leave tracks here and there upon the islets.

By the sound of Buck's machine it was in hot pursuit, gaining on them, and just out of sight behind them. They ran in a fairly straight line for a while—as straight as was possible climbing up and down, over islets and through the brush and reeds—until they came to a place where the water was especially deep. "The perfect place for our tracks to suddenly end," Faas beamed. Here he uncovered a coracle he had stashed under some brush on the side of an islet. Beside it was a double ended paddle. This coracle was smaller than the others Stella had seen. The two of them could barely squeeze into this tiny boat together. But once they got going she was surprised by the speed Faas could make the thing go.

Soon they were traveling waterways that were so narrow, running through thousands of grass hummocks and high banked islets—she could not imagine Buck's machine being able to follow —even if he had a clue *where* to follow. And the sound of the machine fell further behind them—for now.

Yet somehow, Buck *had* gotten clued enough to approach Faas's outpost. Stella listened to the revving of Buck's machine. It seemed now to be in the area of the deep water, near where they'd gotten the coracle. And there it stayed for quite some time—as though Buck had gotten confused or stuck. The sound faded as they distanced themselves from that area. "Do you think he can track us further?" she asked.

Faas shook his head. "We are safe for now," he informed. But he continued paddling vigorously, without a word, for another ten minutes. This part of the De Da Mua was aglow with purple and yellow flowers. It was beautiful—and different than anything Stella had ever imagined. The islands varied in size from a single grass clump, to about twenty or thirty feet across at the largest. They were close together, separated only by narrow waterways. The entire area looked the same in all directions as far as Stella could see.

"If we're safe," Stella questioned, "why are you still paddling so fast?"

Faas sighed and slowed down. "Buck—and his machine," Faas said, foreboding, "are only a part of something much bigger that is coming."

Stella went silent. She sensed—whatever was coming, it was not only coming for her and Faas. It was coming for everyone. It was like—her little adventure, in fact, her whole life and everything in it, was just a metaphor. And yet, every little metaphor was actually real. All the great stories she had ever read —all the signs she had seen in nature—it was all for her, each moment, reflecting her life, for her...*mythic adventure*. And somehow, for better or for worse, she and all humanity...and all nature...were now coming to the biggest moment ever....

Finally, Faas parked the coracle and led her up onto an island to rest. This island was about fifteen feet wide and maybe twenty four feet long. It was mostly covered with thin saplings, dwarf trees, and bushes; but a trail led up from the water, to a grass and mossy clearing centered around a rather large and ancient looking stump. Stella sat down in the clearing and listened.

The helicopter was clearly gone. Buck's machine still whined in the distance—apparently in about the same spot it had been in when Buck first got stuck or confused. Faas stood listening—his hands cupped over his ears. Dragonflies, butterflies, honey bees, bumbles, bluebirds, cardinals, and woodpeckers fluttered about— each contributing its own songs to the Harmony. In the distance, Buck's machine made three loud, sputtering sounds, then went silent.

Faas raised his brows, his head tilting. "Uh oh—" he said, the familiar impish grin spreading across his face. Now Faas too, sat down and rested.

"What?" Stella raised her brows questioningly. "What's going on with Buck?"

"The Guardians have him," Faas answered, "in a conundry."

"A conundry?" she gave a perplexed look.

"It's a very confusing place," Faas answered. "It will be quite some time before he gets out. And then—he will have no idea how or where he got in. I suspect he will be quite frustrated," Faas smiled, "but a bit too exhausted to be angry, by the time he gets home." Faas sighed. "All the upgrades and implants in his mechanized world will not help him get out sooner, or recover quicker, from the ordeal of a conundry."

"What happens in a conundry?" Stella raised her brows, a concerned look on her face.

"It's always different," Faas answered. "Usually, one finds oneself in a bramble patch with fifteen foot high vines covered with two inch long thorns. Often, these will be interspersed with twelve foot high stinging nettles. Then, there's the poison sumac—but that doesn't get you until the next day. There's pollen...and dusty fungus that gets into your eyes and nose and mouth. There are unpredictable sink holes in the mud—so you're constantly falling and rubbing up against all the poisonous vines and sharp thorns. But that's just the plant life...."

"There can be all sorts of aggressive birds, water snakes, snapping turtles, beavers, otters, leeches, water rats.... But the very worst deterrent...is the insects. There are mosquitoes, gnats, horse flies, and *no-see-'ems* enough to drive *anyone* to utter madness. There are no clothes they cannot penetrate. Finally, there are the bees and wasps—swarms like you could only imagine."

"That's...*horrifying*," Stella exclaimed. "Have *you* ever been in a conundry?"

"Only in practice," Faas answered. "Just for fun, to test them out—see how far I can penetrate."

"You call that *fun?*"

"Conundries don't get you all at once," Faas laughed. "They start out gentle—the plants and creatures sort of guide you out of the De Da Mua. It's only when you're stubborn and try to fight your way in that it starts getting bad. And then it just keeps getting worse and worse until you go in the direction you are guided— out. The vines and thorns start closing in around you—more and more as you fight. And the more you fight—while the way in becomes impossible, even the way out grows more and more difficult."

"Wow," Stella stared about with awe. "I guess MacAwen wasn't kidding when he said the De Da Mua was protected. But Buck *did* manage to get *in* to the De Da Mua," Stella retorted. "And he did get quite close to your outpost."

"He does seem to have made a strange connection with me," Faas sighed. "From now on, I don't suppose it will be safe to remain long in one place."

Stella looked at Faas. He seemed completely unruffled by that thought—as though he was accustomed to living on the run. But the thought of not staying long in one place—it was not anything Stella had ever had to think about. In fact, it was more than she *could* think about. It led to all kinds of other thoughts and fears. Everything was just overwhelming. Yet more than all the craziness —more than she being the Prophet Walker—more than The It Animal ruling every major government, corporation, and institution in the world—more than every law enforcement agency from every government in the world hunting her—more than anything—she missed her mom. "I won't be able to go home, will I?"

Faas closed his eyes. "No," he shook his head.

"So, like—how am I supposed to survive?" she asked. "Do you have places to go? Or do you think you'll be able to teach me —like, how to survive in the wilderness?" She thought of her Uncle Ken; he was going to teach her. She missed him so much— and her knife.

"How to *survive*?" Faas stared at her incredulously. "Stella...*you* won't have to even *try!* Just stick with me—and it will all come naturally," he shrugged. "Everything you need to learn is *totally* fun and easy." He smiled. "You will learn to identify, gather, and store all the edibles you need—ignite fires— build shelters—and craft every useful item you could ever need from wood, stone, bone, plants, and clay!" He leapt to his feet with new excitement, scanning the wetland forest about them.

"Don't worry about *survival!*" he shook his head, almost laughing. "I can teach you how to live in the lap of luxury—with as little as four hours of work—all fun and interesting work—each day! Which is only half the time most modern people spend at *their* tedious and unhealthy jobs each day," he added with an air, "not to mention how much they have to work when they get home —to cook and clean...and prepare for their next day."

"I know...." Stella shrugged. "I'm only thirteen, and I spend, like—six torturous hours at school every day—not to mention the *drudgery* of homework!" Stella leaned back on her elbows, her dreamy gaze following a swirl of fog that rose up from the wetland like a small, gentle twister moving in slow motion, thinning and dissipating into the atmosphere. She was struck suddenly, by a rather uplifting realization; "Well—" she raised her brows, "at least I won't have any homework...."

Her mind mulled over the situation. "I won't have to read any *stupid stuff,*" she nodded. "*And...*" she leaped to *her* feet suddenly, and advanced on Faas. Her thoughts once more were moving in domino fashion—only now, each crashing thought gave her new satisfaction. "I *won't,*" her eyes lit up—a smile spreading across her face, "have *any* more math classes—*ever* again!" She shouted. Her look intensified. Faas raised his brows, appearing somewhat amused, but stepped back from her—apparently, a bit concerned as well.

Stella felt a great, almost uncontrollable sense of mirth and freedom welling up inside her. "Liberty!" she shouted, smiling wildly and throwing her arms to the air.

"Whoa—slow down," Faas cautioned, raising a hand carefully before her—a look of concern and confusion appearing on his strong, young face. But he sighed, showing a bit of a smile and shaking his head.

"I'm glad to discover how resilient you are. But...my deeper concern—" Faas searched her expressions, "is not only you missing your folks...and your friends—and them missing you. But worse—my real fear is…" Faas shrugged, studying her expression very seriously. "What *you* will have to learn to live is not *ordinary wilderness survival.*" Stella eyed Faas questioningly—almost defiantly.

356

"*You,*" he asserted, "will be forced to master the arts of defense—*and* the ways of the scout. *You* will be hunted, relentlessly—anywhere you go on this planet—by the worst and most powerful enemy ever to exist." Faas sighed. "*You* will need true magic."

Stella nodded. But it was clear to both of them, something wild within her was awakening. And rather than feeling daunted, that part of her was excited. Faas, obviously, was striving to keep her emotionally balanced.

"When you do survive long enough—like me—*they* will broadcast to the world that *you* are the most wanted terrorist—and *half the world* will be hunting you—even good people who *unknowingly* serve The It Animal."

"I know," Stella sighed. "I know. But what about Clann Taluv? Who are they? Where are they all? And how many of you are there?"

"You mean, how many of *us* are there," Faas replied. "*You* are one of *us*, Stella." Faas smiled. "And you have friends all over this planet—"

But even as Stella was starting to feel comforted, even excited, by what seemed the first bits of good news Faas had shared all day, his words halted. Faas's expression went wild—and froze.

Stella froze, also. She too, could sense it. It was dead silent, but approaching faster than the speed of sound. Whatever it was, it felt alien, extremely aggressive, and very, very powerful.

She looked to the sky. At first there was nothing visible. Then, out of thin air—a gigantic, circular, silver object appeared. It hovered, completely silent. Its entire mass was illuminated, though no individual lights could be seen upon it.

Suddenly—boom! There was a deafening explosion. Stella nearly collapsed from the shock of it. Then, again, all went silent —now, dead silent...even the birds and insects... even the very winds. And the "space ship" simply hovered above them.

Stella stared, confused as well as awed. "A space ship? What...who?"

"It's not what it appears to be," Faas said, staring also, at the great apparition hovering above them. But before he could say more, the space ship disappeared—and something else came thundering out of the sky, flying very low and heading straight toward them.

"Predator drone!" Faas yelled. "APD! Jump in the water!" He took her by the hand, and they both ran and leaped into the water. The APD: Autonomous Predator Drone flew straight over their heads—then slowed, circling back towards them, barely above the trees.

A huge flock of geese arose from the swamp and flew head on toward it as the drone banked around. *Newfoundlanders,* Stella recalled what Faas had told her, *known to take down jets*. But as the geese approached the APD, they were instantly vaporized to a puff of black smoke and fine ash. No birds or swarms of insects could have an effect on this thing. Stella *was* terrified. But she would *not* be overcome. She looked to Faas.

"Breathe through this," he handed her a large reed. "Stay submerged—right here! I will avert it!" He gave a quick smile. "This is to cool your breath—so no thermal detection," he said, as he shook dry a cold, wet clump of debris he had pulled from under the cold water. He placed it over the top of her reed. "Stay submerged—and as still as you can until I return!"

Stella gave one quick, exasperated look. "Now!" he pushed the reed into her mouth and almost forced her under water. Stella submerged herself and closed her eyes. The world went dark and cold.

Wow—that sort of happened really fast, Stella thought—as she trembled beneath the cold waters, clinging to the roots of reeds on the bank of the island—her heart pounding. But nothing seemed to happen very fast there after—as she waited in darkness and cold.

Her throat tightened—like there was a large lump in it. She had no idea what Faas was doing—or how long it would take—or where he was—or if he was okay. If she'd felt any appeal to being the prophet Walker—it was all gone now.

Of course Stella was frightened, but much more—she felt very, very sad. She felt so much like crying. But if she was even physically capable of crying, without drowning or revealing her position, she didn't know. And she did not want to find out. She held it back. And her throat seemed to tighten further. Her eyes, probably, were releasing tears. But of course she could not feel them under water.

She thought of the whale that had appeared in one of her dreams while she slept in Faas's hut, recovering from her last ordeal. She had swam with it under the De Da Mua's waters. To pass the time she imagined it now, swimming with her again. She looked into its deep, dark eye—so peaceful...but sad. Stella's hands were caressing the whale's face. It felt so familiar—like she really knew this whale. But she *did* know this whale! Although she only ever met it in dream, Stella had a sudden realization; this whale really did live out in the ocean. And it had a name. Or rather, *she* had a name. And *hers* was a long name that could only be expressed in song. No human could sing it. But Stella could hear it—and she understood the meaning, which she translated as best she could into her grasp of modern English: *Melodium-trumpeteeri-um-sumptuous-echo-phonic-sur-la-mer-sea-sauntering-sensuous-madonna-drum-den....*

One day dream led to another. Now Stella was running—somewhere with her friends. They were being chased. She thought of the Cambulls. And then, the image of floating corpses came back to her. Where on Earth was Faas! And what was taking him so long? She felt like a floating corpse herself. She strove to think of other things. Like her sister, Ari—or Uncle Ken....

How long she stayed in that position, having only day dreams to pass the time, she could not fathom. But she never gave up. She contained the urge to burst up. In spite of cold, darkness, and fear. In spite of the shivering. In spite of the overwhelming desire to know what was going on above—with the Predator Drone —with Faas. Instead, she thought of other things: NeeGaia, Clann Taluv, MacAwen....

Stella entered a deep meditation. She was no longer awake —nor asleep. From the deep silence she grew aware of a sound. It was like the sound of millions of snowflakes falling—to super sensitive ears. Or the sound, she imagined, of ten thousand butterfly wings....

"She hears this much," a voice rose out of the darkness. "She's got butterfly wings."

"I've got butterfly wings," she responded in her mind, knowing that "butterfly wings" was some kind of code phrase for a certain level of consciousness.

"She hears us," another voice said. "She's aware of us."

"I *am* aware of you," Stella said. "Who are you?" she asked, thinking maybe they were highly skilled duirkens from Clann Taluv.

"We're your subconscious," one of the voices answered her. And then the voices spoke to each other—as though she could no longer hear them. They were discussing the situation amongst themselves. "She did jump the train...and crash the jet," one voice said, "but no one got hurt." In her deep trance, Stella somehow knew what "jump the train" and "crash the jet" meant. She felt bad about the jet.

"I'm sorry," Stella responded, "for crashing the jet."

"She still hears us," said one of the voices. "She's achieved 333!"

"333?" Stella questioned. But then the voices went silent. They could still hear her thoughts, Stella knew. But they were no longer speaking out loud—or her inner hearing was no longer so deeply attuned. Then again, perhaps she was imagining it all. But...that would make it no less real—because the voices did say they were from her own subconscious. And she did not *consciously* make them up. On the other hand, she imagined, maybe she did not yet have clearance from above to hear more. But...there might be a way to over ride them—go straight to the top.

"Ahh...hum! And straight to the bottom," MacAwen's voice cut in. "Ta the depth o' the matter."

"MacAwen!" Stella opened her eyes—and there was the little brown man, floating before her. But he rather looked like he was hovering in air than floating in water. "I must be dreaming," she said. "But I'm awake."

"Lucid dreaming are ye, Stella. Both awake and in a dream. Now do with it what will ye."

"Oh...yeah.... I will," she promised. "But...MacAwen," she asked, "am I really the Prophet Walker?"

"Ha—" he laughed. "Is't not for anyone else ta answer for ye. If will ye and imagine ye ta be—so shall be ye," he answered.

360

"Are there many forks in the pathways," he smiled. "Is't for each ta decide their own."

"Oh...okay.... But, MacAwen," she asked, "were you really in Washington...D.C.?"

"Ah..." he smiled, suddenly glowing. "Whispering in ears was I. In many ears. And still whispering am I—from the woodwork."

"From the woodwork?"

"Ah...yes! From the woodwork! From secret symbols that spoke I into while prayerfully carving." MacAwen showed her a birch key board with a beautiful design on it. But when she looked closely she could see the hidden symbols.

"Tree letters!" she exclaimed

"Ah," MacAwen nodded, "and Bal Onu Fes." Stella looked closer—and now she saw the *Impaction Reverberation Symbols* MacAwen had also embedded into the design.

The sound of the butterfly wings grew louder. And as she listened more intently, she could hear MacAwens words, whispering from the wooden keyboard—whispering very loud!

"You carved these in D.C.?" she asked hopefully.

"From the *woodwork* on the very walls and halls of wonder and power," MacAwen nodded, "will come influencing voices of transformation."

"Where exactly in D.C. did you carve it?" she asked.

"In museums...in rooms of public and secret councils that themselves are parts of a greater, secret symbolic architecture. And yet, is the greater architecture only a part of an even greater secret symbol." A gentle laugh emanated from MacAwen.

All this was wonderful and hopeful, but...what about Faas! "Where's Faas?" Stella suddenly remembered the reality going on outside her dream.

"Is't but a dream ta me. Is't *yer* reality, Stella! Now do with it what will ye." And MacAwen disappeared.

Stella was alone once more with her thoughts in the dark. Her whole body, she now realized, had gone numb from the coldness of the water. Her breathing had slowed to a barely noticeable rhythm. Time seemed to have almost stopped. And yet, perhaps a lot more time than she imagined had gone by.

After some time a different voice came into her mind. This voice had neither sound nor personality. It was more a stream of thought than a voice. Yet it formed like a voice in her mind. And it stated things she had not known or thought about before:

"The image you perceive of the Little Brown Man really is a holographic projection.... Yet the true MacAwen is much, much more than this image—and Clann Taluv are no more the creators of this image than Dr. Warburger...or you, yourself."

Stella wondered if this voice again, was a part of her subconscious. *It must be*, she thought. Yet this voice was different than the voices she had overheard, conversing with one another inside her mind. This voice seemed more like—more encompassing of her *whole* consciousness. And yet also, it was from beyond *her* consciousness. She felt herself transcending the dream-realities that she dwelt in during the time fragments of her life. And now...she floated in timeless, eternal now....

Finally, there was a great flash from above—and then, an explosion that shook the very De Da Mua! A wave came over the top of her reed, and her mouth filled with water. Stella gasped. She had no choice but to emerge from the water for breath.

What Stella saw was disturbing and frightening. The fog was swirling and billowing violently about the whole region—and was thinning drastically. It was very bright—brighter than she'd ever seen the De Da Mua—like the sunshine might burst straight through any moment. There was no sign of Faas—nor of the autonomous predator drone. But Stella sensed a great disturbance in the Harmony. She looked to the sky.

The cloud cover evaporated—and within moments, blue sky appeared. The cover of the De Da Mua was blown wide open! But it was not a clear blue sky above. Hovering over her were three alien crafts—exactly like the space ship she and Faas had seen, just before the predator drone had thundered in. But these were much lower—and one was descending rapidly upon her.

Whether or not he could save himself, Faas had somehow saved her from the predator drone, but he was not able to return in time to meet this little challenge. Yet even if Faas was with her—these, she sensed, were far more powerful than predator drones. And there were three of them. Above them, the blue sky was criss-crossed with Stealth Cloud forming chemical trails.

There was no point in trying to hide. They already had her position. The only question was, what would they try to do to her? Whatever they tried, she knew she would defy them—somehow. *They are not what they appear to be*, she remembered Faas's words. But what they were in reality now came to her; *Stealth Craft*. Not the type everyone knew about, but some top secret form of stealth technology.

Stella felt a beam of energy projecting down to her from the lowest craft, as it descended. She was affected immediately. She felt dazed. But she raised her fists in defiance, and strove to *see* the energy. If only she had more Duirken Self Defense Training. *The Three Fold Initiative*, she remembered; *Sensing, Illuminating, Transforming*. She *had* sensed this energy beam. And without even thinking of the Three Fold Initiative she had strove to see it, thus illuminate it. Strangely, all she could now *see* was Awen—which she hadn't noticed before. Yet now it was rising from everywhere.

Swirling blue and white sparks formed into great waves of energy; Awen—pulsating, growing, expanding—impregnating the air, the land, the sky. The De Da Mua mists rose up and closed the opening in the sky. The two higher Stealth Craft disappeared in the mists. Stella opened her fists, her palms raised up. She envisioned Awen emanating from her hands—and from all around. She imagined MacAwen's voice, coaching her on how to raise the energy. And then—she could actually hear it:

"Ta be raising the Awen, simply need ye ta be raising consciousness. An' as raise ye that which believe ye ta be yer own consciousness, will realize ye that all consciousness is one consciousness—an' arises the Awen simultaneously from yer self as from all around."

Stella willed and imagined with all her might, Awen rising from all around. And as she did, she saw something else forming into her view. It *was* MacAwen! He was standing on the big stump on the center of the little island beside her, his arms raised to the heavens—working the Awen with Stella.

"Now," MacAwen instructed, "bring up a little Awen here," he waved his arm over the water—and a whole wave rose up out of the De Da Mua. "And bring down a little Awen here," he waved his other arm about the sky, and a beam of sunlight shone down.

"Mix it up here," he added, smiling at Stella as the water and sunbeam coalesced into a huge, swirling cloud pulsating with rainbow colors. "Roll it over here," he directed the cloud around the Stealth Craft. "And fold it over, and turn it away." His cloud folded over—and took the Stealth Craft with it.

"And swirl and turn away," he added, waving his arms in a circular motion over the area where the two higher Stealth Craft had been. For a moment, they reappeared. One of them fired a missile—straight at MacAwen! Instinctively, Stella closed her eyes—then quickly reopened them.

"Ha!" MacAwen laughed. "Close shot!" he exclaimed, peering into the hollow of the stump between his feet. "Yet no deep damage can it cause down there!" Then his laughter and light expression vanished, his attention returning to the two Stealth Craft hovering above.

"Ahh!" MacAwen's voice rose up suddenly, in a long, deep syllable, unlike anything Stella had ever heard—his arms moving in the direction of the two Stealth Crafts. "Hum!" he completed in a great boom. Awen emanated from his outstretched hands until the whole sky was filled with it. And the Stealth Craft were simply gone. "And return ta the Harmony," MacAwen added in his smaller, more typical voice. And then, MacAwen was gone, too. Only the resonating echo of his great "hum" remained.

Stella stood, awestruck, gazing about. All was returned to the Harmony. The only difference between now and before the De Da Mua had been invaded was an increase in the abounding Awen—and that she could still hear, and feel, MacAwen's echoing "Hum."

At last, Faas returned. "I lured it into a conundry," he boasted, smiling. Yet his face was blackened and his body was spattered with small wounds, dirt, blood, and soot. "Those APDs do have a bit more fire power than Ralphy Cambull," he shrugged, "regardless of whether or not they hit the intended target. On the other hand, they do have a pretty good aim. But programmed drones are predictable—easier to manipulate or evade than manned or remotely controlled aircraft."

"It was not easy!" he added in response to her incredulous look. "It was firing on me—and I had to get into a conundry myself, to lure it. But as soon as the drone got too close a sudden whirlwind formed, drawing up water and drawing down air. The drone was drawn in, struck by a bolt of lightening, then swallowed!" Faas smiled wide.

"Unfortunately for it," he added, "the drone didn't have a brain to understand what it was up against—nor a living body for me— or the guardians—to feel any compassion toward. So, how did it go for you?" Faas asked. "I see you're not still submerged."

Stella shook her head. She didn't know how to explain. "Well —I was attacked by three Stealth Crafts. But I managed to fight them off—by harnessing the power of Awen. Oh yeah—and I had a bit of assistance, from MacAwen."

Faas gave her an odd look. "You *are* joking.... Yes?"

"Probably," Stella answered. Certainly, it had seemed very real. But now that she thought it over, it seemed rather *unreal*. And she had been doing a lot of concentrated imagining while waiting the long wait, submerged in the darkness under water. She honestly wasn't sure if she had just imagined it all. *"Always are ye imagining, Stella,"* she heard MacAwen's voice. "But Never do ye *just* imagine." And again she was aware of MacAwen's echoing "Hum."

She looked to Faas. "Did you just hear something?"

"No." he answered. "But I do sense an echoing vibration. Something of MacAwen's energy, I think, *is* watching over us."

"Do you think?" Stella smiled.

"Always," Faas answered. He smiled. "Let's take a nice little break, shall we?"

"I think I can handle that," Stella responded. Not only was she exhausted, but really confused. There was so much she wanted to know—but not now. She just needed to breathe and feel sane.

At last they enjoyed some peace—and quiet—and a snack of dried fruit and venison. The Harmony was fully restored. Solid. It seemed timeless. Stella soaked up the tranquility. It seemed like it transcended time—like all that she had been through, and would yet have to go through, was but a dream. And all that was real was this moment. Remembering the Mother Goddess embodying the Earth, she relaxed to the ground and closed her eyes. Bumble bees droned. Birds chirped and sang. A gentle breeze played on the reeds....

It was good she plugged in so fully and absorbed so much nourishment from so little time. Because it did not last. When she opened her eyes she saw; again, Faas's expression was wild—and yet he stood frozen. Stella got up immediately.

"What is it?" she asked anxiously. Faas did not answer. Stella searched around with all her senses—looking, listening, and sniffing intently. She felt the atmosphere with her fingers. The air was warm and wet. It smelled fresh and healthy—full of life. And so it felt...to her. She could neither see nor hear anything unnatural. The fog was thinning. Birds chirped. Moist green leaves of countless shades and varieties covered the vines, bushes, and scrub trees throughout this part of the De Da Mua. Purple and yellow blossoms were opening everywhere. It was beautiful—and peaceful. Again she looked at Faas.

Faas's eyes were wide and out of focus—as if he was in a trance. He seemed barely to be breathing. "Faas?" she half whispered. Still, he did not respond. "Faas!" she raised her voice. "What is it?"

"Nothing near here," he answered gravely. "*We* are safe," he spoke softly, still half in his trance. "But *something... terrible.*" He crinkled his brow, shaking his head and sighing.

"What?" Stella begged. "Tell me! What do you sense?"

Faas turned to her, shaken and trembling. He blinked his eyes—as if striving to return his focus to the here and now. "A disturbance...in the Harmony," he breathed heavily. "Far from here, yet...more disturbing than anything I have ever felt before." He closed his eyes, his head shaking.

"Can you sense what caused it?" Stella asked.

Faas shook his head. But even as he did, Stella sensed it.

"*A bomb,*" she half whispered, herself in a trance now. And then, she had a vision:

"*People...panicking...striving to escape from the city. Everywhere on the streets...and on all the news...everyone speaking about the bomb....*"

Faas stared intently at her. "You are having a vision. Do you sense a bomb?"

"*No*...not really," Stella answered, snapping out of her trance. "Just the panic...and the news."

"That's just what I suspected," Faas cut in.

Stella stared, expectantly. "Do you know what it is?"

"I am...almost certain," he nodded.

366

"Well?" Stella prodded. "What is it?"

Faas drew in a deep breath, his eyes wide and out of focus. *"The Filth Bungs,"* he half whispered. Then he sighed, his countenance overcome by amazement...and an uncharacteristic expression of horror.

"What...are the *Filth Bungs?"* Stella asked.

Faas looked down, sighing and shaking his head. "The prophesy—" he raised his gaze, as if searching memory. Then he began to recite:

"The first Filth Bung...on The New City falls.
From it rises...the king of kings...who rules unseen...
by all but The It Animal-I...of whom the king of kings...
the blue capped king...is but one play thing."

"All these years..." Faas shook his head. "It has been spoken of as one of the final warnings in The Prophesy. But only in recent times has the term, *Filth Bung* come to the forefront of Clann Taluv's discussions. Some of the Council have been predicting that this might well come to be."

"Do the filth bungs represent...*the bomb?"* Stella questioned in sudden terror. "I mean like...*nuclear?"* her face contorted with horror and disgust.

"No!" Faas shot her a wild look—then sighed. "Not exactly." He shrugged. "It's not *that* terrible. But it *is* terrible." Faas sighed heavily. Then he shot her a sudden intense look—like *the looks* he used to give her. "Do you sense..." he searched her aura, "that it may be? Like, that it may be nuclear?"

Stella shook her head. "No! That thought just came to me— from you! When you described the *Filth Bungs."*

Faas let out a sigh of great relief. "The main purpose of the Filth Bungs, we think, is to terrorize rather than cause real devastation. But that does not mean they are not lethal," he shrugged. "We don't know—they *probably* are bombs—and maybe with *some* nuclear *waste* attached to them. But their purpose, and their most powerful effect, will be mass mind control —through terror."

"Mind control? I don't get it," Stella said, screwing up her face. "What does terror have to do with mind control?"

Everything," Faas answered. *"False Flags,"* he stated, as though it should be obvious. Stella stared blankly.

"Oh—of course," Faas shrugged. "They would not teach you their own tricks in the school system they themselves designed. The term, False Flag, comes from an old practice of deception. A ship's flag would be exchanged for a flag that misrepresented it—so it might falsely appear to be an enemy ship. Then it would be used to commit a crime that would be blamed on the enemy."

"But modern false flag operations don't necessarily use flags —or ships. It is simply a method of deception, used by conspirators, to make it look as though some *other* government, corporation, or group of individuals has committed their crime. As to the point of Mind Control—when used in a way that not only fools, but also terrorizes the population mass. False Flag operations work on this premise: *Problem—Reaction—Solution.* This is one of the oldest, yet still most effective tricks in The It Animal's book."

"First; agents of The It Animal create a problem. For instance: *they* detonate a bomb that releases small amounts of radiation into a major city. Then *they* name a terrorist organization that's responsible, and let their media convince the public that *the terrorists* mean to strike again. Second; with some measure of panic, the public reacts, demanding a response: *hunt the terrorists down—destroy them—whatever it takes.* Third; agents of The It Animal, through the media they control, present their *desperate* solutions: *we need more laws—more control—more military spending—more secrecy for the MIF—less privacy and privileges for common people...."*

"The real Problems *they* create usually aren't nearly as big as a *Filth Bung.* But there are *many* problems that *they* create. So people give up freedoms, *incrementally*, for what they're told is greater security."

Stella shook her head. "Where on Earth did this *It*-thing come from? And what does *It* actually want?"

"It is said to have come, *not from the Earth*, but *from the heavens,"* Faas answered. For untold millennia *It* has dwelt underground. But more and more, *It* is re-emerging. It should not be confused with other entities and forces from the heavens that dwell in the Earth. Many others are, and will be emerging, also. I will speak of those later. But as for the It Animal, what *It* wants is a micro-chipped slave race: a workforce/army of *real* zombies—

people who are smart and capable enough to serve, but not to think independently."

"*That*...is just like—*insane*." Stella breathed in deep—and out, violently. "But..." she sighed, "if it's true...and the Filth Bungs are blowing off now...."

"What I am reading," Faas said, "is the first *Filth Bung,* spreading out now, over *The New City.*" Faas sighed. "What was predicted...in The Prophesy," Faas shook his head, reciting:

"When agents of The It Animal release the bungs—
terror will paralyze the people.
Freedom to travel will cease."

Faas went quiet. There was pain in Faas's expression like Stella had never seen. He drew in a deep breath, then recited the verse again—as if to reexamine the meaning:

"The first Filth Bung...on The New City falls.
From it rises...the king of kings...who rules unseen...
by all but The It Animal-I...of whom the king of kings...
the blue capped king...is but one play thing."

"They have released *The first Filth Bung...on The New City.*" Faas stared blankly into the sky—as though still in shock.

"But I don't get it," Stella confessed. "I mean, compared to everything else The It Animal has done, the Filth Bungs don't seem *that* terrible. I mean, they *are* terrible, but like—you seem so...*shocked.*"

Faas turned to Stella with a start—his eyes snapping into focus. His look was wild, but sad and filled with compassion. Faas breathed in deep, looked up—and from memory, continued reciting further:

"The next Filth Bung...makes angels scream—
from their city dream...where the West does end...
and cease to be...the West believed.

The third Filth Bung...with the fourth and fifth—
all fall at once...and tear asunder...
the Northern Lake...the Southern Sea...and the Eagle's Heart...
and so begins...The Singularity."

"*The Singularity*—" Faas said, his head nodding briskly— "it has begun!"

The Singularity? Stella searched within, struggling to recall everything Faas had revealed to her. *Like, the end of the world?*

Stella stared at him, struck with shock and awe. "You can sense this? Are you sure?" But even as she asked, she realized that *she* was sensing something again: *The New City*—it was New York! And...*the next Filth Bung...makes angels scream*—she just knew it was directed at *the City of Angels.* That part was obvious. But the third, fourth, and fifth Filth Bungs—they would be directed in such a way that nowhere would seem safe.

Faas was nodding, pacing. "We know this has been in Its tentative plans for a long time. But the timing—now—I think it is because—" he paused, eying Stella. "Because *you* escaped—and It has failed to retrieve you."

Stella said nothing. The gravity of this situation was too much.

"Now," Faas thought out loud, "of course, the agents of The It Animal will blame this terrorism on some made up group—or worse, on some real, but innocent group. Probably, they will link it to some militant survivalist group, to instigate the hunt for Clann Taluv. This will be their excuse—those agents seated in positions of power will use this event as a pretext...to implement *Martial Law.* And after *this*—" Faas sighed, "it is likely the masses, in their panic, will accept Martial Law with barely a question. Many will be begging for it—even demanding it!"

"But I don't understand—" Stella stuttered. "Since they *are* a terrorist organization—" But even as she started forming the question, the answer came to her. Of course. She already knew, and yet she kept forgetting. Agents of The It Animal had infiltrated all the governments of the world long ago, and instigated the creation of the world's spy agencies. *It* had total control over...not only the MIF; the *Middle Information Front*, but also.... Stella thought of every spy group she had heard about: MI5, *Middle Information 5*—MI6, *Middle Information 6*—the LIA, *Lower Information*—the UIA, *Upper Information*—the KGB, *Committee for State Secrecy*—the MSA, *Mandatory Secrecy Agency*—the CFI...she couldn't even remember what that one stood for. Not that it mattered; the names were just fronts to deceive people. The It Animal was the eye at the apex of every major spy agency in the world.

Even if ninety nine percent of the agents knew next to nothing about this—even some who were supposedly at the top—The It

Animal used them. *It* had total control over forces that common people believed to be at odds or at war with one another. It was all a ploy. An excuse for taking away freedom. A confusion confounded with fear to get people to give up their own freedom. Freedom was the only true opposition to *It*. Everything else was phony—*controlled opposition*. The whole world had been *double crossed*.

Now *they* would be able to hunt her more easily. Now *they* would have the excuse to hire a thousand Buck Cambulls. Now, on top of all the secret special forces, they would have millions of volunteers and concerned citizens after *her*...and Faas...and all of Clann Taluv!

"What do we do?" Stella asked.

"I don't know—exactly," Faas answered. "You are obviously not yet ready to read The Prophesy. Yet we are clearly running out of time. We must meet with the full Council—of Clann Taluv. Together we will decide. I *can* tell you this much though—we *will* be acting very fast. Your training will be intense. For The Prophesy was very clear about this point: *After the Filth Bungs— the Death Clouds will follow swift.*"

"*Death Clouds?*" Stella questioned. "I don't like the sound of *that*. And I don't know how much more of this prophesy I can take!"

"It's not all bad," Faas responded. "I promise. In fact, much of The Prophesy is filled with hope and wonder. There are various possibilities of *Golden New Ages* of Freedom, Peace, Prosperity, and Harmony for all life, following The Singularity," he sighed. And although The Prophesy *is* written in stone, in the end—in fact, at every fork in the trail—it is all about the choices we make."

"Alright then," Stella sighed. "Go ahead. Tell me. What are the *Death Clouds?*"

"It is complicated," Faas answered. "Not even the full Council yet has all the answers to this question. Only The It Animal knows. But I *can* tell you what I myself was able to translate from the Prophet Walker's tracks:

"From the body of The It Animal there arose a horde of silver birds, giant sized, flying all over the world—leaving trails of poisonous dust and vapor across the sky, in long parallel lines and

371

crisscross patterns. The dust trails spread out—and slowly covered the sky with a poisonous cloud covering all the Earth."

"The Death Clouds represent one of the many forks in humanity's pathways," Faas explained. "It is a time of momentous choice. If the masses notice and are roused by this blatant wake up call—and act passionately and intelligently—it could be the end of The It Animal—and the dawn of a wondrous new age."

"But—" Faas continued, "if the *Death Clouds* appears for all to see in the sky—and the masses of people *still* do not wake up and stop it—then *the great destruction* will be nigh upon us. For the Death Clouds are a direct attack on *life itself*—against Mother Earth—against all humanity—against the very life force we call Awen—even against *the Great Spirit of Creation!*" Faas exclaimed, shaking his head."

He looked suddenly very fierce. "If the sleeping masses do not protest this attack—they will have gone beyond hope. And then we can expect to see the final sign—*the bleeding heavens.*"

Stella was struck cold. She had seen *the Death Clouds* already! She was sure of it. The *Stealth Clouds* fit this description perfectly—obviously! But how could Faas be unaware it? Faas, of all people?

He did live under the protective atmosphere of the De Da Mua. But he often ventured outside the De Da Mua. And even from within it, he was acutely aware of what was going on in the skies beyond his realm. How could he not sense this gigantic disturbance in the Harmony? It made no sense. These thoughts raced across Stella's mind as her heart pounded slow and her blood ran cold. But she did not speak of it. She would not. She could not. She just hoped that she was wrong. She dared not inquire. For the moment, she suppressed her thoughts and just listened—as Faas recited more of The Prophesy:

"When the Death Clouds prevail—over the once blue, life-giving sky—the harvest moon does rise—and from it there rains...the Bleeding Heavens."

"If we follow the pathways to where *The Bleeding Heavens* comes to pass," Faas continued, "The Prophesy says that Clann Taluv must then retreat to the farthest wildernesses: *and live Underland, as did the ancient primitives.* The It Animal will hunt us—and *Its* agents will try to poison us. Bugs and sickness, *they*

372

will have created that will be spread by ticks, mosquitoes, birds, and other animals. Partly, to weaken our immune systems—*but more, to terrorize potentials of Clann Taluv out, and away from the wilderness.*"

Stella was starting to feel sick. "God! That is... *horrible*," she cried, rather feebly—swallowing hard, but feeling instead like spitting or throwing up. She thought of the Lyme Disease Epidemic, and how Dr. Warburger had used it as an excuse to keep kids away from the natural world. And it seemed really strange how Lyme Disease had never existed in New Hampshire, until like, about the time Stella was born.

"It *is* horrible, yes,: Faas conceded. "But *this* will backfire on them," he said soothingly. "According to the prophecy, many *will* die, but:

In this time of need, as ever, new plant allies will appear—
plants invading from far off lands.
Into the bodies of the Children of the Earth
will *these plants help grow new defenses....*
Yet the agents who create these diseases,
in the end, will die from them—
and even The It Animal Itself, to its core,
will be weakened and left wretched by this action."

Faas sighed, nodding and eyeing Stella up and down. "If I haven't said too much, then I have certainly said enough—for now," he nodded. "Though I've only scratched the surface." He smiled. "Before the end, it will be *you*, Stella, who informs the rest of us to all the prophecy's details—and of the final piece."

She shook her head. "To follow in the footprints...of the Prophet Walker..." She continued shaking her head. "It's a path I can hardly imagine—"

"And yet you have already begun," Faas smiled. "If you only look behind you," he gestured to her footprints coming from the water to where she now stood, "you will see that you have been on the pathways to becoming what you are destined to become—for quite some time. Your inklings, your interests...and your inspirations, have led you along these paths."

Stella nodded, slightly. "Yet without MacAwen," she raised her brows sympathetically, "we would never have known about tracks...or the Shadow Beast...or anything. And without *you*...I wouldn't be alive."

"Without your openness to nature's true magic you would never have seen nor heard MacAwen," Faas answered. "No one, ever, has even taught you. Yet—" he studied her earnestly, "you are *so* gifted...." Faas's eyes went out of focus, staring off into some faraway place.

"Now listen—" he snapped back to the present. "If anything happens—and you find yourself alone—remember: It is the business of the Prophet Walker—on behalf of all humanity—on behalf of the Harmony of all life on Earth—to perform the greatest act of defense ever—in response to the darkest magic forged against the Harmony of life in all the history of the world."

Faas eyed Stella very seriously and intensely. "Remember the threefold directive: *Sensing; Illuminating; Transforming.* These three, in this order, are what is required of the Prophet Walker...on the grandest scale."

"I do understand," Stella nodded. "Only...I feel there is one over-arching...*initiative*...you haven't spoken of." She turned to Faas.

Faas eyed her curiously. "What is it?"

"Love," Stella answered, feeling it in her heart and throughout her being as she spoke the word.

Faas went silent.

The Awen pulsating in the atmosphere increased. Or Stella's consciousness of it increased. But of course, she realized, her consciousness of Awen *was* Awen. And pure love, more than anything, was what raised it.

"Love..." she breathed reverently, her arms lifting into the atmosphere. "It's what it's all about, really. Isn't it?" she glanced at Faas, then her eyes swam about the heavens, her body vibrating with the Awen all about her. "I mean, everything comes from love. And everything strives for love—however messed up that love might be."

Faas continued staring at her in silence.

Stella suddenly felt re-connected to the Great Consciousness that had reached into her while she had waited, submerged under the De Da Mua's water. And from this consciousness, there streamed into her now, a flow of information:

"There is a greater, underlying conspiracy—not only to keep The Prophesy from all humanity—and keep hidden, the Prophet Walker's tracks, from the Prophet Walker—but to hide everyone's tracks, from themselves. Not only their footprints, but their DNA, even the unique patterns of their electrons. For all these things connect everyone to the greater web, to the prophesy that was written—and beyond...."

"On a deep level, each and every one plays a part in this greater underlying conspiracy, feeding the Shadow Beast to monstrous proportions. Not only The It Animal. Each and all hold the code."

This information entered Stella's mind, not as a voice, but a stream of thought. It came not from any *other* mind, but simply from *universal* mind. Her own mind, she knew, was simply part of this. Yet she felt this universal mind very closely related to the *mindfulness* of MacAwen. His presence, his essence, was very near.

"The code of The It Animal," Stella's stream of thought continued, *"is a construct with parts identical to the human code--"*

It's DNA! Stella suddenly realized, *The It Animal is mostly human! It even has a soul!*

As these words came to her, and passed through her, Stella realized; not even Faas knew some of the things that just came to her in moments like this. It wouldn't have made sense—knowing how he could tap into the world wide web of tracks and trails. But in these moments, she realized; she was not just Stella.

"Wow!" Stella blurted out loud, returning to herself.

Faas was still silent, still staring at her. He raised a brow.

"Wow...like—the poor It Animal. Nobody loves it. It's part human, too!"

Faas looked shocked, for a moment, then confused, almost amused—as though unsure whether she was joking or totally serious.

"On some level," Stella said, her body swaying as she spoke, her head swimming in the atmosphere as she eyed the world up

375

and down, near and far— "even The It Animal is part of...the *Universal* Harmony." Her gaze went wide to the heavens.

Faas stared dumbly—then smiling, nodded slowly. *The look* had returned to his face, but he said nothing—as though overcome with an amazing mixture of awe, reverence, and amusement.

"We are all part of this...this *play*," Stella continued. "We are all...*complicit*" —the perfect word just came to her, and she wished Patrick was there to hear it. "On some level—" Stella's gaze penetrated to deep layers of the atmosphere— "I imagine some *higher part* of The It Animal—and its agents—they actually want to get caught. They *want* to be figured out," she raised her brows intensely. "They want the Prophet Walker to succeed! Their work—in the end—will all have been part of the awakening of us all...to greater and higher vibrations..."

"I don't know about them *wanting* to get caught," Faas raised *his* brows. "After all, *they* and *It* have been going to the greatest of lengths, for thousands of years, to insure they do *not* get caught— at least, not until they, and It, are so powerful it won't matter." He looked at her thoughtfully—still with reverence and awe, but now with concern rather than amusement.

"Be careful, Stella. You see and feel deep into the depths of souls. But it is not what is in the depths, but rather that which lies just below the surface which is the most deceiving...and treacherous."

"I will be careful," Stella promised. "I don't know how I know," Stella said, her head still swimming in the atmosphere, "but..." she breathed deep—feeling a sudden intensity of emotion moving through her. "Now I know—I *will* walk the prophesy."

With that, Faas sighed, staring at her reverently and confidently. "And you *will* fulfill the journey," he nodded.

Stella could only imagine what that journey would be. *Yet—in a way*, she thought, *I am walking it, even now.* She nodded to herself, eyeing her own tracks, leading to where she now stood. Though what the outcome of her walk would be, she could not truly foresee. There were many forks in the path.

"I will go with you," Faas said, "*all the way*...." He nodded, his gaze meeting hers, intense and sincere. "Whatever it takes...wherever you go.... I will see to it that you succeed...*and* return safely. For if ever I had a shred of doubt about who and what you are," he shook his head, "nothing now could be more clear."

Stella felt such gratitude, such warmth, such love—she threw her arms around him.

But that moment, as they embraced, she had a terrible vision —and a premonition. She saw Faas's death:

He looked a few years older—but very scarred and haggard. Someone was trying to shoot her, but Faas leapt between and took the bullets. Faas died to save her!

She stepped back from him—as though she had been shocked. "It isn't true!" she exclaimed. "It can't be! I won't let it!"

"What is it?" Faas eyed her, confused for a moment. She looked at him, wild eyed and worried. And from her look, he seemed to understand—she had a vision. "You needn't speak of it," he held up his hand. "Whatever it is," he said, "remember— there are many forks in our paths."

Stella closed her eyes, shaking her head. She breathed in deep, and sighed. He was right. She looked into his eyes and nodded. "Many forks," she sighed again. "And maybe...some-times," she added hopefully, "we just see our own fears—not true visions."

Faas nodded, looking deep into her eyes. He put a hand on her shoulder and smiled—then turned quickly away.

Stella eyed Faas up and down—from his filthy feet to his wild, tangled hair. He was strong and awesome...and beautiful. She could not bear the thought of losing him. She felt like she'd lost everyone else—and that would have included her self, if not for Faas saving her. Now he meant everything to her. She would just die without him.

I will not let it happen, Stella vowed within as she sighed with determination, eyeing the stain on her palm and remembering the goddess's gift. She reached into her pocket and clutched her amulet. *For Love,* she thought to herself, *for Awen, and for pure skies....*

"So—" she shrugged. "Here we are." She looked at Faas, expectantly. "What do we do now?"

"We need to to go," Faas answered shortly.

"Okay," Stella sighed. She glanced about the De Da Mua. "Which way?"

"Down," Faas smiled with enthusiasm, gesturing to the huge, hollow stump on the center of the small island they were on. "We journey *Underland,*" he nodded with a bright gleam in his eyes.

"*Underland?*" Stella eyed the ancient, hollow stump with growing wonder and amazement—and was struck with a sudden vision of networks of tunnels and caverns spreading throughout the inner regions of the Earth at various depths. Her eyes lit up. "Where to?"

"First, to the *Bruigh Comhairli*, to meet with the full council of Clann Taluv. And then..." he looked to Stella with wide eyes, as if to say; *your guess is as good as mine.*

The *Bruigh Comhairli*? It rang a bell. That name—somehow, it was familiar. Somehow, she just knew; *it was the gathering place of Clann Taluv.*

"Where we're going now...is beyond anything you have ever imagined." Faas nodded, smiling. "It can't be described—from up here."

Stella peered down, into the hollow stump. It was a long, dark tunnel. But there was a green glow that seemed to be emanating from the rotting wood.

"Foxfire," Faas said, breaking a chunk of the wood from the hollow, and showing her that it was in fact the wood that glowed. He tossed the chunk of wood and gestured for her to enter. "After you," he said, and offered his hands to lower her into the stump.

Stella looked to the sky for one glorious moment. It was pulsating as she had never imagined, with the wild energy of Awen. The Awen was deep blue, blending with white high in the sky, and with emerald green all around them, which seemed especially to be emanating from the stump. She took Faas's hands, then climbed into the stump. He lowered her to his arms reach, and she could still feel no bottom.

"Just relax and enjoy the ride," Faas said. And before she had time to respond, Faas released her....

Stella fell through the darkness, whizzing down in a blur of green light. A rush of damp air blew past her. Adrenaline coursed through her blood. Her heart thumped. A dazzling flash of thoughts and feelings raced through her mind and body.

For one moment, again, she saw the distant vision of Ben Bel Tienne. The sides of the volcanic mountain were inscribed with The Prophet Walker's tracks, scrolled out in the design of a myriad branching vine—trans-burgeoning pathways. The whole image had symbolic meaning, as did as did every branching segment of the Prophet Walker's trails. Yet Stella's vision was drawn now, to zoom in on the minutest details. Embedded within each footprint she glimpsed the Impaction Reverberation Symbols that, as BAL ONU FES, spelled out the multitude of various tidbits that made up The Great Prophesy:

If only she could translate the meanings....

Yet still, she was falling. And, again, thoughts from her subconscious formed into words: *"There are things Faas has not yet told you. And other things, Faas does not yet know."*

Then out of the deep green darkness, a flash of insight burst upon her vision like a bolt of white lightening, striking her right between her brows. All she saw, emblazoned before her, was a single tree letter:

And she knew it was the letter "**D**," and that it represented the Oak Tree...and a door into other worlds. That door was waiting for those who would crack the codes, translating the tree letters...and the BAL ONU FES.

Yet still, she was falling...free falling toward unfathomable depths.

Well, I guess seventh grade is over, she mused. So was life—as Stella knew it. In fact, life, *as everyone knew it*, was over. Somehow, amazingly, *they* just didn't know it...yet.

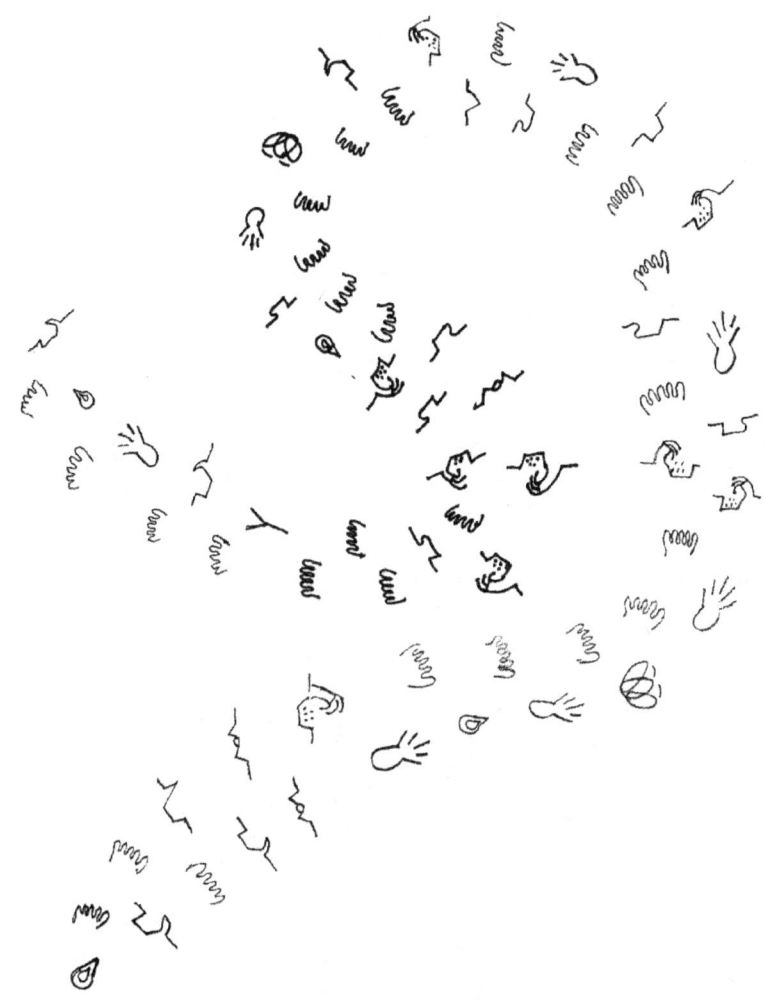

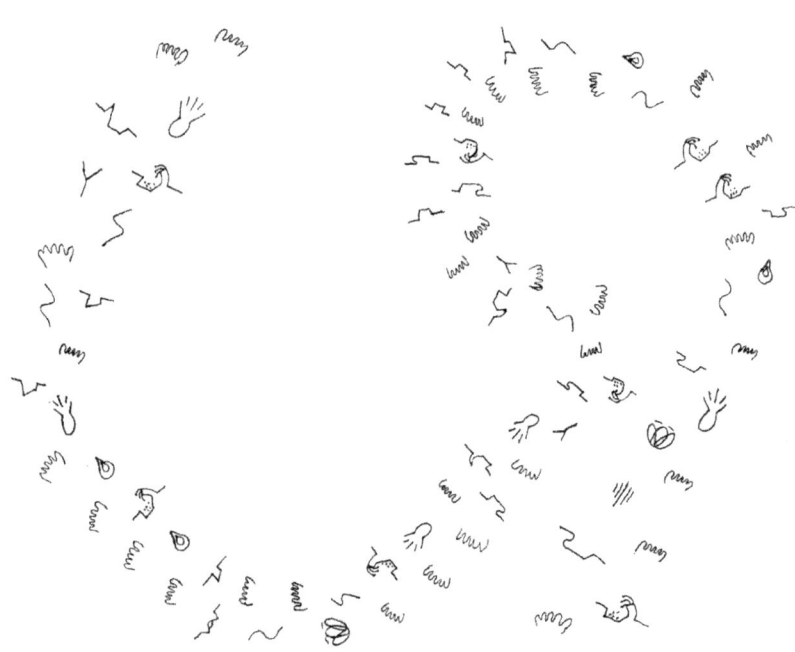

Afterword

The Prophet Walker series continues with Book II: *"Rites of Passage...."*

Stella is going to have to grow up—rather quickly. In fact, if she is to survive, Stella must learn—not only how to live in the wild—but also, the way of the Stealth Warriors of Clann Taluv. She must master the arts of camouflage, stalking, trapping, hunting, and self defense—not only in the physical realm, but also, in the realms of spirit, mind, and energy. For though he would die trying, Faas cannot always be there to look after her. And MacAwen, though always with her in essence, is proving far more mysterious a creature than she had imagined, and is seeming more and more to be as busy elsewhere and with other matters as he is with her.

Further, she must master the Bal-Onu-Fes; the esoteric alphabet of Clann Taluv. Not only as reader, but also, as author—she must master the ways of the walk. For it is from her footprints that Clan Taluv must translate the final piece of the prophesy: they must learn the deepest secrets behind The It Animal's monster conspiracy and receive the final instructions of how to combat it.

The Shadow Beast grows to monstrous proportions, overwhelming the minds of the masses with confusion, entertainment, electromagnetic brainwave interference, Stealth Clouds, mass drugging, and many forms of deceit. For the few who resist the psychic assault, Martial Law is instituted in every country on the surface of the Earth, enforced by the Gestapo-like World Police. The excuse: imminent threat from the most deadly worldwide terrorist group ever to exist; Clann Taluv! The war for the minds of everyone on the planet erupts. All the while, Stella is hunted....

But not all those who follow her tracks are of like mind. You, the reader, have tracked Stella this far. You have traversed

The Trans-Burgeoning Pathways. To go through the Rights of Passage you must take up the battle within yourself and the world around you. Know that you can make a difference—and to save your world, you must. Remember the Three-Fold Initiative.

Stella Childs alone can read the prophesy to its depths and breadths. But she alone cannot inform the world of our destiny, of our choices, and of the ways that we may avert The It Animal's designs. It is up to you.

Tread the word....

To help Stella spread the awareness...of The Mysterious Creature...of The Shadow Beast...and of The Terrible War that has erupted—join Clann Taluv. Go to: www.thededamua.com.

Spread the awareness. Gain access to further levels of the De Da Mua. Become active in the World Freedom Revolution. Encourage as many as you can to follow Stella's tracks through the Pathways—and in turn, to tread the word again, for others.

It may seem absurd; but this could be our greatest hope.

"If at first it does not seem absurd, it doesn't stand a chance." Albert Einstein

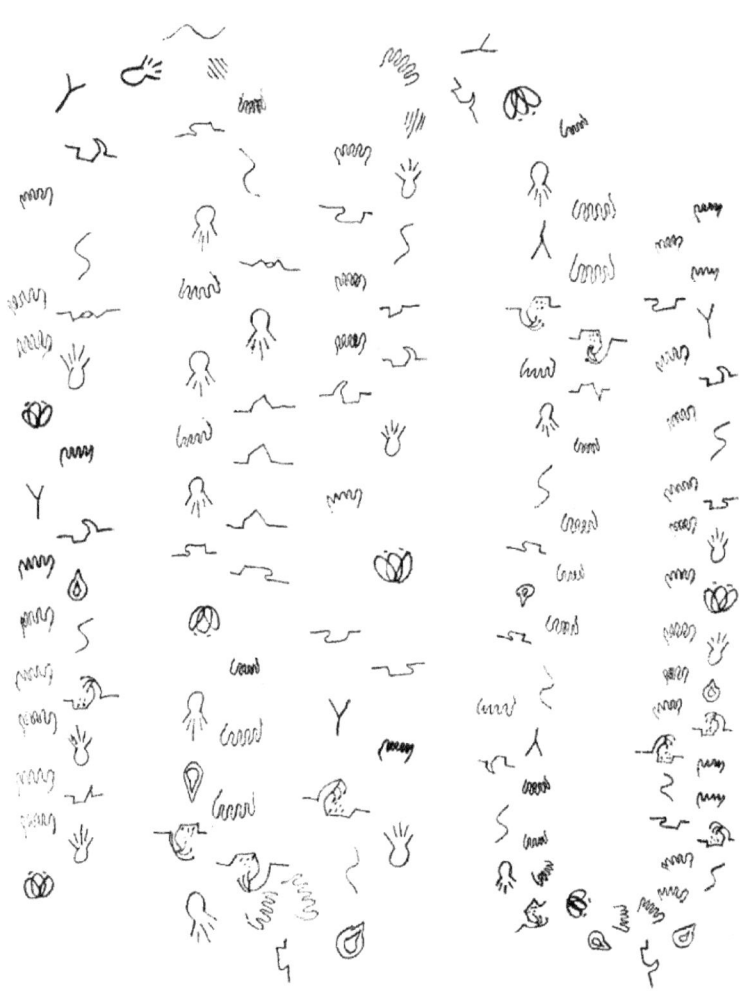

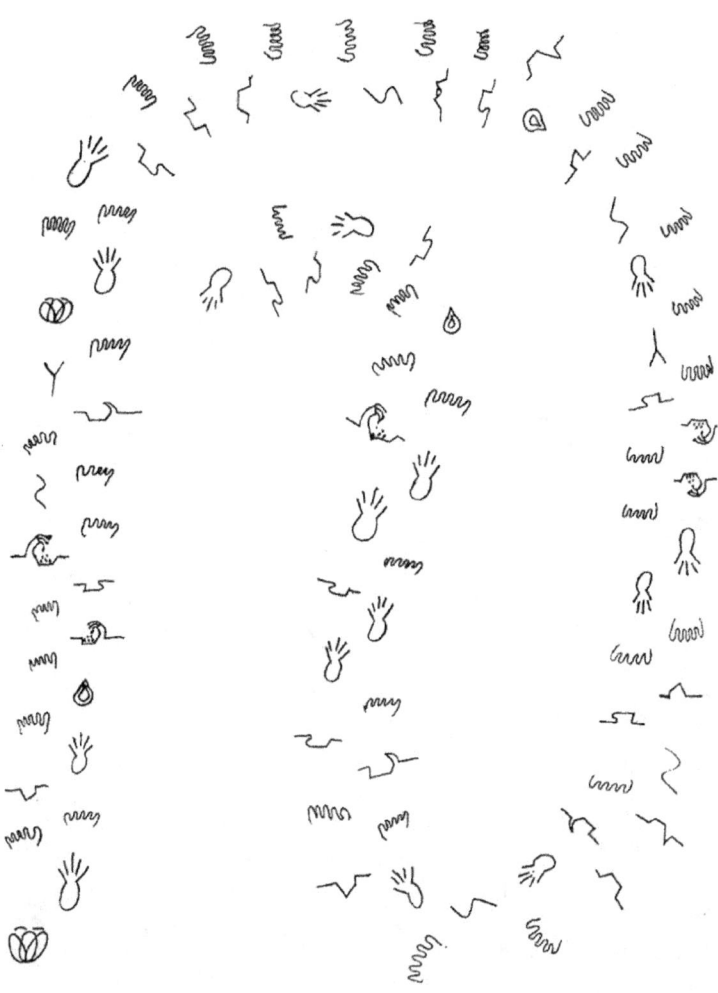

387

BAL ONU FES

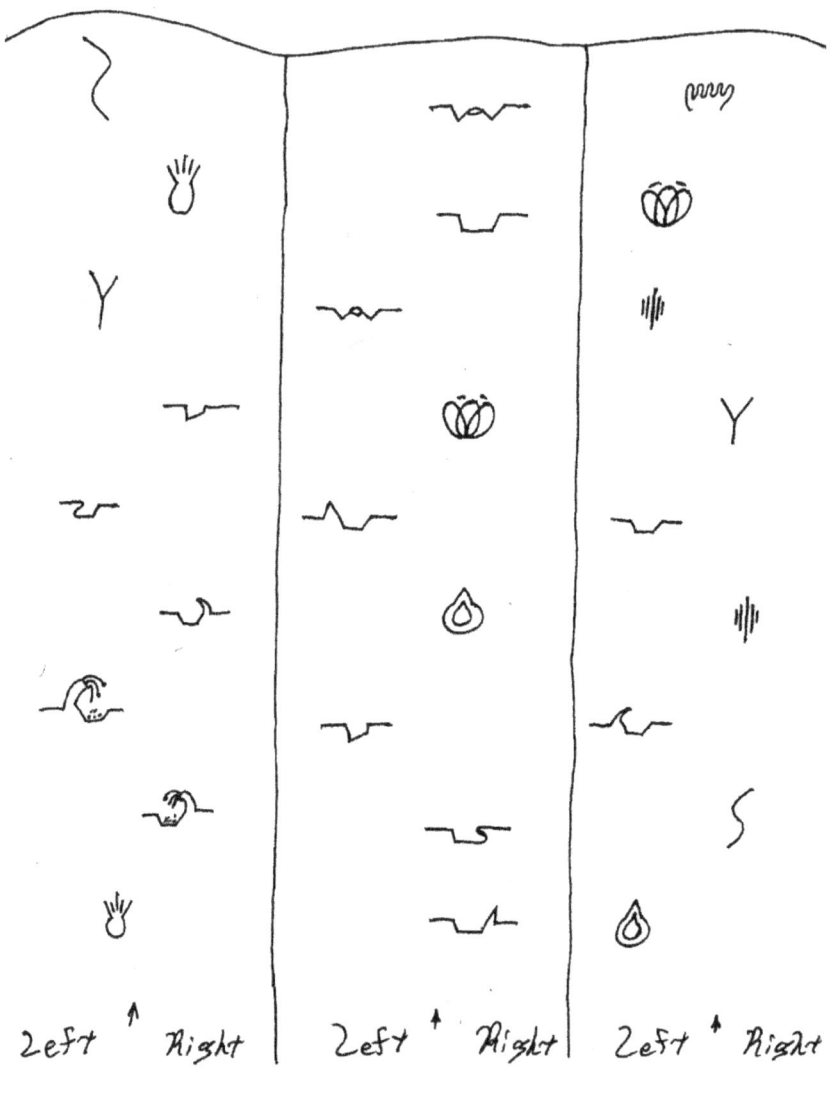

Left   ↑ Right   Left   ↑ Right   Left   ↑ Right

Ogham: Celtic Tree Letters
(Robert Graves Translation. *P, Y, & V/W addendum* D. M.)

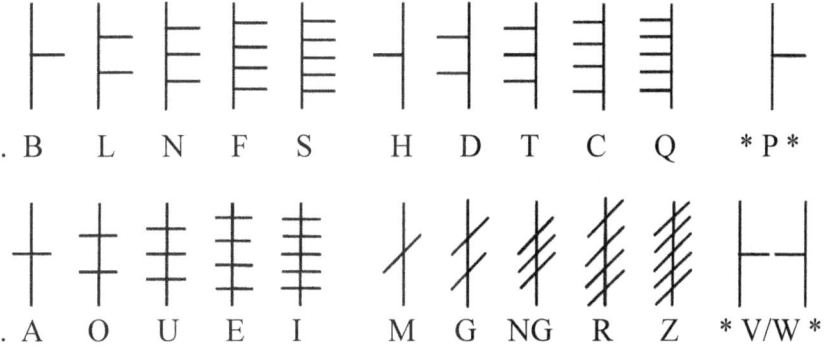

The Living Ogham
(Phonetic English)

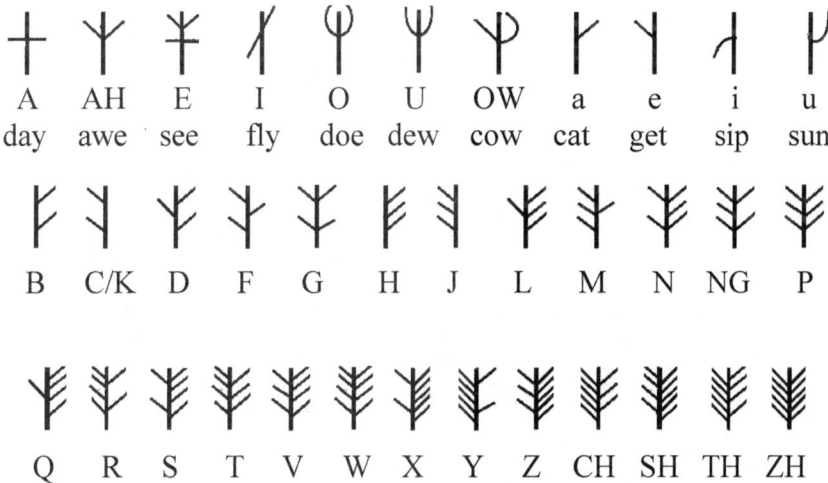

Dan Mac is a wilderness guide, an inspired and learned proponent of **Natural Education,** a tracker, designer/builder/woodworker, teacher, poet, historian, piper, brewer of magical meads, and a purveyor of Awen. His wife says he is the Renaissance man of the twenty-first century. He claims only to be the discoverer of the Basic Formula of the Universe--and a very fast runner. Currently, while continuing the nine part "Prophet Walker" series, he is allegedly finishing his house, working on a nonfiction book entitled, "Natural Education," and a **Mythic Reality** novella entitled, "De-Coding The Lord of the Rings." He lives with his clan on "the land" in Temple, NH, where he offers Wilderness Workshops and Mythic Adventures.

Angus Ryan is a graduate of the Cape Ann Waldorf School and currently attends High Mowing high school in Wilton, NH where he is enrolled in The Naturalist Program and where his artwork is both renowned and infamous. His early childhood introduction to, and immersion in, nature observation and primitive skills started in his backwoods--which were also the home of *Wild Ways.*

www.ingramcontent.com/pod-product-compliance
Lightning Source LLC
Chambersburg PA
CBHW071645260626
47170CB00001B/242